MARVELOUS

A Novel

by

Lampert x Griffin Urban Universe™

MARVELOUS

FOREWORD

First and foremost, we give all glory and thanks to God, without whom none of this would be possible. When we were lost in our own coma dreams, He woke us up and showed us the way.

To our families—our real-life Cherrys, Larrys, Titos, and Uncle Donnys—thank you for showing up. Every single day. Even when we were wearing metaphorical purple suits and refusing to accept reality. You loved us anyway. You stayed anyway. That's what family does.

To our readers—you magnificent humans who took a chance on a book about a guy who got hit by a truck because of a pigeon—thank you. Your willingness to laugh at life's absurdity while crying at its beauty makes this whole thing worthwhile. May you never back up into traffic while photographing churro-eating birds. But if you do, may you wake up marvelous.

"The pigeon won the battle, but we won the war—by being ourselves."

— *Minghao Liu (probably)*

Now go be marvelous. For real.

CHAPTER 1

Born Broke, Died Rich, Rose Again

⚓

Da Marvelous McCall didn't just walk into a room—he arrived like an eviction notice with a theme song, like a tax bill that learned how to breakdance.

Gold chains swinging, mink coat so voluminous it needed its own zip code, he sank into his clawfoot bathtub filled with Crown Royal and announced to the universe: "Behold... the greatest motherfucker this city ever produced."

And because the universe was scared of his loud ass—and maybe also impressed by the sheer audacity of bathing in premium liquor—it listened.

The bathroom was the size of most people's apartments. Marble floors with veins of gold running through them like the arteries of a wealthy corpse. Mirrors on every wall because one reflection of greatness wasn't enough. A chandelier that looked like it sold dope on the side hung overhead. Beneath it, a gold rug shaped like a lion's head that seemed perpetually disappointed in its life choices.

Above the sink, a neon sign proclaimed:

DA MARVELOUS WAS HERE BEFORE YOU

"Talk to me, bubbles," Marvelous murmured, lifting a handful of purple foam. "Y'all ever seen anybody more legendary than this?"

The bubbles said nothing. Even bubbles knew when to shut up and appreciate greatness.

A knock rattled the bathroom door.

"Yo, Marvelous! You decent?"

"I ain't been decent since 1987," he shouted back. "And I was three years old then. Come on in, Lil' Breadcrumb, before your thoughts evaporate. I know they on a timer."

The door burst open and Lil' Breadcrumb stumbled in, practically vibrating with nervous energy usually reserved for chihuahuas on expired energy drinks.

Short, skinny, all knees and elbows like God had sketched him in a hurry. He wore a bright yellow hoodie so aggressively neon it seemed to glow. Dreadlocks stuck out in every direction like he'd been personally electrocuted by the concept of fashion.

One sock on, one sock off, for reasons unknown to God, man, or any deity in between.

His sneakers were two different brands—the left one a Nike, the right one appeared to be a Croc that someone had spray-painted black and attached shoelaces to. It was like his feet were in an argument his brain wasn't aware of.

"Damn, boss. You really bathing in Crown again?"

Marvelous stretched in the purple liquor. "This ain't a bath. This is a marinade. I'm letting the greatness soak in through my pores so my haters can smell it when I walk by. It's science, Breadcrumb. It's alchemy."

Breadcrumb nodded like that was the deepest thing he'd ever heard. "Facts. Big facts." He paused, scratching his head. "Wait... can you get diabetes from bathing in alcohol? Like, through your skin?"

"No."

"You sure?"

"Breadcrumb, I swear to God—"

"Okay, okay!" Breadcrumb pulled out a crumpled napkin. "Anyway, we got three situations. Three whole situations requiring your immediate attention."

"Last time it was two. We escalating?"

"Life moves fast. Situations multiply."

"I'm listening."

"First situation: Cherry Bomb at the club talkin' about you late. She say she ain't taking the stage again till you show up and 'breathe superstar in her direction.' Her exact words." He held up the napkin proudly. "I wrote them down."

Marvelous squinted at it. "Breadcrumb, that says 'breef sooperstar.'"

"Okay but you know what I meant though."

"That ain't how spelling works."

"It's phonetic documentation, boss. I'm preserving the essence of her words."

5

"The essence is spelled wrong."

"But you felt it though."

Marvelous grinned despite himself. "What's situation number two?"

"Pastor Stacks outside. Say he need a word and also a front. Said it's urgent." He pulled out another crumpled napkin. "'Spiritual economic importance.' Also he brought his choir. They in the driveway. They been harmonizing for forty-five minutes."

"His choir?"

"Twelve of them. They doing that thing where they sing but it sound like questions? Like they disappointed in you but musically? I think it's called passive-aggressive gospel."

"Why he bring his whole choir to ask for a front?"

"He said—and I'm reading directly—'The Lord provides but the Lord also requires collateral, and twelve voices of heavenly guilt is better than paperwork.'" Breadcrumb squinted. "Actually that might say 'pancakes.' My handwriting fall apart when I'm scared."

"You was scared of the choir?"

"Boss, the altos was looking at me like they knew my browser history."

"A front," Marvelous repeated slowly. "This man sell salvation on Sunday and still need credit on Thursday? That's just bad business."

"What's situation number three?"

Breadcrumb's face shifted to worry. "The goat back."

Marvelous felt his eye twitch. "What goat."

"The one that been hanging around the dispensary? Ate through the back fence last week? He back. And boss..." He swallowed hard. "He brought a friend."

"Why was you running from a goat, Breadcrumb?"

"That goat got eyes. Like he knows things. Like he seen my credit score and found it personally offensive."

"Get rid of the goat."

"I tried! Called Animal Control three times! Third time they said 'We don't do goats no more, not since the incident.' Then they hung up!"

"What incident?"

"They wouldn't say! It's classified goat information!"

"Handle it," Marvelous said. "I don't care how. But when I come back,

I don't wanna see, hear, smell, or spiritually sense anything goat-related."

"Say less, boss. I'ma handle that goat like it owes me money."

(The goat situation would not be handled. It would, in fact, get significantly worse. The goat—whose name was Larry—was at that very moment teaching his new friend how to unlock simple latches. He was a goat of ambition, and his ambitions were just beginning.)

"Now," Marvelous said, raising one dripping hand. "Before you leave—how my empire look today? Any drama?"

Breadcrumb perked up like a dog hearing the word "walk."

"We good, big bro. Strip club packed—had to turn people away. Fire marshal showed up but we gave him a VIP pass and two drink tickets, and suddenly he couldn't count no more. Dispensary got a line around the block. And the laundromat—" He paused, smiling. —"laundromat got three machines that almost work now. We up seventeen percent!"

"Hold on. Three machines out of how many?"

"Thirty-six."

Marvelous did the math. "So we at like eight percent functionality?"

"Yeah, but that's up from five percent last month! That's progress!"

"How a laundromat with ninety-two percent broken machines making money?"

"Oh that's easy—we converted the back room into a casino. Craps, poker, that thing where you spin the wheel—"

"Roulette?"

"Nah, we got the wheel where it falls over and everybody argues about what number it landed on. People take that shit seriously. Made four thousand dollars last Tuesday alone."

Marvelous stared at the ceiling. "I have created an empire built on nothing but confidence and faulty appliances. I am a mogul of malfunction."

"It's beautiful," Breadcrumb said, wiping away what might have been a tear. "It's like the American Dream but with more legal violations."

"Get out my sight."

"Too late! You been questioning reality since page one!"

The door closed—well, Breadcrumb kicked it three times before it finally latched—and Marvelous was alone with his thoughts, his bubbles, and approximately forty dollars worth of Crown Royal he was currently sitting in.

His phone buzzed. Cherry Bomb.

"You late, mutha—" Her voice cut through the speaker like lip gloss with razor blades in it, smooth and sharp simultaneously.

"Baby girl, time bend around me. I exist outside the normal flow of temporal reality. I'm not late, I'm dramatic."

"You dramatic, alright. That stage getting cold. Your money getting lonely. You left both them bitches sitting by theyselves."

"I'm in the tub, baby. I gotta be ripe for the people. They can't handle me fresh."

"You better not be in there with no other bitch."

"This tub only hold me, my liquor, and my genius. That's a three-person capacity and two of them is intangible concepts."

She sucked her teeth so loud he had to pull the phone away. "Hurry up. I'm giving you one hour before I start fusion dancing with a rival pimp outta pure boredom and also for dental."

The line went dead.

Marvelous stared at his phone. "Love a woman with threats. That's healthy communication right there."

He stood slowly, Crown Royal cascading down his body in purple streams, glistening under the chandelier like he was a discount mythological creature emerging from a lake of very expensive mistakes.

His left foot hit the marble.

His right foot followed.

And then physics, that hating-ass bitch, reminded him that wet marble plus premium liquor plus excessive confidence equaled a near-death experience.

His legs went in two different directions—one toward the toilet, one toward the door—and for exactly 1.3 seconds, Da Marvelous McCall looked like a very expensive wishbone about to snap. His arms windmilled. His chains swung with the momentum of regret. One ring flew off his finger and pinged against the mirror.

He reached out desperately and caught the towel rack.

The heated towel rack. The one that cost four thousand dollars because it was "imported from Italy."

It came out of the wall with a sound like marble screaming.

The whole thing—rack, towels, mounting bracket, and a small chunk of wall—came down with him, depositing him in a heap on the lion rug, which slid across the floor like it was trying to escape.

For a moment, he just lay there. Covered in towels. Surrounded by Crown Royal. The chandelier swinging overhead like it was judging him.

A piece of wall plaster landed gently on his chest.

"That," he said to the ceiling, "did not happen. History will not record that."

He pulled himself up using the toilet as leverage, which felt like a metaphor for something but he refused to examine what.

"That was a test," he announced to his reflection. "A test of my reflexes. I passed. The colors were purple and also embarrassment but we focusing on the purple."

⚓

His walk-in closet was less a closet and more a retail space that had given up on customers. The size of a bodega, possibly larger. Racks of mink coats in every color: red, purple, electric blue, a particularly aggressive orange that looked like a traffic cone had evolved into luxury. Velvet suits in neat rows. Leather pants that squeaked when he walked.

"What's tonight's vibe?" he asked the room. "What says 'I'm important but also approachable but also you can't afford me'?"

He pulled out a mustard-yellow suit. Shook his head. "Too 'Black James Bond goes to court for tax evasion.'"

He grabbed a red leather trench coat. Considered it. Rejected it. "Too 'Satan got a mixtape and it's actually fire but also damns your soul.'"

Finally settled on a deep purple velour tracksuit, customized with "DA MARV" stitched across the back in gold thread, and white Air Forces so pristine they practically glowed. Added a gold chain thick enough to tow a vehicle, rings on seven fingers, and a watch that could pay off a small country's debt.

"Perfect. This says 'I'm successful but I'll still fight you at a gas station if you disrespect me.'"

⚓

An hour later, Marvelous emerged from the brownstone in full regalia.

Purple velour tracksuit that cost more than most people's car payments.

9

Gold chains layered so thick they had their own gravitational pull. White sneakers so clean they made people's eyes water.

His fleet waited: three black SUVs with tinted windows so dark they violated at least six laws in four states.

The courtyard was chaos. His crew, his employees, his hangers-on—people lounging on steps, leaning against vehicles, smoking things that weren't strictly legal but nobody was checking because everyone who might check was also present and also smoking.

The afternoon sun hung low and golden, painting everything in that specific Los Angeles light that made even garbage look like it had potential.

Off to one side, Pastor Stacks stood with his arms crossed, twelve choir members arranged behind him in perfect formation, humming "Wade in the Water" in a key that felt like a personal attack. Every time Breadcrumb walked past, the altos shifted slightly, tracking him like spiritual predators.

"That's unsettling," Breadcrumb muttered to no one in particular.

A dude was selling incense out of a duffel bag, each stick allegedly blessed by "a real shaman, or at least a guy who knew a shaman's cousin." His product line included "IRS Audit Protection (lavender)," "Baby Mama Drama Neutralizer (sage)," and his newest creation, "Landlord Confusion Blend (makes them forget rent is late for up to 72 hours)."

"What you got for me today?" Marvelous asked him.

The man's eyes lit up. He pulled out a velvet pouch. "Boss. Made this one special. Just for you. It's called 'Empire Energy.'" He waved the stick. "Smell that? That's sandalwood, myrrh, and—this the secret ingredient—I burned some money. Real money. A twenty-dollar bill. Andrew Jackson himself. You're smelling a dead president's face converted into spiritual power."

Marvelous inhaled, nodding like a sommelier. "You burned a twenty to make this?"

"For YOU, boss. Anything for you."

"...Give me three."

Another man had set up bootleg DVDs with masterfully misspelled labels: "SHRECK 5: the shrekening," "star tracks: the wrath OF CONS," "FROZEN BUT IT'S JUST ELSA (2 HOURS)," and a mysterious disc labeled "GOOD MOVIE (TRUST ME)" with a handwritten guarantee that read "If you don't like it, too bad, no refunds, but I'll feel bad about it."

Near the gate, a teenager was selling "Authentic Marvelous Merch" that was absolutely not authentic—bootleg t-shirts that said "DA MARVELUS" (misspelled), and one that just featured a blurry photo of someone who might have been Marvelous or might have been a tall lamp in a mink coat. Impossible to tell. The lamp theory was gaining traction.

Marvelous had tried to shut down the bootleg merch operation twice. Both times, the kid offered him a cut of the profits. Both times, Marvelous had been too impressed by the hustle to follow through.

In the corner, a woman offered "Spiritual Credit Repair—"for fifty dollars, she'd burn your name on paper and "send your debt to an alternate dimension where it's somebody else's problem." She had a surprisingly long line, mostly because her explanations were convincing and also because everyone's credit was terrible.

"The king has emerged!" someone shouted.

"Marvelous! Looking good, boss!"

"You hiring?"

Pastor Stacks stepped forward, his choir shifting behind him like backup dancers at a very judgmental concert. "Da Marvelous! I require a moment—"

"Pastor, I see you brought the ensemble. That's dedication. Also blocking my driveway." Marvelous held up a hand. "Breadcrumb will set you up with the deluxe repentance package. Coffee, honey buns, the good napkins. We'll talk when I get back. Tell the choir they can stay but they gotta harmonize quieter."

The lead alto made a face that suggested the key changes would intensify.

Breadcrumb scampered ahead. "Clear the path! Make way for your neighborhood overlord, the hood hero with zero fear of RICO charges— DA! MARVELOUS! McCALL!"

People cheered, recorded for Instagram stories they'd never finish editing.

Big Tito fell into step beside Marvelous as they moved toward the SUVs. Tito was the muscle—six-five, built like a refrigerator that had developed opinions, face permanently set to "don't even think about it." He'd been with Marvelous since the beginning, back when "the beginning" was three dudes selling loose cigarettes out of a backpack.

"Pastor want to talk," Tito rumbled, his voice like gravel in a blender.

"Pastor can wait. Pastor brought a whole choir like this a Broadway show."

"He seem stressed."

"Stressed is his brand. He sells stress and then sells the cure. That's his whole business model."

⚓

Club Marvelous stood in the heart of the neighborhood like a monument to bad decisions that somehow paid well.

The building had been a church, then a warehouse, then briefly and disastrously a check-cashing place that exploded for reasons nobody fully understood. Marvelous had bought it at auction for twelve thousand dollars and a promise he had no intention of keeping.

Now it was his flagship. Purple neon outlined every surface. A marquee sign proclaimed:

CLUB MARVELOUS

"If You Leave Here Happy, We Didn't Do Our Job Right"

Across the street, a billboard featured a personal injury lawyer named Gerald with the tagline "HE'll fight" and a photo where Gerald's shoulders looked suspiciously photoshopped to appear broader. Next to it, a mattress store had a "GOING OUT OF BUSINESS" banner that had been there for six years. At this point, the going out of business WAS the business.

The line to get in stretched around the block—dressed-up people, under-dressed people, people who'd clearly lied about where they were going tonight to someone who cared about them.

Cherry Bomb was waiting at the entrance, arms crossed, heels sharp enough to qualify as weapons in most states. Red hair cascading down her back in waves that looked professionally styled but she'd probably done in fifteen minutes while yelling at someone on the phone. Dress hugging every curve in open rebellion against gravity and common decency.

She was beautiful in that dangerous way, like she could either kiss you or stab you and you wouldn't know which until it was happening.

"You twenty-eight minutes late," she said, her voice sharp enough to cut glass.

"You track time like the FBI." He smiled that smile that usually got him out of trouble or deeper into it. "You that pressed to see me?"

12

She rolled her eyes so hard he worried they might complete a full rotation. But her lips twitched. "The crowd restless."

"Baby, time bend around me. I'm not late, I'm dramatic."

She led him inside.

The air was thick with money, smoke, and dreams on layaway.

Purple and blue lights washed over everything, pulsing with the beat like the whole building had a heartbeat made of bass. Dancers moved on stages with the dedication of people paying off student loans through sheer force of will. One of them—stage name allegedly "Accounts Receivable—" was doing something with her legs that should have required a permit and possibly a zoning variance.

VIP booths lined the walls, glowing behind tinted glass. In one, a man was having a business meeting with a PowerPoint presentation—the slide visible read "Q3 PROJECTIONS" with a graph going in an optimistic direction. In another, someone was definitely asleep, surrounded by empty bottles arranged like Stonehenge made of bad decisions.

The bar stretched along one wall, bottles lined up like soldiers. A neon sign above the top shelf read: "TOP shelf: for people WHO HATE THEIR SAVINGS ACCOUNT."

In the corner, a mechanical dove was supposed to descend from the ceiling every hour as a "symbol of peace and prosperity." It had been broken for three weeks and now just hung there at a forty-five-degree angle, one wing twitching occasionally like it was having a small mechanical stroke. Occasionally it made a grinding sound that suggested both mechanical failure and emotional distress.

"We really gotta fix that dove," Cherry muttered.

"That dove is a metaphor."

"For what?"

"I'll let you know when I figure it out."

"Ladies and gentlemen and questionable individuals of all genders!" the DJ shouted, his voice booming through the speakers. "Your king has entered the premises! Your leader has arrived! Your landlord's worst nightmare is in the building! Make some noise for DA! MARVELOUS! McCALL!"

The place damn near exploded. The roar was physical, a wave of sound that hit him in the chest like validation mixed with bass.

Marvelous raised both hands in a gesture of benediction—or possibly surrender, hard to tell—and did a slow spin, letting everyone see the outfit, the chains, the attitude, the whole package. He walked through the main floor like a politician in a district he actually cared about, like a mayor who remembered people's names. Handshakes, dap, hugs, phones out, bottles lifted like they were toasting his existence.

"Yo, Marv, can I get a selfie?"

"My mama wanna meet you!"

"You remember me? I'm Darnell's cousin's friend's brother!"

He stopped in front of a random dude holding a drink that glowed blue.

"You pay your rent this month?" Marvelous asked.

The guy paused, uncertain if this was a trick question. "Almost. Like, almost."

"Ain't no almost in my vicinity. We either broke or we balling, pick a lane."

He moved on before the guy could respond.

He slid into his VIP booth overlooking center stage. The table was already covered in bottles—champagne, vodka, and some bottle that just said "PREMIUM" with no other information.

Cherry leaned in close. "You gon' say something to the people, or you just gon' sit here looking like a screensaver of a better life?"

He grabbed the mic and stood up on the couch.

"Yo! Shut the hell up! Let me talk my truth!"

The music dipped. People turned, faces tilted up.

"First of all, I wanna thank everybody for coming out to Club Marvelous, where we respect women—"

"Most of the time!" someone shouted.

—"where we disrespect bank accounts, and believe in second chances as long as the first one was fun."

Laughter rippled through the crowd.

"I remember when I ain't have shit. Just a dream, a durag that had seen better days, and some off-brand sneakers that squeaked when I walked too fast. Made me sound like a mouse with ambition. Made me sound like a rodent with goals. Now look at me—velvet on my ass, ice on my neck, gold on my wrists, and a line of people outside tryna give me they paycheck for a chance to stand near my energy."

Cheers, whistles, bottles raised.

"So tonight, we celebrating survival, success, and symptomatically poor

14

decision-making. If you broke, drink like you rich. If you rich, act like you broke and tip like you compensating for emotional issues your therapist don't know about yet."

He paused, surveying his kingdom.

"If you came here to find love—" he gestured at the dancers, —"it's probably the wrong building but we admire your optimism."

Someone cheered.

"If you came here to forget your problems—" he raised a bottle, — "congratulations, tomorrow you'll have the same problems plus a hangover. That's growth. That's what economists call 'expanding your portfolio of regret.'"

More cheers.

"And if anybody came in here with hate in they heart, with negativity in they spirit, with broke energy in they aura… we got security trained in emotional support ass whoopings. They'll hug you. Then they'll escort you outside. Then they'll hug you again. You will leave here feeling LOVED and removed. We practice AGGRESSIVE HOSPITALITY."

Someone in the back screamed "AGGRESSIVE hospitality!" and it immediately became the night's catchphrase. Another person got it tattooed on their arm by 2 AM, misspelled.

The club roared, the sound shaking the walls, probably disturbing the neighbors who'd long since given up calling the police.

He handed the mic back, sank onto the couch, and spread his arms like a king.

Cherry slid in next to him, close enough that their thighs touched. "You ridiculous."

"I'm legendary," he corrected.

"Same thing."

"It absolutely is NOT."

From across the club, there was a commotion near the mechanical dove. Someone was trying to fix it with a coat hanger and determination.

"Should we…?" Cherry started.

"Nope."

The dove made a grinding sound, lurched, and dropped three inches. Its one working wing began flapping with manic, desperate energy, like it was trying to escape its own mechanical prison.

"That seem like a metaphor," Cherry observed.

"Everything in my life a metaphor," Marvelous said, settling deeper into the couch, Crown Royal still faintly sticky on his skin. "I just choose which ones to pay attention to."

He closed his eyes, let the bass vibrate through his bones, let the chaos of his kingdom wash over him.

"Let the evening ruin itself," he whispered to nobody in particular, to the universe, to fate.

And it did.

(The goat, for the record, was at that exact moment learning how to open padlocks. He had already mastered simple latches and was now advancing to more complex mechanisms. His friend—whose name was also somehow Larry, which was statistically improbable but narratively convenient—was keeping watch. Nobody knew this yet. Nobody would know until it was far, far too late.)

⚓

⚓

CHAPTER 2

The Origin of a Legend (That's Mostly Lies)

⚓

Hours later at Club Marvelous—after the crowd had thinned to just the hardcore drinkers, people who'd lost track of time and several important life decisions, one guy who'd fallen asleep standing up like a passed-out flamingo, and approximately fourteen people who'd come to "just stay for one drink—"Marvelous held court in his VIP booth like a king addressing subjects about the sacred texts: his own childhood, exaggerated to the point of mythology.

The booth smelled like expensive alcohol, cheap perfume, and the lingering ghost of decisions that would be regretted tomorrow.

The mechanical dove in the corner twitched once, its broken wing flapping with sad, irregular energy. Nobody acknowledged it. The dove had become like a family member everyone was too polite to mention had a problem.

Cherry Bomb sat next to him, red hair slightly disheveled, counting money with the focused intensity of an accountant who'd seen too much. Her fingers moved through bills with practiced efficiency, making neat stacks.

Breadcrumb was on the floor—not sitting, actually on the floor—organizing bottle caps by "vibe energy," which required absolute silence and probably a psychological evaluation.

His phone buzzed. His face went pale.

"Boss," he said quietly, "the goat guy texted. He said Larry learned how to open the dispensary's back door."

"We're not talking about goats right now," Marvelous said firmly.

"But he said Larry looked satisfied. Like a goat who achieved his goals—"

"BREADCRUMB. Origin story. Focus."

A new girl—Cinnamon, fresh to the game—sat at the edge of the booth, eyes wide with innocence that was about to get obliterated.

"Marvelous," she said, "how you get started? Like, for real for real?"

He took a slow sip of Crown Royal. "You really wanna know?"

Cherry sighed without looking up. "Here we go."

"I was born," Marvelous began, pausing for dramatic effect, "during a thunderstorm so disrespectful that the sky itself had to file an apology with the city council. Property values dropped. Insurance premiums went up."

"Your first word was 'juice,'" Cherry interrupted, still counting. "Your mama told me personally. You said it wrong too. Said 'doos' like you had a speech impediment. You was THREE. That's not even early."

Cinnamon blinked. "Wait—"

"DETAILS!" Marvelous waved dismissively. "The spirit of the story is true. Facts are for scientists and tax auditors. Vibes are for legends."

"He was born on a regular-ass Tuesday at 3:14 PM in County General Hospital," Cherry said, pulling out her phone. "Bald as a boiled egg. The doctor's notes said—and I QUOTE—'unusually loud, possibly dramatic.' I got the birth certificate screenshotted and backed up to three clouds."

"Marketing is just lies that went to business school," Marvelous said.

"That's the smartest dumb thing you've ever said."

Real childhood DeShawn—the ACTUAL version—wasn't fearless.

Not even close. Not even in the same zip code as fearless.

He was allergic to bees, which he discovered after trying to harvest honey from a hive because he'd watched a documentary and thought "that looks easy." It was not easy. He spent three hours in the emergency room. His mama spent the entire time saying "I TOLD you" in seventeen different vocal tones.

He was terrified of heights, which made it unfortunate that they lived on the third floor and the elevator broke approximately once a week. He once spent forty-five minutes on the landing between floors two and three, having a philosophical crisis about whether falling was really that bad compared to the effort of climbing.

He was lactose intolerant but refused to accept it, kept drinking milk like it was a personal challenge, kept suffering the consequences, kept blaming it on "bad chicken" or "spiritual attacks from haters."

His asthma had asthma. His childhood asthma had filed for disability benefits. His lungs wheezed when he walked up stairs, when he thought about walking up stairs, when someone mentioned the concept of elevation in casual conversation.

(Years later, he would claim his asthma was "strategic breathing." It was not. It was just asthma.)

His mama, Mrs. Gloria "Don't Try Me Today" McCall, raised him alone while working two jobs—a day shift at County General Hospital and an evening shift at the post office. She loved him fiercely but didn't tolerate nonsense even microscopically.

Her favorite phrases, delivered with the precision of a sniper, included:

\- "Boy, I will knock the cartoon sound effects out yo head and send them to another dimension"

\- "Keep playing with me and see what Jesus do—spoiler alert, Jesus working with ME today and He brought tools"

\- "I brought you IN this world, I can take you out and make another one that LISTENS"

\- "Don't make me come over there" (this one was the scariest because of its vagueness—where was "over there"? Nobody knew)

\- "I can show you better than I can tell you" (the nuclear option, never deployed)

They lived in Apartment 3B of Riverside Gardens, which had "Gardens" in the name but no actual gardens—just concrete stretching in every direction and one sad tree that looked like it had depression and needed therapy.

The apartment building was painted a color that might have been beige once but had evolved into "municipal surrender." The lobby smelled like floor cleaner, someone's cooking from 1987, and broken dreams. A handwritten sign said "ELEVATOR broken" and had been there so long the paper had yellowed and someone had added "STILL" underneath.

Their apartment had exactly:

\- One working burner on the stove (the front left; the other three had been broken since Reagan)

\- A refrigerator that hummed constantly like it was trying to become a rapper

\- A bathtub faucet that whistled every time somebody lied nearby—which meant it whistled A LOT

\- Walls so thin you could hear the neighbors' whole life story

\- Windows that didn't quite close, letting in a draft that felt personal

But little DeShawn had big dreams. MASSIVE dreams. Dreams that didn't fit in Apartment 3B.

When most kids drew stick figures, he drew mansions with infinity pools that had pools inside them. He called this "pool inception."

When kids traded Pokémon cards, he ran what he called a "Limited Edition Market Exchange," which was actually just a scam using words like "projected value" and "investment opportunity."

The scam lasted three days before his mama found out.

She made him write seventeen apology letters. He learned to spell "apologize" wrong in fourteen different ways. His mama made him rewrite them all.

He cried. She didn't care.

"You gonna learn today," she said.

(He did learn. He learned to run his scams more carefully and never leave a paper trail. This was not the lesson she intended.)

⚓

"My first step to greatness," Marvelous said in the booth, gesturing with his drink like it was a scepter, "began on a hot summer day. The kind of hot that made the asphalt smell like ambition and bad decisions having a baby."

"It was regular July," Cherry said flatly. "Eighty-four degrees. Average temperature. Normal, unremarkable summer day."

"Exceptional July. Historically significant July."

"It changed nothing."

"It changed ME."

"That's not a historical event, that's personal delusion."

"Personal delusion IS history, Cherry. Who do you think MADE history? Delusional people who believed they could change things."

She paused her counting for exactly one second. "That's the smartest dumb thing you've ever said."

Young DeShawn—age eleven, asthmatic, wearing a tank top his cousin had outgrown three years ago—sat on the front stoop fanning himself with a torn magazine featuring Janet Jackson looking significantly more put-together than anyone in a three-mile radius.

His beat-up Coleman cooler waited beside him—the one he'd found in the dumpster behind Building C and cleaned with dish soap and ambition.

The sun beat down with aggressive intensity, making the concrete shimmer. The air smelled like hot garbage, someone's barbecue, and melting plastic.

That's when Mrs. Henderson waddled over, sweating like a sinner in court who'd just been asked if they'd committed the crime they definitely committed.

"You got any cold water, baby?"

Eleven-year-old DeShawn looked at her with the kind of assessment that suggested his brain was calculating something. Then at his cooler. Then at the universe opening a door.

A door that said "CAPITALISM" in neon letters ten feet tall.

A door that whispered "this is your moment" in a voice that sounded like every motivational speaker from 3 AM infomercials.

"No ma'am," he said, suddenly sitting up straighter, putting on his "business voice." "But I got business opportunities. I got refreshment solutions for your hydration needs."

She blinked, confused. "Baby, what?"

He pulled out a lukewarm Sprite. Not cold. Not even cool. Room temperature approaching hot.

He held it up like it was made of diamonds.

"Fifty cents."

"Chile, that ain't even cold."

"It was cold this morning," he said, which was technically true but misleading in ways that a lawyer would call "problematic." "And cold is a mindset, Mrs. Henderson. Temperature is just a number. You drink this with the right attitude, it gonna feel like it came straight from the Arctic. Plus, I'm an entrepreneur. You supporting small business. The American dream. You wouldn't deny me the American dream, would you?"

She sighed—a long, defeated sigh that suggested she knew she was being hustled but was too hot to care.

Pulled out two quarters.

Cracked it open and immediately made a face like she'd been betrayed by life itself.

"This taste like disappointment."

"That's the entrepreneurial spirit you tasting. That's the flavor of capitalism in liquid form. That's PROGRESS."

She walked away shaking her head, drinking it anyway because sunk cost fallacy is real.

DeShawn looked at his two quarters.

Two whole quarters.

Fifty cents.

Most people would see coins.

He saw a VISION.

Lightning struck his soul. Thunder rolled through his consciousness. Angels sang briefly but then got distracted.

He went inside, got every beverage in the fridge, put them in the cooler, and by sunset had made \$4.50.

By the end of the summer, he'd made \$143.50 selling lukewarm beverages at markup to neighbors too hot and tired to walk to the corner store. His mama found his stash and made him put half in savings.

But she also looked at him different after that—like maybe she'd raised something unusual.

Something either brilliant or criminal.

Possibly both.

Then came Pastor Stacks.

Tall, wide, wearing a suit that cost more than the average monthly rent. He walked up to DeShawn's card table one Sunday morning, his choir of twelve arranging behind him like backup dancers.

"Young man," Pastor Stacks said, "whatchu got for me today?"

"Pastor, I got Sprites, Cokes, and opportunity." DeShawn gestured to his setup. "See, you a businessman. Your congregation gonna see you supporting young Black entrepreneurship. That's good PR. That's what the Lord would want. Probably."

Pastor Stacks stared at him. Then started laughing—big, booming laughter.

"How old are you, son?"

"Twelve."

"And you tryna negotiate with ME?" He pulled out a five-dollar bill. "Keep the change. Not because your pitch was good—which it was—but because you got AUDACITY."

Three steps away, he turned back. "That Sprite ain't cold, is it?"

"No sir."

"But you sold it anyway."

"Yes sir."

Pastor Stacks nodded slowly. "You gon' either be very successful or very arrested. Possibly both."

⚓

By age fifteen, puberty had hit DeShawn like it had been waiting outside with a baseball bat, brass knuckles, and a list of humiliations it had been saving just for him.

He grew three inches in six months, which sounds impressive until you realize his pants couldn't keep up—spent half of tenth grade showing ankle like a scandalous Victorian gentleman.

His voice dropped an octave overnight, then got confused and went back up, then dropped again. It cracked at random moments like a puberty yo-yo controlled by someone with shaky hands. He once cracked mid-word during a class presentation and the word came out in three different octaves.

His mustache tried to come in but got lost halfway, leaving him with what can only be described as "a failed attempt at facial hair that looked like pencil marks." Patchy, uneven, refusing to connect in the middle like there was a tiny border dispute happening on his upper lip.

But despite all this physical chaos, something SHIFTED in him.

He started wearing cracked sunglasses indoors (even though they were broken on one side, so he just squinted through and called it "mysterious").

Started walking different—slower, with more shoulder movement, like he'd studied how cool people walked but only got 40% of the information. He called it his "mogul stride." Everyone else called it "what's wrong with your back?"

He started telling girls things like:

\- "You ain't never met a future mogul before? Lemme change yo life"

\- "I'm destined for greatness, you can get in on the ground floor"

\- "Your beauty is an investment opportunity and I'm the hedge fund"

None of this made sense. He said it anyway. Multiple times. To multiple confused girls who backed away slowly.

He was delusional. Completely, utterly, magnificently delusional.

But he was charismatic.

That combination—delusion plus charisma—is weapons-grade dangerous.

That combination starts MOVEMENTS.

That combination gets people to follow you even when you're heading in the complete wrong direction.

⚓

The name "Marvelous" came from a basketball accident.

"The name," Marvelous said in the booth, standing up dramatically, "came to me during a LEGENDARY moment of athletic excellence."

"You mean during AN accident," Cherry corrected.

"A DESTINED accident. A prophetic collision of fate and a basketball."

It was Lincoln High versus Roosevelt Prep. Sixteenth game of the season, Tuesday afternoon.

The gymnasium smelled like old socks and broken dreams and whatever industrial cleaner the janitor had given up measuring correctly. Approximately forty-seven people in attendance—parents who had to be there and students skipping other classes.

DeShawn was on the team not because of talent but because Coach Wallace believed in participation and also didn't have enough players who could legally be on a roster. DeShawn spent most games on the bench, watching, occasionally waving a towel when it seemed appropriate.

But that day, with three minutes left and Lincoln losing 47-52, Coach turned to look at his bench.

His eyes landed on DeShawn.

DeShawn's eyes widened.

"McCall," Coach said, the word carrying the weight of a man who had made peace with whatever was about to happen, "you're in."

"Coach, I don't think—"

"NOBODY thinks, McCall. We just DO. Get out there."

DeShawn walked onto the court with the confidence of a man walking to his own execution but trying to look casual about it.

Thirty seconds left.

Lincoln ball.

Somehow—through a series of passes that seemed designed by someone having a stroke—the ball ended up in DeShawn's hands.

He was open.

Wide open.

The kind of open that happens when the other team has decided you're not a threat and has stopped guarding you entirely out of pure basketball disrespect.

He had practiced this shot. In his bedroom. Using a waste basket. Successfully approximately 12% of the time, and that percentage was GENEROUS.

He threw it.

The ball went up.

And up.

And UP.

Way higher than it should have. Higher than any basketball had a right to go on a shot from the three-point line. It was like the ball was trying to escape the gymnasium entirely, like it had decided basketball wasn't for it and was pursuing a career in ceiling exploration.

It hit the backboard with a sound like hope dying.

Bounced to the rim.

Rolled around in that terrible, tantalizing way that makes everyone hold their breath.

Everyone leaned in.

And then—

The ball came straight back down.

Directly onto DeShawn's head.

The impact was not gentle. The impact suggested the universe had been waiting for this moment. The ball bounced off his skull with a hollow THOCK that echoed through the gymnasium.

DeShawn went down like someone had cut his strings.

Flat on his back.

Stars exploded across his vision—not metaphorical stars, actual visual phenomena that suggested a concussion or at minimum a really bad headache.

The gymnasium lights swirled like a disco he hadn't consented to attending.

From somewhere far away, he heard someone shout: "THAT WAS MARVELOUS!"

Actually, they shouted "THAT was MARVELOUSLY STUPID!" but his concussed brain only processed the first two words.

When he came to in the nurse's office, ice pack on his head, the word "Marvelous" was bouncing around his skull like it lived there now.

From that day forward, DeShawn Marquell McCall became Da Marvelous McCall.

He told everyone the name came from "the legends of his achievements."

It actually came from head trauma and selective hearing.

Nobody stopped him.

Nobody should have encouraged him.

But nobody stopped him either, which is basically the same as encouragement when you're seventeen and have a mild concussion.

⚓

The "pimping" thing started by accident.

At twenty-two, Marvelous had exactly: a studio apartment above a laundromat, \$340 in savings, and a laptop he'd won in a raffle that definitely wasn't rigged.

He taught himself basic web design watching YouTube at 2 AM.

Started making websites for small businesses—\$50 here, \$100 there.

Then Miss Crystal, a dancer at Club Paradise, asked if he could make her a "professional website."

He did.

It was terrible.

But it had her photo, her rates, and a "booking inquiry" form.

She loved it.

Her friends wanted websites too.

Within months, he was the hood's unofficial web developer for sex workers.

Then came the question: "Marv, you ever think about managing more than websites?"

Miss Crystal sat next to him. "Making sure we safe. Handling the money. You already doing half the work."

And that's how Marvelous accidentally became a pimp.

Not because he sought it out. But because he was good at websites, decent at scheduling, and had a face that made people think he knew what he was doing.

Confidence plus ignorance plus showing up equals success.

Cherry Bomb entered his life six months later like a storm that had hired a lawyer.

She walked into Club Paradise for amateur night and brought the HOUSE down.

Afterward, she walked straight to him.

"You Marvelous?"

"That's what they call me."

"I don't need a pimp," she said. "I need a BUSINESS PARTNER. Seventy-thirty split. I keep seventy."

"That's not how this usually—"

"That's how it works with ME. Because I'm the product, the talent. You provide infrastructure."

Most pimps would've laughed. But Marvelous recognized something.

This woman was GOING places.

It was better to have 30% of HER success than 50% of someone else's failure.

"Deal."

Her grip was firm, like sealing a blood oath.

From that day forward, Cherry was the only person who could tell him he was being stupid and he'd actually listen. Sometimes.

Then came his greatest rival: Madame Pancake.

"And then," Marvelous said in the booth, his voice dropping to something approaching genuine storytelling, "I met my GREATEST rival. My nemesis. My breakfast-themed adversary."

"Madame Pancake," Breadcrumb whispered with reverence.

"Don't say her name like that," Cherry said. "She don't deserve the dramatic pause. She rides a scooter and wears a pancake hat."

But Madame Pancake was DANGEROUS.

She ran girls in the East Side, dressed head-to-toe in breakfast-themed fashion—pancake earrings, syrup-colored wigs, dresses patterned with eggs and bacon. She carried a purse shaped like a butter dish. Her business cards smelled like maple syrup.

She rode a modified Vespa scooter painted to look like a stack of pancakes, with a license plate that said "FLPJCK" and handlebar streamers that looked like dripping syrup.

She'd run the East Side for fifteen years, survived four police investigations, and allegedly made a rival "disappear" by having him deported to a country he wasn't even from. The rumor was she had connections in immigration offices. Nobody confirmed this. Nobody wanted to try.

Their first confrontation happened outside Club Paradise at 2 AM.

Marvelous was leaving, feeling good, twelve thousand in his pocket from a good night.

That's when he heard it.

The sound of scooters.

Multiple scooters.

Approaching with the menace of a breakfast-themed motorcycle gang.

Madame Pancake pulled up with her crew—the "Syrup Squad—"six women on matching scooters with underglow lighting that pulsed in butter-yellow. They wore matching outfits. Waffle-textured jackets. Bacon-striped leggings.

It should have looked ridiculous.

It was terrifying.

"So YOU'RE Marvelous," Madame Pancake said, removing her helmet—which was shaped like an egg. Looking him up and down. "I expected someone taller. And less... tacky."

"And I expected someone who didn't dress like IHOP had a baby with a Fashion Nova clearance rack."

Her eye twitched.

"You think you funny?"

"I think I'm HILARIOUS. And successful. And better dressed than a Denny's menu—"

"Your HEAD is a waffle," she snarled, cutting him off. "syrup receptacle skull. butter TRAY BRAIN. UNSEASONED TOAST OF A MAN. I will POUR misfortune on you like WARM MAPLE—"

"Is that a threat or a brunch menu?" he interrupted.

"BOTH." She leaned forward. "You've been expanding into my territory. MY girls. MY blocks. You think I don't notice? I notice EVERYTHING. I am CONSEQUENCE in pancake form."

"I go where the business takes me—"

"The business is about to take you to a HOSPITAL," she said sweetly. "Or maybe just somewhere... quiet. Somewhere nobody would find you. Somewhere the only thing you'd hear is the sizzle of a griddle. Metaphorically. Or maybe literally. I haven't decided."

She revved her scooter. "You got six months. Then I'm taking everything you built. Consider this your... PANCAKE NOTICE."

The Syrup Squad revved their scooters in unison, a chorus of tiny engines that somehow sounded menacing.

"We'll see," Marvelous said, his voice carrying more confidence than he felt.

She smiled. It was not a nice smile. It was the smile of a woman who had made men disappear and still had room for breakfast.

"Yes," she said. "We will."

She drove away, the sound of six scooters fading into the night like a breakfast-themed nightmare.

Marvelous stood in the empty street.

He was terrified.

But he was also, somehow, exhilarated.

He had a nemesis now.

A real one.

With a theme and everything.

⚓

Back in the booth, the mechanical dove made a grinding sound and dropped another two inches. Its wing twitched with increasing desperation.

Cinnamon stared at him. "So you went from selling warm Sprite to… THIS?"

"Baby girl," Marvelous said, spreading his arms wide, "I went from a one-bedroom apartment with a whistling faucet to a MANSION with a bathtub I fill with Crown Royal. From asthma and bee allergies to being the man everyone in this city know by name. From getting hit in the head by my own basketball to being called a legend."

He paused, looking around at his empire—the club, his crew, the money, Cherry still counting stacks.

"You know what the difference is between where I started and where I am now?"

Cinnamon shook her head.

"I BELIEVED," he said, pointing at his temple. "Even when nobody else did. Even when the evidence said I was delusional. Even when warm Sprites and concussions were my whole resume. I believed I was Marvelous. And eventually? The world believed it too."

He leaned back, twelve thousand dollars in his hand.

"Tonight I'm Da Marvelous McCall. King of the hood. Emperor of delusion. Sultan of confidence. Believer in my own mythology."

And completely, utterly, magnificently convinced this would last forever.

Spoiler alert: it wouldn't.

But for now, in this moment, he was exactly who he'd always claimed to be.

Marvelous.

(Outside, in the parking lot of the dispensary three blocks away, Larry the goat had successfully opened his fourth padlock of the night. His friend— also named Larry, because the universe has a sense of humor—was learning from his technique. They had plans. The plans were not good, but they were ambitious.

30

Their moment was coming.

Nobody was ready.)

⚓

\# Chapter 3: A Day in the Empire (Or: How to Run Five Businesses Into the Ground Simultaneously)

MONDAY, 9:47 AM - CLUB MARVELOUS, OFFICE OF BROKEN DREAMS

Da Marvelous McCall woke up on the velvet couch in his office wearing yesterday's emerald-green tracksuit and a headache that felt like it had been personally crafted by his enemies, shipped express, and delivered directly to his brain with a hammer.

The couch smelled like regret, Crown Royal, and the tears of good decisions that had died here.

Sunlight stabbed through the window like it was actively trying to murder him.

His mouth tasted like he'd licked a carpet that had been used as a dance floor by people who didn't believe in soap.

Sunday nights at the club always ended the same way: too much Crown, too many promises nobody intended to keep, Cherry Bomb yelling at him about "fiscal responsibility" while he yelled back about "living in the moment," and Breadcrumb asleep in the storage closet spooning the mop bucket like it was his emotional support cleaning tool.

His phone buzzed on the table.

Vibrated with the urgency of seventeen missed calls.

"Oh God," he muttered, reaching for it with the coordination of a drunk baby giraffe. "Oh God oh God oh God."

He scrolled through the messages with growing horror:

Cherry (6:23 AM): The dispensary is on fire again.

"AGAIN?!" he shouted at the phone like it had personally set the fire.

Tito (7:15 AM): Boss, the laundromat flooded. We got a situation. Actually multiple situations. Actually it's all one big situation that has smaller situations inside it like nesting dolls of problems.

Breadcrumb (8:02 AM): BOSS THE GOAT ESCAPED AND I THINK HE STEALING

Breadcrumb (8:04 AM): BOSS HE DEFINITELY STEALING

Breadcrumb (8:07 AM): BOSS LARRY GOT KEYS I DON'T KNOW HOW

Pastor Stacks (8:34 AM): Son, we need to discuss your "financial consulting services." The IRS called the church. Again. They sound angry. Very angry. Biblically angry. Wrath of God angry.

Madame Pancake (9:12 AM): I know what you did. We need to talk. NOW. Or I'm coming to your club with CONSEQUENCES.

Marvelous sat up slowly, each movement causing his brain to protest by sending pain signals that spelled out "YOU drank too MUCH YOU ABSOLUTE FOOL" in Morse code made of suffering.

"Just ONCE," he said to the empty room, to God, to whoever was listening and clearly ignoring him, "I wanna wake up with zero problems. Just ONE morning. ONE peaceful, problem-free morning where nobody calling me about fires, floods, or livestock theft."

His phone rang.

Cherry.

Of course it was Cherry.

He answered with the enthusiasm of a man facing a firing squad. "How bad?"

"Which fire?" she asked, voice sharp enough to cut through his hangover and several layers of denial. "The dispensary fire or the dumpster fire that is your ENTIRE LIFE?"

"THE dispensary FIRE, CHERRY!"

"Oh, THAT fire. Small. Manageable. Breadcrumb left the vaporizer on overnight. again. Burned a hole through the counter. AGAIN. The same counter we just replaced. AGAIN."

"Is it OUT?"

"Yeah, Tito put it out with the fire extinguisher. But now the whole place smells like burnt weed, chemical foam, and broken dreams. Customers are CONCERNED. One lady asked if we were 'going through something emotionally.'"

"So..." Marvelous said hopefully. "Like normal?"

"Baby, NO," Cherry said with the exasperation of someone who'd had this conversation forty-seven times. "Like WORSE than normal. It smell like if sadness was a store."

He rubbed his face hard enough to possibly remove the top layer of skin. "What about the laundromat?"

"Washing machine number four—the ONE machine that was working good—exploded. Water EVERYWHERE. Three inches deep. The casino in the back? Flooded. People's poker chips floating like little life rafts of bad decisions. Someone's lucky rabbit's foot floating past like it had DROWNED. That rabbit foot gave UP."

"Did we lose money?"

"We ALWAYS losing money," Cherry said. "That's our business MODEL at this point. But yes, MORE money now. Significantly more. The kind of more that has CONSEQUENCES."

"And the goat?"

Cherry sighed so hard he could hear her soul leaving her body through the phone.

"Larry escaped again. Third time this WEEK. Breadcrumb thinks he's at the farmer's market eating organic produce and POSSIBLY committing identity theft, we're not sure yet."

"AGAIN?!" Marvelous stood up too fast, got dizzy, sat back down. "How does he keep finding the farmer's market?! It's THREE MILES AWAY!"

"Larry got better navigation skills than Breadcrumb," Cherry said.

"That's a LOW bar! That's a bar on the ground! That bar is in a HOLE!"

"Nevertheless."

"Don't 'nevertheless' me! How does a GOAT have keys?!"

"I don't KNOW, baby! Larry mysterious! He operate on a level we can't comprehend! He might be MAGIC!"

Marvelous stood up again, more carefully this time, and started pacing.

"You coming in or you gon' hide in the club all day?" Cherry asked.

"I'm not HIDING, I'm STRATEGIZING."

"You HUNGOVER and AVOIDING."

"Strategically hungover and tactically avoiding."

"Get your ass to the dispensary. We got customers waiting and they KNOW something's wrong because there's scorch MARKS and the door is CROOKED."

"It's ON FIRE!"

"It WAS on fire. Now it's just... damaged. Structurally questionable. Aesthetically concerning."

"That's WORSE!"

"Everything about your businesses is worse!" Cherry shouted. "That's not NEW information! come FIX IT ANYWAY!"

She hung up.

Marvelous stared at his phone.

Took a deep breath.

Tried to remember why he'd thought owning multiple businesses was a good idea.

Failed to remember.

"Alright," he said to himself, straightening his tracksuit like he was preparing for battle. "Let's go see what's on fire today."

⚓

10:32 AM - THE DISPENSARY/BARBERSHOP (SCENE OF FIRE #3)

When Marvelous arrived at Marvelous Medicinal Solutions & Premium Fade Headquarters (the sign said both things because he couldn't decide which business he wanted it to be), the damage was worse than Cherry had described.

WAY worse.

Like "insurance company would laugh and then cry and then call the police" worse.

Half the counter was GONE—not damaged, GONE, like it had been deleted from reality.

Black scorch marks covered the wall in a pattern that looked suspiciously like the Grim Reaper.

The ceiling tiles had melted into sad droopy shapes.

The air smelled like someone had hotboxed a chemical plant while it was having an emotional breakdown.

And somehow—SOMEHOW—inexplicably, against all logic and reason...

There was a LINE of customers outside.

Twenty deep.

Waiting patiently.

Like this was NORMAL.

"Why they still HERE?!" Marvelous asked, gesturing at the line with both hands like he was trying to physically push away the absurdity.

"Because you the ONLY dispensary in walking distance," Tito said, standing in the doorway looking like a disappointed father whose son had just wrecked the family car for the third time. "They desperate. This neighborhood need weed like it need OXYGEN."

"We can't serve people in a CRIME SCENE!"

"Then lose the money," Tito said flatly.

"How much money?"

"Lotta money."

"Define 'lotta.'"

"Two thousand, maybe three, standing in that line right now. Cash. Immediate. Money we NEED because we three months behind on—"

"DON'T say IT!"

—"rent."

"YOU said IT!"

Marvelous looked at the waiting customers, most of whom were checking their phones and looking annoyed that their weed emergency was taking longer than expected.

Then at the fire damage that looked like abstract art if abstract art was created by failure and negligence.

Then at his bank account which was currently screaming in terror.

"...Open the side door," he said finally. "Serve 'em from the barbershop section."

"Boss," Tito said carefully, the way you'd talk to someone about to make a terrible decision that would definitely end badly. "The barber quit last week. After you told him his fades 'lacked vision.'"

"Then I'LL cut hair!"

Tito stared at him.

Just stared.

With eyes that said "I've seen you try to cut a sandwich and fail."

"Boss. YOU don'T know HOW TO CUT HAIR."

"I'LL improvise!" Marvelous said with the confidence of someone who'd never actually improvised anything successfully. "How hard can it be?! It's just… SCISSORS! And SHAPES! And… HAIR!"

"Boss—"

"Tito, I once sold a man a car that didn't RUN and convinced him it was 'vintage.' I can cut ONE head of hair!"

"You sold your COUSIN that car and he STILL mad at you!"

"He got OVER it!"

"He didn't! He bring it up at EVERY family function!"

"That's UNRELATED! Get me the clippers!"

⚓

11:15 AM - THE HAIRCUT DISASTER (CARLOS WILL REMEMBER THIS)

Cutting hair, it turned out, was VERY hard.

Significantly harder than Marvelous had assumed.

Harder than selling lukewarm Sprites.

Harder than fixing WiFi by unplugging things.

Possibly harder than theoretical physics.

The first customer—a man named Carlos who made the CATASTROPHIC mistake of trusting Marvelous with sharp objects near his head—asked for a "simple fade."

"Simple fade," Marvelous repeated confidently, holding the clippers like a sword he didn't know how to use. "Got it. I understand completely. Fade. Simple. Easy."

He did not understand.

He did not got it.

Nothing about this was simple or easy.

Fifteen minutes later, Marvelous stepped back to admire his "work."

What Carlos received could only be described as "a cry for help rendered in hair."

One side was shorter than the other by at LEAST an inch—and not in an artistic way, in a "this person doesn't understand geometry" way.

The lineup—the MOST important part, the part that makes or breaks a fade—looked like Marvelous had used a ruler from a funhouse that was actively having a nervous breakdown.

There was a random bald patch near the back that looked like someone had sneezed while holding the clippers.

The fade itself didn't fade so much as it JUMPED from one length to another like it was being chased.

And somehow—and Marvelous would never be able to explain this—there was a ZIGZAG pattern on the left side that he definitely hadn't meant to create but had DEFINITELY created anyway.

Carlos looked in the mirror.

The silence that followed was profound.

The kind of silence that exists before someone calls a lawyer.

The kind of silence that has WEIGHT.

"Bruh," Carlos said finally, voice small and broken, like his soul had just filed for bankruptcy. "What… WHAT… is THIS?"

"That's the…" Marvelous cleared his throat, scrambling for words, any words, words that could save this situation that was beyond saving. "That's the EXPERIMENTAL style. Very avant-garde. Very fashion-forward. This is what they doing in PARIS."

"Ain't NOBODY doing this in Paris!" Carlos shouted, standing up. "This look like a ACCIDENT!"

"Art IS accidents!" Marvelous insisted, which was something he'd heard once and didn't understand but it sounded deep. "All great art starts as MISTAKES!"

"this ain'T art!" Carlos was yelling now, pointing at his head with both hands like he was presenting evidence. "this A hate crime! THIS is assault WITH A CLIPPER! THIS IS—I CAN'T GO TO WORK LIKE THIS! I WORK AT THE BANK!"

"You could say it's a STATEMENT about—"

"about what?! ABOUT how I LET AN UNQUALIFIED MAN TOUCH MY HEAD?!"

Tito grabbed Marvelous by the arm and physically pulled him away from Carlos and the clippers and the possibility of making things even worse, which seemed impossible but Tito wasn't taking chances.

"Boss," Tito said quietly. "Stop. Please. I'm BEGGING you. Before you get sued, arrested, or BOTH."

"I'm TRYING to save the business!" Marvelous hissed back.

"You DESTROYING that man's will to LIVE!"

Cherry walked in from the dispensary side, took ONE look at Carlos's head, and gasped.

"Baby. Baby NO. What did you DO?"

"I gave him a FADE!"

"You gave him TRAUMA!"

Carlos was looking in the mirror again, touching his head gently like he was mourning the loss of a loved one.

"I had plans tonight," he whispered. "A DATE. I was gonna propose. I bought a ring. Now I look like I survived a ENCOUNTER."

"You can wear a HAT!" Breadcrumb suggested helpfully from the corner where he'd been watching this disaster unfold like a Greek tragedy.

"THE restaurant DON'T ALLOW HATS!" Carlos screamed.

They gave Carlos:

\- A full refund

\- A free eighth of their best strain (which was mid at best)

\- An apology card that Breadcrumb made that said "Sorry for Aesthetic Harm"

\- A hat ANYWAY (a nice one)

\- And fifty dollars in cash to "emotionally recover"

Carlos left wearing the hat pulled down LOW, muttering about "unqualified individuals with weapons" and "how is this LEGAL" and "I'm telling my LAWYER."

"That went well," Marvelous said, putting down the clippers like they'd betrayed him.

"THAT went TERRIBLE," Cherry said. "You basically ASSAULTED that man!"

"I was HELPING!"

"You gave him POST-traumatic FADE DISORDER!"

"Is that real?"

"IT is NOW!"

Tito locked the clippers in a drawer.

"Boss," he said. "You banned from cutting hair. Forever. Permanently. We putting it in WRITING."

"That's EXCESSIVE—"

"We putting it in a CONTRACT that you gotta SIGN!"

⚓

12:03 PM - THE LAUNDROMAT FLOOD (LARRY RETURNS)

The laundromat—officially named Marvelous Wash & Fold & Definitely Don't Ask About The Back Room—was a DISASTER of biblical proportions.

Three inches of standing water.

Actual WAVES sloshing between the washing machines.

Poker chips floating everywhere like the saddest confetti.

Someone's UNDERWEAR stuck to the ceiling (nobody knew how, nobody wanted to know how, it was remaining a mystery).

A playing card—the King of Hearts, ironically—drifted past like it had given up on everything.

And in the corner, standing on TOP of washing machine number seven like he was surveying his conquered kingdom, was Larry the goat.

Majestic.

Unbothered.

Moisturized.

Happy.

In his lane.

Focused.

Flourishing.

Around his neck was a keychain with THREE distinct keys, jangling like a tiny jailer's collection.

"HOW did he GET IN HERE?!" Marvelous yelled, pointing at Larry with accusation and also mild respect.

"HE got KEYS SOMEHOW!" Breadcrumb yelled back, equally confused and significantly more impressed.

"GOATS don'T HAVE KEYS!"

"LARRY DO!"

"WHERE did HE GET THEM?!"

"I DON'T know! he DON'T TELL ME STUFF!"

"he'S A goat, HE CAN'T TELL YOU STUFF!"

"MAYBE that'S why HE DON'T TELL ME!"

Marvelous waded through the water toward Larry, shoes making sad sloshing sounds.

Larry watched him approach with eyes that contained ancient wisdom and also mild contempt.

"Larry," Marvelous said gently, like he was negotiating with a hostage-taker. "Where did you get those keys, buddy?"

Larry bleated once.

It sounded like "wouldn't YOU like to know."

"Larry, I'm serious. Those are KEYS. You're a goat. Goats don't need keys. You don't have PROPERTY. You don't have POSSESSIONS. What do you even UNLOCK?"

Larry bleated again, louder, more insistent.

It definitely sounded like "THAT'S for ME TO KNOW."

"Is he… TALKING?" Breadcrumb asked, voice filled with wonder.

"He's BLEATING," Tito said. "Y'all giving him too much credit."

"Nah, he TALKING," Breadcrumb insisted. "Larry got SECRETS."

As if to punctuate this statement, Larry jumped down from the washing machine, landed perfectly in the water without splashing (how?), and walked toward the front door with the confidence of someone who'd just completed a successful heist.

He paused at the door.

Looked back at Marvelous.

Bleated once more—definitely saying "SEE you LATER, SUCKERS—"and walked out into the street like he had APPOINTMENTS.

Important appointments.

Business meetings.

A SCHEDULE.

Marvelous stared after him, mouth open, brain struggling to process what it had just witnessed.

"I'm gonna sell that goat," he said finally.

"YOU can'T!" Breadcrumb cried, genuine distress in his voice. "He part OF THE TEAM! He ESSENTIAL PERSONNEL!"

"He's a CRIMINAL!"

"He's MISUNDERSTOOD!"

"He's STEALING!"

"He's ENTREPRENEURIAL!"

"THOSE are THE SAME THING!"

"NOT when LARRY DO IT!"

Cherry waded over, holding her purse above her head to keep it dry.

"Baby," she said. "We gotta drain this water before the building COLLAPSES."

"With WHAT? We don't got a pump!"

"Call the LANDLORD!"

"The landlord HATE ME!"

"I WONDER why!" she shouted. "Maybe because you three MONTHS BEHIND ON RENT!"

"Don't YELL at me in front of Breadcrumb, he get NERVOUS!"

"I'M ALREADY nervous!" Breadcrumb said, voice cracking. "I'M always NERVOUS! THAT'S MY DEFAULT!"

1:47 PM - LUNCH WITH PASTOR STACKS (THE IRS CONVERSATION NOBODY WANTED)

Pastor Stacks met Marvelous at Mama Lou's Soul Food Kitchen, a place where the portions were massive, the prices were fair, and the judgment was FREE and ABUNDANT.

The Pastor was wearing his finest polyester suit—the purple one with gold buttons that looked like it had been purchased from a catalog called "Prosperity Gospel Quarterly."

His expression was grave.

Not "I'm worried" grave.

"I'm actively attending your funeral in my mind" grave.

"Son," Pastor Stacks began, folding his hands on the table like he was about to deliver a sermon at a funeral for Marvelous's financial future. "We need to discuss your tax situation."

Marvelous, who'd been about to bite into a chicken wing that smelled like heaven's waiting room, froze.

"I don't GOT a tax situation," he said carefully.

"Son," Pastor Stacks said, voice heavy with the weight of bad news and Old Testament wrath. "That IS the situation. The lack of taxes IS the situation."

"What you mean?"

"I mean," Pastor Stacks leaned forward, voice dropping like he was revealing classified information, "you been running FIVE separate businesses for two years and ain't filed nothing. Not ONE tax return. Not ONE legitimate form. Not ONE piece of paperwork that would indicate you understand how the LEGAL SYSTEM works."

Marvelous set down the chicken wing very slowly.

"…Define 'nothing.'"

"ZERO," Pastor said, holding up his hand in the shape of a zero. "zilch. nada. The mathematical and legal concept of ABSENCE. You got more NOTHING than most people got SOMETHING."

"But I got… receipts?"

"RECEIPTS written on NAPKINS DON'T COUNT!" Pastor Stacks shouted, then caught himself and lowered his voice because they were in Mama Lou's and Mama Lou didn't tolerate shouting during lunch hour. "They don't COUNT, son!"

"Some are on GAS station RECEIPTS!" Marvelous protested.

"THAT'S worse! That's worse, son! You can't run a BUSINESS on GAS STATION RECEIPTS!"

"But they GOT NUMBERS!"

"THEY got THE WRONG NUMBERS!"

Marvelous took a breath.

"Okay. Okay. But like… the IRS probably don't even know I exist, right? They got bigger fish to fry, right? They going after BILLIONAIRES and CORPORATIONS and—"

"They called the CHURCH," Pastor Stacks said, cutting him off.

Silence.

Heavy, thick silence.

The kind of silence that makes your ears ring.

"They… what?" Marvelous asked quietly.

"The IRS," Pastor Stacks repeated slowly, "called new covenant word OF FAITH AND FINANCIAL LITERACY CHURCH asking about YOU."

"WHY?!"

"Because," Pastor said, rubbing his temples like he was trying to massage away a migraine that had a BIRTH certificate, "you listed the CHURCH as your business address on THREE different forms! THREE!"

"I needed an address that sounded LEGITIMATE!"

"YOU committed fraud," Pastor Stacks hissed, leaning across the table, "using the lord'S HOUSE! You used GOD'S ADDRESS for TAX EVASION!"

"I thought that was NETWORKING!"

"NETWORKING?!"

"Yeah! Using my CONNECTIONS! You told ME to use my connections!"

"I meant SOCIAL connections, not HOLY REAL ESTATE!"

"WHAT'S the DIFFERENCE?!"

"THE difference is one IS LEGAL AND ONE IS FEDERAL PRISON!"

Pastor Stacks ordered a double whiskey even though it was 2 PM on a Monday.

The waitress didn't judge.

Mama Lou's had seen worse.

"So what do I DO?" Marvelous asked, genuine fear creeping into his voice now.

"You get a LAWYER," Pastor said. "A real one. Not your cousin who got his degree from the INTERNET."

"Carlos Ruiz is a LEGITIMATE—"

"He got his degree from a website called LAWSCHOOL4REAL dot NET!"

"The 4REAL part sound HONEST!"

"IT was run BY A MAN IN PRISON!"

Marvelous put his face in his hands.

"I'm SCREWED," he muttered.

"You're BEHIND," Pastor corrected. "But you can catch up. You just need MONEY. REAL money. Like… fifty thousand MINIMUM to sort this out, pay back taxes, get right with the government."

"WHERE I'm supposed to get fifty THOUSAND?!"

Pastor Stacks shrugged, sipping his whiskey.

"That's YOUR problem, son. I'm just the messenger. The messenger who's spiritually concerned about your immortal soul and also your legal status."

⚓

3:22 PM - MADAME PANCAKE CONFRONTATION (BREAKFAST VIOLENCE DECLARED)

Marvelous was walking back to the club, mind racing with IRS problems and money problems and Larry problems and haircut trauma when—

SCREEEEEECH.

A pink scooter appeared out of NOWHERE and screeched to a stop directly in front of him, close enough that he felt the breeze of aerodynamic fury.

Madame Pancake.

Neon purple wig styled like cotton candy that had achieved consciousness.

Sunglasses bigger than her entire face, possibly bigger than some small aircraft.

Pink leather jacket with "SYRUP QUEEN" bedazzled on the back.

And an expression that could curdle milk, spoil wine, and make babies cry from a distance.

"We need to TALK," she said, voice sharp enough to cut diamonds and also feelings.

"I'm BUSY—" Marvelous started.

"You STOLE TIFFANY," she interrupted, revving her scooter menacingly (which shouldn't be possible but she made it work).

"Who?"

"TIFFANY!" Pancake shouted loud enough that people across the street turned to watch. "my top earner! the girl WHO MADE ME FIFTEEN HUNDRED A WEEK! She came to YOUR club LAST WEEK and now she working for YOU!"

"I didn't steal NOBODY!"

"She said," Pancake continued, pulling out her phone and reading directly from a text message, "'Marvelous offered me better opportunities, dental insurance, and a vision plan.'"

"I DON'T even got DENTAL FOR MYSELF!"

"THEN why SHE SAY THAT?!"

"I DON'T know!" Marvelous yelled back. "Maybe she lying! Maybe she CONFUSED! Maybe I was DRUNK and PROMISED stuff I can't DELIVER!"

"So you DID recruit her!"

"I DON'T REMEMBER!"

"YOU don'T remember STEALING MY EMPLOYEE?!"

"I DON'T remember last tuesday AT ALL! It's a BLUR! There was CROWN ROYAL!"

Madame Pancake revved her scooter again, this time creating a small cloud of exhaust that smelled like anger and motor oil.

"This means WAR, Marvelous," she said, voice dropping dangerously low.

"We ALREADY at war!"

"Then this means ESCALATED war! war 2.0! THE SEQUEL!"

"You can't ESCALATE what's already ESCALATED!"

"WATCH me!" she screamed. "I'M gonna escalate so hard YOU WON'T EVEN KNOW WHAT PEACE LOOKS LIKE ANYMORE!"

She peeled out, leaving tire marks on the street, the smell of burning rubber and burning bridges, and one flip-flop that had fallen off her foot during her dramatic exit.

Marvelous picked up the flip-flop.

It had pancakes on it.

Of course it did.

Cherry walked up from the club entrance where she'd been watching.

"What was THAT?" she asked.

"Pancake think I stole her girl."

"Did you?"

"MAYBE? I don't know! I was DRUNK! You know I recruit when I'm drunk!"

"Baby, you GOTTA stop recruiting when you drunk!" Cherry said, exasperated. "That's how we got three PEOPLE we can't AFFORD to pay!"

"That's when I'm MOST CHARISMATIC!"

"That's when you're MOST DELUSIONAL!"

"SAME ENERGY!"

⚓

5:15 PM - EMERGENCY MEETING (AKA: THE COUNCIL OF POOR DECISIONS)

Back at Club Marvelous, in the office that smelled like desperation and very old carpet, Marvelous called an emergency meeting.

Present:

\- Cherry Bomb (CFO of Reality Checks)

\- Tito (VP of Telling Marvelous No)

\- Breadcrumb (Director of Confusion and Bottle Cap Art)

\- And somehow, inexplicably, Pastor Stacks (self-invited, as always)

"Alright," Marvelous began, standing at the head of the table like a general addressing troops before a battle they were definitely going to lose. "We got MULTIPLE problems."

"Just multiple?" Cherry asked, eyebrow raised.

"The dispensary BURNED. again. That's fire number THREE this year, for those keeping track."

"I'm keeping track," Tito said, pulling out a notebook labeled "MARVELOUS'S DISASTERS - VOLUME 4."

"The laundromat FLOODED. There's water damage. Structural concerns. poker chips IN THE WALLS."

"The goat's a CRIMINAL with KEYS," Breadcrumb added helpfully.

"The IRS is investigating me because I used the CHURCH ADDRESS!"

"I told you that was gonna BACKFIRE!" Pastor Stacks said.

"You TOLD ME to use my connections!"

"Not LITERALLY!"

"And," Marvelous continued, voice rising, "Madame Pancake has declared ESCALATED war because I ALLEGEDLY stole her employee while I was drunk and don't remember!"

"That's a LOT of problems," Tito observed.

"I KNOW it'S A LOT OF PROBLEMS!"

"Also," Tito continued calmly, flipping through his notebook, "we three months behind on rent. Every property. All of them. The club, the dispensary, the laundromat, AND the petting zoo building."

Silence.

Thick, uncomfortable silence.

"…How behind?" Marvelous asked carefully, like he was asking a doctor about terminal diagnosis results.

Tito flipped a page. "Club: three months, \$9,000. Dispensary: three months, \$7,500. Laundromat: FOUR months, \$8,000."

"HOW is it FOUR?!"

"The landlord forgot about us for a month," Tito said. "He just… didn't remember we existed."

"That's not GOOD!" Marvelous shouted. "That's sad! That means we so INSIGNIFICANT he FORGOT!"

"Nevertheless," Tito said. "When he remembered, he sent a letter. Says if we don't pay by end of month, he's EVICTING all three properties. Simultaneously."

"CAN he DO THAT?!"

"He OWN the buildings, so YES!"

Pastor Stacks cleared his throat loudly, commanding attention.

"Son," he said, voice carrying the weight of spiritual concern and also financial TERROR. "I say this with love and with the lord'S guidance: your empire is held together by NEGLIGENCE, PRAYER, and what I can only describe as DIVINE CONFUSION."

"And CHARISMA!" Marvelous added desperately.

"Charisma don't PAY BILLS!" Pastor shouted.

"It pays SOME bills!"

"NAME ONE!"

Marvelous thought HARD.

Brain working overtime.

Searching through memories.

"...The phone bill that time I flirted with the customer service lady and she gave me a discount?"

"THAT was A one-TIME PROMOTIONAL OFFER!"

"She WINKED at me!"

"YOU can'T see WINKS OVER THE PHONE!"

"I HEARD IT!"

Cherry put her hand on Marvelous's shoulder, voice gentle but firm.

"Baby," she said. "We need REAL money. soon. Like, by end OF MONTH soon. Like, \$25,000 MINIMUM soon."

"I KNOW!"

"So what's the PLAN?"

Marvelous stood up.

Paced.

Ran his hands through his hair.

Looked at the ceiling like God might drop down some answers.

God did not.

THINK.

THINK HARDER.

What would a REAL businessman do?

What would someone COMPETENT do?

What would someone who UNDERSTOOD BUSINESS do?

"We need an EVENT," he said finally, stopping mid-pace, finger pointed up like he'd just discovered fire.

"What kind of event?" Cherry asked carefully.

"Something BIG. Something that brings in real money. FAST money. Something that puts us on the MAP and also in the BLACK."

"Like what?" Tito asked.

Marvelous's eyes lit up with the kind of dangerous enthusiasm that preceded most of his worst decisions.

"A GALA," he said.

Everyone stared.

Long stares.

The kind of stares that communicated "this is the dumbest thing you've ever said" without words.

"A… gala?" Cherry repeated slowly, like she was trying to make sure she'd heard correctly.

"YES!" Marvelous said, getting excited now, gesturing wildly. "A high-class, black tie, celebrity-studded event that puts us ON THE MAP! We charge for tickets, get sponsors, make it FANCY! Rich people LOVE galas!"

"Boss," Tito said gently, carefully, like he was explaining reality to a child. "We can't even afford to fix the COUNTER. How we gon' afford a GALA?"

"We'll FIGURE it OUT! We always do!"

"We always BARELY SURVIVE!" Breadcrumb corrected, voice cracking with truth.

"SAME ENERGY!"

"IT'S NOT!"

Pastor Stacks stood up, shaking his head.

"I'm out," he said. "Y'all on your own with this nonsense. This is BEYOND even my ability to enable through prayer and willful ignorance."

He walked toward the door.

"Pastor, wait—" Marvelous called.

"NO!" Pastor said, turning back. "I enabled enough! This is where I DRAW THE LINE! At the GALA!"

He left.

The door slammed.

"He'll be back," Marvelous said confidently, sitting down.

"Why you think that?" Cherry asked.

"Because we pay him in CASH and he got a gambling problem and a WEAKNESS for redemption narratives!"

"That's..." Tito paused. "That's actually accurate."

"He'll be back by TOMORROW," Marvelous said. "Probably earlier. Definitely before dinner."

⚓

9:33 PM - END OF THE DAY (SOMEHOW STILL ALIVE)

Marvelous sat in his office alone, lights dimmed, exhausted in ways he didn't know a person could be exhausted.

The club thumped with music below, bass vibrating through the floor.

His phone buzzed with sixteen new problems he was ignoring.

But for one quiet moment, he just sat there.

Breathing.

Existing.

Somehow still running an empire that was more chaos than empire.

And despite EVERYTHING—the fires, the floods, the goat theft, the IRS, the haircut trauma, the escalated war with a breakfast-themed rival—he smiled.

Because even though everything was chaos...

Even though nothing worked right...

Even though he was drowning in debt and problems and bad decisions...

He was building SOMETHING.

Something messy.

Something impossible.

Something ridiculous.

Something MARVELOUS.

Cherry walked in quietly.

"You good?" she asked.

"Yeah," he said. "Just… thinking."

"About what?"

"How we gon' pull off this gala."

She walked over, sat on his lap, wrapped her arms around his neck.

"You serious about that?" she asked.

"Dead serious. We NEED it. Like, existentially NEED it."

"Then we'll make it happen," she said softly. "We always do."

"We always barely survive," he corrected.

"Same energy," she said, repeating his words back to him, smiling.

He kissed her.

Long.

Slow.

Real.

Tomorrow they'd start planning.

Tomorrow they'd figure out funding (somehow).

Tomorrow they'd tackle the impossible (again).

But tonight?

Tonight they had survived another day in the empire.

And that was enough.

For now.

CHAPTER 4

The Gala That Shouldn't Happen (But Definitely Will! Because Nobody Can Stop This Man)

⚓

Planning a hood gala with no money, no venue, and no actual event planning experience is like trying to perform surgery with a spoon—technically possible if you're really committed and nobody's watching too closely, but everyone involved knows it's going to end badly.

Marvelous didn't care.

He woke up the morning after announcing the gala with the energy of a man who'd just invented electricity, even though he'd barely slept three hours, even though his body was screaming for rest and his brain was filing formal complaints about being asked to function on caffeine and delusion alone.

The gala.

THE GALA.

His salvation. His solution. His extremely poorly thought out answer to every problem—the IRS, the fires, the floods, the criminal goat syndicate, and a breakfast-themed rival who'd weaponized city bureaucracy.

(Outside his window, Larry and Larry 2 were watching from across the street. They'd been monitoring his sleep patterns. They had concerns. They also had the petty cash from last week, which they'd invested in what Larry 2 called "diversified organic produce holdings.")

"CHERRY!" he yelled into his phone before she even answered.

"It's 7 AM on a tuesday," she answered, voice thick with sleep and murder. "Why are you AWAKE? Why am I AWAKE? Why does consciousness EXIST?"

"THE gala! We got two WEEKS! That's FOURTEEN DAYS! That's like… A LOT of minutes! MANY minutes!"

"I'm hanging up."

"WAIT! I made a list!"

Silence. Heavy, suspicious silence.

"You don't know how to make lists," Cherry said finally. "You've NEVER made a list. I've known you for years and I've never seen you complete ANY organizational task."

"I MADE one ANYWAY!" He grabbed a crumpled paper from his nightstand—covered in what might have been Crown Royal. "Number one: venue. Number two: entertainment. Number three: food. Number four: more food because the first food might not be enough—"

"Wait—"

"Number five: drinks. EXPENSIVE drinks. Number six: dessert! multiple desserts! Number seven: appetizers, which I KNOW should come before dessert but I only thought of it AFTER—"

"Is this list just food items after number three?"

"NUMBER eight: SNACKS—"

"MARVELOUS!"

"NUMBER ten is A chocolate FOUNTAIN BECAUSE EVERY GALA NEEDS A CHOCOLATE FOUNTAIN—"

She hung up.

The mechanical dove in the corner of his bedroom—wait, when had THAT gotten there?—twitched once and dropped a feather.

"Don't look at me like that," he told the dove. "I got PLANS. I got VISION."

The dove made a sound like a disappointed robot sighing.

THE FIRST PLANNING MEETING: A MASTERCLASS IN ORGANIZED CHAOS

By noon—after Marvelous had called Cherry seventeen more times, sent forty-three text messages, and threatened to show up at her apartment with a megaphone he'd bought from a man on the street who definitely stole it— she'd agreed to one meeting.

One meeting.

With conditions.

Condition one: No megaphone.

Condition two: No lists that were just food items.

Condition three: She could leave at any time if she felt her blood pressure rising above "concerning" levels.

The crew assembled in the back office of Club Marvelous, a room that smelled like old cigarette smoke, spilled drinks, and the accumulated anxiety of bad business decisions.

Cherry Bomb sat at the table with a legal pad, three pens of different colors (black for facts, red for problems, blue for things that would never happen but Marvelous would insist on anyway), and her "calculator of doom—"the big one, the serious one, the one she called "The Reaper" because it delivered death to dreams. It had a small scratch on the side from the time she'd thrown it at the wall during the last budget meeting.

Tito stood by the door, already looking tired, already regretting being here. He'd brought a flask. Nobody questioned the flask. The flask was reasonable.

Breadcrumb sat cross-legged on the floor with a notebook that had "GALA ideaz" written on the cover in green crayon because he'd lost the black one and "green is the color of money and GROWTH and also GRASS which is NATURAL which means my ideas are ORGANIC."

Nobody had the energy to unpack that logic.

Big Mike stood silently in the corner like a piece of furniture that could throw you through a wall if necessary.

And somehow, inexplicably, Larry the goat had gotten into the building and was standing by the window, watching with the intensity of a board member who owned significant shares.

"Why is Larry here?" Cherry asked.

"He showed up," Tito said. "We couldn't stop him. He has keys."

"To THIS building?"

"To EVERY building apparently. We've stopped questioning it."

Larry bleated once. It sounded like "I have vested interests in this operation's success."

"Did that goat just—" Cherry started.

"We don't TALK about what the goat says," Tito interrupted. "It's easier that way."

"Alright," Marvelous said, standing at the head of the table like a CEO who'd never read a business book but had watched half a ted Talk once and felt inspired. "Let's talk budget. Cherry, what we working with? Give me the

REAL numbers."

Cherry looked at her notes—actual notes, with actual numbers, written in ink that meant actual consequences.

"We got twelve thousand in the account."

"PERFECT! See? We got capital! We got RESOURCES! We got—"

"That's not perfect," Cherry interrupted, her voice carrying the patience of someone explaining gravity to a flat-earther. "That's RENT. That's rent for ALL the businesses. The club, the dispensary, the laundromat—"

"Okay but what if," Marvelous said, leaning forward with the expression of someone about to suggest something brilliant or catastrophically stupid, "we just… don't pay rent this month? Use that money for the gala, MAKE money at the gala, then pay rent. It's not avoiding rent, it's strategically DELAYING rent. It's INVESTMENT rent. It's rent that's taking a VACATION."

"MARVELOUS."

"I'm BRAINSTORMING!"

"You're COMMITTING financial SUICIDE!"

"It's called INVESTMENT!"

"It's called EVICTION!"

"It's called VISION!"

"It's called the landlord GROUP chat that Madame Pancake set up! They're ORGANIZED now! They have MEETINGS!"

Larry bleated from the window. It sounded distinctly like "even I pay my debts, and I'm a goat."

Tito cleared his throat. "Boss, how much you think this gala gon' cost? In ACTUAL dollars. Money that won't accept napkins or vibes."

"I don't know. How much DO galas cost? Ballpark. Estimate. Vibe."

"'Vibe' is not a unit of currency," Cherry said.

"It SHOULD be."

"But it ISN'T."

Cherry pulled out her phone, typed rapidly, her face going progressively paler as she scrolled, like she was watching someone die slowly on screen.

"Marvelous. A proper gala. Venue rental, catering, entertainment, decorations, security, insurance, permits…" She paused. "Fifty thousand dollars. MINIMUM. That's the 'we cutting corners everywhere and praying nothing catches fire' budget."

The room went silent.

Not just quiet. SILENT.

The kind of silence that happens in movies right before someone gets bad news from a doctor.

Even Larry stopped chewing whatever he'd found to chew.

"Fifty thousand?" Marvelous said slowly, carefully, like he was testing whether the words meant what he thought they meant.

"Yes."

"As in five followed by four zeros?"

"That's what fifty thousand means, yes."

"As in more than we've ever HAD? As in more than we've ever SEEN?"

"I don't know how many different ways you need me to say the same number."

Marvelous nodded slowly, like gears were turning in a machine that hadn't been serviced in years.

"Okay," he said finally. "We can do that."

"WITH what MONEY?!" Cherry's voice cracked, achieving notes previously reserved for opera.

"The money we ABOUT to make!"

"FROM where?! Is there a MONEY TREE I don't know about?!"

"I DON'T know YET! But money WANTS to come to us! Money is ATTRACTED to our energy!"

"MONEY don'T have desires! MONEY IS AN INANIMATE CONCEPT!"

"That's what POOR PEOPLE think!"

"WE are poor PEOPLE! We're so poor the POOR PEOPLE feel bad for US!"

Cherry put her head on the table with a THUNK that suggested she was considering just staying there forever.

"I'm going to have an aneurysm. They're going to write PAPERS about what your decisions did to my neurons."

Breadcrumb raised his hand slowly, like a student who knows his answer is probably wrong.

"I got an idea. What if we do a FUNDRAISER for the gala?"

Everyone turned to look at him with deep suspicion.

"A fundraiser..." Tito said slowly, "...for a party?"

"YEAH! Like, we charge people to help us throw a party that they eventually get invited to!"

"That's just... tickets," Cherry said flatly. "You just described selling tickets. With extra steps."

"WITH extra STEPS! See? I'm INNOVATIVE!"

Larry bleated. It sounded like agreement with Breadcrumb, which was concerning.

"Two hundred dollars each," Cherry said, sighing. "Early bird tickets."

"Two hundred?!" Tito said. "Who paying two hundred dollars to come to a party thrown by people who've had THREE FIRES this month?"

"People with two hundred dollars," Marvelous said confidently. "Rich people. Fancy people. People who want AUTHENTICITY."

"That's not a demographic. That's a DELUSION."

"It's a demographic now. I'm MANIFESTING a demographic."

Big Mike spoke for the first time, his voice like gravel wrapped in velvet: "I'll handle security. For FREE. Because this gon' be entertaining either way."

"That's..." Cherry paused. "Actually the most reasonable thing anyone's said today."

⚓

VENUE HUNTING: A COMEDY OF REJECTIONS

They spent three days calling every venue in the city.

Cherry made a spreadsheet with columns for: Venue Name, Reason for Rejection, Level of Mockery Received, and "Did They Laugh At Us (Y/N/Audibly)."

That last column filled up fast.

Call #1 - The Riverside Hotel:

"It's for Marvelous Enterprises! The EMPIRE!"

Long silence.

"Sir, are you the establishment that was on the news for the… chicken incident?"

"THAT was one TIME! And technically it wasn't CHICKENS, it was ROOSTERS, and the fire wasn't directly RELATED to the roosters—"

Click.

"What chicken incident?" Breadcrumb asked.

"WE. don'T. TALK. ABOUT. IT."

Call #2 - The Grand Ballroom:

"I'm sorry, but we're booked that evening. Madame Pancake's annual fundraiser. She's quite professional. Very organized. Pays in advance. Has INSURANCE."

"THAT'S my RIVAL!"

"Sir, I'm going to have to ask you to—"

"YOU tell madame PANCAKE THAT DA MARVELOUS MCCALL SAID—"

Click.

Call #3 - Community Center:

"Do you have insurance?"

"…Define insurance."

"In case of fires."

"What if we PROMISE not to damage anything? What if we pinky PROMISE?"

"Sir—"

"WHAT if we sign A CONTRACT SAYING WE DON'T BELIEVE IN FIRE?"

"You don't believe in FIRE?"

"AS A concept! Fire is CANCELLED in our organization!"

Click.

Call #4 - Mama's Function Hall:

This one was promising. The lady sounded nice. Maternal.

"Baby, what kind of event you throwing?"

"A gala, ma'am. Very sophisticated."

"That sounds lovely! Have you ever hosted an event before?"

"I throw parties at my club—"

"What kind of club?"

"A… nightclub. Strip club sometimes. Also a barbershop on Mondays. And a dispensary on Tuesdays. And there's a casino in the back of the laundromat on Thursdays but that's not TECHNICALLY—"

Long silence.

"Baby," she said finally, heavy with grandmother's disappointment, "I'm gone pray for you."

Click.

At least she offered prayers. That was more than most.

⚓

MADAME PANCAKE STRIKES

Day four. Marvelous's phone rang with a number he didn't recognize but somehow knew meant trouble.

"Hello, Marvelous." That voice. Smooth like syrup. Dangerous like a breakfast food that wanted you dead. "This is your COMPETITION calling."

"PANCAKE."

"I hear you planning a little… EVENT. A gala of some kind. In a parking LOT." She laughed, a sound like butter sizzling in a pan. "How quaint. How ADORABLE. Like watching a child play business."

"WE ain'T PLAYING! This is REAL!"

"Oh, I KNOW it's real. That's why I called. To tell you I've made some moves."

Marvelous's eye twitched. "What kind of moves?"

"I booked dj Stutter. You know, the DJ you were trying to book? The one with the broken equipment you promised to fix but never did? I bought

59

him brand NEW equipment. Top of the line. Fifteen thousand dollars worth. Pioneer. The good stuff. He's VERY grateful. Very EXCITED to work with a PROFESSIONAL operation for once."

"But... but he was OUR dj! He OWES us!"

"He owed you money. I PAID him money. Money wins, baby. That's capitalism. That's business. That's how the world WORKS for people who aren't living in a fantasy."

She continued, twisting the knife: "Since we both throwing galas the same night, people gon' have to CHOOSE. Your parking lot with... what entertainment you got again? A bluetooth SPEAKER? A phone connected to Spotify? Or MY gala with an actual DJ, actual food, actual EVERYTHING? What you think they gon' choose?"

Marvelous opened his mouth. Closed it. Opened it again.

No words came.

His brain was buffering.

"That's what I THOUGHT," Pancake said. "Oh, and Marvelous? I'm offering you one final chance. Because I'm magnanimous. Because I got CLASS. Fifteen thousand dollars. Cash. For you to CANCEL your event. Admit defeat. Acknowledge that I'm the SUPERIOR businesswoman. Walk away with your dignity... MOSTLY intact. With your kneecaps... ENTIRELY intact."

"FIFTEEN THOUSAND?!"

"That's GENEROUS considering your circumstances. Considering your debt. Considering your irs situation that I DEFINITELY know about."

Fifteen thousand would solve SO many problems.

Pay the IRS something.

Fix the dispensary.

Get permits.

Maybe even make rent.

But...

"No," he said quietly.

"I'm sorry, what?"

"NO," he said louder, finding something in his chest, some spark of stubborn idiocy that refused to die. "I ain't taking your money. I ain't canceling. I ain't QUITTING."

"Don't be STUPID—"

"I'M STUPID already! Might as well commit to it! Being stupid is my BRAND! Being stupid is my IDENTITY! I'm PROFESSIONALLY stupid at this point!"

"You'll LOSE everything!"

"Then I'll lose EVERYTHING! But I won't lose it because I QUIT! I'll lose it because I TRIED! At least I'll have that!"

Pancake was silent for a moment.

Then she laughed.

Not a mean laugh.

Almost… respectful?

"You know what, Marvelous? You ridiculous. You DELUSIONAL. You operating a business on vibes and PRAYER and probably WITCHCRAFT at this point." She paused. "But you got HEART. Stupid heart. Stubborn heart. Heart that should've stopped working years ago from all the stress."

"Is that a compliment?"

"It's an OBSERVATION. And a warning." Her voice hardened. "I'm going to destroy your gala. I'm going to take every customer. Every DOLLAR. December fourteenth will be remembered as the night Madame Pancake ENDED Da Marvelous McCall. They're going to write ARTICLES about how bad I beat you."

"We'll SEE about that."

"Yes. We will."

She hung up.

Marvelous stood there, phone to his ear, eye twitching like it was trying to send Morse code signals of distress.

Tito appeared in the doorway. "Boss? I heard yelling. Even for you, lot of yelling."

"She… she booked DJ Stutter."

"Damn."

"And she throwing her gala THE same NIGHT."

"Double damn."

"And she offered to buy me out for fifteen thousand."

"That's… actually a lot of money. Did you—"

"I said NO."

Cherry Bomb walked in, somehow knowing—she always KNEW—when things got worse.

"This is war," she said quietly, before he could explain.

"THIS is PERSONAL!" Marvelous shouted. "She want to DESTROY me!"

Breadcrumb poked his head in. "What if we sabotage her event?"

"No," Cherry said immediately.

"What if we LEGALLY sabotage—"

"That's not a thing, Breadcrumb. That's like saying 'jumbo shrimp' but for CRIMES."

Larry appeared in the doorway, having returned from wherever he went when he wasn't present.

He bleated once.

It sounded like "I could help, but my fee has increased."

Nobody asked what that meant.

THE BUDGET MEETING: WHERE DREAMS GO TO DIE

Cherry pulled out The Reaper—her serious calculator, the one with the memory function that remembered all your bad financial decisions and judged you for them.

"Okay. ACTUAL math. Real numbers. Real consequences. Real TEARS, probably."

"I hate math," Marvelous muttered.

"I KNOW. That's why we in this situation. That's why we drowning. That's why the IRS knows your NAME and ADDRESS and probably your SLEEP SCHEDULE."

She started writing numbers, each one hitting like a small funeral:

"Venue: parking lot is free BUT we need permits—five hundred if we can even GET them approved, which is a MASSIVE if.

Entertainment: since Pancake STOLE dj Stutter like a VILLAIN—"

"She IS a villain," Marvelous interjected.

—"we gotta find someone else. Someone willing to work with us despite our REPUTATION. Minimum fifteen hundred. more if they've Googled us. SIGNIFICANTLY more if they know who we are."

"What if they just heard RUMORS?"

"Then maybe twelve hundred. Depends on which rumors."

She continued, calculator clicking like a death march:

"Food: actual catering, not sandwiches from the corner store, not pizza from the place that got a C rating. Three thousand for two hundred people. That's the 'we serve chicken but don't ask what KIND of chicken' budget."

"What kind of chicken WOULD it be?"

"That's why you don't ASK."

"Decorations: Breadcrumb's budget is—"

"ONE million dollars!" Breadcrumb shouted from the floor, where he'd been staring at the ceiling like it contained the secrets of the universe. "I need ONE MILLION DOLLARS to execute my VISION! My vision involves LASERS!"

"Breadcrumb."

"And WATERFALLS! Indoor waterfalls that sparkle! And a light SHOW that syncs with music! And DOVES! LIVE doves that fly around and—"

"BREADCRUMB."

—"and maybe a HOLOGRAM of me welcoming people! Like Tupac at Coachella but it's me! But alive! A hologram of a LIVING person welcoming people to a LIVE event! It's INNOVATIVE!"

"BREADCRUMB!"

He stopped, looking hurt. "What?"

"We don't have a MILLION dollars. We don't have a thousand dollars for decorations. We got FIFTY dollars. What can you do with fifty dollars?"

"fifty?! FIFTY DOLLARS?!"

"Fifty. Five-zero. The cost of a nice dinner that we ALSO cannot afford."

Breadcrumb's face crumbled like a cookie in a blender.

"Fifty dollars… is… is NOTHING! That's one balloon! Maybe two balloons! What kind of GALA has TWO BALLOONS?!"

"OUR kind of gala! The affordable kind! The 'we grateful to HAVE balloons' kind!"

"But my VISION—"

"Your vision costs fifty dollars. Your vision IS fifty dollars."

"What about my LASERS?"

"No lasers."

"What about ONE laser?"

"How much does one laser cost?"

Breadcrumb pulled out his phone, searched, his face falling. "…three thousand dollars."

"Then NO laser."

"What about… a flashlight? That I move around REAL fast? That's like a POOR MAN'S laser!"

Cherry stared at him for a long moment.

"You know what? Fine. You can have a flashlight."

"YES! my VISION LIVES!"

"Your vision is a FLASHLIGHT, Breadcrumb."

"MY flashlight VISION LIVES!"

Marvelous pinched the bridge of his nose. "Can we focus?"

Cherry added up the numbers. "Total minimum: roughly twelve thousand dollars. That's the 'everything goes perfect and nothing catches fire' budget."

"We got twelve thousand!"

"That's rent, Marvelous! That's RENT we HAVE to pay or we get EVICTED from all THREE properties!"

"So we need… MORE than twelve thousand."

"We need about fifty thousand to do this RIGHT. We need about thirty thousand to do it acceptable. We need about fifteen thousand to do it in a way that doesn't ACTIVELY EMBARRASS US."

The room went quiet.

"Where we gonna get that kind of money?" Tito asked.

⚓

THE SOLUTION: PASTOR STACKS' "CONNECTIONS"

They needed money. Fast money. The kind that didn't ask questions and definitely didn't report to the IRS.

"There IS one option," Cherry said slowly, hating that she was saying it. "Pastor Stacks."

"Pastor Stacks? What's HE got to do with—"

"His OTHER business. The one we don't talk about. The one where he's not Pastor Stacks, he's just… Stacks."

Marvelous's eyes went wide. "You mean—"

"The 'seminar.' The 'business consulting.' The 'investment opportunities' that come with… SPECIFIC terms."

Everyone knew what she meant.

Everyone had heard the rumors.

Pastor Stacks ran the biggest church in the neighborhood by day. But by night—and sometimes during Wednesday Bible study—he ran something else. Something that involved loans. Interest. And consequences for non-payment that weren't spiritual.

"They took a SEMINAR on conflict resolution," Tito added. "They got a BROCHURE now. Very professional. Says 'We Value Your Partnership' on the front. Got a picture of two hands shaking. Very corporate."

"What's on the BACK of the brochure?" Breadcrumb asked.

"Terms and conditions. Interest rates. And a small disclaimer about 'alternative collection methods.'"

"What kind of alternative—"

"We don't ASK, Breadcrumb."

"But—"

"WE. don'T. ASK."

"We can't go to the MOB," Marvelous said.

"It's not the MOB. It's… organized community lending with aggressive collection practices."

"THAT'S the MOB!"

"It's the mob with a MISSION statement! They tithe! They have a 501(c)(3)! Technically they're a NONPROFIT!"

"A nonprofit that BREAKS KNEECAPS!"

"OCCASIONALLY breaks kneecaps. And they give you three

warnings first. Very professional. Very by-the-book. Their book, but still."

Larry bleated from his corner. It sounded like "Tell them Larry sent you."

"Did that goat just offer us a MOB REFERRAL?!"

"We don't TALK about Larry's connections! We don't acknowledge Larry's connections! Larry is just a GOAT as far as anyone asking questions is concerned!"

The room fell silent.

Everyone processing.

Everyone calculating.

Everyone trying to figure out if this was brilliant or suicidal.

Marvelous stood in his club, staring at the numbers Cherry had written, staring at the hole they were in, staring at the two choices before him: quit and let Pancake win, or go to the mob and maybe win but also maybe end up with broken legs.

"Call Pastor Stacks," he said quietly. "Tell him I want a meeting. About his… 'seminar.'"

Cherry nodded slowly. "You sure about this?"

"No. Not even a little bit."

But he was going to do it anyway.

Because that's who he was.

A man who made bad decisions with confidence.

A man who ran toward disaster like it owed him money.

A man who was definitely, ABSOLUTELY going to regret this.

He smiled.

Tired smile.

Possibly delusional smile.

Definitely stubborn smile.

Because what else could he do?

Quit?

Give up?

Let Pancake win?

Accept that he was just a small-time hustler who'd gotten too big for his britches?

"Nah," he said to the empty room, to God, to the universe, to whatever force governed the fate of fools and dreamers. "We doing this."

Tomorrow he'd meet the mob.

Tomorrow he'd borrow money he probably couldn't pay back.

Tomorrow he'd start planning an event that would either save his empire or destroy it completely.

But tonight?

Tonight he was still standing.

Still breathing.

Still believing—against all evidence, against all logic, against all reason, against the advice of everyone who loved him—that somehow, some way, this would work out.

(Outside the club, Larry made his way through the night streets. He had calls to make. Contacts to reach. The goat crime syndicate had assets that might be relevant to the gala's success. Larry 2 would want to know about these developments. There might be opportunities here.

The goats were INVESTED now.

For better or worse.

Mostly worse, probably.

But that was their brand at this point.

And somewhere across town, Madame Pancake sat in her breakfast-themed headquarters, looking at her own spreadsheets, her own plans, her own victory that felt more certain with every passing hour.

She didn't know about Pastor Stacks.

She didn't know about the mob meeting.

She didn't know that Marvelous was about to do something incredibly stupid that might actually work.

But she would find out.

They all would.

December fourteenth was coming.

And nobody was ready for what was going to happen.)

⚓

CHAPTER 5

The Offer (or: When Desperation Meets Opportunity Meets Definitely the Mob But With Excellent Espresso)

⚓

WEDNESDAY, 2:47 PM - GRIMALDI'S RESTAURANT

Marvelous sat in the back booth wearing his best suit—emerald velour with gold pinstripes that screamed "I make questionable choices but EXPENSIVE questionable choices—"and enough cologne to violate the Geneva Convention's rules about chemical warfare.

The cologne was called "Executive Power" and cost \$9 at the swap meet.

It smelled like someone had tried to bottle confidence but accidentally bottled aggression mixed with synthetic musk and the ghost of better decisions.

He'd applied it liberally. Too liberally. AGGRESSIVELY liberally.

The air around him shimmered slightly, creating a small weather system of poor choices.

A waiter three tables away sneezed and looked around accusingly.

Grimaldi's was OLD school Italian. Not "family-friendly with breadsticks and that weird unlimited soup deal" Italian. OLD school. The kind of place where:

\- The red leather booths had seen crimes but stayed quiet about it

\- The lighting was dim enough to hide facial recognition

\- The waiters looked like they'd buried bodies but had excellent tip-based amnesia

\- The marinara sauce was rumored to contain ACTUAL secrets

\- Cash only, no questions, receipts came pre-aged to look innocent

\- The music was Frank Sinatra but like, THREATENING Frank Sinatra

The walls were covered in black-and-white photos of people who looked important and also like they could have you disappeared with a phone call.

He checked his watch. 2:47 PM. Thirteen minutes early.

He'd never been early to anything in his life—not church, not meetings, not his own BIRTH according to his mother—but terror made him punctual.

Terror was an excellent motivator.

His leg bounced like it was trying to escape his body.

Sweat gathered at his hairline despite the restaurant being cool.

(Outside the restaurant, Larry and Larry 2 were stationed across the street. They'd followed him. They did that now. They were INVESTED. Larry 2 had binoculars, somehow. Larry had a notepad, somehow. They were taking notes on the meeting they couldn't see or hear. Their intelligence-gathering methods were questionable but their dedication was not.)

A waiter appeared—elderly, seventy if he was a day, white mustache waxed to perfect points that could probably be used as weapons, dead eyes that had witnessed the fall of empires and personally helped push a few of them over.

"You want anything while you wait?"

"Just water," Marvelous said, voice cracking like a teenager's. "And maybe a PRIEST if this go wrong. Or a LAWYER. Can you get both? Is there a combo deal?"

The waiter didn't smile. Not even a little.

"We don't do priests. Health code. Spirits are one thing, but clergy is another. Different permit."

"That's concerning."

"Many things are concerning, my friend. The state of the world. The economy. Your suit, which I assume was a choice you made deliberately." He leaned in slightly. "The water is not one of them. Water is safe. Water we can promise. Perhaps consider the water a friend. Perhaps the water is the ONLY friend you have in this establishment."

"WHY you emphasize water like everything ELSE might kill me?!"

"I emphasize nothing. I merely provide information."

"THAT'S worse! That's somehow WORSE!"

He disappeared, moving silently despite appearing to be approximately ninety-seven years old.

He returned with water in a glass so clean it looked suspicious, so clear it seemed too perfect, like water in a movie about water.

Marvelous sniffed it carefully.

What if it's poisoned? What if poison don't HAVE a smell? What if that's the POINT of good poison? What if rich people poison is like expensive perfume— subtle?

He took the tiniest sip.

Tasted like… water. Really good water actually.

What if it's SLOW poison? What if the symptom is excellent HYDRATION and then DEATH?

"You gonna drink that or MARRY it?" a voice said behind him.

Marvelous jumped so hard he almost flipped the table.

A man had slid into the booth across from him WITHOUT making A SOUND.

Late fifties, maybe sixty—one of those ageless faces that could be anywhere between "distinguished" and "personally CAUSED some shit."

Sharp Italian suit that probably cost more than Marvelous's car. Gray, perfectly tailored, not a wrinkle.

Salt-and-pepper hair slicked back with enough product to waterproof a boat.

Gold watch on his left wrist—expensive, understated, the kind that cost six figures but didn't announce it.

Gold ring on his right hand—thick, substantial, possibly weighted for hitting people.

Gold TEETH—just a flash when he smiled.

This man was SERIOUS.

"Marvelous McCall," the man said.

Not a question. A statement. Like he was reading Marvelous's obituary early.

"That's me. And you are?"

The man smiled—the kind of smile that knew where bodies were buried because it had personally helped DIG the holes.

"Someone who can help you."

Pause.

"Or hurt you."

Longer pause.

"Depending on this conversation."

"You… you a COP?" Marvelous asked desperately.

The man's smile widened slightly—just a millimeter, but it made everything worse.

"Worse. I'm in BUSINESS."

"What kind of business?"

"The kind you don't discuss in LOUD voices. Or court. Or with people wearing WIRES."

"So… ILLEGAL business."

"LEGITIMATE business conducted in creative ways with OCCASIONAL violence and MOSTLY legal paperwork."

"That's just illegal with syllables, commas, and THREATS."

"Tomato, tomahto. What matters is RESULTS."

The man leaned back. "Let me be direct. I represent interests. POWERFUL interests. We've been watching you."

"That's NOT creepy at ALL."

"It's BUSINESS. We have cousin Vinny who lives next to your club. excellent hearing. You just happen to be INTERESTING."

"I don't WANNA be interesting! Interesting gets you DEAD!"

"Only if you're STUPID interesting. You're entertaining interesting. Entertainment has VALUE."

The man pulled out a small leather notebook.

"You run five businesses," he said. "All failing. All three months behind on rent."

"HOW you KNOW THAT?!"

"I KNOW things. You owe nine thousand on the club. Seven-five on the dispensary. Eight on the laundromat. You bounced three checks last month—which is impressive since most people don't still WRITE checks."

"Who ARE you? cia? FBI? IRS in a SUIT?"

The man signaled the waiter—just two fingers raised—and two espressos appeared instantly.

"You can call me Mr. Gallo. I work for the Castellano family."

"THE Castellanos?! The ones my grandmother used to whisper about and then do that thing with her hand to ward off evil?!"

"We prefer 'connected businessmen with diverse portfolios and strong community relationships.'"

"That's MAFIA with MARKETING!"

Mr. Gallo sipped his espresso like he was tasting Marvelous's future.

"The Castellanos are LEGITIMATE business owners. Restaurants, construction companies, waste management, entertainment venues, import-export operations…"

"That's every mob business EVER! That's like a bingo CARD of criminal activity! You just missing money laundering!"

"Our accountants prefer 'creative financial structuring.'"

"THAT'S LAUNDERING!"

"It's AGGRESSIVE ACCOUNTING."

"Do those accounts involve CEMENT?"

"Some of our construction ventures do involve cement, yes. Quality cement. Union cement."

"I meant cement SHOES!"

"Oh." Mr. Gallo smiled. "Those are more of a METAPHOR these days. Environmental concerns. Bodies are terrible for the ecosystem. We're very green now. We care about SUSTAINABILITY. We planted trees. We're carbon neutral."

"THAT'S not COMFORTING!"

"It should be. We're thinking LONG TERM."

Mr. Gallo set down his cup.

"Now. Let me make you an offer. You're planning a gala. December fourteenth."

"HOW—who told YOU THAT?! You got BUGS in my office?!"

"No bugs. Your assistant talks VERY loud on the phone. Cousin Vinny has thin walls. He makes RECORDINGS."

"That's SURVEILLANCE!"

"That's ARCHITECTURE. Maybe invest in soundproofing."

Mr. Gallo tapped a folded paper.

"I'm prepared to FUND your event. Thirty-five thousand dollars. Plus we cover all your current fines—that's another thirty-eight thousand hitting you TODAY actually. Seventy-three thousand total. Cash. Immediate. No credit checks—which is good because yours would CRASH our computer."

Marvelous gripped the table.

"Seventy-three thousand dollars."

"What you WANT?" he asked quietly. "What's the REAL price?"

Mr. Gallo leaned forward, voice dropping.

"The event succeeds. You make money. LEGITIMATE money. You pay us back our initial investment plus thirty PERCENT within ninety days."

"THIRTY percent?! That's LOAN SHARKING!"

"That's VENTURE capital with AGGRESSIVE collection policies. We WANT you to succeed. Our return depends on it."

"What if I CAN'T pay back?!"

Mr. Gallo smiled that smile again. The one that suggested buried knowledge.

"Then we discuss ALTERNATIVE arrangements. Maybe you work for us. Maybe we become partners. Maybe we take OWNERSHIP of your businesses. Maybe cousin Vinny gets a new NEIGHBOR."

"And if I say NO?"

"Then you say no. Free country. Your businesses close in thirty days when the fines come due. You lose EVERYTHING. And Madame Pancake wins by DEFAULT." He sipped his espresso. "Which would be disappointing. I have FIVE THOUSAND bet on you succeeding."

"You BET on me?!"

"We bet on MANY things. You're currently at six-to-one against. I believe in UNDERDOGS."

Marvelous's hands shook.

"I need TIME."

"Twenty-four hours. After that, the offer EXPIRES." Mr. Gallo pulled out a business card—heavy cardstock, embossed lettering—and placed it on the table.

CASTELLANO FAMILY ENTERPRISES

Mr. Anthony Gallo - Senior Business Consultant

"Solutions for Complex Situations"

(Allegedly)

"Did you PUT 'Allegedly' on your business CARD?!"

"Legal recommended it. Makes things CLEANER in court. Very professional."

"This is INSANE!"

"This is BUSINESS!" Mr. Gallo adjusted his jacket. "Call me before 2 pm tomorrow. Your choice. Your FUTURE. Your kneecaps—METAPHORICALLY speaking, we don't do that anymore, too PRIMITIVE."

He walked away, moving through the restaurant like he owned it.

He probably did.

The waiter reappeared.

"You want anything else?"

"Therapy. Professional therapy. Maybe medication. Definitely a TIME MACHINE."

"We only got dessert. The tiramisu is excellent. Many people have their last—I mean their MOST MEMORABLE tiramisu here."

"Did you almost say LAST?"

"I said MOST MEMORABLE. English is my fourth language."

"THAT'S not COMFORTING!"

"Tiramisu is comforting. Consider the tiramisu."

THE EMERGENCY MEETING

3:47 PM - BACK AT THE CLUB

Marvelous called an emergency meeting because WHERE ELSE could you call an emergency meeting when all your businesses were questionable and your office smelled like fear and Crown Royal?

Cherry arrived first, immediately sensing disaster like she had a sixth sense specifically calibrated to detect his bad decisions—a sense she'd developed over years of exposure, like how some people develop immunity to poison but she'd developed sensitivity to STUPIDITY.

Tito came next, bringing silence and judgment in equal measure, also bringing his flask because he'd learned.

Breadcrumb showed up with a bucket of chicken wings from somewhere because of COURSE he did, because who DOESN'T bring chicken wings to an emergency meeting about mob money and possible death?

"It's comfort food!" he explained. "For COMFORT! In these times of DISCOMFORT!"

Pastor Stacks arrived uninvited—which was becoming a pattern—wearing his purple suit and eating wings from Breadcrumb's bucket without asking permission.

"These wings are BLESSED," he said, mouth full. "I'm blessing them as I eat them. retroactive SANCTIFICATION."

"That's not how blessings WORK," Cherry said.

"Everything's negotiable with the LORD."

The mechanical dove that had somehow migrated to this office—they kept appearing in new locations, nobody knew who was moving them—twitched in the corner and dropped another feather.

"Okay," Marvelous said, pacing. "I got news. Good news and BAD news."

"Start with the bad," Cherry said, pulling out her serious notebook, the one with the black cover that meant CONSEQUENCES.

"The bad news is we probably gon' owe money to the MOB."

Everyone froze.

Mid-chew.

Mid-breath.

Mid-EXISTENCE.

Breadcrumb had a wing halfway to his mouth, frozen in place like a screenshot.

Pastor Stacks stopped blessing.

Even the mechanical dove seemed to pause its deterioration.

"The GOOD news," Marvelous continued quickly, "is we get seventy-three thousand dollars to fix EVERYTHING and throw the BEST gala this city ever seen!"

"WHAT?!" everyone yelled simultaneously, creating a harmony of horror.

"Also there might be a betting pool on whether I succeed or fail and Mr. Gallo has five thousand on me succeeding so really he's INCENTIVIZED to help—"

"WHAT?!"

"And his business card says 'Allegedly' on it which is actually pretty funny if you think about—"

"MARVELOUS!"

Cherry stood up, hands on hips, eyes narrowed to slits that could cut glass. "Explain. NOW. In detail. Leave NOTHING out. Include the parts you're thinking about leaving out because you think they'll make us angrier—include THOSE especially."

Marvelous explained the meeting. The offer. The thirty percent interest. The ninety-day deadline. Mr. Gallo's smile (terrifying). The business card with "(Allegedly)" printed on it (oddly charming). The tiramisu (excellent, possibly his last tiramisu).

By the end, Cherry was gripping the table so hard her knuckles turned white.

"You considering TAKING mob money," she said slowly, each word landing like a small bomb. "Money from connected businessmen. Money from people who put ALLEGEDLY on their business cards because their LAWYERS said so. Money from people who have BETTING POOLS on your SURVIVAL."

"It's an OPTION!"

"It's a DEATH SENTENCE!"

"It's ENTREPRENEURSHIP!"

"It's INSANITY!"

"SAME ENERGY!"

"NOT if we dead! Dead people don't have ENERGY! That's the whole POINT of being DEAD!"

Pastor Stacks raised his hand slowly, wing sauce on his fingers like evidence of a delicious crime.

"I have concerns. Serious concerns. Biblical concerns. LEGAL concerns. spiritual concerns. ETERNAL DAMNATION concerns."

"Name ONE concern that's ACTUALLY helpful!"

"Accepting money from criminals is a SIN punishable by damnation, hellfire, and eternal torment! Saint Peter keeps RECORDS!"

"They ain't CONFIRMED criminals! They ALLEGEDLY criminals! That's legally DIFFERENT! That's what the business card SAYS!"

"CASTELLANO family?!" Pastor Stacks stood up dramatically, wing in hand like a prophet. "That's like being named mafia mafia INCORPORATED! That's like calling yourself CRIME FAMILY CRIME BUSINESS LLC!"

"That could be COINCIDENCE! Lots of people named Castellano!"

"ALL connected to the same family! That ain't COINCIDENCE, that's a CRIMINAL ENTERPRISE with GOOD BRANDING!"

Breadcrumb whispered, "Boss... even I know that's mob. And I don't know NOTHING about nothing."

"YOU ain'T even KNOW WHAT DAY IT IS!"

"It's Wednesday!" Breadcrumb said confidently.

"IT'S THURSDAY!"

"SEE?! I was close! one day OFF! THAT'S WITHIN THE MARGIN OF ERROR!"

Tito held up both massive hands. "LISTEN. Real talk. We take this money, we owe them. Forever. FOREVER. My cousin Rico took mob money once. Know where he is now?"

"Where?" Breadcrumb asked, eyes wide.

"I DON'T know. nobody know. that'S THE POINT! He disappeared! Just GONE! His mama still get birthday cards from SOMEONE but the postmarks are from PLACES THAT AIN'T ON MAPS!"

"Maybe he just MOVED—"

"TO where?! NARNIA?! Did he find a WARDROBE?!"

Marvelous knew they were right.

He KNEW taking mob money was a terrible, horrible, no-good, absolutely-should-not-do-this idea.

He knew it in his BONES.

But he also knew they were broke.

The kind of broke where you start considering which organs you can sell.

The kind of broke where you look at the goat and think "does Larry have RESALE VALUE?"

"Gimme twenty-four hours," he said quietly. "Lemme think. Lemme explore OTHER options."

"THINKING is how you got IN this mess!" Cherry said.

⚓

THE INSPECTORS ARRIVE

As if the universe wanted to provide IMMEDIATE context for his desperation, as if fate had been waiting for the perfect moment to kick him while he was down and then stomp on him, his phone EXPLODED with texts.

Not figuratively. EXPLOSIVELY. Buzzing so hard it vibrated off the table.

From Tito: INSPECTORS at the club. fire MARSHAL. SHE LOOK ANGRY. SHE BROUGHT A CLIPBOARD.

From Carlos: INSPECTOR at dispensary freaking out. FOUND THE STORAGE CLOSET. THIS IS BAD.

From Diego: THEY shutting down the laundromat RIGHT NOW. THEY FOUND THE BACK ROOM.

From Larry the Goat: BAAAAAA (someone had taught the goat to text, which was concerning on MULTIPLE levels)

From Larry 2: BAAA baa BAAAA (apparently Larry 2 ALSO texted now, this was an escalation)

"THEY hit all of them at ONCE!" Marvelous screamed. "EVERY BUSINESS! SIMULTANEOUSLY! THIS IS COORDINATED! THIS IS WARFARE!"

"This is PANCAKE!" Cherry grabbed her phone. "who else would COORDINATE FIVE INSPECTIONS AT ONCE?!"

They split up. Had to. Disaster management protocol. The "everything is on fire but the fires are in different locations" protocol.

⚓

The fire marshal found SEVENTEEN violations at the club.

\- Faulty wiring that could start a fire "TOMORROW. Or today. Possibly RIGHT NOW."

\- Blocked fire exits with boxes of T-shirts ("Those are DEATH TRAPS in cardboard form")

\- Emergency lights missing bulbs or hanging by wires

\- Sprinkler system not tested since 2019

\- Capacity sign wrong by fifty people

\- Expired fire extinguisher from 2021

\- Electrical outlets with scorch marks, one shaped like a skull

Final count: \$8,000 in fines

Marshal Torres handed Cherry the violation notice. "This building is in the top five for 'most ways to burn down.' Fix EVERYTHING or I'm shutting you down PERMANENTLY."

⚓

The health inspector at the dispensary found the storage closet where Larry had been living.

He found a FILING cabinet. With LABELS. With FILES on everyone.

"THIS goat has BETTER RECORDS THAN YOUR BUSINESS!" Inspector Chen screamed.

He found a CALENDAR. With Larry's APPOINTMENTS marked.

"THE goat has A calendar! THE GOAT IS MORE ORGANIZED THAN YOU!"

He found cross-contamination between hair products and edibles, expired permits by EIGHT months, and evidence Breadcrumb had been sleeping in a back corner (laundry everywhere, a sleeping bag, three boxes of cereal, a small ALTAR to a Beyoncé poster).

Total dispensary fines: \$12,000

⚓

The laundromat inspection found the back room casino. The poker tables. The chips. The wheel. The whole operation.

Total fines: \$18,000

⚓

Grand total hitting them TODAY: \$38,000

    Exactly what Mr. Gallo had predicted.

    Almost like he KNEW it was coming.

    Almost like he'd ARRANGED it.

⚓

THE DECISION

8:47 PM

Marvelous sat alone in his office, staring at the business card.

(Allegedly)

Such a small word for such a big threat.

    Such a ridiculous disclaimer for such serious people.

    Cherry's calculator—The Reaper—had delivered the final verdict earlier that evening:

    Current debt: \$67,000 (before today)

    Today's fines: \$38,000

    New total: \$105,000

    Available funds: \$2,400

    Difference: "WE're all going TO PRISON OR DIE BROKE OR BOTH"

    The numbers didn't lie. That was the problem with numbers—they were brutally, devastatingly honest.

    The mechanical dove in the corner had fallen completely off its perch during the day's chaos. It lay on the floor now, one wing twitching occasionally, making small grinding sounds of distress. It looked exactly how

Marvelous felt—broken, grounded, still somehow trying to function.

He poured himself a glass of Crown Royal. Not because he wanted it. Because he NEEDED it. Because what he was about to do required either courage or stupidity, and alcohol made it hard to tell the difference.

He pulled out his phone.

Stared at the number on the card.

His thumb hovered over the dial button.

Every part of him screamed DON'T.

His brain screamed DON'T.

His survival instincts screamed DON'T.

His grandmother's ghost, somewhere in the afterlife, was probably screaming DON'T while making that hand gesture she used to make, the one that warded off evil spirits and bad decisions.

But what choice did he have?

Close everything down? Admit defeat? Let Pancake win? Go back to being nobody?

He pressed call.

One ring.

Two rings.

Click.

"Mr. McCall." Mr. Gallo's voice, smooth as silk, dangerous as everything. "I was hoping you'd call. You're four hours early. I respect punctuality. Especially in people who are usually CATASTROPHICALLY late. I had money in the pool for you calling at 1:47 AM in a panic. You just cost my cousin Angelo fifty dollars."

"I'm in," Marvelous said quietly. "I'll take the money."

"Excellent choice. The RIGHT choice. The ONLY choice, really, but you came to it on your own, which shows character. Or desperation. Usually the same thing."

"I got CONDITIONS."

Pause. Interested pause. The kind of pause that suggested he'd said something unexpected.

"I'm listening."

"The gala succeeds or fails on MY terms. You fund it, but I run it. No mob... I mean no FAMILY members showing up and scaring my guests. No 'associates' doing 'favors' that involve threats. This gotta look LEGITIMATE."

"Reasonable."

"And if I pay you back on time—WHEN I pay you back on time—we're DONE. Clean slate. No 'oh by the way' requests later. No 'one more thing' situations. No surprise visits from cousin Vinny."

"Also reasonable. Cousin Vinny will be disappointed—he enjoys visits—but we can accommodate this. You've clearly thought about this."

"Also I want that in WRITING."

Mr. Gallo laughed. Actually LAUGHED. A real laugh, surprised and almost warm.

"Mr. McCall, we don't do WRITING. Writing is for people who don't trust each other. Writing is for people who need courts. We're going to be FAMILY now. Unofficially. ALLEGEDLY. Family doesn't need contracts. Family has UNDERSTANDING."

"That's EXACTLY what worries me."

"It should. Worry keeps you SHARP. Worry keeps you alive. Worry makes sure you pay on time. Worry is HEALTHY in our line of association."

"When do I get the money?"

"Tomorrow morning. 9 AM. A representative will visit your club with the funds. Her name is Isabella. She's my... associate. She handles TRANSACTIONS."

"She dangerous?"

"Everyone's dangerous, Mr. McCall. Some people are just more EFFICIENT about it. Isabella is very efficient. Very organized. Very... motivating. You'll like her. Or you'll be terrified of her. Most people are both. I myself am both."

"Great. GREAT. Looking forward to being TERRIFIED by someone named Isabella."

"Welcome to the family, Mr. McCall. Unofficially. Allegedly. We're very happy to have you. Very INVESTED in your success."

The line went dead.

Marvelous sat there, phone in hand, staring at nothing, feeling everything.

He'd done it.

He'd actually done it.

He'd made a deal with the Castellano family.

With people who put "Allegedly" on their business cards.

With people who sent associates named Isabella who were "slightly terrifying."

With people who had cousin Vinny listening through walls.

With people who kept FILES.

With people who had BETTING POOLS on his survival.

There was no going back.

The gala was happening.

Everything—EVERYTHING—depended on it now.

His businesses. His reputation. His future. Possibly his kneecaps (metaphorically speaking, they didn't do that anymore, they were GREEN now).

And somewhere across the city, in her breakfast-themed empire, Madame Pancake was DEFINITELY laughing.

Probably while eating pancakes.

Definitely planning her next move.

The war had escalated.

And Marvelous had just armed himself with mob money to fight it.

(Outside the club, Larry and Larry 2 convened in the shadows. They'd watched the whole thing through the window. They'd UNDERSTOOD—goats were excellent lip readers, apparently. The goat crime syndicate now had information. They had concerns about this development. But also they saw OPPORTUNITY.

Larry bleated a series of instructions to Larry 2.

Larry 2 nodded—actually NODDED, with his goat head, like he understood every word.

They had work to do.

The gala was happening.

Everyone was invested now.

Including the goats.

ESPECIALLY the goats.

They disappeared into the night, two shadows with hooves, two criminals with fur, two entrepreneurs with better business instincts than most humans.)

This was either genius or suicide.
Possibly both.
Definitely both.

CHAPTER 6

The Money Arrives (And So Do the Strings, the Conditions, and Someone Who Makes the Mob Look Friendly)

⚓

THURSDAY, 9:47 AM - CLUB MARVELOUS

Marvelous sat at the main table wearing his best "meeting with possibly-the-mob" outfit: a deep purple suit with gold buttons that looked like they'd been stolen from a very fancy hotel.

The suit had cost him \$200 at a thrift store called "Don't Ask—"which was its actual NAME.

Around the table sat:

\- Cherry Bomb (skeptical, arms crossed, Calculator of Doom charged and waiting)

\- Tito (worried, silent, emanating concern like a lighthouse warning ships)

\- Breadcrumb (confused, eating dry cereal from a ziplock bag like this was a MOVIE)

\- Pastor Stacks (uninvited but present—his BRAND now—eating an \$18 breakfast burrito)

The mechanical dove sat in the corner where someone had placed it after it fell last night. It was propped against the wall like a drunk friend at a party, occasionally twitching, one eye flickering on and off like it was sending Morse code.

"She should be here any minute," Marvelous said, checking his watch for the seventeenth time.

"'She'?" Cherry asked. "I thought we was dealing with Mr. Gallo."

"Mr. Gallo said his 'associate' Isabella would handle operations. Daily operations. Oversight operations. Probably SURVEILLANCE operations."

"So we meeting the mob's secretary?" Tito asked.

"She ain't no SECRETARY! She a 'operational liaison' and 'someone you should definitely not cross' and 'makes me look friendly.'"

"That's a secretary with a GUN," Pastor Stacks said through a mouthful of burrito. "That's hr but the H stands for HOMICIDE."

(Outside the club, Larry and Larry 2 had positioned themselves near the dumpster with a clear sightline to the front door. Larry had his notepad. Larry 2 had what appeared to be a tiny camera, somehow. The goat crime syndicate was documenting EVERYTHING now.)

The front door opened.

Everyone froze.

Breadcrumb dropped his bag of cereal, Cheerios scattering across the floor like tiny fleeing witnesses.

A woman walked in.

Late thirties, possibly early forties but had the kind of face where aging seemed like a choice she'd simply declined to make, like she'd received a memo about getting older and marked it "return to sender."

Immaculate black pantsuit—designer, obviously designer, the kind where the price tag causes cardiac events and possibly requires financing.

Hair pulled back so tight it looked legally binding, like a contract enforcement hairdo, like her hair had signed a non-disclosure agreement.

Briefcase that probably cost more than Marvelous's car, possibly more than his car AND his rent combined.

Sunglasses despite being indoors, despite it being unnecessary, despite it making her look like she was about to repo someone's entire life and had already filed the paperwork.

She moved with the kind of confidence that suggested she'd never been told "no" in her life, or had been told "no" once and that person had relocated to a country without extradition treaties.

She radiated "I will ruin your life professionally, thoroughly, and possibly also personally just for efficiency."

The air temperature seemed to drop five degrees.

The mechanical dove stopped twitching entirely, possibly out of respect.

Even the Cheerios on the floor seemed to roll away from her path.

"Good morning," she said, voice smooth as expensive whiskey, cold as expensive ice, sharp as expensive knives used for expensive crimes that never made the papers. "I'm Isabella Castellano."

Dead silence.

Absolute silence.

The kind of silence that happens in movies right before someone dies or signs something they'll regret.

Then Breadcrumb whispered: "She PRETTY."

Cherry elbowed him so hard he wheezed, air escaping his lungs in a gasp that communicated regret and pain.

"OW! I was just OBSERVING—"

"OBSERVE quietly! your MOUTH HAS LOST OBSERVATION PRIVILEGES!"

Isabella walked to the table with footsteps that sounded expensive— her heels clicking on the floor like tiny hammers of judgment, like a metronome counting down to something bad—and set down her briefcase with the precision that suggested military training, expensive private school, or possibly both plus a PhD in intimidation.

She removed her sunglasses with one smooth motion, folded them with a click that sounded like a gun being cocked.

Her eyes were dark, sharp, and looked like they'd calculated everyone's net worth, debt-to-income ratio, credit score, likelihood of success, and probability of failure in approximately three seconds.

They were the eyes of someone who'd seen balance sheets that made grown men cry.

They were the eyes of someone who'd CREATED balance sheets that made grown men cry.

"Mr. McCall," she said, extending a hand with perfectly manicured nails that could probably double as weapons and were definitely tax-deductible as business equipment.

Marvelous shook it. Her grip could've crushed diamonds, pulverized rubies, possibly reorganized the molecular structure of weaker gemstones.

"Miss Castellano. Welcome to my... establishment."

"Your allegedly illegal establishment," she corrected, sitting without being invited, without asking permission, without acknowledging that permission was even a concept that applied to her. "Let's be accurate about the legal status. Precision matters in business and in court."

"I like her already," Pastor Stacks whispered to Tito, beans dripping.

"You like ANYONE with legal knowledge," Tito whispered back.

"That's because legal knowledge is SEXY!"

"That's because you got WARRANTS!"

"THOSE are UNRELATED!"

She opened her briefcase with decisive motion—inside: folders color-coded by threat level, documents organized by urgency, tablets, pens that probably cost more than Breadcrumb's monthly rent, and something that was definitely NOT a gun but looked concerning anyway.

She pulled out a thick folder. VERY thick. The kind of thickness that suggested someone had done extensive research, possibly illegal research, definitely thorough research, research that had research of its own.

The folder had tabs. COLOR-coded tabs. With TYPED labels. Professional labels.

Marvelous felt his future contracting.

"Let's discuss terms," she said, placing the folder on the table like presenting evidence at a trial.

"Before we do that," Cherry interrupted, leaning forward, pen poised, "we got questions. LOTS of questions."

Isabella turned to her with a professional smile—not warm, the kind that suggested she found this mildly amusing but would become significantly less amused if it wasted her time.

"You must be Cherry Bomb. Mr. Gallo mentioned you were the smart one. The competent one. The one who actually understands basic accounting. The only reason we're investing at all, frankly."

"He talk about ALL of us?"

"Extensively. We do thorough background checks. It's policy. It's tradition. It's how we avoid investing in people who will embarrass us." Isabella opened the folder, revealing pages of typed notes. "Shall I demonstrate?"

She pointed at Cherry. "You're the competent one who holds this operation together with duct tape, prayer, and impressive spreadsheet skills considering your lack of formal training. Degree from a community college that closed three years ago. Outstanding student loans you've been paying responsibly. Credit score of 680 despite your association with—" she gestured at Marvelous —"this operation. You're the reason this investment is happening."

Cherry blinked. "That's... actually accurate."

"I know."

She pointed at Tito. "Former semi-professional boxer, 14-3 record, retired due to shoulder injury. Never convicted of anything despite three arrests, all charges dropped. Loyal to a fault. Also, you owe \$347 to a gym in East LA."

Tito shifted uncomfortably. "How you know about the gym?"

"We know about EVERYTHING about the gym. We know your locker combination. We know which weight machine you prefer."

She pointed at Breadcrumb. "Real name Marcus Williams. Average IQ of… let's just say 'room temperature' and move on. Failed three businesses before this one, all food-related, all involving fires. Currently living in what you describe as a 'studio apartment' but is actually a converted storage unit not zoned for residential use."

Breadcrumb opened his mouth to protest.

Cherry elbowed him again.

"OW! stop DOING THAT!"

"Then stop SAYING things that need ELBOWING!"

She pointed at Pastor Stacks. "Unlicensed therapist who keeps showing up uninvited to meetings, eating other people's food, and providing spiritual guidance that's legally questionable. Ordained online through a website shut down by the FTC."

"SPIRITUAL advisor!" Pastor Stacks corrected indignantly. "I provide COUNSELING! FAITH-BASED support!"

"Unlicensed," Isabella repeated flatly, each syllable hitting like a gavel. "You charged Mrs. Henderson fifty dollars for marriage counseling. You charged Mr. Torres seventy-five for 'spiritual financial advice' that was mostly lottery numbers. That's illegal in this state."

"The LORD don't need CREDENTIALS!"

"The STATE does."

She pointed at the mechanical dove in the corner. "And that's a malfunctioning animatronic from a 2019 promotional event. Technically stolen property from a company that went bankrupt, so no one's pursuing it."

Everyone stared at the dove.

The dove's eye flickered once, as if in confession.

"Y'all did RESEARCH research," Breadcrumb whispered.

"We did RESEARCH research. We do EVERYTHING research. It's policy."

She pulled out a cashier's check and slid it across the table.

Everyone leaned forward. Synchronized. Like magnets being pulled toward money.

\$15,000

"This is the FIRST installment," Isabella said. "This covers immediate needs: venue deposit, vendor retainers, marketing materials, and paying your most urgent fines before the city shuts you down permanently."

"And the OTHER fifty-eight thousand?"

"Released in STAGES as you hit milestones. Venue secured? Five thousand. Entertainment booked? Five thousand. The remaining thirty-eight thousand covers fines directly—we pay those ourselves to ensure they're actually PAID."

"You don't trust us to pay the fines?"

"We don't trust you to pay ANYTHING without supervision. That's not an insult. That's statistical analysis based on your payment history, which is… creative."

She pulled out a contract. Thick. Professional. Multiple pages. Tabs. Appendices. Possibly a glossary.

"Standard terms. You throw the event as specified. We're listed as primary sponsor. Our representatives get VIP seating. And…" She paused. "…first option on any future business ventures you undertake."

"Future ventures? You want CONTROL of stuff I ain't even THOUGHT of yet?"

"We want OPPORTUNITY. Think of it as professional courtesy. Partnership. A mutually beneficial relationship that definitely won't feel like control if you don't think about it too hard."

"What KIND of consequences if we decline?" Cherry asked.

"Financial consequences. Professional consequences. The kind where other investors mysteriously lose interest. The kind where permits become harder to obtain. The kind where insurance premiums increase unexpectedly. Nothing illegal. Just… unlucky. Coincidentally unlucky. Repeatedly unlucky."

"That's EXTORTION!" Breadcrumb said.

"That's NETWORKING. Extortion requires explicit threats. This is just karma, but with lawyers."

"What if we say no?" Cherry asked quietly. "Give the check back? Walk away?"

Isabella smiled. Colder than before.

"Then you pay your thirty-eight thousand in fines with money you don't have. You lose all five businesses by next week. And we never speak again."

She leaned back.

"OR, you sign. You throw a successful event. You pay us back with REASONABLE interest—twelve percent annually."

"Twelve percent?" Cherry did the math quickly, pen flying. "That's... actually not that bad. That's better than most credit cards. That's better than some LEGAL lenders."

"We're professionals. We're not loan sharks. We're businesspeople who happen to have connections and resources and a certain reputation for creative problem-solving. There's a difference. One has an HR department. One has dental benefits. One has a 401(k) match."

"Y'all have a 401(k)?" Breadcrumb asked, genuinely curious.

"We have EXCELLENT retirement benefits. We believe in taking care of our people. Long-term."

Marvelous looked at Cherry. Cherry looked at the check. \$15,000. Real money. Right now. Salvation or damnation on paper. Probably both.

"Where we sign?"

Isabella smiled—a real smile this time, small but genuine, the kind that suggested she'd won something.

"Page seven. Initial pages three, five, and nine. Sign and date page twelve. Use the blue pen—it scans better. And read the arbitration clause on page fourteen—actually, don't read it. It's fine. Just sign."

"Should we read it?" Cherry asked.

"You should. You won't understand it. Sign anyway."

AFTER THE SIGNING

Isabella packed up with the signed contract, now official, now binding, now extremely real.

"Congratulations. You're now officially in business with the Castellano family. Try not to embarrass us. We have a reputation to maintain. A reputation built over generations."

"We won't!" Marvelous said, probably lying, almost definitely lying.

"You will," Isabella corrected. "Statistics suggest you'll embarrass us at least twice before the event. Our actuaries have calculated a 73% probability of minor embarrassment and a 34% probability of major embarrassment. Try to keep it MINOR. Nothing that makes the news. Nothing that requires our legal team to work overtime. They bill by the hour and they're VERY expensive."

She headed for the door, stopped, turned back.

"Oh, and Mr. McCall? Don't disappoint Mr. Gallo. He rarely gives second chances. And when he does, they come with CONDITIONS that make the first chance look appealing. They come with INTEREST that compounds in ways you won't enjoy."

"Understood."

"Good." She put her sunglasses back on despite it still being unnecessary indoors. "You have my number. Call if there are problems. Don't call if there aren't. I charge for phone consultations—\$200 for the first fifteen minutes, \$150 for each additional fifteen. Text is free but I don't respond to emojis. Email is acceptable but expect a 24-hour response time."

"That's... very specific."

"I believe in clear communication and billable hours."

She left.

The door closed.

Heavy silence.

The silence of people who'd just signed something binding with people who had "Allegedly" on their business cards and actuaries calculating embarrassment probability.

(Outside, Larry and Larry 2 watched Isabella leave. Larry made a note. Larry 2 nodded respectfully. They recognized a professional when they saw one. The goat crime syndicate had OPINIONS about the Castellano organization. Mostly positive. Very organized. Good documentation. The kind of operation Larry aspired to build.)

"So," Breadcrumb said finally. "We in the mob now?"

"We in BUSINESS with the mob," Cherry corrected. "There's a difference."

"Is there?"

"Legally? Yes. Practically?" She paused, looking at the check in Marvelous's hands. "We'll find out. Probably soon. Probably dramatically."

Marvelous held the check to the light like it might be fake. It wasn't. It was VERY real. \$15,000 of very real, very mob-adjacent, very contractually-obligated money.

"We should celebrate," he said.

"We should PANIC," Cherry corrected, pulling out her Calculator of Doom. "Because we about to spend all this money in approximately six hours and then we gonna need MORE money."

"That's not celebrating energy."

"That's REALITY energy. That's MATH energy. That's the energy of someone who's done a budget before."

⚓

THE BUDGET REALITY CHECK

Cherry spread out a legal pad, three pens (color-coded by expense category), and her Calculator of Doom—the Reaper, the Bringer of Mathematical Death.

"Okay," she said, voice taking on that professional quality that meant she was about to destroy everyone's optimism with MATH. "Let's make a real budget. With NUMBERS that mean things."

"We got fifteen thousand. MINUS two thousand we gotta pay immediately on fines or they shut us down tomorrow."

\$13,000 AVAILABLE

"That's still a LOT!" Marvelous said.

Cherry gave him THE look. The one that killed optimism and buried it in a shallow grave.

"Venue. Tito, your tent guy?"

Tito called. Five minutes of negotiation in Spanish, lots of "hermano" and "por favor" and what sounded like begging.

"Three thousand. Big tent. White. Holds three hundred. Includes setup and takedown. Basic lighting. Portable generator. Plus five hundred deposit

93

we get back if we don't destroy it."

Everyone looked at each other. Everyone knew. Everyone had SEEN what happened to things they touched.

"We ain't getting that deposit back," Cherry said flatly. "Let's budget for DESTRUCTION."

VENUE/TENT: \$3,500

"That leaves ninety-five hundred for EVERYTHING ELSE."

"Catering. Food for two hundred people. REAL food. Not hot dogs. GALA food. Food that rich people and mob representatives and Madame Pancake's spies will see and judge."

She started calling catering companies.

Call #1: "Hi, we need catering for two hundred people... December fourteenth... What's your rate?"

Her face fell.

"FOUR thousand dollars?!" She listened more. "The premium has garnishes?! FOUR THOUSAND DOLLARS FOR GARNISHES?!"

Call #2: "Thirty dollars per person MINIMUM?" Calculator clicking. "That's SIX THOUSAND for just FOOD!"

Call #3: "Mystery meat sandwiches? What makes the meat MYSTERY? ...I don't WANT to know?! THAT'S NOT REASSURING!"

Call #4: "I can't serve hot dogs at a GALA! ...What makes a hot dog FANCY?! TRUFFLE OIL?! That's still a HOT DOG with DELUSIONS!"

Call #5: Actually promising—until: "We EXCLUSIVELY cater events that haven't had fire department incidents in the past six months."

They all looked at each other. Six months would be a RECORD for no fire incidents.

Finally, Pastor Stacks raised his hand.

"Sister Washington. Church catering. The LADIES. They can do it for fifteen hundred if we provide ingredients."

"Church ladies?" Cherry asked skeptically.

"You ever had CHURCH lady food? You ever had Sister Washington's mac and cheese? That mac and cheese is structural. That mac and cheese is LOAD-BEARING. Engineers have studied it. They have QUESTIONS about how it defies physics. Architects have tried to replicate it for BUILDINGS."

CATERING: \$2,500 (with ingredient estimates)

Entertainment was next.

"My cousin know a DJ," Tito offered. "He cheap. REAL cheap. He'll work for three hundred dollars and unlimited wings."

"Done," Marvelous said immediately.

"Shouldn't we get someone GOOD?" Cherry protested.

"We BROKE! We can't afford good! We can afford ENTHUSIASTIC and HUNGRY! That's the budget!"

"His name literally DJ Discount," Tito added. "He got business cards that say 'Why Pay More?' with a picture of himself looking sad."

"That's not ENCOURAGING!"

Breadcrumb raised his hand. "My cousin's boyfriend's sister can SING."

"Can she sing WELL?"

"She can sing LOUD. She once shattered a GLASS."

"Was that on PURPOSE?"

"…No. But it shows POWER!"

"Volume and talent are DIFFERENT MEASUREMENTS!"

"I also know a guy who does MAGIC! He make stuff disappear! Like credibility. And sometimes wallets. And occasionally watches. And one time a whole PURSE but that was an accident he says."

"NO theft MAGICIANS!"

"He got business cards! They say 'Magic by Marcus - Now You See It, Now You Don't (Terms and Conditions Apply)'!"

"BUSINESS cards don'T MAKE YOU LEGITIMATE!"

(Outside, Larry watched through the window. Larry had opinions about theft. Larry was a PROFESSIONAL. Larry didn't need magic—Larry had SKILL.)

ENTERTAINMENT: \$650 (including estimated wing expenditure)

Cherry calculated rapidly.

INSURANCE: \$1,200

PERMITS: \$700

SECURITY: \\$500

MARKETING: \\$1,000

Total spent: \\$9,550

Remaining: \\$3,450

"We got thirty-four hundred left for decorations, emergencies, and ANYTHING ELSE that goes wrong."

"That's almost FOUR THOUSAND!"

"That's one ambulance ride! That's ONE LAWYER for ONE HOUR! That's ONE DISASTER and we're BROKE AGAIN!"

She gestured around at the sparking mechanical dove, the water-damaged ceiling, the wobbling chair.

"WE are living PROOF of things going WRONG!"

⚓

THE CALL

Marvelous's phone rang. Unknown number. Blocked caller ID.

He almost didn't answer. But he answered. (He always answered. That was his PROBLEM. That was ALWAYS his problem.)

"Da Marvelous McCall speaking, emperor of—"

"I know about the money, darling."

His blood went cold. Ice cold. Antarctic cold. Colder than Isabella's smile. Colder than Cherry's look when he said "same energy."

Madame Pancake.

"I don't know what you talking about," he said carefully, hand gripping the phone tighter.

"The FUNDING, baby. The seventy-three thousand dollars from our very connected friends. The Castellanos? VERY interesting business partners for someone who claimed they were 'legitimate.'"

"How you—who TOLD you?!"

"Baby, I got EYES. I got ears. I got sources. The hood TALKS. The streets WHISPER. People tell ME things because I pay them to tell me things. And the hood is VERY chatty about who's taking mob money. You trending, baby. In the WRONG circles."

She paused, and he could hear her smiling through the phone.

"You desperate enough to owe THEM? That's delicious. That's tragic. That's EXACTLY what I hoped you'd do. I was COUNTING on you doing something STUPID and baby, you DELIVERED."

"We ain't OWE nobody nothing!"

"You owe them EVERYTHING now, darling. You think they just gave you money out of KINDNESS? You think the castellanos invested in your little parking lot party because they BELIEVE in you?"

She laughed. Rich laugh. Full laugh. The laugh of someone winning. The laugh of someone who had already seen the end of the movie.

"They own you now, Marvelous. They own your businesses. They own your FUTURE. They got that 'first option' clause you probably didn't read properly because reading isn't your strength. And when you can't pay them back—and you WON'T—they'll take EVERYTHING. Your club. Your dispensary. Your laundromat. Your DIGNITY."

"How you KNOW about the contract?! How you KNOW about the clause?!"

"I know EVERYTHING, baby. I got someone CLOSE to you. very close. Someone who TELLS me things. Someone who keeps me INFORMED about every little decision you make. Every move. Every mistake. And baby, you make a LOT of mistakes."

The line went dead.

Marvelous stood there, phone in hand, blood cold, brain racing.

Someone in his crew was a mole.

Someone was feeding Pancake information.

Someone he TRUSTED.

He looked around the room at Cherry. Tito. Breadcrumb. Pastor Stacks.

One of them?

Someone else?

How deep did this go?

How long had it been going on?

Cherry looked up from her calculations. "You look like you seen a ghost. What happened? Who was that?"

"Nothing," he said automatically.

Lying.

Badly.

Poorly.

She wasn't buying it. Nobody was buying it.

"We got a problem. A BIG problem."

"Bigger than being sixty thousand in debt to the mob?"

"Maybe. Possibly. Probably."

Cherry stared at him. "You gonna tell me what kind of problem?"

He looked at his team. His crew. His family.

One of them was betraying him.

Or was it someone else entirely?

"Later," he said. "Not now. Not here."

Cherry's eyes narrowed. She knew he was hiding something. She ALWAYS knew when he was hiding something. That was her superpower. That was why she was the competent one.

"You stupid," she said.

"I'm Marvelous," he corrected.

"SAME THING."

"Hey—"

"That time it WAS same energy."

Outside, the sun was setting over Los Angeles, painting the sky in shades of orange, purple, and consequences.

Somewhere across town, Madame Pancake was planning her counter-event, probably laughing, definitely plotting, absolutely winning at this moment in time.

Somewhere in an expensive office, the Castellano family was watching, waiting, calculating their return on investment, possibly already planning what to do if this failed.

Somewhere in a storage closet, Larry was reviewing his notes, updating his files, possibly sending encrypted bleats to Larry 2.

And somewhere in the future—though nobody knew it yet—a garbage

98

truck was warming up its engine, preparing for a route that would change everything.

But for now?

For now, Da Marvelous McCall had \$15,000 deposited, a signed contract that might doom him, twenty-eight days to prove himself, a team of people who believed in him despite all evidence suggesting they shouldn't, and a mole feeding information to his enemy.

The gala was happening.

Ready or not.

Probably not.

Definitely not.

But happening anyway.

God help them all.

The Castellanos certainly wouldn't.

CHAPTER 7

The Ticket Hustle (or: How to Fail at Marketing While a Dolphin Watches)

⚓

FRIDAY, 10:17 AM - THREE WEEKS AND FIVE DAYS UNTIL GALA

Marvelous stood in front of Club Marvelous holding five hundred pieces of paper that could only be described as crimes against graphic design.

The trees had died for THIS.

Somewhere, a forest was weeping.

The designer—Breadcrumb's cousin's girlfriend who "took a Photoshop class once" (actually a YouTube tutorial she'd watched halfway through before getting distracted by cats)—had created promotional materials that looked like a ransom note designed during an earthquake in a glitter factory.

The flyer, when examined closely (which hurt to do, which caused actual physical pain), featured:

\- THREE different fonts, all terrible, all conflicting, all screaming at each other like divorced parents at a custody hearing

\- One font was Comic Sans, which should be illegal, which WAS illegal in several countries with taste

\- Marvelous's face poorly cut out from his DMV photo where he looked hungover, angry, and definitely questioning his life choices

\- The cut-out had a VISIBLE white BORDER because nobody had taught this woman about feathering edges or professional standards or dignity

\- Glitter effects applied so heavily everything became unreadable, like someone had vomited sparkles onto important information

\- The word "GALA" spelled wrong as "GALAH" in letters three inches tall—like they were hosting an event about Australian parrots who enjoy fine dining

\- Event details printed in font size 4, requiring a microscope or supernatural vision or just giving up entirely

\- A clip art tuxedo DEFINITELY still watermarked with "SHUTTERSTOCK" across the chest

And inexplicably:

A STOCK PHOTO OF A DOLPHIN JUMPING OUT OF WATER IN THE BOTTOM CORNER

Not small. PROMINENT. Taking up 20% of valuable promotional space. Mid-leap. Water spraying. Sunset behind it. Living its best life while Marvelous's business died.

(Outside, Larry and Larry 2 had obtained one of the flyers. They had OPINIONS. The goat crime syndicate had better marketing.)

"Why there a DOLPHIN?" Cherry asked, witnessing a crime.

"She said it represent GRACE," Breadcrumb explained. "And ELEGANCE. And ocean vibes?"

"OCEAN vibes?! We in a PARKING LOT!"

"It represent FAILURE!" Cherry grabbed the flyer. "It represent the fact that your cousin's girlfriend needs to APOLOGIZE to Adobe!"

The mechanical dove made a grinding noise that sounded like agreement.

Tito held up a flyer. "I can't read the address. Is this BEHIND the blood-drip font?"

"It's next to the dolphin's FIN."

They'd paid \$300 for this disaster.

Then Cherry checked the date. Her eyes widened with new horror.

"It says March 14th. That's THREE MONTHS from now!"

"BREADCRUMB!"

"I TOLD her the date!"

"You probably told her the WRONG date because you thought today was WEDNESDAY yesterday!"

They spent three hours writing "December 14th" on five hundred flyers by hand while the dolphin watched.

Since they couldn't afford legitimate advertising, professional marketing services, or anything resembling competent promotional strategies, they resorted to what Marvelous called "grassroots community engagement" and what was actually just "putting up flyers illegally on every surface we could find while hoping nobody noticed the dolphin, the misspelling, or our general existence."

Tito drove the SUV—his personal vehicle that he was increasingly regretting volunteering, that he was starting to understand would never recover from this experience—while Marvelous and Breadcrumb hung out the windows like teenagers doing something stupid, which they were, holding duct tape rolls and stacks of dolphin disasters.

"THERE!" Marvelous yelled, pointing at a telephone pole like he'd spotted treasure, like this was the pole, the pole that would change everything. "THAT'S A PREMIUM POLE!"

Tito slowed down to approximately five miles per hour, which was still probably too fast for the illegal activity they were attempting to commit.

"This is ILLEGAL!" Tito said for the seventeenth time that afternoon.

"Only if we GET CAUGHT!"

"THAT'S not how laws WORK! Laws work whether you get caught OR NOT! That's the WHOLE POINT of laws!"

"It's how MY laws work!"

"YOUR laws AREN'T REAL!"

(Behind them, at a safe distance, Larry and Larry 2 followed in a wagon they'd obtained somewhere. Nobody knew where. Nobody asked. They were taking detailed notes on Marvelous's distribution strategy, and from their bleating and head-shaking, they were NOT impressed. This wasn't how you ran a grassroots campaign. You needed targeted bleating. You needed FINESSE. You needed to not be constantly VISIBLE.)

They hit every pole, bus stop, and flat surface within a three-mile radius of Club Marvelous.

The Tally:

\- Telephone poles: 47 flyers (12 overlapping other flyers for garage bands and missing cats, creating a layered disaster)

\- Bus stops: 23 flyers (commuters stared, nobody looked interested, several took photos for the wrong reasons)

\- Random walls: 31 flyers (one property owner came out yelling, they drove away quickly)

\- Abandoned storefronts: 18 flyers (sad, desperate, perfect)

\- One very patient tree: 4 flyers (nature could not escape marketing)

By noon, they'd posted 147 flyers across the neighborhood like the world's saddest treasure hunt, like they were leaving breadcrumbs for nobody, like they were marking territory but the territory didn't want to be marked.

By 12:15 PM, a city worker named Jerome—who moved with the efficiency of someone who had seen the dolphin, had PROCESSED the dolphin, and had QUESTIONS about the dolphin but was too professional to ask—had removed 83 of them.

By 12:30 PM, Marvelous's phone rang. Official-sounding number. The kind of number that means you're in trouble, that means consequences, that means someone with a clipboard and AUTHORITY has noticed you.

"Is this Da Marvelous McCall? This is Code Enforcement. We've received eighty-three complaints about illegal flyers in the last HOUR. Eighty-three individual complaints. People are CALLING about you."

"Oh." The sound of doom.

"You're facing a five-hundred-dollar fine PER FLYER removed."

Cherry, who was somehow listening (she had sixth sense for disaster math), pulled out her Calculator of Doom and started typing. Her face went through several stages of horror.

"Seventy-three thousand five hundred dollars," she announced flatly, like announcing the end of the world.

"HOW you KNOW IT'S US?!"

"Sir, your face is ON the flyers. In full color. From what appears to be your dmv photo. Your NAME is on the flyers. In THREE different fonts. And you SIGNED one when a Code Enforcement officer in plain clothes asked if you were 'the flyer man.'"

"I WAS being personable! I WAS ENGAGING with the COMMUNITY!"

"You signed your crime for her. You AUTOGRAPHED your violation." Pause. Professional judgment. "Also, why is there a dolphin?"

"IT represents GRACE!"

"It represents POOR decision-MAKING. Remove all materials within two hours or the fines DOUBLE."

They spent the next two hours removing their own promotional materials, driving the same route BACKWARDS, peeling off flyers while the dolphin stared at them from every single one. Always watching.

The tree was particularly sad. The four flyers fluttered in the wind like surrender flags.

Final Accounting:

\- Lost: \$300 on printing (dolphins cost money)

\- Lost: 3 hours of time (could've been spent literally anywhere else)

\- Lost: 5 gallons of gas (Tito's gas, Tito's regret)

\- Lost: Dignity (immeasurable, possibly infinite)

\- Gained: 0 ticket sales (zero, nothing, the void)

\- Gained: A reputation as "the dolphin people" (will follow them forever)

\- Gained: Entry into Code Enforcement database (permanent record)

One elderly woman named Mrs. Chen showed up at the club two hours later asking about the "dolphin event."

"Ma'am, there's NO dolphins."

"But the FLYER shows a dolphin! It looks so free! So MAJESTIC!"

"The flyer was a MISTAKE! A TERRIBLE mistake!"

"Will there be dolphins at the event?"

"We're in a PARKING lot. In los ANGELES. There's nowhere to PUT a dolphin. There's no WATER for dolphins. Dolphins need OCEAN."

"But the dolphin looked so HAPPY..."

She left disappointed. Dolphin-less. Without buying a ticket. The dolphin had cost them \$300, three hours, their dignity, and gained them exactly zero sales and one sad elderly woman with crushed marine mammal dreams.

But then—MIRACLE. Pastor Stacks called Saturday.

"I got you an interview! On Hot 97.3! THE radio STATION!"

This was HUGE. Legitimate exposure. Real marketing. Actual people who could buy tickets.

They had one shot.

(Narrator voice: They were absolutely going to mess it up.)

They arrived twenty minutes early. Marvelous wore his purple suit—the good one, with only two stains, both mostly hidden if he kept his arms down.

Cherry brought talking points on index cards: ticket prices, event date, venue location, things to NOT mention (dolphins, fires, mob connections, Larry, that thing with the hot dog cart).

The DJ—Trent, who looked perpetually tired like he'd been doing this job for seventeen years too long—welcomed them into the booth.

"Alright, folks, we got Da Marvelous McCall here promoting his upcoming gala!"

"THANK you FOR HAVING ME!" Marvelous shouted directly into the mic, causing feedback that made everyone wince and probably several listeners turn down their radios.

"Little quieter, buddy. The mic is sensitive. So what's this event about?"

"EXCELLENCE!"

"…Okay. And when is this excellent event?"

Marvelous's mind went blank. Completely, utterly blank. Empty. Void. The mental equivalent of the TikTok comment section. The date—the ONE thing he needed to remember—vanished from his consciousness like it had never existed.

Cherry whispered urgently: "December fourteenth."

"DECEMBER FOURTEENTH!"

"And where is this happening?"

Another blank. Total blank. The dolphins had taken the information with them.

Cherry mouthed: "Behind Club Marvelous."

"BEHIND club MARVELOUS! in A tent! A big tent! LIKE A CIRCUS BUT CLASSIER! CIRCUS-SIZED BUT GALA-STYLED!"

"Is it… a circus?" Trent asked, genuinely confused now.

"NO! It's a gala! But with circus SIZE! Think circus dimensions meets gala sophistication meets PARKING LOT VIBES!"

"...What?"

"And ticket prices?"

"Two hundred dollars!"

"What do people get for two hundred dollars?"

He'd never actually made a clear list. He'd never THOUGHT about this question in specific terms that could be articulated to strangers.

"CULTURE! community! champagne! VIBES! CULTURAL COMMUNITY CHAMPAGNE VIBES!"

"That's four C's and vibes."

"I GOT more C's! CELEBRATION! CREATIVITY! CHAOS!"

"Chaos?" Trent's eyebrow raised dangerously.

"CONTROLLED chaos! chaos WITH PERMITS! PRE-APPROVED CHAOS!"

"Do you actually have permits?"

"We have SOME permits! We have conceptual permits! We have permits in our HEARTS!"

"Permits in your hearts?"

"It's a JOURNEY! Permits are a JOURNEY!"

Trent looked at Cherry for help. "Is he okay?"

"He nervous. He doesn't do interviews well. This is his first one."

"THEN why IS HE YELLING?!"

"THAT'S just my VOICE! This is my INSIDE VOICE!"

The interview continued for eight of the longest, most painful minutes in radio history.

Marvelous mentioned "dolphins" twice for reasons nobody understood including himself. The word just... appeared. Like his subconscious was haunted by marine mammals now.

He accidentally said "Madame Pancake" three times when trying NOT to mention her.

He forgot to mention where to buy tickets.

He mispronounced his own business name.

And when Trent asked—"Why should people come to YOUR gala instead of Madame Pancake's event the same night?"—Marvelous froze.

Fifteen seconds of dead air.

On radio.

Fifteen seconds feels like YEARS on radio. Like geological time. Like the formation of continents.

Then, FINALLY: "because I'M MARVELOUS AND SHE PANCAKES!"

Silence. Profound silence. The kind that contains judgment, regret, and questions about life choices.

"…That's not a reason," Trent said carefully, like speaking to someone having a breakdown.

"IT is in my HEART! I'm MARVELOUS! She PANCAKES! That's a FUNDAMENTAL DIFFERENCE! That's PHYSICS!"

"Okay, folks, that was Da Marvelous McCall. Tickets are… somewhere. Probably. Good luck with your event. You'll need it."

"THANK you! come TO THE GALAH—I MEAN GALA!"

Within hours, someone uploaded the audio. Within days: 5,000 views.

"I'M MARVELOUS AND she PANCAKES" was becoming a meme.

Someone made a REMIX. It was catchy. Infuriatingly catchy.

People were putting it on T-shirts.

⚓

THE DANNY DEVITO ACQUISITION

One bright spot: Breadcrumb arrived Tuesday carrying something MASSIVE.

A FULL-size cardboard CUTOUT OF DANNY DEVITO.

4'10" of cardboard celebrity in a tuxedo, looking distinguished and slightly confused.

"WHY is THERE A DANNY DEVITO?!" Cherry screamed.

"It was FREE! Nobody was USING it!"

"WHERE did YOU GET IT?!"

"IT fell OFF A TRUCK! A truck that may or may not have been coming from a promotional event! The universe PROVIDED!"

Marvelous examined it like fine art. Danny DeVito stared back. Eyes full of cardboard wisdom. Face frozen in slightly amused expression that suggested he'd seen worse.

"…We keeping it."

"WE can'T keep STOLEN DANNY DEVITO!"

"It's not STOLEN, it fell! Finders keepers! That's LAW!"

"He got CLASS! He got confidence! That's danny DEVITO ENERGY! That's MARVELOUS ENERGY! SAME ENERGY!"

They set him up in the corner. Within hours, he'd become the most popular thing they owned. People took photos. Someone bought him a drink. Breadcrumb made a name tag: "DANNY - official MASCOT & SPIRITUAL ADVISOR"

Larry visited that evening. Stood before Danny for three minutes. Bleated once. It sounded like respect.

⚓

CORPORATE SPONSORSHIPS (THE GOAT MAN EMERGES)

After the promotional disasters, Pastor Stacks suggested corporate table sales. "Companies got BUDGETS! Accountants need DEDUCTIONS!"

Cherry created actual professional sponsorship packets—Platinum (\$5,000), Gold (\$2,500), Silver (\$1,000).

"We need FIVE platinum sponsors," Cherry said. "That's twenty-five thousand dollars."

"Easy! Platinum sponsors probably LINING UP!"

"Or TEN gold sponsors."

"Also easy!"

"Or TWENTY-FIVE silver sponsors."

"…That's a lot."

Marvelous's first call: Big Tony's Auto Body Shop.

"BIG TONY! It's Da Marvelous—"

Long pause. "Who?"

"DA MARVELOUS! We met at the community thing—"

"Oh. The guy with the goat."

THE goat. They remembered THE GOAT.

"Listen, I got an OPPORTUNITY—"

"Not interested. Last time I sponsored your event, health inspector showed up at MY shop asking about MY permits. Does the goat still work for you?"

"He's more of an INDEPENDENT CONTRACTOR—"

"The goat is ALWAYS relevant. Goodbye."

Click.

The Pattern Emerged:

Call #2 - Rosa's Restaurant:

"WE don'T want WHATEVER YOU SELLING!"

"I ain't SELLING! I'm OFFERING! There's a difference!"

Click.

Call #3 - Discount Furniture:

"Is this a pyramid scheme?"

"NO! It's a GALA!"

"Galas are just pyramid schemes for fancy people."

Click.

Call #4 - Chen's Dry Cleaning:

"You the goat man?"

"I HAVE a goat, but I'm also a BUSINESSMAN—"

"No thank you."

Click.

Call #5 - Riverside Deli:

"How you get this number?"

"Phone book from 2015!"

"That's STALKING!"

"That's MARKETING!"

Click.

Call #6 - Kim's Electronics:

"Oh! The guy from the radio! 'I'M MARVELOUS AND she PANCAKES!'"
The person was LAUGHING. Full belly laughs. "My daughter has it as her
RINGTONE! Hold on—"

Marvelous heard, faintly, a remix of his own voice with a BEAT behind
it. His failure had become MUSIC.

"Isn't that GREAT?! You're so FUNNY!"

"Can we talk about TABLES?"

"Oh, you're selling something? No thanks!"

Click.

Call #7 - Martinez Plumbing:

"Ain't you the guy who spammed everybody?"

"That was my ASSISTANT! I fired him!"

"You ain't fire him. I saw him in your TikTok video!"

Click.

Call #10 - Washington Legal Services:

"Are you calling to HIRE a lawyer or to get SUED by one?"

"...Neither?"

"Then why you calling a LAW firm for EVENT SPONSORSHIP?"

"You got MONEY though, right?"

Click.

By 10:30 AM:

\- Calls made: 17

\- Interested: 0

\- Hang-ups: 17

\- Recognized as "the goat man": 8

\- Recognized from the meme: 6

\- Threatened with legal action: 2

\- Called "the spam guy": 4

\- Success rate: 0.0%

\- Soul remaining: 12%

"This ain't WORKING!"

Cherry called. "How many sponsors?"

"…Define 'got.'"

"HOW many SAID YES?!"

"Zero."

"ZERO?!"

BREADCRUMB'S EMAIL MASTERPIECE

After the phone massacre, Breadcrumb arrived. "Mass emails! I got FIVE thousand addresses from the LIBRARY!"

"That sound ILLEGAL!"

"It's PUBLIC! That's legal-PLUS!"

"LEGAL-plus IS NOT A THING!"

Too late. Breadcrumb had typed the email, added all 5,000 addresses to "To"—not BCC—so everyone could see everyone's private information.

Subject: AMAZING BUSINESS OPORTUNITY! (GALA)! \[NOT SPAM\]

Dear Business Owner/Manager/Person/Human,

Come to DA MARVELOUS gala on December 14th! We have tables for sale! This is a LEGIT event (NOT A SCAM) with entertainment, food, and also a Danny DeVito cardboard that we found!

Also we are NOT affiliated with any goats anymore (mostly). The goat situation is HANDLED.

Sincerely,

Da Marvelous McCall

Emperor of Business

CEO of Excellence

(Allegedly)

P.S. If you seen a goat with keys please call us.

⚓

"BREADCRUMB! You spelled OPPORTUNITY wrong!"

"I was RUSHING!"

"You put ALLEGEDLY in our BUSINESS EMAIL!"

"That's LEGAL PROTECTION!"

"THAT makes US LOOK GUILTY!"

"SAYING 'not A scam' MAKES IT LOOK LIKE A SCAM!"

Responses flooded in like a tsunami of judgment:

Response #1: Please remove me from this list.

Response #2: This is spam. Reported.

Response #3: UNSUBSCRIBE

Response #4: How did you get my email? This is a violation of privacy.

Response #5: Is this a joke?

Response #6: You spelled opportunity wrong. And everything else wrong. Did you even TRY?

Response #7: What's with the goat reference? Why would a goat have keys? WHAT KEYS? I HAVE QUESTIONS.

Response #8: "Emperor of Business"? Who calls themselves that?

Response #9: This violated CAN-SPAM Act. My lawyer will be in touch. Expect documents.

Response #10: I'm calling the police. Seriously considering it.

Response #11: DANNY DEVITO CARDBOARD? THAT YOU FOUND?

Response #12: "Allegedly"?? This is the most suspicious email I've ever received and I get emails from Nigerian princes.

Response #13: Why would you put everyone's email in the TO line? Now we all have each other's contacts. You just created a privacy nightmare. I'm connected to 5,000 strangers now.

Response #14: Is this the pancakes guy from the radio? I love that video! (unhelpful but at least positive)

Response #15: I'M MARVELOUS AND SHE PANCAKES I have it as my ringtone! (extremely unhelpful)

Response #16: "NOT A SCAM"—only scams say that. Only criminals say "trust me." Only liars say "I'm honest."

Response #17: Emperor of Business? CEO of Excellence? Are you okay? Should someone check on you?

Response #18: I showed this email to my marketing class as an example of what NOT to do. My professor wants to know if you're available for an interview about failure.

Then ONE response stood out:

From: madamepancake@syrupandsuccess.com

Marvelous,

This is sad. Genuinely, profoundly sad. You're SPAM EMAILING now?

Also you misspelled OPPORTUNITY. And you put "Allegedly" in your signature. And everyone can see everyone's email.

P.S. - I got twenty-three calls from YOUR list asking if I'm affiliated with you. My lawyers are reviewing.

- Madame Pancake

Actual Businesswoman

Not Allegedly

⚓

Within an hour:

\- 847 unsubscribed

\- 234 reported as spam

\- 67 threatened legal action

\- 0 interested in sponsoring

"We've achieved NEGATIVE reputation," Cherry said. "We're in reputation DEBT."

⚓

Just when hope seemed lost…

Pastor Stacks walked in with THREE people. Professional people. In SUITS.

"I brought SPONSORS! REAL ones! Ones who didn't get your email!"

First person: "Marcus Williams. Brother Marcus Insurance. I'm interested in a Silver Table." He wrote a check for \$1,000.

Second: "Jennifer Kim, IT consultant. Gold Table. It's a tax deduction. Plus I owe Pastor a favor from that thing we don't discuss."

"WHAT THING?!"

"The thing we DON'T DISCUSS!" they said simultaneously.

She wrote a check for \$2,500.

Third: "Councilman Donald Patterson. Platinum Table. Five thousand. I'm running for mayor. I need the Black vote."

He wrote a check for \$5,000.

Marvelous stared at three checks totaling \$8,500.

He'd made seventeen calls: zero dollars.

Breadcrumb sent 5,000 emails: zero dollars.

Pastor Stacks made three calls: \$8,500.

"How you DO that?!"

"I ASKED people who owe ME. I built RELATIONSHIPS. I didn't SPAM people."

THE BIRTH OF FRANK

Domingo's truck pulled up Wednesday afternoon with a tent that was immediately, catastrophically wrong in ways that suggested God had a sense of humor and that sense of humor was MEAN.

The tent was:

\- Smaller than promised (holds 150 people, not 300, and that's optimistic, that's if everyone breathes in)

\- White (more accurately: "off-white with a history" or "beige with trauma" or "that color things turn when they've given up")

\- Damaged (visible tears, mysterious patches, one pole held together with what appeared to be a leather belt, possibly Gucci but probably not)

\- Concerning smell (musty, possibly mold, definitely something had died in storage and nobody had found it yet)

And across the front, in LARGE cheerful letters that mocked their existence:

"HAPPY 50TH BIRTHDAY FRANK"

Not small letters. Not discreet letters. LARGE letters. Three feet tall. Bright cheerful colors. Permanent. Built into the fabric. impossible to miss. IMPOSSIBLE to ignore. Frank's birthday celebration, immortalized in tent form, forever.

Frank—whoever he was, wherever he was (possibly dead)—would live on through this tent. His 50th birthday would outlast them all.

(Larry and Larry 2, watching from across the street, exchanged a look of deep judgment. Even by THEIR standards of criminal incompetence, this was amateur hour. Larry bleated something that might have been "this is what happens when you don't plan properly" or possibly "I could've gotten a better tent through my connections.")

"Why it say 'HAPPY 50TH BIRTHDAY FRANK'?!" Marvelous's voice went up three octaves.

"I forgot to mention!" Domingo said with the cheerfulness of someone who had definitely NOT forgotten, who had known this would be a problem. "This tent from a birthday party rental company that went out of business! I got it cheap! VERY cheap! SUSPICIOUSLY cheap! Some might say CRIMINALLY cheap!"

"It say FRANK! In BIG letters! With EXCLAMATION POINTS!"

"That's CHARACTER! That's charm! That's a CONVERSATION STARTER! People will ASK about Frank! 'Who's Frank?' they'll say! And you'll say... something! You'll figure it out!"

"THAT'S A problem! I don'T know FRANK! NOBODY KNOWS FRANK! FRANK COULD BE ANYBODY!"

"Maybe Frank will COME! Maybe he'll see his tent and be HAPPY!

Maybe he'll buy a ticket! Boom, one ticket sold!"

"FRANK HAD his party ten YEARS AGO! Frank might be DEAD! Frank might be in FLORIDA! Frank might not even EXIST!"

"Then it's a MEMORIAL! A celebration of FRANK'S LIFE! Frank LIVES ON through tent! Through CANVAS! Frank is IMMORTAL now!"

"IT'S vintage!" Domingo continued, pivoting strategies. "Vintage is IN! Vintage is TRENDY!"

"This isn't VINTAGE, it's a stranger'S birthday party we're INHERITING! It's SECONDHAND CELEBRATION! It's USED JOY!"

"Vintage is just sad with marketing! That's the WHOLE INDUSTRY!"

Cherry walked around the tent slowly, examining it like a detective at a crime scene, like she was gathering evidence for a trial, like she was documenting war crimes but the war was against good judgment.

She found:

\- Three tears in the fabric (one patched with duct tape from 1987, one patched with what appeared to be a Sublime t-shirt, one patched with hope and prayer)

\- Multiple stains of indeterminate origin (best not to ask, best not to KNOW, ignorance was survival)

\- One pole bent at a 15-degree angle (structural engineer would weep, building inspector would condemn, OSHA would have QUESTIONS)

\- Support ropes that looked original to Reagan's first term

\- Evidence of previous occupants (bird nests? raccoon situation? SOMETHING had lived there, SOMETHING had loved there)

\- And FRANK. Always FRANK. Eternally FRANK. FRANK FOREVER.

"Can we paint over Frank?" Cherry asked with the desperation of someone drowning and seeing a life preserver made of concrete.

"The fabric don't take paint good. You'll just make it look SUSPICIOUS. Like you're hiding something. Like you murdered Frank. Better to just OWN Frank. EMBRACE Frank. BECOME Frank."

Tito made seventeen calls. Every tent rental company in the city: BOOKED. December was wedding season. Quinceañera season. Corporate holiday party season. Bar mitzvah season. Literally every celebration that required shelter.

And Madame Pancake had rented the GOOD tent three months ago— the white tent, the clean tent, the tent without BIOGRAPHICAL

INFORMATION on it—and had paid DOUBLE to ensure nobody else got it.

"HOW she KNOW?! How she ALWAYS know?!"

"She knows EVERYTHING! She got SOURCES! She got spies! She probably knew about the dolphin before WE did!"

Marvelous closed his eyes. Tried to find inner peace. Tried to meditate. Tried to channel Buddha, Jesus, Oprah, anybody with wisdom. Found only rage. And Frank. Always Frank.

"So we stuck with FRANK."

"We stuck with Frank."

Silence. The silence of acceptance. The silence of defeat. The silence of Frank.

"…We'll EMBRACE Frank," Marvelous decided, finding strength somewhere, maybe from Danny DeVito's cardboard spirit. "Frank is our theme. Frank represents persistence. Frank represents LEGACY. Frank represents the CELEBRATION OF LIFE. Frank is our BRAND now."

"FRANK REPRESENTS us getting the cheap TENT! FRANK REPRESENTS POOR PLANNING! FRANK REPRESENTS EVERYTHING WRONG WITH THIS EVENT!"

"FRANK REPRESENTS opportunity! spelled CORRECTLY THIS TIME!"

"FRANK REPRESENTS BANKRUPTCY!"

"FRANK REPRESENTS… FRANK!"

Danny DeVito, still standing in the corner of the club, watched all of this with cardboard patience. He'd seen worse in his long cardboard life. He'd been to Breadcrumb's cousin's apartment. Frank was NOTHING compared to some situations Danny DeVito had endured. Frank was actually kind of charming in a deeply sad way.

"Danny DeVito doesn't judge Frank," Breadcrumb observed quietly, speaking wisdom from a place of unexpected depth. "Danny accepts Frank."

"Danny DeVito is CARDBOARD! He can't JUDGE!"

"He can judge with his ENERGY! With his aura! With his CARDBOARD SPIRIT!"

⚓

The installation crew arrived in Domingo's cousin's truck: Domingo himself (who mostly supervised from the shade while eating churros and providing ADVICE but not labor), his teenage nephew Diego (definitely high, moving at 0.3x speed like he was underwater or possibly on another planet entirely, giggling at nothing, at EVERYTHING, at the concept of EXISTENCE), and Steve who "used to work construction" approximately twenty years ago and hadn't touched a tent since.

"This seem SIMPLE!" Diego said, looking at the tent like it was an ancient puzzle, like it was ikea furniture but bigger, like it contained MYSTERIES.

It was not simple.

The tent collapsed twice during installation.

The first time, Diego pulled the wrong rope—specifically, the LOAD-bearing rope, the ONE rope you don't pull, the rope that HOLDS EVERYTHING UP.

HAPPY 50TH BIRTHDAY FRANK kissed the dirt with surprising grace. The whole structure folded like someone giving up on life.

"DIEGO! That was the load-BEARING ROPE!" Domingo yelled from his lawn chair, not moving, just OBSERVING.

"They all LOOK the same!" Diego protested, genuinely confused about why ropes would have different FUNCTIONS. "How I supposed to KNOW which rope is which? They didn't label them! That's bad DESIGN!"

"CONTEXT! physics! BASIC ENGINEERING!"

"I don't know those words!"

The second collapse happened when Diego, while making lightsaber sounds because he'd found a tent pole and imagination is a hell of a drug, accidentally POKED A HOLE through the side of Frank.

"VRRRMMM. VRRRMMM. I'm Luke. This is my... what's the word... light stick?"

"LIGHTSABER!"

"Yeah. That. VRRRMMM—" PUNCTURE. "Oh. Ohhhhh. That's not good."

Frank now had a wound. Frank had been STABBED. Frank's 50th birthday tent had been ASSAULTED.

They patched it with duct tape. More duct tape. So much duct tape. Different COLORS of duct tape because they ran out of silver. Now Frank had a rainbow scar. Frank had been through something.

The duct tape had duct tape. It was duct tape all the way down.

"How much duct tape did you USE?!" Cherry asked, staring at what appeared to be 75% of a roll on a single patch.

"ENOUGH!" Diego said proudly, like he'd accomplished something, like he'd created art. "It's not coming OFF now! That hole is SEALED! Frank is SECURE!"

"Frank look like he been in SURGERY!"

"Cosmetic surgery! Frank got a FACELIFT!"

Installation was supposed to take two hours. It took six. Diego got distracted seventeen times. Once he sat down and stared at clouds for eleven minutes. Steve's back went out. Domingo ate three full meals from the food truck across the street and provided COMMENTARY but never actually touched the tent.

Installation cost \$500 extra because "unexpected complications" and "Diego's time is valuable" (debatable) and "Steve's back injury is a workplace hazard" (legitimate concern).

"FIVE hundred?! For this?! For DIEGO?! Diego was HIGH! Diego doesn't KNOW where he IS! Diego thought the pole was a LIGHTSABER!"

"He still SHOWED up! That's PROFESSIONAL! That's COMMITMENT!"

"That's the BARE MINIMUM of existence!"

But Frank was up. Frank stood. Frank persisted. HAPPY 50TH BIRTHDAY FRANK stared at the sky, at the neighborhood, at the future, at the gala that would happen beneath its cheerful letters.

Frank was their destiny now. Frank was their BRAND. Frank was forever.

THE MOB CALLS

Isabella called Monday at exactly 9:45 AM with timing that maximized anxiety.

"Mr. McCall. Status update."

"We GREAT! Everything on TRACK!"

"Ticket sales?"

Marvelous looked at Cherry. She held up eleven fingers spread across two hands.

"ELEVEN!"

Heavy silence. The silence of red spreadsheets.

"Eleven. Your agreement specified one hundred tickets by Friday. That's FOUR days. You have eighty-NINE to sell."

"We got STRATEGIES!"

"Your strategies include a viral meme, spam emails, and a tent that says 'HAPPY BIRTHDAY FRANK.' We know EVERYTHING."

"We turning it AROUND! We got corporate sponsors! Eight thousand dollars!"

"That's… actually progress. Unexpected progress." Pause. "Don't make me regret believing in progress, Mr. McCall. If you miss Friday's milestone, we send OBSERVERS. Daily operations. APPROVAL power over decisions—including what you eat for lunch."

"What KIND of conditions?"

"The kind where your business is less YOURS and more OURS."

She hung up.

Danny DeVito watched from the corner, offering cardboard solidarity.

"How bad?" Cherry asked.

"Bad. We got four days to sell eighty-nine tickets or the mob sends OBSERVERS."

But they had corporate sponsors. They had Danny DeVito. They had FRANK.

They had a plan.

If they got lucky. If people said yes. If the universe stopped punishing them.

If the dolphins stayed gone.

RUNNING TALLY:

\- Tickets Sold: 11

\- Corporate Sponsors: \$8,500 (34 more ticket-equivalents)

\- Total Progress: 45 of 100 tickets

\- Days Remaining: 4

\- Dignity Remaining: Negative

\- Dolphins in Marketing: 1 (too many)

\- Franks Embraced: 1 (exactly right)

CHAPTER 8

Sabotage Begins (or: Larry Commits Agricultural Terrorism While Madame Pancake Plays Chess)

⚓

SATURDAY, 7:23 AM - TWELVE DAYS UNTIL GALA

Marvelous stood in front of a whiteboard in Club Marvelous's makeshift office—a converted storage room that smelled like old beer, regret, and whatever had been stored here before (probably more regret)—holding a red dry-erase marker like it was a weapon.

On the board, in increasingly desperate handwriting that got smaller and more frantic as it went down:

TICKETS SOLD: 45 (11 individual + \$8,500 sponsors)

TICKETS NEEDED: 55

DAYS LEFT: 12

PANIC LEVEL: MAXIMUM

HOPE LEVEL: QUESTIONABLE

DANNY DEVITO STATUS: STILL STANDING

FRANK STATUS: ETERNALLY CELEBRATING

LARRY STATUS: ?

DIGNITY STATUS: DECEASED

Cherry Bomb sat at the folding table with her laptop, Calculator of Doom, and stress-eating supplies (chips, cookies, an entire sleeve of Oreos, family-size Flamin' Hot Cheetos, three different types of chocolate—the architecture of despair).

Tito leaned against the wall, arms crossed, face showing exhaustion.

Breadcrumb scrolled mindlessly on his phone.

(Outside, Larry 2 was conducting surveillance from across the street. Larry 2 had noticed Larry's absence. Larry 2 had CONCERNS. Larry 2 was taking notes in a small notebook that nobody knew goats could use. Nobody was watching Larry 2. This was a mistake.)

"We need a NEW strategy!" Marvelous announced. "FRESH IDEAS! INNOVATION!"

"We need a MIRACLE," Cherry corrected.

"Same energy!"

"NOT the same energy! A miracle is supernatural intervention! Strategy is planning! We need planning! Not just VIBES and HOPE!"

Tito raised his hand slowly. "What if we just... gave up?"

The room temperature dropped three degrees.

"GIVING up ain'T IN MY VOCABULARY!"

"Boss," Tito said gently, "you can't spell 'vocabulary.'"

"THAT'S beside THE POINT!"

Then Breadcrumb's phone dinged. His face went pale—actually pale, color draining like someone pulled a plug. "Uh... boss? Larry's trending on Twitter."

"WHAT?!"

On the screen: A video. Of Larry. At the Saturday farmer's market. 47,000 views. And climbing fast.

THE LARRY SITUATION (AGRICULTURAL TERRORISM)

The video started with beautiful organic vegetables. The kind that cost \$8 a pound and came with backstories. The kind that had FEELINGS.

Then: hooves. The unmistakable sound of hooves on pavement. Clip-clop. Clip-clop. The sound of destiny arriving, of chaos manifesting, of someone's weekend getting RUINED.

Larry walked into frame. Just standing there. Four blocks from Club Marvelous. Looking directly at the camera like he KNEW he was being filmed. Like this was his TED talk. His manifesto. His moment.

"That's LARRY!" someone yelled. "The one from Club Marvelous! The one that picked locks! The CRIMINAL GOAT!"

Larry spotted a vegetable stand selling organic kale, heritage tomatoes, microgreens—the expensive stuff, the stuff farmers treat like children, like INVESTMENTS—and CHARGED.

Like a tiny woolly missile with a grudge.

Kale: gone in seconds, demolished with extreme prejudice. Arugula: obliterated (and that stuff is \$12 a pound). Heritage tomatoes: destroyed, juice everywhere, seeds flying like confetti at a disaster party. Microgreens: completely annihilated (and those were \$15 a container, \$15 for GRASS basically).

The vendor—a bearded man in overalls who probably talked to his vegetables, who probably sang to them—tried to stop Larry.

Larry headbutted him. Not hard. But effectively. Professional headbutt. Practiced headbutt. The headbutt of someone who'd done this before.

Someone tried to grab him. Larry KICKED. THWACK. Direct hit. That person sat down, rethinking their life choices.

Someone else approached with a rope, clearly thinking "I can catch a goat, I'm a capable human adult."

Larry DODGED—with agility suggesting either military training or supernatural ability or both—knocked over a display of artisanal honey jars. The handmade, \$25-per-jar kind with little handwritten labels about local bees and sustainable farming. Twelve jars. \$300 of honey. Spreading across the pavement like liquid gold dreams dying, like someone's small business evaporating in real-time.

Someone screamed "MY bees worked SO HARD ON THAT!" With actual tears. Real tears about bee labor.

Larry did not care about the bees. Larry had never cared about the bees. Larry had philosophical objections to bee labor.

The video ended with Larry running off-screen, mouth full of heirloom carrots (the purple kind, \$7 a pound), while someone yelled: "THAT goat has A taste FOR CRIME! SOMEONE CALL ANIMAL CONTROL!"

The hashtags were comprehensive and devastating:

\- #LarrytheTerror (17K tweets, climbing every minute)

\- #ArrestLarry (8K tweets demanding justice, pitchfork emojis)

\- #GoatCrimes (new category created specifically for Larry)

\- #LarrysNotSorry (accurate, Larry had never been sorry)

\- #FreeTheBees (collateral damage activism)

Marvelous's phone rang. Unknown number. Government-adjacent number. The kind that means TROUBLE.

"Is this Da Marvelous McCall, legal owner and registered guardian of Larry the goat?"

"...Who asking?"

"This is Janet from City Animal Control. We have your goat in custody."

Marvelous's stomach dropped like an elevator with cut cables. "You ARRESTED Larry?!"

"We DETAINED him. Legal difference. Arrest implies charges. Detention implies... holding. Temporary. Expensive holding."

"How MUCH?!"

"Two hundred dollars detention fee, three hundred dollars vendor damages, forty-eight-dollar administrative processing fee. Total: five hundred forty-eight dollars. Twenty-four hours to claim him or he goes to public auction."

"AUCTION?! who out THERE BUYING CRIMINAL GOATS?!"

"You'd be surprised. He's FAMOUS. We've had SEVEN inquiries already. One from a petting zoo that wants 'an attraction with personality.' One from someone who just said 'I love chaos' and wouldn't elaborate. One from what appears to be another goat—we got a phone call that was just bleating and we're not sure how to process that legally."

"That's LARRY 2! That's his ASSOCIATE! His business PARTNER!"

"Your goat has ASSOCIATES?"

"It's COMPLICATED! Their relationship is complex! Look, he AIN'T FOR SALE!"

"Twenty-four hours, Mr. McCall. The clock started at 7:45 AM. Have a nice day."

Click.

Larry was in goat jail. Larry needed bail. Larry needed five hundred forty-eight dollars by 7:45 AM tomorrow or he'd be auctioned off to the chaos person.

⚓

THE GREAT LARRY DEBATE

"They charging us FIVE hundred FORTY-EIGHT DOLLARS to get Larry back," Marvelous whispered.

Cherry looked up, face completely flat, the expression of someone beyond feeling, beyond hope, beyond the capacity for surprise. "Then leave him."

"WHAT?!"

"Leave him. We don't got five hundred dollars. We NEED every dollar for the gala. Larry is a luxury we can't afford. He's a LINE ITEM we need to DELETE from the budget. Let the petting zoo have him. Let the chaos person adopt him. Let Larry 2 orchestrate a prison break."

"WE can'T LEAVE LARRY!"

"WHY not?! He's a criminal goat who keeps ESCAPING! He's eaten through THREE fences! He's picked LOCKS—plural locks, multiple lock types! He left a DRAWING when he escaped that time! A drawing with a HELICOPTER in it! What does that even MEAN?! How does a goat know what helicopters ARE?!"

"BECAUSE he'S LARRY! He's OUR Larry!"

Danny DeVito watched from the corner, cardboard face neutral, offering no judgment but also no solutions. Sometimes Danny just observed. Sometimes observation was enough.

Frank's tent, visible through the window, continued celebrating his 50th birthday, oblivious to the chaos, to Larry's situation, to everything. Frank's tent just WAS. Frank persisted.

"Boss… she got a point," Tito said quietly, like someone delivering bad news at a funeral. "Five hundred dollars is insurance money. Decorations budget. Medical staff for when Sister Kim faints during the gala."

"I'm getting him back," Marvelous said firmly, not yelling for once, just stating a fact. "I don't care about the math. I don't care about logic. Larry's family."

"WITH what MONEY?!"

"I'll RAISE it! I got twenty-FOUR HOURS! That's a WHOLE DAY! That's OPPORTUNITIES!"

He grabbed his jacket, headed for the door, stopped, turned:

"Y'all coming or not?"

Tito sighed the sigh of someone who'd signed up for a job and somehow ended up in a lifestyle. "...I'm coming. Larry's annoying but he's OUR annoying."

"Me too," Big Mike said, speaking for the first time that morning. "Larry headbutted me once but I respected it. Clean headbutt. Professional form."

"I'M IN!" Breadcrumb yelled, jumping up. "Justice for Larry! goat SOLIDARITY!"

Cherry stayed seated, closing her laptop slowly. "...Fine. But I'm DOCUMENTING every dollar. And when this fails—when, not IF—I'm saying I told you so. With CHARTS. Graphs. PowerPoint presentation. The works."

Mission: Save Larry.

Budget: Zero.

Time limit: Twenty-three hours.

Success probability: Extremely low.

Determination level: Maximum.

⚓

FUNDRAISING MONTAGE (DIGNITY'S FUNERAL)

10:15 AM - EMERGENCY CAR WASH (OPERATION: NEGATIVE ROI)

They set up in the Club Marvelous parking lot with equipment that inspired zero confidence:

\\- A hose (kinked in three places, leaking in two more, probably older than Breadcrumb, possibly older than the BUILDING)

\\- Five buckets (one cracked down the side, one missing its handle entirely, one with something growing at the bottom that might be sentient, might have consciousness, definitely had OPINIONS)

\\- Dish soap (not car soap, the kind that strips paint and wax and

128

protective coatings and hope and dreams)

\- Sponges (suspicious origin, possibly from someone's kitchen circa 2015, definitely harboring bacteria colonies with their own civilizations)

\- Rags (formerly t-shirts, one said "FAMILY REUNION 2009," one was a Sublime shirt, one was just… sadness in fabric form)

\- A sign made by Breadcrumb: "CAR wash - \$10 - SAVE LARRY THE GOAT" (with a badly drawn goat that looked like a confused dog with a tumor, possibly dying, definitely not encouraging donations)

"That don't look like Larry," Tito observed, stating objective facts with the energy of someone too tired to lie.

"It REPRESENTS Larry! It's impressionistic! It's POST-MODERN! It's ARTISTIC!"

"It represents a DOG with PROBLEMS! Medical problems! Oncological problems! Terminal problems!"

"Larry look like that from CERTAIN ANGLES!"

"Larry don't look like that from ANY angle! Not even ABSTRACT angles!"

First customer at 10:23 AM: Mrs. Chen, 1998 Honda Civic, original owner, treated that car like her third child.

"You washing cars?"

"YES ma'am! Ten dollars! Professional results! GUARANTEED! SATISFACTION ASSURED!"

"Professional?" She looked at their setup with the appropriate level of skepticism that would've saved the Titanic. "You got DISH soap. That's DAWN. I can see the DUCK on the bottle. The DUCK is judging me."

"Soap is SOAP! Chemistry is chemistry!"

"Dish soap strips WAX! My cousin used dish soap on her car and it looked like she took it through a sandstorm! Through HELL ITSELF! Through multiple dimensions of suffering!"

She looked at the sign, at the sad dog-tumor-goat drawing, at their desperate faces, at the kinked hose, at the bucket with sentient growth.

"What Larry do to deserve this?" she asked, voice soft with genuine concern for goat welfare.

"Ate vegetables! WITHOUT permission! Terrorized organic farmers! Assaulted small business owners! Destroyed artisanal honey! The bees are TRAUMATIZED!"

"That's a crime?"

"IN this economy! Apparently! The justice system don't care about CONTEXT! Don't care that Larry was HUNGRY! That vegetables are NATURAL goat food!"

She sighed the sigh of someone who'd lived seventy-three years and seen humanity at its best and worst and this was definitely somewhere in the middle-to-worst range. "Fine. But be CAREFUL. This car is vintage. It's been with me twenty-six years. It has MEMORIES. It has HISTORY."

"It's from 1998! That's the NINETIES! That's barely VINTAGE!"

"VINTAGE is A STATE OF MIND! Just... don't hurt her."

They were not careful.

Marvelous grabbed the hose with confidence he absolutely did not deserve. Turned the water on. The hose jumped in his hands like a living thing.

Water pressure they didn't know existed—apparently the hose had been WAITING for this moment—water went everywhere at once. Hit the car. Hit the ground. Hit Mrs. Chen's window (still completely open because she was WATCHING THEM, she was SUPERVISING).

Water FLOODED the interior. Soaked the seats. Soaked her purse. Soaked HER directly in the face.

"my seats! I'm wet! MY PURSE! I JUST HAD MY HAIR DONE!"

"WE're sorry! water IS AGGRESSIVE TODAY! WATER HAS OPINIONS!"

Meanwhile, Breadcrumb had grabbed the dish soap—Dawn, with the duck logo, the duck that represented cleaning and also apparently betrayal—and started soaping the hood.

He squeezed.

TOO MUCH came out. Way too much. An amount of soap that suggested he'd never used soap before, never understood proportions, never grasped the concept of "less is more."

SUDS. Immediate suds. Expanding suds. Suds that had ambitions. Suds cascading down the sides like a bubble party, like a foam rave, like someone had weaponized soap for psychological warfare.

"That's a LOT of soap!" Tito yelled over the sound of rushing water and Mrs. Chen's distress.

"More soap equals MORE clean! That's CHEMISTRY! That's SCIENCE!"

"that'S not how chemistry works! THAT'S NOT HOW SCIENCE WORKS! THAT'S NOT HOW ANYTHING WORKS!"

"It's working RIGHT now! Look at these BUBBLES! These are MAXIMUM BUBBLES!"

Tito, attempting to be helpful, grabbed a sponge from the bucket—specifically, he grabbed the sponge that had somehow accumulated SAND inside its porous structure, like it had been to the beach, like it had a VACATION planned.

He started scrubbing the roof.

SCRATCH.

Visible scratch. Immediate scratch. Scratch that appeared like magic, like the universe had decided this car specifically needed suffering.

"What was that sound?" Mrs. Chen asked from inside her wet car, from inside her new mobile swimming pool.

"NOTHING! cleaning SOUNDS!"

"That sounded like SCRATCHING!"

"That's... advanced cleaning! That's FRICTION! That's PHYSICS!"

scratch. SCRATCH. SCRATCH.

"YOU're scratching it!" Mrs. Chen yelled, opening her door (water poured out, actual pools of water). "I CAN SEE THE SCRATCHES! From IN HERE! They're VISIBLE! They're NUMEROUS! They're MULTIPLYING!"

"They were ALREADY there! Those are old scratches! VINTAGE scratches!"

"MY car didn'T have scratches five MINUTES AGO! IT HAS SCRATCHES NOW! THE MATH IS SIMPLE!"

Big Mike, trying to be helpful, trying to contribute, trying to DO SOMETHING, grabbed a rag to dry the windows.

The rag was FILTHY. Whatever it was (formerly a t-shirt, currently a biological hazard), it left streaks. Made the windows WORSE. Somehow made them DIRTIER than before cleaning.

"Are you using a DIRTY rag?!" Cherry yelled from her observation post.

"IT looked CLEAN!"

"IT'S brown! rags AIN'T SUPPOSED TO BE BROWN!"

"SOME rags ARE BROWN!"

"NOT cleaning rags! NOT RAGS TOUCHING PEOPLE'S PROPERTY!"

By the time they finished—and "finished" is generous, "gave up" is more accurate—Mrs. Chen's car looked demonstrably, objectively, scientifically WORSE:

\- Interior seats completely soaked (she was literally sitting in a puddle, water squished when she moved)

\- New scratches on roof and hood (visible from space, probably visible from the MOON)

\- Soap streaks on ALL windows (abstract art but the bad kind, the kind that makes people angry)

\- Antenna bent at a 23-degree angle (Breadcrumb leaned on it "for balance" while soaping)

\- Mirrors slightly askew (HOW?! How do you mess up mirrors?! They just SIT THERE!)

\- Door handle somehow soapy inside (again: HOW?!)

\- The duck logo from the Dawn bottle had transferred to her paint somehow (actual logo, like a tattoo, like a brand)

"You OWE me ten dollars," Mrs. Chen said flatly, voice completely emotionless, beyond anger, in the realm of pure acceptance of humanity's failure.

"WE owe you?! We WORKED! We LABORED! We SWEATED!"

"FOR making it worse! trying ain'T ENOUGH WHEN TRYING CREATES DAMAGE! When trying creates NEW problems! When trying summons the DUCK LOGO onto my PAINT!"

"That logo will wash off!"

"WITH what?! you're the car WASH! YOU'RE THE ONES WHO PUT IT THERE!"

She drove off without paying, water sloshing inside her car with every turn, muttering in Cantonese, probably cursing their descendants unto the seventh generation, possibly placing hexes, definitely telling this story to everyone she knew forever.

They attempted seven more cars over the next two hours. Results varied from "disaster" to "catastrophic disaster" to "is this a crime?"

Car #2: Customer saw Mrs. Chen leaving and drove away before they could even approach. Net: \$0, pride: wounded.

Car #3: Breadcrumb broke the antenna completely off while using it as a "handle." Paid \$15 in damages. Customer threatened to call police. Net: -\$5.

Car #4: SUCCESSFULLY WASHED! First success! Actual success! Customer PAID! They CHEERED like they'd won the Super Bowl! (\$10 earned! Profit! Actual profit!)

Car #5: Breadcrumb dropped sponge in dirt, watched it fall, shrugged with the energy of someone who'd given up on life, picked it up, used it anyway despite EVERYONE screaming "DON'T USE THAT! BREADCRUMB NO! STOP!"

He did not stop.

Scratched the paint like a mountain lion attack. Like someone took keys to it. Like VIOLENCE had occurred.

Customer's husband was BIG. Very big. Intimidatingly big. "You scratched my WIFE'S car."

"It was an ACCIDENT!"

"Accidents cost MONEY. Twenty dollars. Now."

They paid. Customer's husband watched them leave. Made sure they LEFT. Net: -\$10.

Car #6: Customer took one look at their setup, at Breadcrumb holding the dirty sponge, at the hose kinked in seven places now, and said "I'm good" and drove away. Wise decision. Probably saved their car's life. Net: \$0.

Car #7: SUCCESS! Clean! No damages! No scratches! No flooding! A MIRACLE! (\$10 earned!)

Car #8: Big Mike slipped on soapy ground—the ground was now MORE soap than concrete—fell backward, landed IN the bucket with the sentient growth, stayed there for eleven seconds questioning every decision that led to this moment, questioning his EXISTENCE, wondering if this was rock bottom or if there were deeper depths to explore.

Customer watched this happen, said "I've seen enough," drove away mid-incident while Mike was still IN the bucket. Dignity destroyed. Spirit broken. Bucket unchanged.

Car Wash Final Tally (12:37 PM):

\- Cars attempted: 8

    \- Cars successfully washed: 2

    \- Cars made worse: 5

\- Cars that fled: 1

\- Damages paid: \$35

\- Revenue earned: \$20

\- Net total: -\$15

\- Dignity remaining: 0%

\- Sentient bucket status: Still sentient

"WE going backwards!" Cherry yelled, documenting everything in her spreadsheet of doom, creating graphs of failure, charts of catastrophe. "We worse off than when we STARTED! We'd have been better off doing NOTHING! NOTHING would have been PROFITABLE compared to this DISASTER! We've achieved NEGATIVE VALUE! We've created a DEFICIT in the UNIVERSE!"

"At least we TRIED!" Marvelous said weakly.

"TRYING cost us money! TRYING MADE THINGS WORSE! TRYING IS EXPENSIVE!"

⚓

1:00 PM - BAKE SALE SALVATION

Pastor Stacks called with an idea: "BAKE SALE! Call Sister Rodriguez! She owes me a favor from that thing we don't discuss!"

Sister Rodriguez arrived forty-five minutes later in her church van with:

\- Two dozen chocolate chip cookies (still warm, smelling like heaven)

\- Three pies (apple, cherry, pecan—a PIE TRILOGY)

\- One pound cake (massive, could feed an army)

\- Brownies (full pan, military precision squares)

\- Lemon bars (bonus item, not requested but appreciated)

\- Her grandson Marcus (age 12, youth group shirt: "JESUS loves you BUT I'M HIS FAVORITE")

"PASTOR stacks called ME!" she announced. "He said you need money for that VIRAL goat! The TERRORIST goat."

Marcus drew a better goat picture—actually looked like a goat, recognizable, sympathetic, with big sad eyes and a sign around its neck that said "HELP."

"That's GOOD!" Tito said, genuinely impressed. "That looks like a goat people would SAVE! That looks like LARRY!"

"I watch a lot of YouTube tutorials," Marcus said modestly.

Customers started arriving, drawn by the smell of salvation and the story of criminal justice.

First customer bought three cookies: "Free Larry. Goats gotta eat."

Second customer bought pie: "I saw the video! Sixty-two thousand views now! I'm team Larry."

Third customer: "Y'all really doing a bake sale to bail out a GOAT? That's the dumbest thing I heard all week." He pulled out his wallet. "I'll take two brownies. I LOVE dumb causes. This is PEAK dumb. This is MAGNIFICENT dumb."

Then Pastor Stacks showed up. 4:30 PM. Because he could sense baked goods from three miles away like a shark sensing blood.

"I HEARD there was baked GOODS!"

"You ORGANIZED this!"

"That mean I get a DISCOUNT! Organizer discount! clergy discount! TAX-EXEMPT discount!"

Everyone noticed he had chocolate on his fingers. On his shirt. Crumbs on his chin. He'd been "browsing" for ten minutes.

"That was SAMPLING!" he said defensively. "quality control! TESTING the product! FOR THE LORD!"

"That was THEFT! That's twenty DOLLARS worth of brownies!"

"The Lord wanted me to verify the brownies! The Lord and I have an ARRANGEMENT!"

He bought one brownie (\$5) after eating four (\$20 worth).

Bake Sale Final: \$180

Running Total:

\- Bake sale: \$180

    \- Car wash: -\$15

    \- Door-to-door begging (not shown): \$287

    \- Random donations: \$98

    \- TOTAL: \$550

They had enough. Barely. With \$2 to spare.

At 6:47 PM, Marvelous walked into Animal Control, paid \$548, and Larry walked out.

Larry bleated once. It sounded like "thanks" but was probably "I'll do it again."

⚓

THE TV INTERVIEW DISASTER (MONDAY MORNING)

5:17 AM

Marvelous had been awake since 4 AM—not by choice, but because anxiety had decided to throw a full-blown house party in his brain. Complete with DJ. Strobe lights. Loud guests who wouldn't leave. A fog machine. Someone doing karaoke badly in the corner of his consciousness singing "I Will Survive" off-key.

He'd tried sleeping. Gave up around 4:30 AM after the seventeenth time checking his phone to confirm that yes, the TV crew was really coming today, and yes, this was really happening, and yes, he could absolutely embarrass himself on live television in front of the entire city.

By 5:17 AM, he was standing in his bathroom—tiny, mirror slightly cracked (from that time he punched it celebrating a deal that fell through the next day), light flickering like it was possessed by a spirit who had opinions about his life choices—practicing his TV presence.

"Hi, I'm Da Marvelous McCall," he said to his reflection, trying different smiles. Too stiff. Too robotic. Like a robot who'd learned human behavior from YouTube tutorials made by other robots.

He tried again: "What's good, I'm Marvelous." Too casual. Too street. Like he was selling mixtapes outside a convenience store.

Third attempt: "Greetings! I'm Marvelous McCall—"

"WHO says greetings?!" Cherry Bomb's voice came through the wall, loud and judgmental and tired. "It's 5 AM and I can HEAR your failure through DRYWALL! Through INSULATION! Through PLASTER!"

"I'M PRACTICING!"

"You sound like a ROBOT! A weird robot! A robot that other robots don't invite to parties! A robot with SOCIAL PROBLEMS!"

"I'm being PROFESSIONAL!"

The door opened—she'd just WALKED in, she had a KEY apparently, this was news to him.

Cherry stood there in pajamas, holding coffee, radiating the specific energy of someone who'd been woken up by their friend practicing terrible TV introductions at 5 AM on a Monday when the world was dark and cruel.

"Just be yourself," she said, walking in like she lived there.

"myself don't know how to act on tv! MYSELF never been on TV! MYSELF went viral for saying 'I'M MARVELOUS AND SHE PANCAKES'! That's MYSELF'S track record! That's my RESUME!"

"Then be the CONFIDENT version of yourself! The version that talks big! That takes risks!"

"That's the version that got us INTO this mess! That's the version that owes the mob money! That's the version that bought a goat with a CRIMINAL RECORD!"

Cherry sighed the sigh of someone managing a disaster. "Marvelous. Listen. You SAVED a goat from public auction. You're hosting a gala despite everything. You got CORPORATE sponsors who gave you real money. You got Danny DeVito. You survived Old Betsy's explosion without DYING. Just... tell the story. Don't overthink. Don't say 'greetings' like you're an ALIEN making first contact."

"But what if they ask about the code violations? The seventeen code violations?"

"They WON'T."

"What if they ask about the fires? The MULTIPLE fires?"

"They WON'T."

"What if they ask about the spam email? 'Emperor of Business, Allegedly'? What if they ask about the dolphin? What if someone brings up the dolphin FLYER?!"

"They DEFINITELY won't because that's embarrassing for everyone involved! For humanity AS A WHOLE!"

10:47 AM

His phone rang. He'd lost track of time practicing—FIVE HOURS of talking to himself.

"Mr. McCall? Our crew is running fifteen minutes EARLY. Is that okay?"

"FIFTEEN minutes?! I ain'T READY! I'M PSYCHOLOGICALLY UNPREPARED!"

He looked down. He was still wearing his purple bathrobe with "MARVELOUS" spelled out in rhinestones across the back. Custom-made. Pride and joy. Completely inappropriate.

"THIS my thinking robe!" he yelled at Cherry, who was now sitting on his couch eating cereal. "MY MEDITATION ROBE! MY PROCESSING ROBE!"

"IT'S A bathrobe with rhinestones! It's what FAILED BOXERS wear when they give up! It's what MAGICIANS wear when they're between gigs! GET YOUR SUIT!"

He ran to his bedroom, throwing clothes everywhere like a tornado made of panic, searching for his best purple suit (the one that said "successful businessman" and not "person who talks to himself at 5 AM").

⚓

11:02 AM - THE CREW ARRIVES

The Channel 7 News van pulled up—white van with the station logo, satellite equipment on top, the kind of vehicle that screamed "we're about to make you look either very good or catastrophically bad on television and we don't know which yet."

Out stepped three people:

Tracy Chen - Reporter, early 30s, perfect hair that defied wind and gravity, professional smile that she could turn on like a light switch, the energy of someone who'd done a thousand human interest pieces and could do them in her sleep, possibly had DONE them in her sleep.

Derek - Cameraman, late 40s, seen EVERYTHING in his career, completely unfazed by anything life could throw at him. Nothing surprised Derek. Derek had filmed things. Terrible things. Beautiful things. Mostly terrible things. Derek just WAS.

Mike - Sound guy, 30s, currently eating a breakfast burrito despite it being almost noon (time is an illusion, breakfast is whenever), concerned only with audio levels and absolutely nothing else, not feelings, not drama, just clean audio, just sound quality, just doing his job.

Marvelous stood outside wearing:

\- His best purple suit (dry-cleaned THREE times, pressed with military precision, looking good, looking EXPENSIVE)

\- Gold chains (polished with Windex because he'd read that online, shining like tiny suns, catching light)

\- Sunglasses (completely unnecessary for the overcast day, but ICONIC, but image, but BRAND)

\- And anxiety levels that could power a small city, possibly a medium city, definitely enough to keep several factories running

Cherry, Tito, Breadcrumb, and Big Mike stood off to the side like a support crew, or possibly an intervention team, or possibly witnesses at a trial.

Danny DeVito (cardboard, eternal, wise) had been positioned near the entrance for maximum visibility, for BRAND SYNERGY, for moral support.

Frank's tent was visible in the background, still celebrating his eternal 50th birthday, leaning its characteristic 5 degrees like the Tower of Pisa but sadder.

Larry was somewhere. Probably. Hopefully contained. Definitely planning something. Definitely scheming. Larry was always scheming.

"Mr. McCall!" Tracy said, extending her hand like a professional. "Thanks for having us!"

"Call me Marvelous!" he said, shaking her hand WAY too enthusiastically, nearly pulling her off balance, nearly dislocating her shoulder, putting his whole body into it. "thanks for coming! I'M EXCITED! ARE YOU EXCITED?! THIS IS EXCITING!"

"Very excited," Tracy said carefully, reclaiming her hand, flexing her fingers to confirm they still worked, that they hadn't been permanently damaged.

Mike walked over with his breakfast burrito in one hand and a microphone pack in the other, multitasking at an Olympic level.

"I need to mic you up," he said around a mouthful of eggs and chorizo.

"Mic me WHERE?" Marvelous's voice went up an octave.

"Your collar." He demonstrated on his own shirt, professional despite the burrito.

"What if I gotta scratch something?"

"Don't."

"What if I GOTTA though? Like emergency gotta? Like MEDICAL NECESSITY gotta?"

"Hold it."

"FOR how LONG?!"

"However long the interview takes. Seven, maybe eight minutes. Every breath, every swallow, every stomach growl—we hear EVERYTHING. Every private moment becomes public. Every prayer becomes BROADCAST. We hear it ALL."

Marvelous's collar suddenly felt very tight. His throat felt very dry. His stomach felt very active.

He looked at Cherry, who gave him a thumbs up and a look that said "you'll be fine or you won't, either way I'm watching and possibly recording for blackmail purposes."

Very reassuring. Extremely comforting.

"Where's the goat?" Tracy asked, looking around, notepad ready.

"LARRY! WE got visitors! TV PEOPLE! IMPORTANT PEOPLE!"

A moment passed. Silence. Maybe Larry wasn't coming. Maybe this would be fine.

Then: the sound of hooves. Clip-clop. Clip-clop. Clip-clop. The sound of destiny arriving, of fate manifesting, of someone's carefully laid plans about to be DESTROYED.

Larry walked around the corner—casual, unhurried, like he was the celebrity and everyone else was supporting cast, like HE was the one being interviewed, like this was HIS show.

He looked at the TV crew. At the camera specifically. At Derek specifically. At the expensive equipment specifically. Then at Tracy. Then at her PURSE.

And if goats could smile—if goats had that facial muscle capacity—Larry was DEFINITELY smiling. Larry was PLOTTING. Larry had seen something he wanted.

"He's perfect," Tracy said, genuinely charmed, falling into the trap that everyone fell into. "Very photogenic. Great for television."

"He's a STAR!" Marvelous said proudly, like a father at a school play. "Natural performer!"

"He's also a criminal," Tito muttered from the side, trying to warn her, trying to prevent disaster.

"REFORMED criminal! He paid his debt TO SOCIETY! He's

REHABILITATED!"

Larry walked closer to the camera, looked directly into the lens with those horizontal goat pupils that suggested ancient knowledge or possibly evil, bleated once.

Translation (probably): "Hello, viewers. I regret nothing. I plan to regret nothing. Watch this."

⚓

11:15 AM - THE INTERVIEW (CATASTROPHIC)

Tracy stood next to Marvelous in front of Club Marvelous. Behind them: the sign with three bulbs out (five if you counted the ones that flickered), Frank's tent leaning its characteristic 5 degrees, Danny DeVito watching with cardboard wisdom.

"Ready?" Tracy asked.

"ready! born READY! MAXIMUM NATURAL! EXTREMELY CASUAL!"

"Maybe… less enthusiasm? And less words that don't make sense?"

Derek counted down with his fingers. "In three… two… one…"

Tracy's face transformed into Professional News Face—the face that had interviewed mayors and criminals and everything in between. "I'm Tracy Chen, and I'm here with Da Marvelous McCall, local businessman and the man behind the viral goat rescue that captured hearts across the city. Marvelous, tell us about Larry."

"Larry is… a free spirit," Marvelous started, voice only slightly shaking. "On Saturday, he got out—ALLEGEDLY the locks failed naturally, mechanical failure, act of God possibly—and he walked to the farmer's market and ate some vegetables because he was HUNGRY. Because vegetables are natural goat food. Because INSTINCT."

"Organic vegetables. Worth approximately two hundred dollars," Tracy added, reading from her notes.

"He got EXPENSIVE taste! refined palate! CULTURE! He's not eating regular vegetables, he eating HERITAGE tomatoes! He knows QUALITY!"

"He also headbutted a vendor."

"That was… allegedly. Self-defense possibly. The vendor was allegedly

141

in Larry's personal space. Larry has personal space NEEDS."

Larry bleated. Loudly. Right next to the camera. Right into the microphone.

Everyone looked.

Larry was eating something.

A strap. A leather strap. Expensive leather. Connected to… Tracy's purse. Her COACH bag. Her three-hundred-dollar bag that she'd saved for, that she'd EARNED.

"Larry…" Marvelous said slowly, voice filled with growing horror, with dawning realization, with the knowledge that this was about to become a SITUATION. "Larry, what you got there, buddy?"

Larry made direct eye contact with the camera—with AMERICA—with the world—and YANKED.

HARD.

The purse flew off the ground. Airborne. Like a bird. Like a terrible leather bird with expensive contents.

Tracy screamed. Actually screamed. Professional composure GONE. "my purse! that'S A coach bag! three HUNDRED DOLLARS! MY WALLET'S IN THERE! MY PHONE! MY KEYS! MY LIFE!"

"LARRY NO!" Marvelous dove forward, arms outstretched like a goalkeeper, like someone trying to stop a disaster that was already in motion.

Too late.

Larry RAN. Purse in mouth like a trophy. On live television. On CHANNEL 7 NEWS. During the NOON BROADCAST.

Past the camera. Past Derek (who kept filming because CONTENT). Past the van. Past any hope of dignity.

The camera followed him automatically because Derek's instincts kicked in, because Derek recognized TELEVISION gold, because THIS was why he became a cameraman, for moments like THIS.

Larry ran straight to Frank's tent. Disappeared inside FRANK'S DOMAIN. Emerged thirty seconds later.

Purse completely empty. Contents GONE. Eaten possibly. Destroyed definitely. Obliterated completely.

Wallet: gone (contained \$73, three credit cards, her driver's license, her social security card, and photos of her dog).

Phone: gone (iPhone 12, \$600 value, all her contacts, all her LIFE).

Keys: gone (car keys, house keys, office keys, her ENTIRE ability TO ACCESS BUILDINGS).

Lipstick: gone (expensive lipstick, \$35, perfect shade).

Pepper spray: gone (hopefully not activated inside the goat, hopefully Larry was okay, hopefully this wouldn't require VET BILLS).

Emergency tampons: gone (seriously Larry? SERIOUSLY?).

He dropped the purse—now just a hollow leather shell, a ghost of its former self—looked at the camera, looked at Tracy, looked at AMERICA, and bleated once.

Long bleat. Satisfied bleat. Accomplished bleat.

Translation: "I regret nothing. This was ART. This was performance. This was COMMENTARY on consumer culture. You're WELCOME."

Tracy's face was frozen in horror. The interview was still LIVE. Still BROADCASTING. Still going into people's homes across the city.

Mike the sound guy was still holding his microphone, still recording, had not moved, had not BLINKED, was just doing HIS JOB.

"Well," Tracy said finally, voice shaking, professionalism cracking like ice in spring, "that's... Larry. Criminal goat. Still criminal apparently. Not reformed. Back to you in the studio, Steve. Please. GET me OUT OF HERE."

The camera cut. The red light went off.

Tracy looked at Marvelous. "You're paying for my purse. And my wallet. And my keys. And my phone. ALL of which were IN that purse. Plus locksmith fees. Plus phone replacement. Plus emotional damages. Plus therapy probably."

"I... yes ma'am. How much?"

"Three hundred for the purse. Six hundred for the phone. Seventy-three dollars cash. Credit card replacement fees. Locksmith at my house. DMV fees for new license. I'm adding it up. I'll send you a bill. With INTEREST."

Cherry appeared from inside the club, having watched the whole thing. "We just raised five hundred dollars for this? For this goat? For THIS MOMENT? For LIVE TELEVISION PURSE THEFT?!"

Larry sat down in front of the tent. Looked satisfied. Looked accomplished. Looked like someone who'd just completed their life's work on LIVE television during MONDAY LUNCH NEWS.

Frank's tent swayed slightly in the wind. HAPPY 50TH birthday

FRANK. Frank had seen it all. Frank did not judge. Frank just WAS.

⚓

MADAME PANCAKE STRIKES (PHASE ONE)

Tuesday morning. 7:23 AM. Marvelous's phone rang.

"Boss, we got a PROBLEM."

"What NOW?!"

"The dispensary. The one that was sponsoring us. Health inspector showed up. UNANNOUNCED. Found violations. shut US DOWN."

"WHAT VIOLATIONS?!"

"All of them. Every violation that exists. Plus some new ones they invented SPECIFICALLY for us."

Marvelous drove over. Yellow tape. CLOSED by order OF HEALTH DEPARTMENT sign.

A note taped to the door. Handwritten. Fancy handwriting.

"Such a shame about your business. Such unfortunate timing. - M.P."

Madame Pancake.

She'd sent the health inspector.

The war had officially begun.

⚓

RUNNING TALLY:

\- Tickets Sold: 56 (was 45, gained 11 from TV exposure despite disaster)

   \- Tickets Needed: 44

   \- Days Remaining: 10

   \- Larry Status: Free but costly

   \- Dispensary Status: CLOSED

\- Pancake's Sabotage: PHASE one COMPLETE
\- Reputation: Damaged but somehow increasing
\- TV Coverage: Viral for wrong reasons
\- Dignity: Still deceased

⚓

CHAPTER 9

Betrayal & Desperation (or: When Your Pastor Sells His Soul for Breakfast Money)

⚓

TUESDAY, 8:47 AM - NINE DAYS UNTIL GALA

Marvelous woke up to his phone buzzing. Not normal buzzing. AGGRESSIVE buzzing. VIOLENT buzzing. The kind that suggested someone had died or was currently dying or the world was ending in real-time.

47 missed calls.

Forty-seven. From everyone. From people who NEVER called unless it was urgent, people who'd rather TEXT because calling was "millennial trauma" and "too much commitment."

His stomach dropped—actually physically dropped, organs rearranging themselves in preparation for catastrophic news.

17 voicemails.

Nobody left seventeen voicemails unless someone was dead or dying or his business was ACTIVELY on FIRE.

He played the first one. Tito's voice, urgent, stressed, borderline panicking: "BOSS. call me. now. it'S EMERGENCY. REAL EMERGENCY. NOT LARRY EMERGENCY. WORSE. SO MUCH WORSE."

Second voicemail. Cherry Bomb, panicked, breathing hard like she'd run somewhere: "MARVELOUS WHERE are you?! the dispensary— it'S— JUST CALL ME BACK! NOW! IMMEDIATELY! THIS ISN'T A DRILL!"

Third voicemail. Breadcrumb, actually CRYING—voice cracking, emotional breakdown in progress: "I'm so sorry boss I'm so sorry I didn't know I didn'T KNOW this is my fault oh god the dolphin flyer was my fault and the spam email was my fault and now THIS is my fault—"

Fourth voicemail. Pastor Stacks, somehow already knowing: "THE lord told me THERE'S TROUBLE! Also Mrs. Chen texted me! She in my Bible study! She got PICTURES! I'M PRAYING! I'm praying HARD! MAXIMUM PRAYER!"

Fifth voicemail. His mother (how did she even know?!): "minghao! I saw something on the news! About your business! Call your MOTHER! your MOTHER WHO GAVE BIRTH TO YOU! WHO RAISED YOU!"

He jumped out of bed so fast he tangled in his sheets and fell. Hard. Face-first onto hardwood. His nose hit the floor. Pain exploded through his face. He tasted carpet fibers and desperation and possibly blood.

He grabbed mismatched clothes—jeans inside out, shirt backwards, one sock, couldn't find the other sock, screw it, no socks—and dialed Tito while hopping around trying to find shoes.

"WHERE you BEEN?!"

"I WAS asleep! it'S EIGHT AM! WHAT HAPPENED?!"

"You need to get down here RIGHT now. The dispensary. now. Not later. Not 'in a bit.' NOW. IMMEDIATELY. YESTERDAY."

"WHAT about IT?!"

"Just come SEE. Words can't... words don't do it justice. Words don't have enough CAPACITY."

He made it to the dispensary in seven minutes flat, running three red lights (sorry officer, emergency, life falling apart), making turns that physics suggested shouldn't work, and parallel parking in a way that was less "parking" and more "controlled collision with the curb plus maybe a mailbox."

And found a crowd gathered outside. Not a good crowd. Not a "something fun is happening" crowd. The kind that gathers around car accidents and public embarrassments and situations where someone's life is visibly falling apart in spectacular fashion.

Mrs. Chen from down the street patted his shoulder with genuine sympathy. "I'm so sorry, baby. I'm so sorry. This is TERRIBLE."

"SORRY for what?! Mrs. Chen! SORRY FOR WHAT?!"

"You'll see, baby. You'll see. It's... you gotta see for yourself."

He pushed to the front of the crowd. And stopped dead.

His soul—his ENTIRE soul—evacuated his body. Left through his feet. Went straight down through the concrete. Descended to hell. Came back up. Looked around. Said "nope, can't deal with this" and left again. His soul was gone. Soul had ABANDONED him.

The dispensary's front window—the BIG window, the one they'd paid \$800 to replace after the chicken incident that nobody discussed anymore—was completely covered.

Not with boards. Not with plywood. With a MASSIVE vinyl banner. Professional. Official. Government-issued. Visible from space. Visible from the MOON. Visible from OTHER PLANETS probably.

The banner read, in letters that screamed FAILURE:

\> "CLOSED BY ORDER OF LOS ANGELES COUNTY HEALTH DEPARTMENT"

\>

\> VIOLATIONS DOCUMENTED:

\> - Mold contamination (SEVERE - BLACK MOLD IDENTIFIED IN STORAGE AREA - HAZMAT LEVEL)

\> - Unauthorized livestock on premises (MULTIPLE VIOLATIONS - GOAT NAMED "LARRY")

\> - Structural damage from unreported fire (SAFETY HAZARD - CEILING COMPROMISED - POTENTIAL COLLAPSE)

\> - Operating without current health permits (EXPIRED 8 MONTHS - MARCH 2024 - FLAGRANT DISREGARD FOR LAW)

\> - Improper food storage (TEMPERATURE VIOLATIONS - FOOD POISONING RISK)

\> - Pest control violations (EVIDENCE OF RODENT ACTIVITY - EXTENSIVE)

\> - Emergency exit blocked by cardboard cutout (FIRE CODE VIOLATION - DANNY DEVITO SPECIFIC)

\>

\> DO NOT ENTER - VIOLATORS SUBJECT TO ARREST AND PROSECUTION

Even listing Danny DeVito's crimes against fire code. Danny DeVito had a RAP SHEET now.

"No," he whispered, voice small, broken, the voice of someone watching their dreams die in real-time. "No no no no no—"

Cherry appeared at his side, face grim, exhausted, devastated. "They came at 6 AM. Full health department inspection team. five people. Clipboards. Cameras. Official badges. They were here for two HOURS. They

148

found EVERYTHING. They found things WE didn't even know about. Things we didn't know EXISTED."

"EVERYTHING?!"

"Mold in the back storage room—black mold, the BAD kind, the kind that can kill people, the kind that requires hazmat suits. Larry's entire setup—all unauthorized because apparently you can't have livestock in a commercial food establishment, who knew. The fire damage we just painted over—they took STRUCTURAL SAMPLES. Expired permits—our health permit expired EIGHT MONTHS AGO and neither of us renewed it."

"I THOUGHT you RENEWED IT!"

"I THOUGHT you RENEWED IT!"

"WHO was supposed TO RENEW IT?!"

"BOTH of us! That's the problem with having NO ACTUAL ORGANIZATION! That's the problem with running a business on VIBES and CHAOS and HOPE!"

"HOW they know to look?!" Marvelous grabbed her arm, grip tight with desperation. "How they know about the mold? The fire damage? ALL THIS?! Health department don't just SHOW UP at 6 AM with a DETAILED LIST!"

Cherry pulled a crumpled paper from her jacket. "Anonymous tip. Filed yesterday at 3:47 PM. Look at the details. Look how SPECIFIC."

ANONYMOUS REPORT #8847

Violations suspected:

\- Black mold in back storage room (northwest corner, behind metal shelving, estimate 3'x4')

\- Goat living in back area (named "Larry", brown and white coloring, documented criminal history)

\- Fire damage concealed with paint (ceiling joists weakened, structural compromise)

\- Cardboard cutout blocking emergency exit (celebrity likeness - Danny DeVito approximately 4'10")

Additional note: This business is associated with a gala event planned for December 14th. Public safety concern.

Specific locations. Specific measurements. Larry's NAME. Larry's criminal history documented. Danny DeVito's HEIGHT noted. Information only someone who'd been INSIDE would know. Someone who'd MEASURED. Someone who'd taken NOTES.

"Pancake," Marvelous whispered, understanding crashing down like cold water, like reality breaking through delusion.

"Phase 3," Cherry confirmed flatly.

Tito walked over, hands in pockets, face grim. "Minimum thirty days to reopen. AFTER we fix everything. Mold removal—professional, certified, expensive, takes WEEKS. Structural repairs—engineers, contractors, permits. New permits—applications, inspections, bureaucracy."

"How much total?"

Cherry consulted her phone, scrolling through estimates, calculations, DOOM. "Minimum six thousand five hundred dollars. Maximum ten thousand. Maybe more. Probably more. Definitely more knowing our LUCK."

"JUST the NUMBER!"

"Six-five to ten thousand. And that's OPTIMISTIC. That's best case SCENARIO. That's IF everything goes PERFECTLY."

Marvelous sat down on the curb. Right there. In front of everyone. In front of the crowd. In front of the BANNER of SHAME.

"We're doomed," he said quietly, voice empty.

"We BEEN doomed," Tito said, sitting next to him like they were at a funeral and the funeral was for their lives. "This just makes us PREMIUM doomed. The DELUXE doom package. With complimentary shame banner visible from space."

⚓

THE PANCAKE PHONE CALL (GLOATING AS ART FORM)

His phone rang. Unknown number but he KNEW. He knew in his BONES.

"Pancake."

"I heard about your… situation," Madame Pancake said, voice dripping with false sympathy so thick you could spread it on toast. "The health department closure? That's TERRIBLE. Truly. Devastating."

"You DID this! YOU called them! YOU gave them EVERYTHING!"

"Me? I would NEVER." Pure innocence. Academy Award-winning innocence. "Although... I did happen to NOTICE some concerning health violations when I visited last month. Just happened to look around while I was there. Took mental notes. Drew a little MAP in my mind. Measured things with my EYES."

"You took NOTES?! You MAPPED my violations?!"

"Organization is key to success, Marvelous. You should try it sometime. Maybe after you reopen. In thirty to sixty days. AFTER you spend ten thousand dollars fixing everything. IF you survive that long."

"You PLANNED this! Phase 3!"

"I don't know what you're talking about. What happened to YOUR business is just... consequence. Karma. The universe correcting itself. Natural selection but for businesses."

"WE ain'T RUN IT POORLY!"

"You got mold. black MOLD. In a place that serves food. You got a GOAT living in your storage room. A goat that's been on the NEWS for stealing purses ON LIVE TELEVISION. You got Danny DeVito blocking an emergency exit!"

"Danny DeVito is a FIXTURE! He's part of the ambiance! He's SPIRITUAL GUIDANCE!"

"He's a FIRE hazard. Just like everything else you do. Just like your whole LIFE."

"Old Betsy didn't EXPLODE! She passed dramatically! With HONOR!"

"SHE exploded! There was foam everywhere! WITNESSES! VIDEO! The DJ has PTSD!"

"COMMEMORATIVE foam! legacy foam! HISTORIC FOAM!"

"You got sixty tickets and NINE days left. I got one hundred seventy-two. Almost sold OUT. My venue is BOOKED. My food is CATERED. My entertainment is PROFESSIONAL. So tell me: who does the community REALLY want?"

"MY gala WON'T BE EMPTY!"

"It'll be empty ENOUGH. Empty enough to humiliate you. Empty enough to make you a cautionary tale. Empty enough that the Castellanos call in your debt. And when they do—because they will—I want you to remember this moment. Remember that you could've just QUIT. Could've walked away with DIGNITY. But you INSISTED on fighting. And now you're about to lose EVERYTHING."

She hung up.

"What she say?" Cherry asked, already knowing it was bad from his face.

"She admitted EVERYTHING. Took notes. Drew a MAP. Called the health department. And she enjoyed telling me about it. She REVELED in it."

He looked at the banner. At the crowd still watching. At his failure made PUBLIC.

And felt something shift. Not despair. Something else. Something that felt like SPITE but productive. Something that felt like RAGE but FOCUSED.

"We gonna SELL tickets. We gonna raise MONEY. And we gonna make her WATCH while we succeed."

"It might ACTUALLY kill us," Cherry said realistically.

"THEN we die SPITEFULLY! We die with STYLE! We die with DIGNITY!"

"We already lost dignity," Tito pointed out.

"THEN we'll find NEW DIGNITY! DIGNITY 2.0! UPGRADED DIGNITY!"

⚓

PASTOR STACKS' MIRACLE (TEMPORARY)

They were having an emergency meeting—really just sitting around being SAD—when Pastor Stacks walked in. Unannounced. Uninvited. As tradition. The man had supernatural ability to appear whenever there was FOOD or DRAMA.

"I HEARD about the tragedy! The banner OF SHAME! The PUBLIC HUMILIATION!"

"How you ALWAYS know?!" Marvelous yelled, genuinely curious, genuinely impressed.

"The LORD tells me! Also Mrs. Chen texted me. She's in my Bible study. She got pictures. MULTIPLE ANGLES. Good lighting too."

"Of COURSE she does."

Pastor Stacks clapped his hands together with surprising energy for someone who'd just learned about disaster. "Y'all look TERRIBLE! Y'all look like you at a funeral but you're the CORPSE! Multiple corpses! A corpse convention!"

"We just acknowledging reality! Reality is AGGRESSIVE right now! Reality is attacking US!"

"Well I got GOOD NEWS!"

Everyone stopped. Stared. GOOD NEWS was not a phrase that happened anymore.

"I'm bringing my ENTIRE CONGREGATION to your gala!"

Silence. Complete silence. The silence of not believing, of not DARING to believe.

"...What?" Marvelous said quietly.

"I announced it Sunday! Stood at the pulpit! Said 'Y'ALL need to support brother MARVELOUS! He got PROBLEMS! He got HEALTH VIOLATIONS! He got a CRIMINAL GOAT! But he got HEART! He got DETERMINATION! He got a tent that says HAPPY BIRTHDAY FRANK!'"

"How many you think will actually BUY tickets?"

"At LEAST twenty! Maybe thirty! Maybe FORTY if Sister Washington brings her whole family!"

"TWENTY to thirty tickets?!" Marvelous jumped up, energy returning, hope emerging like a tiny flame in darkness. "THAT'S HUGE! THAT'S MASSIVE! THAT'S A WHOLE CONGREGATION!"

Pastor Stacks looked around expectantly. "Now—" dramatic pause "—where's the food? I skipped breakfast. The LORD told me there would be food here."

"THE lord ain'T providing! YOU'RE MOOCHING! AS USUAL!"

"IT'S called fellowship! fellowship IS BIBLICAL! IT'S IN THE SCRIPTURES!"

"Eating FOUR brownies worth twenty dollars is not fellowship! That's THEFT! That's ONE OF THE COMMANDMENTS!"

"That was QUALITY control! The Lord wanted me to verify the brownies! To make sure they were WORTHY!"

"The Lord wanted you to PAY for THE BROWNIES!"

"The Lord and I have an ARRANGEMENT about brownies! A COVENANT!"

"CHURCH math AIN'T REAL!"

"CHURCH math is different! It operates on FAITH-BASED PRINCIPLES!"

But twenty to thirty tickets. That was SALVATION. That was hope. That was the difference between success and ABSOLUTE CATASTROPHIC FAILURE.

⚓

INSTAGRAM LIVE: LARRY'S CHAOS HOUR

Marvelous positioned his phone carefully—making ABSOLUTELY SURE the closed dispensary with its shame banner wasn't visible in frame.

Within three minutes, 547 people joined. His highest number EVER. Apparently disaster was CONTENT.

"yo yo YO! IT'S DA MARVELOUS! And I got EXCITING NEWS!"

Comments flooded in immediately:

\> "Why is your dispensary closed?"

\> "I saw the banner"

\> "Is Larry in goat jail again"

\> "Team Pancake tbh she's more organized"

He ignored the hard ones, the TRUE ones, the ones that hurt.

"Larry is FINE! Larry is thriving! And I'm here to announce we got special guests coming to the gala! Including—" he paused for DRAMA "—Pastor Stacks' ENTIRE CONGREGATION! Twenty to thirty people! That's a WHOLE CHURCH! That's DIVINE INTERVENTION!"

\> "Is that legal"

\> "Churches can just do that?"

\> "WHERE IS LARRY"

"And most importantly—" He turned the camera. "—LARRY THE GOAT!"

Larry was eating something that was definitely not food. Possibly a legal document. Definitely something IMPORTANT.

The comments EXPLODED:

\> "LARRY!"

\> "THE LEGEND"

\> "THE MYTH"

\> "THE CRIMINAL"

\> "Larry is my emotional support goat"

\> "Free Larry from the concept of consequences"

\> "Larry 2028"

"We're doing ANOTHER giveaway! one free VIP TICKET! Tag THREE FRIENDS, tell me WHY you wanna meet Larry!"

\> "@jessica \@mark \@tony Larry is my spirit animal, we both make poor decisions and feel no remorse"

\> "@chris \@linda \@pete I need Larry's chaotic energy in my life, my therapist says I should try new things"

\> "@mike \@sara \@dan Larry represents freedom from societal expectations and also crime"

The livestream ran for 47 minutes. Larry attempted to eat the phone (four times). Danny DeVito fell over when Larry bumped him (cardboard casualty). Larry 2 was visible across the street for exactly seven seconds (deeply concerning, nobody mentioned it, pretended it didn't happen).

SIX NEW TICKETS SOLD.

Plus the viral clip of Larry eating what was DEFINITELY a tax document got 127,000 views in two hours.

Current count: 68 tickets. Need 32 more.

THE BETRAYAL (WHEN BREAKFAST WINS)

WEDNESDAY MORNING - TWO DAYS UNTIL ISABELLA

Marvelous was eating a sad gas station sandwich—questionable freshness, mayo that tasted like regret and possibly food poisoning—when Pastor Stacks walked in.

But something was different. He looked... uncomfortable. Which was NOT normal. Pastor Stacks was never uncomfortable. The man had once eaten an entire pie while people watched and made eye contact the WHOLE TIME.

But today? Today he looked guilty. Like a man about to do something terrible. Like a man who'd already DONE something terrible.

"Pastor Stacks! PERFECT timing! Your congregation still coming Saturday, right? Because we counting on those twenty to thirty tickets, we need those tickets, those tickets are our SALVATION—"

"Marvelous." Pastor Stacks' voice was quiet. Serious. Without its usual bombast and volume.

The room's energy shifted immediately. Like a temperature drop. Like the moment before bad news. Like the moment before your life changes forever.

Even Larry, in the back, went still. Larry SENSED it.

"I need to be honest with you."

"Honest about WHAT?"

"I can't sponsor your gala anymore."

The words hung in the air. Heavy. Final. Impossible. Like a gavel coming down. Like a door slamming. Like the universe saying "no."

"...What?" Marvelous said quietly, voice small.

"I'm withdrawing my sponsorship. Effective immediately. The congregation promise. All of it."

"WHY?!" Marvelous's voice went up three octaves. "Pastor, you already committed! We announced it! We got your NAME on everything! You stood at your PULPIT! You made it BIBLICAL!"

"I know. And I apologize. I'll send a check to cover any costs—"

"I DON'T want A check!" Marvelous stepped closer, shaking slightly. "We had a deal! We shook HANDS! You PROMISED! You told me you'd bring TWENTY TO THIRTY PEOPLE! I was COUNTING on that! We're DEPENDING on that!"

"I know what I told you."

"THEN WHY?!"

Pastor Stacks finally looked at him. And Marvelous saw it. Guilt. Deep, obvious, undeniable, HEAVY guilt.

"She got to you," Marvelous whispered, understanding crashing down like cold water, like betrayal made manifest. "Pancake got to you. Didn't she."

It wasn't a question. It was TRUTH.

Pastor Stacks said nothing. Which was answer enough. Silence was CONFESSION.

"DIDN'T SHE?!"

"...She made a generous offer," Pastor Stacks admitted quietly, voice barely above a whisper. "Five thousand dollars. To sponsor her event instead. To bring my congregation to HER gala. To publicly endorse HER. To stand at my pulpit and tell my people to support PANCAKE."

The number hit Marvelous like a physical blow. Five thousand. Five times what he'd offered. Five times what he'd SCRAPED TOGETHER. Five times the cost of loyalty, apparently. Five thousand dollars was the price of a pastor's soul.

"You..." He could barely form words. "You taking FIVE thousand from her after you promised ME? After you ate our FOOD? After you took our BROWNIES? After you said 'THE LORD PROVIDES'?!"

"That was QUALITY CONTROL!"

"THAT was theft! theft with religious justification! and now THIS IS WORSE! THIS IS BETRAYAL! THIS IS JUDAS BUT WITH PANCAKES INSTEAD OF SILVER!"

"Marvelous, I got a CHURCH to run!" Pastor Stacks' voice rose defensively, walls going up. "A congregation to feed! Bills to PAY! The roof needs repairs—we got LEAKS! Water damage! The CEILING is falling!"

"AND I got A mob debt!" Marvelous yelled back, voice cracking, emotion breaking through. "I got employees depending on me! I got a COMMUNITY counting on me! I got the CASTELLANOS waiting to see if I can deliver! And you KNEW THAT! You KNEW ALL OF THAT! And you did it ANYWAY!"

"I'm sorry—"

"YOU ain'T sorry! You're BOUGHT! You're PURCHASED! You're PANCAKE'S PROPERTY now!"

"That's not FAIR—"

"FAIR?!" Marvelous laughed bitterly, the laugh of someone breaking. "You know what Pancake's doing! You know she's trying to destroy me! You know this is phase FOUR of her plan! And you HELPING her! For MONEY! For FIVE THOUSAND DOLLARS! You sold your INTEGRITY for BREAKFAST REVENUE!"

Pastor Stacks' face hardened, defensive walls fully erected now.

"Business is business, Marvelous."

"You're a PASTOR! You're supposed to be better than business! You preach about loyalty and community and FAITH every SUNDAY! You stand at that pulpit and tell people about INTEGRITY! And then you—" His voice broke slightly. "—you're supposed to BE BETTER than this. You're supposed to be DIFFERENT."

"I'm also a MAN with RESPONSIBILITIES!"

"You sold your SOUL for breakfast money! FOR SYRUP! FOR WAFFLES!"

"IT ain'T BREAKFAST—"

"IT'S pancake'S money! BREAKFAST! THEMED! LITERALLY!"

They stood facing each other—Marvelous shaking with rage and betrayal and exhaustion, Pastor Stacks defensive but also ashamed, also KNOWING he'd done wrong.

Marvelous walked to the door. Done. Finished. Over.

"I hope her five thousand dollars is worth it. I hope it fixes your roof. I hope it feeds your congregation. Because you just sold your INTEGRITY for it. You sold your word. And when she's done using you—because she will be done using you, because she uses EVERYONE—you'll remember this moment. You'll remember that you could've had HONOR. Could've had LOYALTY. But you chose MONEY instead."

"Marvelous—"

"get out! GET out of my club! go eat pancake'S brownies! SEE IF THEY TASTE AS GOOD AS OURS! SEE IF THEY'RE MADE WITH BETRAYAL! SPOILER: THEY ARE!"

Pastor Stacks left. The door closed. Silence filled the room like poison.

"Did Pastor Stacks just betray us?" Cherry asked, needing confirmation, needing someone to say it out loud.

"Yes."

"The CHURCH man?! The man who said 'the LORD PROVIDES'?! The man who ATE OUR BROWNIES?!"

"The Lord apparently provides five thousand dollars from Pancake," Big Mike muttered darkly.

"This is Phase 4," Cherry said quietly. "She's not just competing. She's attacking our SUPPORT system. Buying everyone who matters. Destroying us from the INSIDE."

"How many tickets we at?"

"Seventy-four. We need twenty-six more. With NO Pastor Stacks support. No congregation. No church miracle."

Cherry checked her calculator. "And we're negative thirteen hundred dollars. We owe more than we have. We're in DEBT to OURSELVES."

Marvelous sat down slowly. Put his head in his hands.

"We can't do this," he said quietly. And everyone stared because Marvelous NEVER said that.

"The math doesn't WORK."

⚓

THE TEAM REFUSES TO DIE

Cherry stood up—slow, deliberate, ANGRY. Not at Pastor Stacks. At MARVELOUS.

"So we quit? We let Pancake WIN? We let her stand in her purple velvet office knowing she BROKE us?"

"MAYBE! Maybe winning isn't possible! Maybe the universe is TELLING US SOMETHING!"

"So the Castellanos call in the debt. We lose EVERYTHING. Possibly our KNEECAPS. And Pancake wins. Forever. She gets to WIN FOREVER."

That word. WINS. It hung in the air like poison.

"I can't let her win," Marvelous said quietly.

"Then what?! Tell me WHAT! Because I see twenty-six impossible TICKETS and TWO DAYS and a NEGATIVE BANK ACCOUNT and NO PLAN!"

"I DON'T have A plan! I don't have ANYTHING! I just know I can't let her WIN! That's ALL I know!"

"That's not STRATEGY! That's just SPITE!"

"THEN I'M spiteful! I'M MAXIMALLY SPITEFUL!"

Marvelous stood up slowly. Something shifting in his face. Something HARDENING.

"We do what we been doing. We grind. We don't think about impossible numbers. We think about ONE TICKET at a time. Twenty-six individual miracles."

"That ain't a PLAN! That's just desperation with WORDS!"

"THEN we're DESPERATE! Desperate people have done AMAZING things! Desperate people climbed MOUNTAINS! Built PYRAMIDS! Invented FLIGHT!"

"Desperate people usually FAIL and DIE!"

"NOT always! sometimes they win! AND WE'RE GONNA BE ONE OF THOSE TIMES!"

He turned to the crew—Tito (skeptical but listening), Big Mike (confused but loyal), Breadcrumb (scared but present, always present).

"We got FORTY-eight hours! twenty-SIX TICKETS! We hit EVERY DOOR! We call EVERY NUMBER! We abandon ALL dignity!"

"We already abandoned dignity," Breadcrumb pointed out correctly.

"Then we abandon it MORE! We find new depths of shamelessness! Depths that haven't been DISCOVERED yet! We're gonna PIONEER shamelessness!"

"I'm in," Tito said firmly. "We came THIS far. Might as well see it through."

"ME too!" Breadcrumb yelled. "Even though I've been having stress DREAMS about Larry chasing me! The dreams are VIVID! He's got my PHONE! And my WALLET! Dream Larry is AMBITIOUS!"

They all looked at Cherry. Waiting. Needing her to say YES.

She sighed the sigh of someone who knew better but was doing it anyway.

"Y'all are RIDICULOUS."

"We KNOW!"

"We're running on NEGATIVE money."

"YUP!"

"And you still wanna FIGHT?!"

"WE don'T know how to DO ANYTHING ELSE! FIGHTING IS ALL WE GOT!"

"Fine. I'm in. But when this fails—WHEN, not if—I'm saying I told

160

you so. LOUDLY. REPEATEDLY. For the rest of our LIVES. Or until the Castellanos end our lives, whichever comes first."

They bumped fists. All of them. Even Breadcrumb, who missed the first time and had to try again.

Frank's tent, visible through the window, swayed slightly in the wind. HAPPY 50TH BIRTHDAY FRANK. Frank had seen it all. Frank persisted. They would persist too.

$$\text{\textmusicalnote}$$

RUNNING TALLY:

\- Tickets Sold: 74

    \- Tickets Needed: 26

    \- Days Remaining: 2

    \- Hours Until Isabella: 48

    \- Pastor Stacks: BETRAYED THEM

    \- Dispensary: CLOSED

    \- Pancake's Phases Complete: 4

    \- Dignity: Still deceased

    \- Hope: Questionable but present

    - Spite: MAXIMUM

CHAPTER 10

Everything Falls Apart (or: The Kitchen Fire That Ended Dreams)

⚓

THURSDAY, 5:47 AM - SEVEN DAYS UNTIL GALA (ONE DAY UNTIL ISABELLA)

Marvelous didn't go to bed. Why pretend? Why engage in the fiction that his brain would allow rest when Isabella Castellano was arriving in approximately 32 hours and they were still 26 tickets short of certain death?

Sleep was a luxury for people without mob debt, closed businesses with giant shame banners, criminal goats actively eating furniture, and approximately 73 different crises happening simultaneously in real-time.

So he'd spent the entire night:

\- Refreshing the ticket website every 3 minutes (obsessively, compulsively, desperately)

\- Drinking coffee until his hands developed a permanent tremor (currently on cup twelve, heart doing arrhythmia)

\- Practicing his pitch to the bathroom mirror (the mirror remained deeply unconvinced, possibly concerned)

\- Googling "how to sell tickets fast legally" (results: underwhelming, mostly MLM schemes)

\- Googling "how to sell tickets fast" (results: definitely illegal, surprisingly creative)

\- Praying to every deity he could think of, including Larry (no response yet, Larry has never responded to prayers)

By 5:47 AM, he looked like a man possessed by anxiety itself. Bloodshot eyes that looked like road maps to hell. Three-day stubble achieving consciousness. Hair pointing in directions that violated physics. The specific exhaustion that comes from running entirely on caffeine, spite, and the fear of kneecap removal.

CURRENT STATUS:

TICKETS: Sold: 74 \| Needed: 26 \| Percentage: 74% (PATHETIC)

MONEY: In bank: \$1,200 \| Owed to vendors: \$1,900 (tent payment today) \| Net status: NEGATIVE \$700 before we even START

PROBLEMS: Dispensary: closed (shame banner visible from space) \| Mental state: fragile, possibly shattered \| Pancake status: WINNING EVERYTHING \| Larry status: ALIVE and DESTRUCTIVE \| Pastor Stacks: JUDAS \| Dignity: DECEASED, no funeral planned

Cherry Bomb arrived at 6 AM looking equally haunted—dark circles like someone had punched her, messy ponytail that had given up being a ponytail, yesterday's clothes (or possibly last week's), carrying the largest coffee cup legally sold to civilians.

"Did you sleep?" she asked, voice hoarse from exhaustion.

"Sleep is a SOCIAL construct invented by people who don't have mob DEADLINES and HEALTH VIOLATIONS and CRIMINAL GOATS!"

"That's not an answer but also fair."

"NO. I didn't sleep. Did YOU?"

"Two hours. Had nightmares about Isabella. She smiled at me while methodically breaking both my kneecaps. WHILE smiling. Maintained eye contact the WHOLE TIME. Very specific. Very detailed. My subconscious has OPINIONS about our situation."

"That's ACCURATE. That sounds exactly like what she'd do. Your subconscious is PROPHETIC."

"Twenty-six tickets," Cherry whispered, staring at the whiteboard like it contained the secrets of the universe and those secrets were TERRIBLE.

"TWENTY-six tickets!" Marvelous yelled, sudden manic energy from nowhere (probably the caffeine finally achieving critical mass in his bloodstream). "That's nothing! That's like… THIRTEEN COUPLES! Or TWENTY-SIX INDIVIDUALS! Or some COMBINATION! The math is SIMPLE!"

"WHERE we finding them?! who'S LEFT?! We've hit every coffee shop! Every door! Every CONNECTION! We're out of HUMANS!"

"Then we find MORE humans! Los Angeles has four MILLION people! SOME of them want to meet a criminal goat! STATISTICALLY!"

THE BATTLE GEAR (PREPARING FOR VICTORY OR

DEATH)

They assembled like soldiers preparing for the final battle of a war they were definitely losing.

Marvelous wore: His best purple suit (wrinkled from sleeping in a chair, possibly sentient at this point), all his gold chains (fake but SHINY), sunglasses (even though sun wasn't up yet—COMMITMENT to the IMAGE), his "CONFIDENCE COLOGNE" called "Executive Decision" that smelled like capitalism mixed with poor choices and desperation, and lucky socks (had holes, multiple holes, but LUCKY holes that had gotten them this far).

Tito showed up at 6:15 AM wearing TACTICAL GEAR. Actual tactical gear. Black vest with seventeen pockets. Combat boots that could kick through walls. Tactical backpack containing God knows what. Looking like he was about to invade a small country.

"Why you dressed like SWAT?!" Marvelous yelled, genuinely confused, genuinely impressed.

"This a MISSION. Military operation. Missions require gear. PREPARATION. TACTICAL ADVANTAGE."

"We selling TICKETS to a gala! To meet a GOAT!"

"HIGH-stakes sales. Could go WRONG. Could get VIOLENT. People get AGGRESSIVE when you interrupt their morning coffee. I've seen THINGS."

"WHO'S getting violent AT A COFFEE SHOP?!"

"You never KNOW. preparedness is SURVIVAL."

Breadcrumb stumbled in at 6:27 AM wearing: Pajama pants (SpongeBob themed, possibly the same ones from yesterday, possibly he LIVES in them now), hoodie (inside out, tag visible, deeply wrinkled), mismatched shoes (one sneaker, one slide), the expression of someone woken against their will by forces they didn't understand and couldn't fight.

"I'm HERE! I'm PRESENT! I'm— what we doing again?"

"COFFEE shop blitz! We hitting every morning SPOT in the city! People who NEED coffee to FUNCTION might make BAD FINANCIAL DECISIONS while UNCAFFEINATED! That's the STRATEGY! Exploit WEAKNESS!"

Five people. Twenty-six tickets needed. Thirty-two hours until judgment. Zero plan except "aggressively bother strangers about a goat with

164

a criminal record."

⚓

THE COFFEE SHOP GRIND (DIGNITY'S THIRD FUNERAL)

COFFEE SHOP #1: "DAILY GRIND" - 6:34 AM

Strategy: AGGRESSIVE KINDNESS

Expected success rate: 30%

Actual success rate: TBD (ominous music plays)

"GOOD morning beautiful PEOPLE!" Marvelous announced to the entire coffee shop, voice projecting like he was on stage, like this was THEATER, like this was NORMAL.

It was 6:34 AM.

Twenty-three pairs of tired eyes looked up. Twenty-three expressions that universally, immediately, instinctively said "please don't talk to me." Twenty-three souls who had not yet consumed enough caffeine to deal with THIS, with him, with WHATEVER THIS WAS.

The barista stopped mid-pour. A businessman dropped his briefcase (minor). A college student actually hissed like a cat (concerning).

A woman in scrubs—nurse, mid-30s, exhausted from night shift, probably saved multiple lives yesterday, probably saw someone die, probably too tired for this—looked up with dead eyes. Eyes that had SEEN things. Eyes that were DONE.

"Are you selling something?" she asked flatly, voice completely monotone, already knowing the answer, already preparing to say no, already regretting eye contact.

"I'm OFFERING something! There's a difference! A fundamental philosophical difference! We're hosting a community gala on Saturday featuring Larry the Goat! He's got a CRIMINAL RECORD! He's been VIRAL! He stole a reporter's PURSE on LIVE TELEVISION! Three million views! Three MILLION!"

"How much?" she asked, already defeated.

"Two hundred dollars! But you're not paying for a TICKET, you're paying for an experience! For a STORY! For MEMORIES!"

She laughed. Bitterly. The laugh of someone who understood numbers and reality and bills. The laugh of someone who made \$32 an hour and had student loans and rent and a car payment and groceries and the specific poverty of being middle class in Los Angeles.

"I can't afford my RENT. I work sixty-hour weeks at a hospital saving lives. I pull double shifts. I eat vending machine food. I haven't had a vacation in three years. I definitely can't afford a two-hundred-dollar party to meet a GOAT. A CRIMINAL goat. With a THEFT PROBLEM."

She went back to her phone. Conversation over. Dream dead. Hope murdered.

"But the goat is REFORMED!" Marvelous tried desperately.

She didn't look up. "So am I. Still can't afford your party."

By 7:15 AM, he'd pitched to 23 people total across the shop:

\- 18 who didn't make eye contact (pretended phones were ABSOLUTELY fascinating, pretended to receive urgent texts, one person actually FaceTimed THEMSELVES to avoid conversation)

\- 4 who said "no" immediately (some with profanity, one creatively involving suggestions about what he could do with his goat)

\- 1 who asked security to "handle this situation" (got escorted out, walked of shame, barista applauded)

Sales: ZERO. Dignity: NEGATIVE. Will to live: QUESTIONABLE.

Cherry pulled him aside outside. "Nobody wanna buy tickets to a goat party at 6:45 AM. People ain't awake yet. They ain't functioning. You're asking pre-coffee humans to make FINANCIAL DECISIONS. That's against the GENEVA CONVENTION."

"What's our ALTERNATIVE?!"

"I DON'T know! But this AIN'T WORKING!"

⚓

COFFEE SHOPS #2-8 (THE GRIND CONTINUES, SOMEHOW WORSE)

They hit seven more coffee shops over the next three hours. Each rejection slightly different. Each failure uniquely painful.

Coffee Shop #2: "BREW HAVEN" - 7:32 AM

\- Pitched to 15 people with increasing desperation

\- Got yelled at twice ("I'M TRYING to work!" "THIS IS HARASSMENT!")

\- One person said "maybe" (the CRUELEST word, false hope wrapped in politeness, meaningless)

\- Barista asked them to "please leave before we call someone"

\- Sales: 0

Coffee Shop #3: "MORNING RITUAL" - 8:04 AM

\- Marvelous accidentally knocked over someone's oat milk latte while gesturing enthusiastically about Larry

\- The latte cost \$7.50 (SEVEN fifty for MILK that's not even from an animal)

\- Customer glared with actual murder in their eyes

\- Had to pay to replace it using money they desperately needed for OTHER things

\- Got banned by manager Jenny (nice woman, doing her job, completely justified) for "aggressive solicitation and beverage violence"

\- Sales: 0 \| Net loss: \$7.50 \| Trauma: SIGNIFICANT

Coffee Shop #4: "ROASTED DREAMS" - 8:41 AM

\- ACTUALLY sold two TICKETS! TWO! DOUBLE DIGITS APPROACHING!

\- Elderly couple in their 70s: "We saw your goat on the news! HILARIOUS! That poor reporter! We're retired! We got time and DISPOSABLE INCOME and we're BORED!"

\- Marvelous almost cried from relief, from gratitude, from the sudden influx of HOPE

\- They paid in CASH, in TWENTIES, counted out slowly with arthritic fingers

\- Sales: 2 (FINALLY! progress! MOMENTUM! VICTORY!)

Coffee Shop #5: "CAFFEINE FACTORY" - 9:18 AM

\- Tito's tactical approach actually worked somehow

\- Didn't TALK, just stood there in his tactical vest looking official and SERIOUS

\- Handed flyers like they were OFFICIAL documents from a GOVERNMENT AGENCY

\- Three people bought tickets just to make him GO away, to stop the tactical STARING, to escape his PRESENCE

\- "Here's four hundred dollars, just PLEASE stop looking at me like that"

\- Sales: 3 \| Method: INTIMIDATION (unintentional but effective)

Coffee Shop #6: "BEAN THERE" - 9:47 AM

\- Breadcrumb tried pitching (MISTAKE, terrible mistake, catastrophic mistake)

\- Got confused mid-pitch, forgot what a gala was, forgot what WORDS were

\- "It's like... a party? But fancy? With like... food? And a goat? Maybe? I think there's a goat? Is there a goat?"

\- "Are YOU okay?" the customer asked with genuine concern

\- "DEFINE okay"

\- Customer walked away mid-sentence, possibly called a wellness check

\- Sales: 0 \| Breadcrumb's dignity: ALSO 0

Coffee Shop #7: "CUP O' JOE" - 10:11 AM

\- Someone recognized Marvelous from the TV disaster (FAME but wrong kind)

\- "You're the guy whose goat ate the reporter's purse! ON live TV! That was AMAZING! Do it again!"

\- "That cost me EIGHT hundred DOLLARS in replacements! Plus emotional damages! Plus therapy for the reporter probably!"

\- "Worth it for the content though, right? For the VIEWS?"

\- "...Maybe"

\- They bought ONE ticket "for the chaos" "for the STORY"

\- Sales: 1 (motivation: SCHADENFREUDE)

Coffee Shop #8: "GRIND TIME" - 10:34 AM

\- Sold FOUR tickets to a corporate group doing team building

\- Manager type in expensive suit: "This sounds terrible enough to be memorable. MEMORABLY terrible. Like that's the goal. We're doing trust falls next week, this is BETTER than that. We're in. Four tickets."

\- Sales: 4 \| Strategy: MARKETED as DISASTER

Running count by 10:47 AM: 84 tickets. Need: 16 more.

They were getting closer. So close they could taste it (tasted like coffee and desperation and broken dreams). Sixteen tickets. Sixteen individual miracles needed. Sixteen strangers who had to say YES.

⚓

THE TENT CRISIS (ONE MINUTE TO SPARE)

Then Marvelous's phone rang at 10:03 AM. Unknown number. The kind that means bad NEWS.

"This is Miguel from Domingo's Event Rentals. I'm calling about your tent. The FRANK tent. We haven't received the second installment payment. Fifteen hundred dollars. Due TODAY by 10 AM."

Marvelous's blood went cold. Actually cold. Ice in veins. Terror in heart.

"I thought we had until SATURDAY!"

"Contract says payment due Thursday. That's TODAY. By 10 AM specifically."

Marvelous checked his watch: 10:04 AM.

"We're FOUR minutes LATE!"

"Exactly. So we're sending a crew RIGHT NOW to collect the tent. Should be there in about thirty minutes. Sorry for the inconvenience."

"YOU can'T take the tent! the GALA'S SATURDAY! WE SOLD A

HUNDRED TICKETS! PEOPLE ARE EXPECTING A TENT!"

"Should've paid on time. Contract's a contract. Business is business."

"WE don'T have fifteen hundred DOLLARS! WE'RE BROKE! WE'RE NEGATIVE!"

"Then you don't have a tent. Have a nice day."

Click.

Marvelous stared at his phone, brain short-circuiting, reality fracturing, universe collapsing.

"What?" Cherry asked, reading his face, seeing the TERROR.

"They... they taking FRANK. The tent. In thirty minutes. If we don't pay fifteen hundred dollars. They're taking our TENT. Our VENUE. Our EVERYTHING."

Everyone stopped. Froze. Processed the implications.

"We don't GOT fifteen hundred," Tito said slowly, doing the math, arriving at DOOM.

"We got twelve hundred in the bank," Cherry said, pulling out her phone, checking their account, seeing the terrible numbers. "We're three hundred SHORT. Three hundred dollars between us and complete CATASTROPHIC FAILURE."

"Can we NEGOTIATE?" Breadcrumb asked desperately.

"MIGUEL already hung UP! NEGOTIATIONS ARE OVER!"

"Then we get the MONEY!" Marvelous started running to the car, thinking faster than ever before. "We got thirty minutes! We PAWN SOMETHING! EVERYTHING! ANYTHING WITH VALUE!"

THE PAWN SHOP (SELLING THE DREAM, PIECE BY PIECE)

They burst into "QUICK cash PAWN" at 10:14 AM, sweating, panicked, desperate, looking like criminals or victims or both or neither or something WORSE.

The shop smelled like desperation and old leather and broken dreams. Display cases full of other people's failures. Wedding rings from divorces.

Guitars from abandoned music careers. Watches from bankruptcies. The physical manifestation of people giving up on things they once loved.

The owner—older Korean man named Mr. Kim, weathered face with story lines, seen everything twice including his own failures, impressed by nothing ever, not even once—looked up from his newspaper slowly. Deliberately. Like he had all the TIME in the world and they had NONE.

"We need to pawn items. FAST. Emergency situation. Life and death situation. Possible kneecap situation. How much for these?" Marvelous's voice cracked slightly on "life and death."

He laid out on the counter with shaking hands, fingers trembling from caffeine and fear and exhaustion:

Three gold chains - The ones he'd bought three years ago when he first thought he was MAKING IT. When he thought he was SOMEBODY. When he thought success was something you could WEAR. Fake gold but he'd believed in them. They'd made him feel POWERFUL. They'd made him feel like DA MARVELOUS.

Two rings - One was costume jewelry, cheap, nothing special. The other was from his uncle Terrence who'd passed away two years ago. Uncle Terrence who'd believed in him when nobody else did. Who'd given him that ring at the funeral and said "make something of yourself." The ring was worth more than money. The ring was worth EVERYTHING.

A watch - Stopped working in 2019 but he'd never gotten it fixed because fixing things cost money and money was always elsewhere. But it was IMPRESSIVE. It LOOKED expensive. It made people think he had his life together. It was a LIE but a convincing lie.

His sunglasses - Real Versace. His FAVORITE possession. His IDENTITY. He'd stolen them from a photo shoot three years ago during his brief "modeling career" (two catalog shoots, both for discount furniture stores, one shoot where he wore the sunglasses and thought "these are MINE now"). He wore them everywhere. Rain. Night. INDOORS. They made him DA MARVELOUS. Without them he was just… Marvelous. Just a guy with problems.

The owner examined them with the care and attention of a jeweler, which he was, which made this worse somehow. He had STANDARDS. He knew what things were WORTH.

"This gold fake," he said, picking up the first chain, examining it under his jeweler's loupe with expert eyes that had seen ten thousand fake chains. "Plated brass. Poor quality plating. Already flaking here." He pointed to a spot Marvelous had never noticed.

"But it LOOKS good! It's convincing gold! Performance gold! THEATRICAL gold!"

"Still fake. Fifty dollars for all three chains. That's generous. Most places would offer thirty. Final offer."

"FIFTY?! I paid three HUNDRED for those! From a vendor on Melrose! From a REPUTABLE street vendor!"

"You got scammed. Bad. They worth fifty at BEST. Probably forty. I'm being KIND at fifty because I recognize desperation when I see it and I been there myself. Take it or leave it."

Marvelous felt something break inside. Something small but important. His chains. His LOOK. Fifty dollars.

"Fine. FINE. The rings?"

The owner picked up the costume jewelry ring first. "Brass. Ten dollars."

Then he picked up Uncle Terrence's ring. Examined it carefully. Actually carefully. With respect even.

"This one's real gold. Small but real. Fourteen karat. Some sentimental value based on your face. Seventy-five dollars."

Seventy-five dollars for Uncle Terrence's belief. For his legacy. For "make something of yourself."

"The WATCH?"

"Doesn't work. Battery dead probably, maybe mechanism broken, hard to tell without opening it and I'm not doing that for free. Twenty dollars for parts. Someone might want the case."

Twenty dollars. For the lie he'd worn on his wrist for four years.

"The SUNGLASSES?"

The owner paused. Actually paused. Set down his loupe. Picked up the sunglasses with both hands. Examined them carefully. Held them to the light. Turned them over. Checked the logo stamp. Checked the serial number etched inside the arm. Checked the hinges. The lenses. The case (which Marvelous had, miraculously, not lost).

"Versace. Real. Model 4361. Discontinued. Good condition despite their... UNCLEAR PROVENANCE that I'm not asking about. Two hundred dollars."

"TWO hundred?! These cost eight HUNDRED new! EIGHT HUNDRED DOLLARS!"

"I'm not buying them new. I'm buying them NOW. From a desperate man at 10:23 am on a Thursday who needs three hundred dollars in the next twenty minutes. In pawn, timing is everything. Supply, demand, and DESPERATION. Two hundred. Final offer. You got eighteen minutes now."

Marvelous did the terrible, painful math:

\- Chains: \$50 (his swagger, his style, his PRESENCE)

\- Costume ring: \$10 (meaningless)

\- Uncle's ring: \$75 (Uncle Terrence's belief, his deathbed gift, EVERYTHING)

\- Watch: \$20 (four years of fake success)

\- Sunglasses: \$200 (his IDENTITY, his brand, DA MARVELOUS himself)

\- Total: \$355

They needed \$300. He had \$355.

Which meant this would work. Which meant FRANK lived. Which meant sacrificing EVERYTHING THAT made HIM LOOK SUCCESSFUL.

Everything he'd built. Everything he'd accumulated to prove he was SOMEBODY. Gone. For a tent. For FRANK's birthday tent. For a venue that leaned seven degrees and said someone else's name.

He looked at Cherry. She nodded slowly. "We gotta."

He looked at Tito. "No choice, boss."

He looked at the items on the counter. His LOOK. His identity. His PROOF that he'd made something of himself.

"Deal," he said, voice hollow, soul evacuating through his feet. "All of it. Take it. Take everything."

The owner counted out cash slowly: Three fifties. Two hundreds. One hundred. Ten twenties. Five fives. \$355 exactly.

Marvelous stared at the money in his hand. Physical proof of his sacrifice. Numbers that represented EVERYTHING.

Behind him, Cherry was quiet. Tito looked away. Breadcrumb said "I'm sorry" and meant it.

"We gotta go," Cherry said quietly, gently, like speaking to someone in shock, which he was. "We got sixteen minutes."

Marvelous took one last look at his possessions on the counter. The owner was already tagging them, pricing them, preparing them for resale.

Someone else would wear his chains. Someone else would wear his sunglasses. Someone else would become who he'd been pretending to be.

They left the pawn shop. The door chimed behind them. Cheerful. Oblivious.

Marvelous touched his bare neck where the chains had been. Touched his bare wrist where the watch had been. Reached for sunglasses that weren't there.

He felt naked. Stripped. Just a man in a wrinkled purple suit running out of time.

⚓

SAVING FRANK (THIRTY SECONDS TO SPARE)

They arrived at the venue with THIRTY SECONDS to spare. Actually thirty seconds. Screeching into the parking lot, tires smoking, definitely breaking multiple traffic laws, possibly traumatizing pedestrians.

The tent removal truck was ALREADY there. Two workers in coveralls were actively unhooking poles, starting the dismantling process, taking down FRANK'S BIRTHDAY.

"wait!" Marvelous yelled, jumping out of the car while it was still moving (dangerous, extremely dangerous, not recommended). "WAIT! stop! we GOT THE MONEY! WE GOT IT!"

The workers stopped, looked at him skeptically, probably thinking "another deadbeat trying to delay the inevitable."

"You got fifteen hundred?" one asked, arms crossed, face showing zero sympathy.

"YES!" Marvelous pulled out cash from everywhere—pockets, wallet, Cherry's purse, Breadcrumb's hoodie pocket (confused about that), Tito's tactical vest (seventeen pockets, apparently some contained cash).

They counted it out on the hood of the truck while Marvelous's heart tried to escape his chest:

\- \$1,200 from the bank (withdrawn at ATM, account now: \$0)

\- \$355 from pawn shop (still warm from his hands, from his SACRIFICE)

\- Total: \$1,555

174

Marvelous counted it again, hands shaking. Recounted. Made sure. Then handed it over. All of it. Every dollar. Their entire financial existence.

The worker counted slowly—agonizingly slowly, impossibly slowly, sadistically slowly—while Marvelous aged seventeen years. One hundred. Two hundred. Five hundred. One thousand. Fourteen hundred. Fourteen-fifty.

Finally: "Fifteen hundred. We're square."

He pocketed the money. Waved to his partner. "Tent stays. Leave it set up."

They packed up their tools. Got in the truck. Drove away.

Marvelous collapsed on the grass next to the tent. Just... collapsed. Lay there. Staring at the sky. Existing. Breathing. Being.

"WE did IT!" he said to the clouds, to God, to the universe.

"We BARELY did it!" Cherry corrected, also collapsing next to him like a puppet with cut strings. "We had thirty seconds! HALF A MINUTE! That's NOTHING!"

"BARELY counts! BARELY IS SUCCESS!"

"We got FIFTY-five dollars left! TOTAL! That's our ENTIRE FINANCIAL EXISTENCE!"

"THAT'S fifty-five more THAN ZERO! THAT'S INFINITE COMPARED TO NOTHING!"

They lay there, exhausted beyond human description, staring up at the tent with FRANK'S NAME looming above them. Ugly. Stained. Leaning 7 degrees to the left. Saying "happy 50TH BIRTHDAY FRANK" in cheerful letters that mocked their suffering. But THEIRS. Saved. Still standing.

"We still need sixteen tickets," Tito reminded them, also lying on grass, tactical vest uncomfortable but committed to the aesthetic.

"I KNOW!"

"And Isabella coming TOMORROW!"

"I KNOW!"

"And we got FIFTY-five DOLLARS total!"

"I know! I KNOW! I KNOW!"

They lay there for five more minutes. Just breathing. Just existing. Just trying to remember what hope felt like before reality murdered it.

Then Marvelous stood up. Dusted off his suit. Adjusted his non-existent sunglasses (phantom limb syndrome but for accessories).

"Back to coffee shops. We don't stop until we hit one hundred."

"You SERIOUS?!"

"SIXTEEN tickets left! We don't stop! We don't QUIT! We keep GOING until the UNIVERSE PHYSICALLY PREVENTS US!"

⚓

THE FINAL PUSH (DESPERATION AS PERFORMANCE ART)

They hit six more coffee shops. Sold twelve more tickets through sheer desperation that was almost charming, through exhaustion that was almost entertaining, through suffering that was compelling content.

Current count by 2:47 PM: 96 tickets. Need: 4 more.

They stood outside Coffee Shop #15, defeated. Four tickets short. FOUR. So close. So impossibly close.

Then—a voice behind them.

"Y'all look STRESSED. Like genuinely TROUBLED."

They turned. It was PASTOR STACKS. Walking down the street. Holding Starbucks. Wearing guilt like a heavy winter coat in summer.

Marvelous's face went DARK. "you. You got some NERVE showing your FACE! After what you DID!"

"I know. I KNOW. I wanted to—"

"You wanted to WHAT?! apologize?! You can'T apologize for BETRAYAL! You can't UNDO selling your integrity for PANCAKE MONEY!"

Pastor Stacks pulled out his wallet. Interrupted the rant with cash.

"How much you need?" he asked quietly, voice small.

Everyone froze.

"…What?" Marvelous asked carefully.

"How. Much. You. Need. Right now."

"Why you CARE?!"

"Because I feel GUILTY. And guilt is EXPENSIVE. And I can't sleep. And I can't preach. And I can't look my congregation in the eyes. Just tell me. How much."

"Four more ticket sales," Cherry said carefully. "Eight hundred dollars."

Pastor Stacks counted out bills. Handed Marvelous \$900.

"Take nine hundred. Extra hundred is… I don't know. Penance. Repentance. SOMETHING."

Marvelous stared at the money. Then at Pastor Stacks. At the obvious shame.

"This don't make us even," he said quietly.

"I know. It don't. But it's… it's SOMETHING."

Marvelous took the money. "We even. But we ain't GOOD."

Pastor Stacks nodded. "That's fair. That's MORE than fair."

He walked away. Shoulders slumped. Carrying his shame.

FINAL COUNT: 100 TICKETS. EXACTLY 100.

They'd done it. By the narrowest margin in history. By thirty seconds and nine hundred dollars and one guilty pastor. But they'd DONE IT.

RUNNING TALLY:

\- Money Remaining: \$55
    \- Chains: GONE
    \- Sunglasses: GONE
    \- Uncle's ring: GONE
    \- Dignity: STILL DECEASED
    \- Frank Status: SAVED
    \- Isabella: TOMORROW
    - Success: QUESTIONABLE but ACHIEVED

CHAPTER 11

The Unraveling (or: When Everything Goes Wrong At Once)

⚓

FRIDAY, 10:47 PM - ONE DAY UNTIL GALA (THE LONGEST NIGHT)

Marvelous couldn't sleep. Again. Still. Forever, apparently.

Sleep had looked at his situation, evaluated the stress levels, calculated the probability of rest occurring, and said "absolutely not, good luck with that."

So at 10:47 PM, he was back at Club Marvelous. Laptop glowing. Coffee brewed (fourth pot, heart doing complex arrhythmias). Stress-eating Flamin' Hot chips (appropriate flavor for his life currently on fire). Calculator showing numbers that refused to make sense no matter how many times he typed them. Spreadsheet full of RED.

Cherry Bomb walked in at 11:03 PM—also unable to sleep, also drawn to the disaster like a moth to a flame that was actively CONSUMING EVERYTHING.

"You're here," she said, not surprised.

"Where ELSE would I be? Sleeping? Making good life DECISIONS? Having PEACE OF MIND?"

They sat in exhausted, defeated solidarity. The solidarity of people who knew tomorrow might destroy them.

Then Marvelous's phone buzzed. Text from Breadcrumb:

\> "Boss I got an idea"

Cherry read it. Sighed deeply. "Oh no. Here we go."

"His ideas are ALWAYS—"

"—expensive, illegal, or stupid," they said together, in perfect sync, like they'd rehearsed it.

Another text appeared:

\> "What if we rob a bank"

"there it is!" Cherry yelled, jumping up. "THERE'S the CRIME! I WAS WAITING FOR THE CRIME! I KNEW it was COMING!"

Marvelous typed: "NO. absolutely not. GO TO SLEEP."

Response: "NO. ABSOLUTELY NOT. GO TO SLEEP."

"He makes a TERRIBLE point," Cherry said.

"The WORST point. But technically A point."

"We're NOT robbing a BANK!"

"I KNOW! I'm just saying… we've done worse things. Maybe not LEGALLY worse. But ethically COMPARABLE."

They started laughing. Exhausted, borderline hysterical laughing. The kind that's one step away from crying.

"We're considering CRIME as backup plans! Like actual FEDERAL CRIMES!"

"We're doomed!"

⚓

SATURDAY MORNING - THE CASCADE OF DISASTERS

Marvelous woke up at his desk at 6:47 AM. Didn't remember falling asleep. Neck hurt. Back hurt. Everything hurt. Soul hurt. Twelve hours until gala. Twelve hours until EVERYTHING.

His phone rang. Unknown number. The kind that means BAD NEWS.

"Is this Da Marvelous McCall?"

"…Yes?" Voice hoarse from exhaustion and chip dust.

"This is Marcus. DJ Marcus. I'm calling to cancel."

The words hit like ICE WATER. Like betrayal. Like the universe saying "no."

"CANCEL?! The event is tonight! IN TWELVE HOURS!"

"I understand that. But I got a better offer. Madame Pancake offered me twice what you're paying. Fifteen hundred dollars. To DJ HER event instead. Tonight. Same time."

Pancake. Of COURSE. phase FIVE.

"But we had a CONTRACT!"

"A verbal contract. Unenforceable. I checked with my lawyer this morning."

"YOUR lawyer?! You charge three HUNDRED DOLLARS and your last speakers EXPLODED and killed Old Betsy!"

"Which is why I upgraded equipment. Thanks to Madame Pancake's generous advance payment. Anyway, I wish you luck—"

"WAIT! I'll pay you MORE! I'll match her offer!"

"Mr. McCall. She's paying me fifteen hundred dollars cash. Up front. Can you match that? Right now?"

Silence. They both knew he couldn't. They both knew his bank account was EMPTY.

"That's what I thought. Good luck tonight."

Click.

Everyone was awake now, staring at him with horror.

"The dj quit. Pancake offered him fifteen hundred to DJ HER event. She BOUGHT him."

"WHAT?!" Cherry jumped up. "how we supposed to HAVE A GALA WITH NO MUSIC?! WITH NO ENTERTAINMENT?!"

Before anyone could answer, his phone rang AGAIN. Sister Rodriguez.

"Marvelous, I'm so sorry. The choir can't perform tonight. Pastor Stacks called an emergency church meeting for ALL members. Seven PM sharp. Required attendance."

"Required— PASTOR stacks?! THAT JUDAS?!"

"He said it's about the church's financial future. Planning session. Everyone has to attend or risk losing their membership standing. I'm so sorry."

Marvelous felt rage building. Pure, focused rage.

"Let me guess. This meeting was scheduled THIS morning? Conveniently? And it happens to be at the EXACT SAME TIME as my gala?"

"…Yes. He sent the email at 6 AM. Oh Marvelous… you don't think he did this on PURPOSE?"

"I KNOW he did! He's working with pancake! He gave me guilt money then stabbed me AGAIN! DEEPER! WITH A BIGGER KNIFE!"

"I'll pray for you?"

"PRAYER don'T pay BILLS! PRAYER DON'T REPLACE CHOIRS!"

He hung up. Maybe too harshly. But rage doesn't care about phone etiquette or Sister Rodriguez's feelings.

"The choir cancelled too. Pastor Stacks scheduled an emergency church meeting. Same time as our gala. EXACTLY the same time. to THE MINUTE."

"That's CALCULATED," Cherry processed, seeing the pattern. "That's coordinated. That's Phase 5 of her plan. She's not just competing. She's DESTROYING our event from the INSIDE."

His phone rang A THIRD time. Because apparently the universe had a QUOTA.

"Mr. McCall? This is David from Domingo's Event Rentals. Your tent security deposit is due today. Before the event starts. Eight hundred dollars. Cash or certified check."

"We PAID the tent rental fee! fifteen hundred DOLLARS! We paid it ONE DAY AGO!"

"The security deposit is SEPARATE from the rental fee. Section 4, paragraph 2, clause C of your contract. It's due the day of the event."

"We don't GOT eight hundred dollars! we don'T HAVE MONEY ANYMORE!"

"Then we collect the tent. Today. Before your event. Truck arrives at noon. That's—" he paused, checking his watch "—five hours from now."

"NOON?! the gala IS TONIGHT! IN TWELVE HOURS!"

"Then I suggest you find eight hundred dollars quickly. Clock's ticking, Mr. McCall."

Click.

Everyone stared in horror.

"They want eight hundred dollars or they're taking the tent. At NOON. In five HOURS."

"Where we getting EIGHT hundred dollars?!" Cherry asked, pulling out her calculator automatically, already knowing the answer was nowhere. "We're negative in the bank! We spent our last money on disaster SHIRTS that say 'MARV IOUS AL'! We got NO ASSETS left to PAWN! NO jewelry! NO watches! NO sunglasses! NOTHING!"

"I know! I KNOW all OF THAT! I KNOW!"

They sat in defeated silence. The silence of people watching their dreams die.

"We got NO dj. NO choir. And in five hours, NO TENT," Cherry listed methodically.

"So the gala can't happen," Breadcrumb said slowly, realizing.

"Which means we DEFAULT on Isabella," Tito added, following the logic to its terrible conclusion.

"Which means she LIQUIDATES everything," Big Mike finished.

"It's over," Cherry said quietly, voice empty. "It's ACTUALLY over. We can't do this. The math doesn't work. The universe doesn't WANT us to succeed."

Nobody argued. Because she was RIGHT.

⚓

THE LAST MIRACLE (REDEMPTION AT 7:13 AM)

Marvelous was staring at nothing—just existing in despair—when someone knocked on the club door at 7:13 AM.

Nobody moved. Moving required HOPE.

"We're CLOSED!" Cherry yelled. "PERMANENTLY probably!"

More knocking. Persistent. Annoying.

Tito walked over slowly, opened it.

Pastor Stacks stood there. Holding an envelope. Looking guilty. Looking TERRIBLE actually—like he hadn't slept, like he'd been CRYING.

"YOU!" Marvelous jumped up, rage replacing despair. "You got some nerve showing your face after what you DID! After scheduling that meeting to SABOTAGE me AGAIN!"

"I cancelled it," Pastor Stacks interrupted quietly.

Everyone stopped. Processed.

"...What?" Marvelous asked carefully, not daring to believe.

"The meeting. I cancelled it. Sent an email twenty minutes ago to the entire congregation. Meeting postponed indefinitely. Everyone's free to attend your gala if they want."

182

"Why?"

Pastor Stacks stepped inside, closed the door behind him.

"Because I couldn't sleep last night. At all. Kept thinking about what I did. About the money I took from Pancake. Seven thousand dollars. About the meetings I scheduled specifically to destroy you. About the man I've become."

"So you ADMIT it was sabotage?! COORDINATED sabotage?!"

"Yes." No hesitation. No excuses. "She paid me two thousand dollars to schedule that meeting at exactly seven PM. To ensure your choir couldn't perform. To ensure your church supporters would be occupied. It was calculated. It was cruel. It was EFFECTIVE. And I did it anyway. For money."

He held out the envelope with shaking hands.

"This is eight hundred dollars. Cash. For your tent deposit. So FRANK can stay."

Marvelous stared at the envelope. At the SALVATION it represented.

"Why?" he asked quietly, genuinely confused.

Pastor Stacks looked at the ground, couldn't meet his eyes.

"Because I've been a man of God for thirty years. I've preached about integrity, about loyalty, about doing the right thing when nobody's watching. And in the last two weeks, I've betrayed everyone who trusted me. For MONEY. Because I was scared. Because the church building needs repairs. Because I convinced myself it was practical. That it was RESPONSIBLE."

He looked up, eyes wet, voice breaking.

"But last night, lying in bed staring at the ceiling, I realized: I can fix the church building later. I can raise money honestly over TIME. What I can'T fix is my SOUL if I keep doing this. Keep HURTING good people for PROFIT."

He pushed the envelope toward Marvelous with both hands.

"So take it. Save your tent. Save FRANK. Have your gala. And maybe... maybe one day you'll forgive me."

Marvelous looked at the envelope. At Pastor Stacks' face—the genuine remorse, the PAIN.

"How much Pancake pay you total?"

"Seven thousand. Between the initial sponsorship withdrawal and the various sabotage payments."

183

"And you're giving us eight hundred of it?"

"I'm giving you eight hundred. I'm giving the REST back to Pancake. ALL of it. Six thousand two hundred dollars. With a letter explaining I can't keep blood money. That I won't participate in destroying someone's livelihood for my own benefit."

He pulled out his phone, showed them the email draft already written, addressed to Madame Pancake.

Cherry read it, eyes widening. "You actually gonna send this? She's gonna be FURIOUS! She might come AFTER you!"

"Already sent. Fifteen minutes ago. I've accepted the consequences."

Pastor Stacks smiled—sad, tired, but GENUINE. The first genuine smile they'd seen from him in weeks.

"But I'll sleep tonight. For the first time in two weeks. And that's worth more than seven thousand dollars. Worth more than a repaired roof. Worth more than EVERYTHING."

Marvelous took the envelope. Looked inside. Eight hundred dollars. Cash. SALVATION in paper form.

"Thank you," he said quietly, meaning it.

"I don't deserve thanks—"

"Thank you ANYWAY. For coming back. For choosing RIGHT."

Pastor Stacks nodded once. Turned to leave. Stopped at the door, hand on the frame.

"For what it's worth: I hope your gala succeeds. I hope you prove everyone wrong. Including me. Especially me."

Then he left. The door closed softly.

"Did that just happen?" Breadcrumb asked, still processing.

"Pastor Stacks gave us EIGHT hundred dollars," Cherry said slowly, calculator brain trying to compute redemption. "AFTER betraying us TWICE. That's CHARACTER DEVELOPMENT. That's an ACTUAL ARC."

"That's REDEMPTION!" Marvelous said, holding up the cash like a trophy, like proof the universe sometimes worked. "We got the tent MONEY! FRANK IS SAVED!"

"We STILL don't got a DJ!" Big Mike reminded them, ever practical.

"Or a CHOIR!" Breadcrumb added.

"We'll FIGURE it out! We got a TENT! We got a VENUE! We got

SEVEN HOURS! Seven hours to make MIRACLES happen!"

"To do WHAT?!" Cherry challenged.

"To make a BLUETOOTH speaker sound like a dj! To convince Cherry to sing! To FAKE IT until we MAKE TWENTY-THREE THOUSAND DOLLARS!"

⚓

OPERATION: FAKE IT 'TIL WE MAKE IT

The Bluetooth Speaker "DJ" (2:14 PM)

Tito set up his phone connected to a Bluetooth speaker (\$47 from Amazon, two-star review, "works sometimes"). He tested it.

Sound came out. TERRIBLE sound. Like a mouse with asthma trying to SCREAM.

"This is what we GOT! We tell people it's ambient! It's INTENTIONAL! It's ARTISTIC!"

⚓

Cherry's Secret Talent Revealed (3:30 PM)

Cherry stood in the empty tent. The crew sat in the front row, waiting skeptically.

Music started—slow, soulful R&B.

Cherry closed her eyes. Took a breath.

And SANG.

BEAUTIFULLY.

Her voice filled the tent—rich, powerful, controlled. She hit high notes cleanly. Sustained notes effortlessly. Added runs and flourishes that sounded PROFESSIONAL.

Everyone's mouths dropped open. Literally. Flies could've entered.

"CHERRY you CAN ACTUALLY SING?!"

"I took lessons for TWELVE YEARS! Started when I was eight! Choir, competitions, almost went to music school!"

"WHY you NEVER MENTIONED THIS?!"

"Because I gave it up! Chose accounting! Chose PRACTICAL over PASSION!"

"Well UN-give-it-UP! You're performing TONIGHT! You're our ENTERTAINMENT!"

She looked terrified. But also... excited? Like something long dormant was finally waking up.

"Fine. But I'm picking the SONGS. And you're paying me EXTRA."

"We don't GOT extra!"

"Then you OWE me extra!"

"DEAL!"

⚓

Hiding Larry (Again) (4:17 PM)

Animal Control called. "We'll be by between 6 and 8 PM to inspect."

They moved Larry to the BACK back storage room with treats, water, towels, and prayer.

Larry bleated once—loud, defiant, a promise of future chaos.

"He's gonna escape," Tito predicted.

"PROBABLY! But he's FAMILY! You don't give up on criminal family!"

⚓

The Grocery Store Dessert Transformation (5:02 PM)

They bought grocery store desserts—sheet cakes, frozen pies, day-old cupcakes, whipped cream, edible glitter—for \$287.43 total.

Cherry transformed them with MAGIC: arranged on platters, topped with whipped cream, sprinkled glitter liberally, added fresh fruit garnishes.

Final result: Looked like a REAL dessert table. If you didn't look too closely. Or think about math.

⚓

THE FINAL HOUR (6:15 PM - 45 MINUTES TO SHOWTIME)

Everyone gathered for final check.

THE VENUE:

\- Tent: Standing (7-degree lean, but standing)

   \- FRANK name: "Famous Italian designer!"

   \- Danny DeVito: Prominently displayed

   \- Chairs: 78 good ones visible

   \- Tables: Set, wobbling minimally

Marvelous looked at everyone. "This is it. Everything we worked for. Everything we LIED for. Everything we FOUGHT for."

"We gonna make it?" Breadcrumb asked.

"I don't know," Marvelous admitted honestly. "But we gonna TRY."

Car headlights appeared at 6:52 PM. Eight minutes early.

The first guests.

"Show time," Cherry whispered.

Everyone took positions. Marvelous straightened his purple tracksuit (only clean clothes left). Put on his BEST smile—the one that said "Everything is perfect and definitely not held together by LIES."

"Let's make some MONEY!"

⚓

THE FIRST ARRIVALS (THEY'RE REAL!)

A woman in a blue dress approached. "Is this… the gala?"

187

"YES! WELCOME!"

"This is a TENT. It says 'FRANK' on it."

"That's the DESIGNER! Frank Tentelli! FAMOUS Italian tent designer! Very sought-after in Europe!"

"…Frank Tentelli."

"VISIONARY! Changed the tent industry!"

She looked skeptical. But walked in anyway.

By 6:59 PM: 32 people inside. Looking around. Examining Danny DeVito. Taking photos.

They were here. ACTUALLY here.

Marvelous walked to the center. 32 pairs of eyes on him.

Standing in a leaning tent that said FRANK, surrounded by broken chairs and grocery store cakes, with a FUGITIVE goat hidden in back and a BLUETOOTH SPEAKER as entertainment—

Da Marvelous McCall felt something unexpected:

ALIVE.

Terrified. Desperate. But ALIVE.

"Ladies and gentlemen," he began, voice smooth, confidence FAKE but CONVINCING…

"Welcome to the event of the YEAR!"

The crowd applauded. Uncertainly. But they applauded.

And at exactly 7:00 PM—right on schedule, despite everything—

The gala began.

CHAPTER 12

The Crash (or: When Dreams Meet Reality)

⚓

SATURDAY, 7:03 PM - THE GALA BEGINS

For the first time in TWO weeks—two weeks of disasters, sabotage, betrayals, fires, health violations, mob debt, and a criminal goat with a WARRANT—things were going RIGHT.

Actually right. Genuinely, impossibly, miraculously RIGHT.

Marvelous stood at the entrance of the FRANK tent (fully embracing Frank now, Frank was FAMILY, Frank was eternal), greeting guests like he OWNED the city, like he was SOMEBODY.

"Welcome! Welcome! Thank you SO MUCH for coming!"

People smiled. ACTUAL smiles. Not pity smiles. Not sympathy smiles. genuine smiles. They took photos—of the tent, the string lights hung with love and duct tape, the Danny DeVito cardboard cutout (which was getting MORE attention than expected, people LOVED Danny DeVito).

A man in a nice suit shook his hand firmly: "This is UNIQUE! Very… authentic!"

Marvelous couldn't tell if that was a compliment or a polite insult. Didn't matter. The man WALKED in. That was a WIN. That was REVENUE.

Cherry worked the merchandise table like a SALESPERSON, arranging the homemade disaster shirts artistically—folded to hide the worst mistakes, positioned under strategic lighting that made glitter sparkle and spacing errors less obvious.

"Limited edition artisanal shirts!" she called out with the confidence of someone SELLING A LIE. "Hand-crafted! One of a kind! Absolutely unique! Only ten dollars!"

A woman picked one up, unfolded it carefully: "I SUR ived da M RVEL US'S G ALA"

The spacing was TRAGIC. The gaps were CRIMINAL.

"Is this... intentional?" she asked, examining it like ART, like it MEANT something.

"ABSOLUTELY!" Cherry lied smoothly, professionally, beautifully. "It's ironic! It's post-MODERN! It's making a STATEMENT about the imperfection of perfection! About how TRYING HARD doesn't guarantee SUCCESS!"

"...That's actually kind of deep," the woman said, processing, considering, BELIEVING.

"We're DEEP people! We contain MULTITUDES!"

"I'll take two."

SOLD. Twenty dollars. Cherry made a mental note: Irony sells. Desperation as art form works.

Breadcrumb managed the raffle with surprising competence—giant jar of tickets, prizes including a TV, gift cards, spa package, and the grand PRIZE that people kept asking about: Private meet-and-greet with Larry the Goat himself.

"Twenty dollars per raffle ticket! Multiple prizes! Including a PRIVATE session with Larry the Criminal—I mean FAMOUS—Larry the FAMOUS goat!"

"The goat from TV?" someone asked, eyes lighting up with recognition.

"The VERY same! Forty-seven THOUSAND views! Internet CELEBRITY! Local LEGEND!"

They bought three tickets immediately. Fifty dollars. Cash. REAL MONEY.

By 7:15 PM they'd sold:

\- 8 disaster shirts (\$80 profit)

\- 47 raffle tickets (\$940)

\- 2 VIP photo packages (\$100)

\- 0 naming rights (nobody wanted their name on a bathroom, even ironically)

Cherry checked her calculator—the Calculator of Doom that usually showed only RED numbers and NEGATIVE SIGNS—and for once, miraculously, it showed GREEN.

"We made one thousand ONE HUNDRED TWENTY DOLLARS in the first fifteen minutes!"

"WE rich!" Breadcrumb yelled, arms raised like VICTORY.

"We need TWENTY-one THOUSAND MORE!"

"DETAILS! Minor DETAILS!"

⚓

7:18 PM - THE BAR RUSH (TITO'S CRIMES AGAINST MIXOLOGY)

Tito's bar got SLAMMED. Folding table. Mismatched bottles. Plastic cups. confidence. Zero professional training. Maximum YouTube knowledge. Pure VIBES.

His bartending methodology:

1\. Pick a random liquor (usually vodka, safest choice)

2\. Pour GENEROUSLY (mostly alcohol, 70% minimum)

3\. Add mixer (barely any, 20% maximum)

4\. Add ice (if remembered)

5\. Charge \$15

6\. Hope nobody dies

His drinks were: 70% alcohol, 20% mixer, 10% prayer, 100% DANGEROUS, and somehow POPULAR.

The first customer took one sip of Tito's "margarita" and GASPED audibly. Eyes watering. Throat burning. Face contorting.

"This is… WOW. This is STRONG."

"That's the PREMIUM blend! Top-shelf tequila! artisanal salt! We import it from SPECIFIC REGIONS of Mexico!"

"It tastes like PAINT thinner mixed with REGRET!"

"IMPORTED paint thinner! From mexico! Premium REGIONS!"

"This could KILL someone! This is MEDICALLY dangerous!"

"It could! But it WON'T! Probably! We've had zero deaths so FAR!"

The man stared at his drink. Processing. Considering mortality. Then: "I'll take another. Make it a double."

By 7:25 PM, Tito had sold:

\- 34 mixed drinks

\- 12 shots (straight poison)

\- 6 "special cocktails" (mystery combinations)

Total: \$714 in revenue. And approximately 8 people who might need medical attention later but were CURRENTLY very happy.

"I'M A BARTENDER!" Tito announced proudly, arms raised.

"You a CRIMINAL!" Big Mike corrected from across the tent.

"Same thing in this economy!"

"You gonna KILL somebody!"

"But PROFITABLY!"

⚓

7:31 PM - THE TENT FILLS (MOMENTUM BUILDS)

The tent filled steadily like HOPE itself was MULTIPLYING:

\- 45 people at 7:15

\- 60 at 7:20

\- 73 at 7:25

\- 82 at 7:31

More than Marvelous had dared hope. More than seemed POSSIBLE given everything.

Someone took a selfie with Danny DeVito. Tagged it #DannyDeVitoAtTheGala. Then another person. Then TEN people. Then a line formed. People LOVED Danny DeVito. Danny DeVito was the STAR.

For just a moment—standing there watching it all happen, watching his VISION become real—Marvelous felt something he hadn't felt in WEEKS:

PRIDE.

Real pride. Not fake pride. Not ego. Actual PRIDE.

It was a DISASTER. The tent leaned. The shirts had spelling errors. The drinks were poison. But it was their disaster. And people were

ENJOYING it. People were HAVING FUN.

Cherry appeared beside him, calculator in hand like always. "Current revenue: FOUR thousand two HUNDRED THIRTY DOLLARS."

"WE're EIGHTEEN PERCENT to our goal!"

"We need EIGHTEEN thousand MORE in THREE HOURS!"

"But we got MOMENTUM! We got energy! We got DANNY DEVITO!"

"Momentum don't PAY debt! Danny DeVito don't make PAYMENTS!"

But she was smiling despite the words. Smiling GENUINELY. Because for once—for once in this entire nightmare—the numbers were going UP instead of DOWN. Progress was HAPPENING.

7:47 PM - CHERRY PERFORMS (THE HIDDEN STAR)

Marvelous grabbed the microphone (borrowed, barely functional, probably illegal). Tapped it. FEEDBACK screech that made everyone WINCE.

"Sorry! Technical difficulties are part of the AUTHENTIC experience!" The crowd laughed. Politely but genuinely. "Thank you all for coming tonight! We got entertainment, we got food that won't kill you PROBABLY, we got the LEGENDARY Danny DeVito—and NOW, we got something SPECIAL! Something NOBODY expected! Please welcome to the stage: CHERRY BOMB!"

Applause. Polite. Curious. Uncertain.

Cherry walked to center stage slowly—each step reluctant, each step carrying twelve years of training and twelve years of suppressed dreams and twelve years of choosing PRACTICAL over PASSION.

She grabbed the microphone with shaking hands.

"Hi everyone. I'm not a professional singer. I'm actually an accountant. I calculate budgets and tell people they can't afford things." Laughs. Genuine laughs. "But tonight, I'm gonna sing for you. Because sometimes you gotta do things that scare you. Sometimes you gotta TRY even when you might FAIL."

She looked at Marvelous. He gave her a thumbs up. She nodded.

Tito pressed play on the Bluetooth speaker. Music started—slow, soulful R&B that filled the tent.

Cherry closed her eyes. Took a breath. Deep. Centering. PREPARING.

And SANG.

Her voice filled the tent—rich, powerful, controlled, BEAUTIFUL—hitting notes with precision that came from years of training she never talked about—adding runs and flourishes that sounded professional not amateur—pouring emotion into every word like she'd been saving it for this MOMENT, for THIS NIGHT, for THIS ONE CHANCE.

The crowd went SILENT.

Not polite silence. Not awkward silence. CAPTIVATED silence.

People stopped talking. Stopped drinking. Stopped MOVING. Just LISTENED.

Marvelous stood at the back, mouth open, tears forming. Because he KNEW Cherry could sing. But he didn't know she could sing like this. Like every spreadsheet and calculator and budget meeting had been HIDING this person underneath. Like she'd been SOMEONE ELSE all along.

She hit a high note—sustained it, clear and perfect and IMPOSSIBLE.

Someone in the crowd said "DAMN!" loudly. Others murmured agreement.

The song built to its climax. She belted the final chorus—voice soaring, powerful, REAL, raw, HONEST—and when she hit the final note, holding it perfect and strong before letting it fade into silence…

The tent ERUPTED.

STANDING OVATION.

People jumped to their feet, CHEERING, whistling, SCREAMING.

"ENCORE!"

"WHERE'S your ALBUM?!"

"FORGET the gala, START A MUSIC CAREER!"

Cherry stood there center stage, breathing hard, eyes wide with SHOCK and disbelief. Because she'd forgotten what this felt like. What it felt like to be SEEN. To be MORE than just the person who calculates budgets and says "we can't afford that" and manages OTHER people's dreams instead of her own.

Marvelous rushed up, grabbed her in a HUG. "cherry! you WERE

194

INCREDIBLE! YOU WERE PERFECT!"

"I... I didn't mess up?" Her voice was small, uncertain, VULNERABLE.

"MESS up?! You were PERFECT! You were AMAZING! You were—you were YOURSELF!"

Three more songs over the next forty minutes:

\- Whitney Houston (nailed every note)

\- Aretha Franklin (KILLED it, made it her OWN)

\- Modern R&B (transformed it, OWNED it)

After her final song, Breadcrumb's hastily set-up tip jar—a plastic cup with "TIPS for CHERRY" written in Sharpie—had \$847 in cash. Eight hundred forty-seven DOLLARS.

She walked off stage shaking, crying slightly, GLOWING with something that looked like JOY.

"You just made us EIGHT hundred DOLLARS by being YOURSELF! By doing what you LOVE!"

"I forgot," she said, voice breaking, tears streaming. "I forgot how much I LOVED this. How much I needed this. I gave it up for practical. For SAFE. For RESPONSIBLE. And I've been MISERABLE."

"Then don't forget AGAIN! Don't HIDE this!"

"But I'm an ACCOUNTANT! That's my job! That's my CAREER!"

"You can be BOTH! You can be whatever you WANT! You can be MULTIPLE THINGS!"

She hugged him. Hard. Crying. "Thank you. For making me do this. For FORCING me to remember."

Revenue update: \$5,077 earned \| Still needed: \$17,923 \| Time remaining: 2 hours 15 minutes

⚓

8:34 PM - THE BLUETOOTH SPEAKER DIES (DISASTER RETURNS)

Tito's phone died mid-song. Just... DIED. Battery: 0%. He'd forgotten to charge it because he was busy, because there was too MUCH happening, because LIFE was CHAOS.

"DOES anybody have A CHARGER FOR AN ANDROID?!"

Three people offered iPhones (useless). Nobody had the right charger.

Someone offered to play music from THEIR phone. Tito connected it. Nothing. The Bluetooth speaker was also dead. Battery ALSO 0%. Because OF COURSE it was.

Silence filled the tent. Awkward. Heavy. EXPENSIVE.

"Technical difficulties!" Marvelous announced with fake confidence. "Very AUTHENTIC! Very REAL!"

Someone yelled: "THIS is PATHETIC!"

Another voice: "I paid TWO hundred DOLLARS for THIS?!"

Marvelous grabbed his phone. Opened Spotify. Hit play. Held it UP in the air like a torch, like SALVATION.

Music played. Quietly. Barely audible. Phone speakers weren't MEANT for this.

"EVERYBODY pull out your phones! Play this SONG! We'll make our OWN sound system! CROWD-SOURCED ENTERTAINMENT!"

People laughed. Then actually DID IT. Pulled out phones. Found the song. Pressed play.

The tent filled with 47 phones playing the same song at slightly different times creating a WEIRD echo EFFECT that was technically MUSIC but also kind of CHAOS.

It was TERRIBLE.

It was also HILARIOUS.

People started DANCING anyway. laughing. ENJOYING the absurdity. Making it WORK.

⚓

9:47 PM - ANIMAL CONTROL ARRIVES (THE RECKONING)

Two Animal Control officers stepped into the tent with the confidence of people who'd dealt with escaped livestock before. Behind them: a police officer who looked EXHAUSTED—the expression of someone called to a "goat situation" at a failing community gala at 10 PM on a Saturday.

"We're looking for a GOAT," the first officer announced loudly, officially, SERIOUSLY. He pulled out a printed photo. "Brown and white. Approximately 80 pounds. Answers to 'Larry.' Wanted for destruction of city property—specifically the rose garden in Washington Park. Four thousand dollars in damages."

The entire venue went SILENT.

Everyone looked at Marvelous.

Marvelous looked at the back room.

A loud "MEHHHHH!" echoed from exactly that direction.

Crystal clear. Unmistakable. 100% goat. 100% LARRY.

"That was a CAR horn!" Marvelous stammered desperately. "Outside! In the parking lot! Sounds JUST like a goat! Common misconception! Very realistic horn!"

"Sir, that was a GOAT."

Another "MEHHHHHH!" Louder. More insistent. More PROUD. Definitely from the storage room. Definitely Larry asserting his PRESENCE.

Madame Pancake—WHO was here, in the back of the tent, recording everything on her phone, glowing with satisfaction—laughed loudly: "Oh this is good! This is CONTENT! Y'all paid TWO HUNDRED DOLLARS to watch this man get ARRESTED for GOAT CRIMES! GOAT CRIMES!"

Cherry grabbed Marvelous's arm urgently. "We gotta give them Larry. RIGHT NOW."

"NO!"

"They got a WARRANT! They got the LAW!"

"Larry is our MONEY maker! He's our star! He generated over a THOUSAND DOLLARS tonight! People came to SEE him!"

"And now he's EVIDENCE in a criminal CASE!"

The officers moved toward the storage room with PURPOSE. Breadcrumb tried blocking them—arms spread wide, the world's least intimidating bouncer, wearing a too-big suit and DESPERATION.

"He's a CELEBRITY! He's got forty-seven THOUSAND VIEWS! He's an ICON! He's CULTURAL!"

"He's a CRIMINAL animal who destroyed PUBLIC PROPERTY!"

"Can't he be BOTH?! Can't things be COMPLEX?!"

They pushed past easily and found Larry sitting in the middle of destroyed supplies, eating a CARDBOARD box like it was gourmet FOOD. He looked up slowly. Chewed deliberately. Made direct eye contact with the officers. SWALLOWED. Then bleated with PRIDE: "Meh."

Translation: "I regret nothing. I would do it again. I AM who I AM."

"This animal is being SEIZED pending administrative hearing and restitution determination."

"SEIZED?!" Breadcrumb cried, voice breaking. "You can't seize Larry! He's family! He's PART OF US!"

They started leading Larry out with a leash and collar. Larry RESISTED—planted hooves firmly, refused to move, bleated loudly with RAGE, kicked back legs at anyone who approached.

"free LARRY!" someone in the crowd chanted spontaneously. Others joined immediately: "FREE LARRY! FREE LARRY! FREE LARRY!"

The chant grew. LOUDER. More people joining. A MOVEMENT forming.

Marvelous saw an opportunity. Jumped onto a chair dramatically: "PEOPLE! If you wanna see Larry stay—if you wanna save our friend—then DONATE! We can pay the FINE right now! We can RESCUE him! TOGETHER!"

People started throwing money. Immediately. Enthusiastically. \$5s, \$10s, \$20s, \$50s. Coins (painful when they hit people). Someone threw a SHOE (unclear why, didn't help). Someone threw their WATCH (generous but weird).

Cherry scrambled on the ground collecting it with Tito and Big Mike, grabbing bills, dodging coins, COUNTING frantically.

"HOW much IS THE FINE?!" Cherry yelled over the chaos.

The officer sighed deeply, checking paperwork. "TWELVE hundred for the roses. Plus two hundred processing fees. Plus THREE HUNDRED boarding costs while we held him. Plus ONE HUNDRED administrative fees. EIGHTEEN HUNDRED DOLLARS total."

The crowd kept throwing money. Energy building. MOMENTUM. Cherry counted frantically, bills everywhere: \$450, \$670, \$920, \$1,100… \$1,340, \$1,480, \$1,620… \$1,790…

"WE got it! We got EIGHTEEN HUNDRED EXACTLY!"

The crowd CHEERED. screaming. celebrating. "we SAVED LARRY! WE SAVED THE GOAT!"

The officer counted the money slowly, carefully, OFFICIALLY.

"Warrant cleared. Citation paid in full. The goat can remain in your custody."

The crowd ERUPTED. screaming. CHEERING. CRYING. People hugging strangers. CELEBRATION.

But Cherry appeared beside Marvelous, face NOT celebrating, face showing math, face showing REALITY.

"Marvelous." Her voice was quiet. Serious. HEAVY.

His stomach dropped. Oh. Oh no.

"We gave away eighteen hundred dollars."

Eighteen hundred dollars we NEEDED. Eighteen hundred dollars for ISABELLA.

⚓

10:32 PM - THE FINANCIAL REALITY (WHEN MATH WINS)

By 10:35 PM, the tent was emptying. The energy had died. People were leaving. The party was OVER.

Only 38 people remained. Die-hard supporters. People too drunk to realize it was over. People who felt bad and wanted to STAY.

Cherry sat with her calculator, adding and subtracting and re-adding and praying the numbers would somehow CHANGE, would somehow be different, would somehow show HOPE.

They didn't.

FINAL REVENUE:

\- Ticket sales: \$20,000

    \- Bar sales (Tito's poison): \$1,240

    \- Merchandise (disaster shirts): \$320

    \- Raffle tickets: \$1,180

    \- Cherry's performance tips: \$847

    \- Larry photo sessions: \$1,150

    \- Auction/donations: \$4,490

TOTAL REVENUE: \$29,227

Marvelous looked at the number. "Twenty-nine thousand? That's MORE than we needed! We did IT!"

Cherry's face said otherwise. "WAS more than we needed. Before Larry's fine. Before we SAVED the goat."

\$29,227 - \$1,800 (Larry's fine) = \$27,427

"We still got twenty-seven thousand! That's GOOD!"

"It's four thousand SHORT of Isabella's requirement. And that's before we pay our expenses. Before we account for what we OWE."

EXPENSES:

\- Venue rental (FRANK tent): \$3,500

\- Bar supplies: \$680

\- Food (grocery store transformation): \$287

\- Decorations/Permits/Equipment: \$2,630

TOTAL EXPENSES: \$7,097

Cherry did the final calculation, the TERRIBLE math, the TRUTH:

Revenue: \$27,427

Expenses: -\$7,097

NET PROFIT: \$20,330

"We made twenty thousand dollars profit," she said quietly, voice empty.

"That's AMAZING! That's SUCCESS!"

"It's THREE thousand SHORT of what we needed. Three thousand short of Isabella's requirement. Three thousand short of SURVIVAL."

"But it's CLOSE!"

"Close don't PAY debt! Close don't stop liquidation! Close don't save our businesses! Close is just another word for FAILURE! Close is NOTHING!"

She stood up slowly. Exhausted. Defeated. DONE.

"We FAILED, Marvelous. We threw a whole gala. We worked for weeks. We survived disasters, sabotage, betrayals, fires, health violations. We gave EVERYTHING. And we came up THREE THOUSAND DOLLARS SHORT."

Around them, the remaining guests trickled out. 5 more gone. Then 8 more. Then 12 more. By 10:45 PM, only 15 people remained in the entire tent. The party was over. The dream was DEAD.

Breadcrumb approached, crying, voice breaking. "I'm gonna lose my JOB. I ain't got no other skills! What am I gonna DO?! How do I PAY RENT?!"

"You'll find SOMETHING—"

"You PROMISED this would work! You said we'd be SUCCESSFUL! You SAID if we tried hard enough, if we worked hard enough, if we BELIEVED hard enough—"

He stood up, still crying, mascara running (when did he start wearing mascara?), and walked toward the exit.

"I'm SORRY!" Marvelous called after him, voice cracking. "I'm so SORRY!"

Breadcrumb didn't turn around. Just kept walking. Into the darkness. Into NOTHING. Gone.

Tito and Big Mike started packing up in SILENCE. Folding chairs. Taking down lights. The quiet work of ENDINGS. Of admitting DEFEAT. Of acknowledging FAILURE.

Cherry approached slowly, eyes red from crying. "I'm SORRY. I let you think you could pull this OFF when it was ALWAYS impossible. I should've TOLD YOU. I should've made you QUIT."

"It WASN'T impossible—"

"YES it was! You ain't a businessman, Marvelous! You're a dreamer! And dreams DON'T PAY BILLS! Dreams don't make PAYMENTS! Dreams don't save BUSINESSES!"

"So I should've just GIVEN up?! Just accepted FAILURE?!"

"YES!" She was crying now, tears streaming, voice breaking. "You should've given up before dragging us ALL down with you! Before making us BELIEVE! Before giving us HOPE!"

She grabbed her purse, her calculator, her DIGNITY. "I'm done. I enabled this. I let myself believe when I knew BETTER. And that was MY MISTAKE. My FAILURE."

"Cherry, PLEASE don't leave—"

"Sometimes trying your hardest still ends in FAILURE! Sometimes the good guys LOSE! Sometimes EFFORT isn't ENOUGH!"

She got in her car. Started the engine. Rolled down the window one last time.

"I'll come by Monday. To collect my last paycheck. If there IS a last paycheck. If there's ANYTHING left."

She drove off. Tail lights disappearing into darkness. Into NOTHING.

Leaving Marvelous standing in the EMPTY parking lot. Alone. COMPLETELY alone.

⚓

10:52 PM - ISABELLA'S CALL (THE FINAL VERDICT)

His phone rang. He knew who it was before looking. KNEW what it meant.

"Isabella—"

"I assume you're calling to tell me you have the money. The full twenty-three thousand."

"We have TWENTY THOUSAND—"

"I required twenty-three."

"Give us MORE time! Just ONE more week! We're SO CLOSE!"

"No." The word landed like a HAMMER. Like death. Like FINALITY.

"Please—"

"I gave you TWO weeks. You promised results. You delivered PARTIAL results. That's not enough. That's FAILURE."

"Isabella, PLEASE! Take everything else! Take the laundromat! Take the dispensary! But let me keep the club! JUST the club!"

"With what income? Your club barely breaks even on its best months. Without the other businesses supporting it, it's worthless. It's NOTHING."

Her voice softened slightly. Almost KIND. "I respect what you tried to do. You're a hustler. You're ambitious. You've got drive. But respect doesn't pay bills. And your ambition exceeded your ABILITY. Your dreams exceeded your REALITY."

"Please—"

"Monday morning. 9 AM. My people will arrive to begin liquidation proceedings. Everything will be sold at auction. The club. The equipment. The furniture. Even your personal items on the premises. EVERYTHING."

"Isabella—"

"I'm sorry, Mr. McCall. I genuinely am. But business is business. And your business is FINISHED."

She hung up. Clean. Final. OVER.

Marvelous stood there feeling his WORLD collapse. Feeling EVERYTHING end.

"She's liquidating," he said to nobody, to NOTHING. "Everything. Monday. 9 am. It's OVER."

⚓

11:03 PM - THE BREAKING POINT (ALONE IN THE DARK)

The night was COLD. The street quiet. The city continuing like NOTHING had happened, like his world hadn't just ENDED.

His phone buzzed constantly:

\[TWITTER\]: #MarvelousGalaFail trending - 47K tweets

\[NEWS ALERT\]: "Local Gala Ends in Chaos - Goat Seized, Money Lost, Dreams Crushed"

\[INSTAGRAM\]: 127 new posts tagging \@DaMarvelous - mostly mockery

He silenced it. Walked to the edge of the block where the sidewalk ended. And just… STOOD there.

The weight of failure pressing down like CONCRETE. Like gravity had MULTIPLIED. Like the universe itself was CRUSHING him.

Everything he'd built—or THOUGHT he'd built—gone. Erased. Liquidated.

He'd never been marvelous. He'd just been DESPERATE. And desperation isn't the same as greatness. Trying hard isn't the same as SUCCEEDING.

He laughed—bitter, broken, the laugh of someone who'd just realized the JOKE was on them, had ALWAYS been on them.

Then he heard it:

TIRES SCREECHING.

⚓

11:07 PM - THE GARBAGE TRUCK (WHEN REALITY CRASHES IN)

A garbage truck. Turning the corner. Coming down the street. FAST. Too fast. WAY too fast.

The headlights were BRIGHT—blinding, overwhelming—like twin suns bearing down, like JUDGMENT approaching.

The driver wasn't paying attention. Looking DOWN. At his phone. Texting probably. not WATCHING THE ROAD. Not seeing ANYTHING.

Marvelous stood at the edge of the sidewalk. Directly in the truck's path. FROZEN.

His brain registered DANGER—alarm bells ringing, survival instincts screaming—but his body didn't MOVE. PARALYZED by exhaustion, by defeat, by the weight of EVERYTHING.

Time SLOWED. Like the universe wanted him to process every detail. Like this moment needed to be REMEMBERED:

The rust on the bumper (years of decay). The dent in the fender (previous accident). The license plate: NYC-8847 (he'd remember that forever). The logo: metro sanitation services (garbage, of course, GARBAGE). The driver's face as he looked UP—eyes WIDENING—mouth opening—REALIZING—too LATE—

Someone yelled from far away: "LOOK OUT!"

But Marvelous didn't move. His body REFUSED. FROZEN in place.

Maybe a part of him didn't WANT to move. Maybe a part of him thought: This is easier. This ends EVERYTHING. This stops the PAIN.

The truck got CLOSER—20 feet—15 feet—10 feet—

The HORN blared: "HOOOOOOONNNNNKKKKKK!"

Impossibly loud. DEAFENING. The sound of DOOM.

Marvelous closed his eyes—accepting, resigned, READY for it to END—

Then—

IMPACT.

Not a sound. Not pain. Just...

IMPACT.

Like the universe PUNCHED him. Like reality exploded. Like everything SHATTERED.

⚓

THE WHITE (TRANSITION)

Everything went WHITE.

Not dark. Not black. WHITE.

Pure, absolute, IMPOSSIBLY bright white.

He felt WEIGHTLESS—no ground beneath him—no gravity pulling—no BODY containing him—

Floating. Drifting. DISSOLVING into NOTHING.

Then—voices. Distant. Muffled. Like hearing through WATER, through walls, through DIMENSIONS:

"—got a pulse—"

"—massive head trauma—"

"—get him to trauma ONE—"

"—losing him—"

Then IMAGES flashed—rapid-fire, fragmenting, BREAKING APART:

FLASH: The club. Dark. Empty. His kingdom that never existed.

FLASH: Cherry's face. Angry. Crying. Leaving. Disappearing.

FLASH: Larry. Bleating. Majestic. Criminal. PERFECT. Impossible.

FLASH: The gala. String lights. People laughing. For ONE MOMENT it was REAL.

FLASH: The tent. FRANK. Leaning. Beautiful. Home. Never home.

All of it SWIRLING—spinning—faster—like water down a drain—FADING—DISSOLVING—DISAPPEARING—

He tried to HOLD on—tried to keep the IMAGES—tried to keep the WORLD—

But they SLIPPED through his fingers like smoke. Like DREAMS. Like they were never REAL to begin with.

Because they WEREN'T real.

None of it was REAL.

And then—

Nothing.

Pure. Complete. Absolute. NOTHING.

Silence.

Darkness.

END.

⚓

\\BEEP. BEEP. BEEP.**

A sound. Steady. Mechanical. Rhythmic. REAL.

BEEP. BEEP. BEEP.

His consciousness STIRRED—like waking from the deepest sleep—like being BORN—like EXISTING for the first time—

His eyes wouldn't OPEN. Too heavy. Glued shut. REFUSING.

BEEP. BEEP. BEEP.

Smells registered: ANTISEPTIC. bleach. MEDICINE. Hospital smells. REAL smells.

His eyes fluttered—struggling against weight, against REALITY—

Bright lights overhead. WHITE. Fluorescent. White ceiling tiles. Institutional. sterile. REAL.

This wasn't his club. This wasn't the gala. This wasn't ANYWHERE he knew.

A voice—female, gentle, CLOSE, REAL:

"Mr. Liu? Can you hear me?"

Who's Mr. Liu?

He tried to speak. His throat was DRY. raw. Like he hadn't used it in FOREVER. Like he'd been SILENT for MONTHS.

"Mr. Liu, if you can hear me, try to squeeze my hand."

He felt something in his hand—soft, warm, REAL, human. He squeezed. Weakly. But he SQUEEZED.

"Good! That's GOOD! You're awake! Mr. Liu, you're in the hospital. Mount Sinai. You were in an accident. You've been unconscious for three MONTHS."

Three months?

No.

That's IMPOSSIBLE.

He'd been at his gala TONIGHT. He'd been with his TEAM. He'd been—

But even as he THOUGHT it—doubt crept in—cold—inevitable—REAL—

Because the voice was too real. The smells were TOO real. The beeping was TOO real.

And his body felt WRONG.

Everything felt WRONG.

207

"Where's Cherry?" His voice CRACKED. Sounded wrong. Different. NOT his voice.

The nurse—name tag: JASMINE chen, RN—frowned gently, sadly.

"I'm sorry... who's Cherry?"

"Cherry Bomb. My business partner. My RIGHT hand. My FRIEND."

"Mr. Liu... you don't have a business partner."

The words hit like ICE. Like truth. Like REALITY crashing in.

"What? YES I do! And Tito! And Big Mike! And Breadcrumb! WHERE'S MY CLUB?!"

"You don't own a club."

"YES I do! Club Marvelous! On 125th Street! I just threw a GALA! I made TWENTY THOUSAND DOLLARS!"

"Mr. Liu—"

"I'M DA MARVELOUS MCCALL! I'm a businessman! I run an EMPIRE!"

She looked at him with sad, KIND eyes—the eyes of someone who'd seen this before, who'd watched people wake up from comas and learn their lives were different, were LIES, were DREAMS.

"No sir. You're not Da Marvelous McCall."

The world STOPPED.

"You're Minghao Liu. You're twenty-eight years old. You're a sanitation worker for the city. You were hit by a garbage truck while on your route three months ago."

His brain SHORT-circuited. crashed. ERROR. DOES NOT COMPUTE.

"What?"

"You've been in a coma. For three months. You just woke up."

Three months?

No.

That's IMPOSSIBLE.

He'd been at his gala TONIGHT. He'd been with his TEAM. He'd been—

"Where's Cherry?" he asked again, voice cracking, DESPERATE for confirmation. "Cherry Bomb! My business partner! She sang! She was INCREDIBLE!"

Nurse Jasmine's face was gentle, sympathetic, but FIRM. "Mr. Liu... there is no Cherry Bomb."

"YES there IS! And Tito! And Big Mike! And Breadcrumb! And LARRY! Where's LARRY?!"

"You don't have a goat."

"I have a CRIMINAL goat! He's got warrants! He's wanted by Animal Control! He destroyed the rose garden! FOUR THOUSAND DOLLARS in damages!"

She looked at him with sad, KIND eyes—the eyes of someone who'd seen this before.

"Everything you remember—your club, your team, your gala—it was a dream. Your brain created it while you were healing. It's called a 'coma dream.' Very vivid. Very detailed. But not real."

"No," he said, but his voice was weaker now. Less certain.

"You're Minghao Liu. You're twenty-eight years old. You're a sanitation worker for the city. You were hit by a garbage truck while on your route three months ago."

The words HUNG there.

Sanitation worker.

Garbage truck.

THREE MONTHS.

He looked at his hands. They were DIFFERENT. Slimmer. Lighter. No rings. No chains. No gold.

He touched his face. Different features. Sharper. Not the face he REMEMBERED.

"But..." His voice was small now, confused, LOST. "But I remember EVERYTHING. Cherry sang Whitney Houston. Larry ate a cardboard box. Pastor Stacks gave us eight hundred dollars. Frank's tent said 'happy 50TH BIRTHDAY FRANK.' Danny DeVito—we had a cardboard Danny DeVito..."

His voice trailed off.

Was that REAL?

It felt REAL.

It felt MORE real than THIS.

"I know it feels real," Nurse Jasmine said gently, squeezing his hand. "Coma dreams often do. Your brain was VERY active. You lived an entire

LIFE in there."

Minghao lay back against the pillow. Stared at the white ceiling.

And felt something CRACK inside.

But not break.

Not YET.

Because even though his hands looked DIFFERENT—

Even though his face felt WRONG—

Even though this woman was telling him it was all a DREAM—

He could still FEEL Cherry's hug after she sang.

He could still HEAR Larry's defiant bleat.

He could still SEE Pastor Stacks' face when he chose redemption.

He could still REMEMBER being DA MARVELOUS.

And if he could REMEMBER it—

If he could FEEL it—

Didn't that make it REAL somehow?

"I need to rest," he said quietly, closing his eyes.

But he wasn't resting.

He was REMEMBERING.

Every detail.

Every moment.

Every person.

Because even if they weren't REAL—

They were HIS.

And nobody—not Nurse Jasmine, not reality, not even the TRUTH—

Could take that away.

THE DREAM DOESN'T END

IT JUST... ADJUSTS

CHAPTER 13

Still Marvelous (or: When You Refuse to Accept Reality)

⚓

DAY 1 AWAKE - 8:47 AM

"Nurse Jasmine!" Minghao called out, snapping his fingers with the confidence of someone who had DEFINITELY not just been told his entire life was a coma-induced fantasy. "Nurse Jasmine, my beloved! I require your IMMEDIATE attention!"

Nurse Jasmine Chen looked up from her clipboard with the exhausted expression of someone who'd been dealing with Minghao Liu for exactly FOUR HOURS and already needed a vacation.

"Mr. Liu, what do you need?"

"First of all, it's DA Marvelous. Or 'Your Excellency' if we're being formal about professional hierarchy. Second, I need you to make THREE phone calls for me."

She sighed. Deeply. From her SOUL. "Mr. Liu—"

"Call number ONE: Contact my business partner Cherry Bomb. Tell her Da Marvelous is alive and operations should continue as normal. She'll know what that means. We had CONTINGENCIES."

"There is no Cherry Bomb."

"Call number TWO: Contact Tito and tell him to check on Larry. Make sure he's got food and water. Goat maintenance is CRITICAL."

"You don't have a goat."

"Call number THREE: Contact Pastor Stacks and let him know I forgive him. COMPLETELY. Man had a whole redemption arc. Beautiful stuff. Brought tears to my eyes."

Jasmine set down her clipboard. Pulled up a chair. Sat with the specific energy of someone preparing for a LONG conversation.

"Minghao—"

"DA Marvelous."

"—we've BEEN through this. You were in a coma. EVERYTHING

you remember was a dream. A very vivid, very detailed dream. But still a DREAM."

Minghao looked at her with the patient expression of someone dealing with a person who CLEARLY didn't understand BUSINESS.

"Nurse Jasmine. I respect you. I APPRECIATE you. You saved my life. But I'm gonna need you to understand something CRITICAL about my situation."

He leaned forward dramatically.

"Just because I woke up in a DIFFERENT body don't mean my empire stops existing. Just because you can't see Cherry Bomb don't mean she ain't REAL. Just because SCIENCE says it was a dream don't mean it WASN'T REAL in the ways that MATTER."

"That's... that's not how reality works."

"Reality is FLEXIBLE! Reality is what we make it! I made an empire! I made FRIENDS! I made TWENTY THOUSAND DOLLARS at a gala! You can't tell me that don't COUNT!"

"It doesn't count because it didn't HAPPEN."

"It happened TO me! In HERE!" He tapped his head. "And that's what COUNTS!"

Jasmine rubbed her temples. "I'm going to call the psychiatrist."

"EXCELLENT idea! I could use someone to discuss my business STRATEGY with! Someone with VISION!"

⚓

THE MIRROR CONFRONTATION (COGNITIVE DISSONANCE BEGINS)

After Jasmine left, Minghao decided he needed to see himself. Needed PROOF. Needed to confirm he was still da MARVELOUS despite what everyone kept SAYING.

He pulled out his IV (against medical advice, definitely shouldn't have done that, small alarm started beeping), stood up on shaky legs (three months in a coma, muscles WEAK), and shuffled to the bathroom.

The mirror was WAITING.

He looked.

And saw...

A Chinese guy.

Skinny. Hospital gown. Messy hair. Confused expression.

NOT Da Marvelous.

"No," he whispered. "No no no."

He touched his face. The mirror face touched back. SAME movements. SAME confused expression.

"This ain't RIGHT! This ain't—where'S MY FACE?!"

He looked CLOSER. Examining every detail.

Different nose. Different chin. Different EVERYTHING.

But the EYES...

The eyes looked TIRED.

The eyes looked LOST.

The eyes looked like someone who'd just lost EVERYTHING.

He looked at those eyes for a LONG time.

Then said to his reflection:

"You may LOOK different. But you still Da Marvelous. you still got the spirit. YOU still got the VISION. YOU still got the EMPIRE even if nobody ELSE can see it."

His reflection didn't respond.

Because reflections don't DO that.

Unless you're having a psychotic break.

Which the psychiatrist would DEFINITELY want to talk about.

"We gonna be FINE," he told the mirror. "We gonna rebuild. We gonna show 'em. We gonna—"

He tried to strike a POSE. A confident pose. A DA MARVELOUS pose.

Lost his balance. Weak legs. Grabbed the sink for support.

Nearly fell. Caught himself. Breathing hard.

"We gonna... we gonna work on that," he said weakly.

The mirror face looked EXHAUSTED.

"But we STILL marvelous," he whispered. "We STILL are."

⚓

THE PSYCHIATRIST ARRIVES (DR. PATRICIA WASHINGTON)

Dr. Patricia Washington entered the room at 10:15 AM with a kind smile, a notepad, and the professional energy of someone who'd seen EVERYTHING twice.

"Good morning, Minghao! I'm Dr. Washington. How are you feeling today?"

"MARVELOUS!" he announced, sitting up straight in bed with as much dignity as a hospital gown allows. "I'm feeling MARVELOUS! Literally! Because that's my NAME!"

She sat down, notepad ready. "I see. And how are you adjusting to being awake?"

"EXCELLENTLY! I've already made plans to resume business operations! I've got calls to make! PEOPLE to contact! An EMPIRE to rebuild!"

"Tell me about this empire."

"GLADLY!" He launched into it. enthusiastically. "I run Club Marvelous. finest establishment in the city! We also got a dispensary—had some health code issues but we was WORKING through 'em—a laundromat, and we JUST threw a gala that made TWENTY THOUSAND DOLLARS!"

Dr. Washington wrote something. "And where is this club located?"

"125th Street! Big purple building! Can't MISS it! Got my name on it in GOLD LETTERS!"

"And your business partners?"

"Cherry Bomb—INCREDIBLE woman, accountant and singer! Tito—tactical genius, makes drinks that could kill a HORSE! Big Mike—strength of TEN men! Breadcrumb—honestly kind of useless but LOYAL!"

"I see. And have any of these people visited you since you woke up?"

Minghao paused. "They... they BUSY. Running operations while I'm recovering. Can't abandon the business just because the BOSS is temporarily INDISPOSED!"

"Minghao—"

"DA Marvelous."

"—I want you to know that what you experienced is called a 'coma dream.' It's very common. Your brain created an elaborate fantasy world while your body healed. These dreams can feel MORE real than reality sometimes."

"It WASN'T a dream! I got details! I got memories! I remember Cherry singing Whitney Houston at our gala! I remember Larry eating a cardboard box while making direct eye contact! I remember Pastor Stacks giving us eight hundred dollars in CASH because he felt GUILTY! You can't DREAM that level of DETAIL!"

"Actually, you can. The brain is remarkably creative during extended unconsciousness. It can create entire worlds, complete lives, complex characters—all to help process trauma."

"So you saying my FRIENDS ain't REAL?!"

"I'm saying your friends were a creation of your subconscious mind. They represented aspects of yourself, or desires you had, or ways you wanted to feel. But they weren't ACTUAL people."

Minghao felt something CRACK. Something PAINFUL.

"But I can REMEMBER them! Cherry's face when she sang! The way she glowed! Tito's terrible bartending! Big Mike's laugh! Breadcrumb's—okay Breadcrumb was ANNOYING but I still REMEMBER HIM!"

"And those memories are REAL to you. They matter. They affected you. But the people themselves... they only existed in your mind."

He looked down at his hands. The WRONG hands. The hands that weren't DA MARVELOUS'S hands.

"So I was NOBODY?" he said quietly. "Just a regular guy who got hit by a truck and dreamed he was SOMEBODY?"

Dr. Washington leaned forward. "You're not NOBODY, Minghao. You're a person who survived massive trauma. You're a person whose mind created something beautiful to help you survive. That takes STRENGTH. That takes CREATIVITY. That's not nothing."

"But Da Marvelous WAS somebody! People respected him! People KNEW him! He had a KINGDOM!"

"And now YOU can be somebody. In REALITY. Not in a dream. You can build a real life. With real relationships. With real achievements."

"But I LIKED being Da Marvelous! I liked the confidence! The SWAGGER! The feeling that I MATTERED!"

216

"Then KEEP those things. Keep the confidence. Keep the swagger. But apply them to your real life. To Minghao Liu. To the person you ACTUALLY are."

He sat there processing. Struggling. FIGHTING against it.

Because if Cherry Bomb wasn't real…

If Larry wasn't real…

If his ENTIRE kingdom was just a FANTASY…

Then what WAS real?

"I need time," he said quietly. "I need to THINK."

"Take all the time you need," Dr. Washington said gently. "But know this: the person you were in that dream? The confident, capable, MARVELOUS person? That's not GONE. That's still in you. You just have to learn how to BE that person without the fantasy."

She left.

And Minghao sat there.

Looking at his reflection in the dark TV screen across the room.

A skinny Chinese guy in a hospital gown.

NOT Da Marvelous.

But maybe…

MAYBE…

Still containing a PIECE of him.

⚓

MOM ARRIVES (REALITY CHECK #1)

At 2:37 PM, his mother walked in.

Mrs. Liu was a small, energetic Chinese woman in her fifties wearing a sensible cardigan and carrying approximately FORTY-seven bags of food because that's what Chinese mothers DO.

"MINGHAO!" she cried, rushing over. "My baby! You AWAKE!"

She hugged him SO HARD his ribs hurt.

"Ma," he said, voice muffled by her shoulder. "Ma, I can't

BREATHE—"

"I SO worried! three months! You in COMA! Doctor say maybe you never wake up! But I KNOW! I KNOW you strong! I PRAY EVERY DAY!"

She pulled back, examining his face with the critical eye of a mother who'd changed his diapers and therefore had PERMANENT RIGHTS to judge everything.

"You SO skinny! Hospital food no GOOD! I bring REAL food! Congee! Dumplings! Char siu bao! You EAT!"

She started unpacking containers. Enough food for TWELVE people minimum.

"Ma, I can't eat all that—"

"YOU eat! You need strength! You been sleeping THREE MONTHS! Body need NUTRITION!"

Minghao watched her bustle around. So NORMAL. So familiar. So... REAL.

"Ma," he said carefully. "Do you know about my businesses?"

She stopped. Looked at him confused. "What business?"

"My CLUB! Club Marvelous! On 125th Street!"

Her confusion deepened. "Minghao... you work for city sanitation. You no have club."

"YES I do! And a dispensary! And a laundromat! I'm a BUSINESSMAN!"

She put down the dumplings. Came over. Put her hand on his forehead.

"You have FEVER? You confused?"

"I'm NOT confused! I remember! I just threw a GALA! Made twenty thousand dollars!"

"Minghao." Her voice was gentle but FIRM. "You garbage man. Good job! Steady! Benefits! But no CLUB. No BUSINESS. Just... regular job."

"NO! I'm DA MARVELOUS MCCALL! I'm—"

He stopped. Because his mother was looking at him with CONCERN. Deep concern. The kind of concern that led to doctor CALLS and MEDICATION ADJUSTMENTS.

"You hit head VERY hard," she said slowly, carefully. "Doctor say you maybe confused when you wake up. Is NORMAL. Brain need time to... to REORGANIZE."

"My brain is FINE! My brain is organized! My brain created an

218

ENTIRE EMPIRE!"

"Minghao—"

"My NAME is DA MARVELOUS!"

She looked at him. For a LONG moment. With the expression of a mother whose son was CLEARLY having a psychological episode.

Then she did what Chinese mothers do best:

She pulled out her phone and started calling doctors.

While shoving dumplings at him.

"You EAT while I call! Eating help brain! Doctor say nutrition very important for coma recovery! You EAT DUMPLING NOW!"

He ate the dumpling.

It was delicious.

REAL delicious.

Not dream delicious.

REAL.

And somehow that made it WORSE.

⚓

THE COWORKER VISITS (REALITY CHECK #2)

At 4:22 PM, a big Mexican guy in a sanitation uniform walked in carrying flowers (awkwardly, like he'd never held flowers before, like the flowers might bite him).

"YO! milo! You AWAKE!"

Minghao looked at him. Tried to place the face. FAMILIAR somehow. But...

"Who you?" he asked carefully.

The guy laughed. "Man, they said you might have memory problems! It's me! TITO! Well, everyone calls me Tito. Real name's Antonio. We work together! You been picking up trash with me for three YEARS, bro!"

Tito.

TITO.

But not HIS Tito. Not tactical vest Tito. Not bartender Tito.

This was... a DIFFERENT Tito?

"You... you work sanitation?" Minghao asked slowly.

"WE work sanitation! Together! You and me and Big Mike and Uncle Donny! Best crew at the yard! Well, ONLY crew that never complains, but still!"

"Big Mike?"

"Yeah! Big Mike Rodriguez! He wanted to come but he working double shift. He send his regards though. Says to tell you 'get your ass back to work, we tired of covering your routes.'"

This was wrong. This was all WRONG. Tito wasn't supposed to be a real PERSON. Tito was supposed to be HIS FANTASY. HIS CREATION.

"You... you KNOW me?" Minghao asked, voice small.

"Course I know you! You my BOY! We been partners for three years! You always the quiet one but you funny when you talk! Remember that time you made that joke about the broken compactor? 'Trash talks, compactor don't'? That was GOOD, man! I laughed for like TEN MINUTES!"

"I said that?"

"You say funny stuff ALL the TIME! You just don't realize it's funny! You got like... ACCIDENTAL comedy genius."

Minghao's head was SPINNING. Because if there was a REAL Tito...

And a REAL Big Mike...

Then maybe...

Maybe his brain had taken REAL people and created FANTASY VERSIONS?

"Tito," he said carefully. "Do you... do you know how to make drinks? Like BARTENDING?"

Tito laughed. "Man, I can barely make KOOL-AID! Why you asking?"

"Just... checking something."

"You SURE you okay? You seem WEIRD. Well, weirder than normal."

"I'm FINE! I'm PERFECT! I'm MARVELOUS!"

Tito looked confused. "Okay... that's definitely the HEAD injury talking. But hey, whatever helps! Doctor says you gonna make full recovery! That's GOOD NEWS, right?"

"Yeah," Minghao said quietly. "That's... that's good news."

After Tito left, Minghao lay back and stared at the ceiling.

Real Tito existed.

Real Big Mike existed.

Which meant his BRAIN had taken real people from his real LIFE and transformed them into fantasy characters.

Which meant…

Which meant NONE of it was real.

Not the way he WANTED it to be real.

"But it felt real," he whispered to the empty room. "Cherry felt real. Larry felt REAL. My CLUB felt REAL."

The ceiling didn't answer.

Because ceilings don't DO that.

Unless you're REALLY having a bad time.

"I'm still marvelous though," he said to himself. To the universe. To whoever was LISTENING.

"I'm STILL marvelous."

Even if nobody else could see it.

MINGHAO LIU: IN DENIAL BUT DETERMINED

Status: Still thinks he's Da Marvelous

Reality Acceptance: 0%

Delusion Level: MAXIMUM

Comedy Potential: INFINITE

CHAPTER 14

The Marvelous Returns (or: When You Try to Pimp Walk in Crocs)

⚓

TWO WEEKS LATER - DISCHARGED FROM HOSPITAL

Minghao Liu stood outside Mount Sinai Hospital wearing:

\- Borrowed sweatpants (his mother's, technically unisex, practically humiliating)

\- A "I ♥ LA" t-shirt (gift shop, last resort)

\- Crocs (the BETRAYAL of footwear)

\- A hospital bracelet he refused to remove (proof he SURVIVED)

NOT the outfit Da Marvelous would've worn.

But Minghao had a PLAN.

Step 1: Go home

Step 2: Find his REAL clothes (the velour suit MUST exist somewhere)

Step 3: Rebuild his empire

Step 4: Prove EVERYONE wrong

His mother pulled up in her 2003 Honda Civic (rust visible, passenger door required special technique to open, smelled like a combination of Tiger Balm and regret).

"Minghao! Get in! I make special LUNCH! Your favorite!"

He approached the car with what he INTENDED to be a confident stride. A MARVELOUS stride. A pimp walk.

What ACTUALLY happened: He shuffled awkwardly because his legs were still WEAK from three months immobile, lost his balance slightly, and nearly twisted his ankle.

The Crocs did NOT help.

"Ma," he said, getting in carefully (his ribs still hurt). "Ma, when we get home, I need to ask you about my WARDROBE."

"Your clothes in closet! All clean! I wash EVERYTHING while you in hospital!"

"No, I mean my GOOD clothes. My purple velour suit. My gold chains. My rings. My—"

She looked at him with CONCERN while pulling into traffic (aggressively, dangerously, like all Chinese mothers driving).

"Minghao, you no HAVE velour suit. You have work uniform. Some t-shirts. One nice button-up for family dinners. That ALL."

"NO! I have a whole WARDROBE! Expensive clothes! Designer stuff!"

"On garbage man SALARY?" She laughed. Not mean. Just... realistic. "You make \$42,000 a year! BEFORE taxes! You barely afford RENT!"

"I'm a BUSINESSMAN!"

"You garbage man!"

"I'M DA MARVELOUS MCCALL!"

She sighed. "We talk to doctor about this. Maybe you need MORE therapy."

HOME SWEET REALITY

Minghao's apartment was a studio in Koreatown. Sixth floor. No elevator. Rent: \$1,350/month (technically too expensive but better than living with Mom).

His mother unlocked the door and they walked in.

Minghao stopped. Looked around.

This was...

This was PATHETIC.

One room containing:

\- A twin bed (TWIN! Like a CHILD!)

\- A folding table with one chair

\- A mini-fridge

\- A hot plate

\- A shared bathroom down the hall (SHARED!)

\- One window overlooking an ALLEY

\- Total square footage: Approximately 300

"This ain't MY APARTMENT," he said, voice hollow.

"This YOUR apartment! You live here three years!"

"NO! My apartment is huge! I got a penthouse! I got marble countertops! I got a GOLD-PLATED TUB!"

"Minghao, you have TOILET down hall shared with five neighbors!"

He walked to the closet. Opened it with DREAD.

Inside:

\- 3 identical work uniforms (orange safety vests, tragic)

\- 5 t-shirts (various states of faded)

\- 2 pairs of jeans (one with hole in knee, not fashionable hole, ACCIDENT hole)

\- 1 button-up shirt (for "fancy" occasions)

\- Work boots (smell visible, metaphorically)

NO purple velour.

NO gold chains.

NO mink coat.

NOTHING that said "da MARVELOUS LIVED HERE."

He sat on the twin bed slowly. It CREAKED ominously.

"This can't be real," he whispered. "This CAN'T be my life."

His mother sat next to him, rubbing his back like when he was CHILD.

"Minghao, I know this HARD. Doctor say you have very vivid dream during coma. Feel very real. But this is real. THIS is your life. Is OKAY life! You have JOB! You have HEALTH! You have FAMILY!"

"But I had MORE! I had an empire! I had PEOPLE who depended on me! I had CHERRY BOMB!"

"Who Cherry Bomb?"

"My business partner! Beautiful woman! Incredible singer! Accountant! She—"

He stopped. Because saying it OUT loud made it sound CRAZY. Made it sound like FANTASY.

Made it sound like what it WAS.

A dream.

"She wasn't real," he said quietly, realizing. ACCEPTING. "Was she?"

His mother squeezed his hand. "No, baby. But she MEANT something. She represent something you want. Confidence maybe. Partnership. success. And you CAN have those things! In REAL LIFE! You just have to BUILD them!"

"How do I build an empire when I'm a GARBAGE man living in a 300-square-foot SHOEBOX?!"

"You start SMALL! You build slowly! Not everything happen like MOVIE! Real life take TIME!"

He lay back on the twin bed (it creaked AGAIN, louder, possibly DYING).

"But I don't WANNA start small," he said to the ceiling. "I wanna be MARVELOUS."

"Then BE marvelous! But be real marvelous! Not DREAM marvelous!"

After his mother left (with seventeen hugs and forty-three reminders to EAT the food SHE LEFT), Minghao stood in his tiny apartment and made a DECISION.

Fine.

FINE.

If this was his REAL life…

If this was his REALITY…

Then he'd MAKE it marvelous.

He'd REBUILD.

Starting NOW.

⚓

OPERATION: MARVELOUS LIFESTYLE (DAY 1)

8:15 AM - THE OUTFIT

Since he didn't have a velour suit, Minghao improvised with his button-up shirt and better jeans.

He looked in the mirror.

He looked like a Chinese guy wearing too many LAYERS.

"Confidence is INTERNAL," he told his reflection. "It's about the attitude not the CLOTHES."

His reflection looked UNCONVINCED.

8:47 AM - THE PUBLIC DEBUT

Minghao walked to the corner store with MAXIMUM SWAGGER.

Or what he HOPED was swagger.

What ACTUALLY happened:

\- He attempted the pimp walk

\- His boots were TOO heavy (work boots, designed for FUNCTION not STYLE)

\- He twisted his ankle AGAIN (same ankle, still weak from coma)

\- Hobbled the last ten feet

The store owner, Mr. Park (knew Minghao for three YEARS, never seen him act like this), stared.

"Milo... you OKAY?"

"The NAME," Minghao announced, leaning against the counter with attempted coolness, "is DA MARVELOUS."

Long pause.

"You hit your head in that accident?"

"My HEAD is fine! My mind is SHARP! My SWAGGER is UNMATCHED!"

Mr. Park looked concerned. "You need medicine? I call ambulance?"

"I don't need AMBULANCE! I need respect! I need RECOGNITION! I am DA MARVELOUS MCCALL!"

"You Minghao Liu. You buy Hot Cheetos here every Thursday."

"THAT'S before! I'm DIFFERENT now! I'm—"

He attempted to lean MORE casually against the counter.

Slipped slightly.

Knocked over a display of beef jerky.

Twenty packages hit the floor.

"That'll be forty dollars," Mr. Park said flatly.

"I don't GOT forty dollars! I got twelve dollars to my NAME!"

"Then you pick up beef jerky."

Minghao picked up the beef jerky. On his hands and knees. While Mr. Park watched with the expression of someone who'd SEEN EVERYTHING.

"The Marvelous don't stay down long," Minghao muttered while gathering packages. "The Marvelous ALWAYS rises. The Marvelous—ow, my back—the Marvelous is ETERNAL."

BACK TO WORK (REALITY CRASHES HARD)

MONDAY, 5:47 AM - SANITATION YARD

Minghao showed up to work for his first shift back. The yard was LOUD. Trucks rumbling. People shouting. Smell of diesel and GARBAGE.

Real Tito saw him and YELLED: "milo! MY BOY! You BACK!"

Real Big Mike (MUCH bigger than fantasy Big Mike, probably 320 pounds of pure muscle and breakfast tacos) came over and hugged him so hard his RIBS creaked.

"Man, we MISSED you! Place ain't the same without your weird-ass commentary!"

Uncle Donny (older Mexican guy, sixty-three, looked like he'd seen the entirety of LIFE twice and wasn't impressed either time) nodded. "Good to have you back, Milo. We was worried."

They were REAL. They were kind. They were his actual COWORKERS.

But they weren't his CREW. They weren't his TEAM.

They were just... regular people who picked up trash for a living.

Like him.

"Thanks, guys," Minghao said quietly. "Thanks for... for covering for me."

"Course, man!" Tito clapped his shoulder. "That's what CREW does! We family!"

Family.

REAL family.

Not fantasy family.

"Let's get you back on your route," Uncle Donny said. "Start you off easy. Light route. Residential area. Nothing crazy."

Minghao climbed into the truck (passenger side, not DRIVING yet, still on medical restriction). Tito drove.

The sun was rising.

The city was waking up.

And Minghao Liu, formerly known as DA MARVELOUS MCCALL, was picking up garbage.

ACTUAL garbage.

For \$42,000 a year.

Before taxes.

"You okay, man?" Tito asked, noticing his expression. "You look SAD."

"I'm fine," Minghao lied. "Just… adjusting."

"Doctor says that normal! You been ASLEEP for three months! Brain probably CONFUSED! Give it time!"

Time.

Everyone kept saying that.

Give it TIME.

But how much time did it take to stop MISSING people who never existed?

How much time did it take to stop FEELING like you'd lost an empire that was never REAL?

How much time did it take to accept that you were just… REGULAR?

The truck pulled up to the first house. Tito hopped out. Grabbed the bins. Dumped them.

The ACTUAL job.

The REAL job.

The job that DA MARVELOUS would've NEVER done.

But Minghao Liu did it every day.

For three YEARS.

And would probably do it for THIRTY more.

Unless he did something DIFFERENT.

Unless he became someone ELSE.

Unless he found a way to be MARVELOUS in REALITY.

"You coming?" Tito called. "We got fifty more stops!"

Minghao climbed out of the truck. Grabbed a bin. Lifted it.

HEAVY. smelly. UNDIGNIFIED.

But REAL.

"Yeah," he called back. "I'm coming."

MINGHAO LIU: REALITY IS WINNING

Status: Trying to be Marvelous, mostly failing

Reality Acceptance: 15% (progress!)

Swagger Level: 2/10 (DOWN from hospital high of 9/10)

Dignity: Buried under beef jerky display

But Still Fighting: YES

CHAPTER 15

The Roasting (or: When Your Coworkers Tell You The Truth)

⚓

ONE WEEK BACK AT WORK - LUNCH BREAK

The break room at the sanitation yard was NOT glamorous. Concrete floor. Fluorescent lights (two flickering, one completely dead). Vending machine that ate dollars. Microwave that smelled like every lunch ever cooked in it SIMULTANEOUSLY. Four plastic tables. Motivational poster that said "TEAMWORK!" with a photo of penguins (unclear why penguins, nobody asked).

Minghao sat at a table with his lunch (leftovers his mother packed, enough food for FOUR people because that's what Chinese mothers DO). Around him: Real Tito, Real Big Mike, Uncle Donny, and Carlos (new guy, twenty-two, always on his phone).

They were ALL staring at him.

"What?" Minghao asked, suddenly self-conscious.

"Milo," Tito said slowly, grinning. "Mike and I been WAITING for you to get your memory back so we could tell you the TRUTH about your accident."

"What truth?"

"The REAL truth. The whole truth. The truth that's gonna make you WISH you stayed in that coma."

Big Mike cracked his knuckles. "This gonna be GOOD."

Uncle Donny sighed. "Y'all don't gotta be so mean about it—"

"WE absolutely do!" Tito interrupted. "This man been walking around talking about being 'DA MARVELOUS' and running empires! He needs a REALITY CHECK! He needs to know what ACTUALLY happened!"

Minghao set down his chopsticks carefully. "Okay. Tell me. How did I get hit by the truck?"

Tito leaned forward, eyes GLEAMING with the joy of someone about to DESTROY someone else's dignity.

230

"So it's June 14th. Three months ago. We're on our regular route in Koreatown. Nice day. Sun shining. Birds chirping. Everything NORMAL. We stop at this apartment building—six-story walkup, no elevator, full bins because nobody in that building understands RECYCLING—"

"Get to the POINT," Minghao interrupted.

"I'M SETTING the scene! Anyway, we pull up. I'm driving. You hop out to get the bins. And then—" Tito paused for dramatic effect. "—and THEN, my boy, you see something that CHANGES YOUR LIFE."

"What?"

"A BIRD."

Minghao blinked. "A… bird?"

"Not just ANY bird!" Big Mike jumped in, barely containing laughter. "A PIGEON! A regular-ass, city pigeon! Nothing special! Probably had diseases! Definitely had attitude!"

"This pigeon," Tito continued, fighting back laughter, "was eating a CHURRO. A whole churro. Just pecking away. And you—you, Milo—you got MESMERIZED. Like you never seen a pigeon before in your LIFE."

"I've seen pigeons—"

"YOU stopped WORKING!" Big Mike was laughing now. "Dropped the bin! Just STOOD there watching this bird! And you said—man, you SAID—'That bird living better than me!'"

The whole table ERUPTED in laughter. Even Uncle Donny was chuckling.

"That AIN'T what happened!" Minghao protested, face heating up.

"IT is exactly what HAPPENED!" Tito wiped tears from his eyes. "Then—and this is the BEST part—you pull out your phone to take a PICTURE of this pigeon! Like it's a CELEBRITY! Like it's gonna make you INSTAGRAM FAMOUS!"

"And THAT'S when it happened," Big Mike said, still laughing. "You backing up to get a better angle. Taking multiple photos. Completely unaware of your SURROUNDINGS—"

"The truck was BACKING up behind you," Tito said, suddenly serious. "Different crew. Different route. Driver wasn't paying attention—looking at HIS phone probably—and you weren't paying attention because you were PHOTOGRAPHING A PIGEON—"

"And WHAM!" Big Mike clapped his hands together. "Truck backs right into you! Knocks you forward! You hit your head on the CURB! Blood everywhere! Pigeon flew away with the churro!"

"The pigeon GOT away?!" Minghao asked, somehow that being the MOST upsetting part.

"The pigeon lived!" Tito confirmed. "YOU almost died! But the pigeon? That pigeon probably still out there, eating churros, living its best LIFE, completely unaware it almost got you KILLED!"

"So let me get this straight," Minghao said slowly, processing. "I got hit by a garbage truck... while photographing... a pigeon... eating a churro."

"YES!" everyone yelled in unison.

"That's the LEAST marvelous thing I ever heard!"

"THAT'S what we been TRYING TO TELL YOU!" Tito was crying with laughter now. "You ain't no kingpin! You ain't no businessman! You a regular-ass dude who almost DIED because of BIRD-WATCHING!"

Carlos, who'd been quiet this whole time, looked up from his phone. "Yo, did anybody get a picture of the pigeon though? Because that would be VIRAL now. 'Pigeon That Almost Killed A Man.' That's CONTENT."

"THAT'S not THE POINT!" Minghao yelled.

"Actually, I think that IS the point," Uncle Donny said quietly, wisely. "You were so busy looking at something else—something you thought was more INTERESTING than your own life—that you almost died. Maybe that's what the dream was about too. Maybe your brain was trying to make your life feel MORE EXCITING than it actually was."

The table went quiet.

That was... that was DEEP.

That was PSYCHOLOGICAL.

That was PROBABLY TRUE.

"But I WAS exciting in the dream," Minghao said quietly. "I was somebody. People knew my name. People RESPECTED me."

"We respect you!" Tito said, suddenly earnest. "You our BOY! You funny! You work hard! You always help when someone needs it! That's RESPECT!"

"But I wasn't MARVELOUS."

"Milo," Big Mike said seriously. "Let me tell you something. You know what's ACTUALLY marvelous? Surviving a three-month coma. Coming back to work even though you probably still hurting. Facing the truth about how you got hurt—which is embarrassing as hell—and not running away from it. THAT'S marvelous."

"Getting hit by a truck because of a pigeon is the OPPOSITE of marvelous!"

"But surviving it? Coming back? That's STRONGER than any made-up empire."

Minghao sat with that. Processing. Struggling with it.

"Y'all got the picture?" he asked finally. "Of the pigeon?"

"Oh, we GOT IT!" Tito pulled out his phone. "Paramedics took it off your phone before they took you to the hospital! They sent it to me in case you died and your family wanted to know what your last photo was!"

He showed Minghao the screen.

There it was.

A blurry photo of a pigeon.

Mid-churro-bite.

Looking directly at the camera.

Looking MAJESTIC, honestly.

Looking MORE marvelous than Minghao currently felt.

"That pigeon is my NEMESIS," Minghao declared. "That pigeon ruined MY LIFE."

"That pigeon didn't ruin NOTHING!" Uncle Donny said. "That pigeon just happened to BE THERE when you weren't paying attention to REALITY."

Another deep statement.

Uncle Donny was FULL of them apparently.

"Can I have the picture?" Minghao asked quietly.

"Why?"

"I don't know. Evidence. Proof. Reminder that I almost died because I thought a BIRD was more interesting than my actual LIFE."

Tito sent him the picture.

Minghao stared at it for a long time.

The pigeon stared back. Judging. KNOWING.

"I'm gonna print this," Minghao said. "Frame it. Put it on my wall. 'THE pigeon that CHANGED MY LIFE.'"

"That's either VERY healthy or VERY CONCERNING," Carlos said, still scrolling on his phone. "I can't tell which."

"BOTH!" Minghao declared. "It's BOTH!"

⚓

THE VIRAL VIDEO (HUMILIATION CONTINUES)

"Oh, and there's one more thing," Tito said, trying not to laugh again. "The accident got RECORDED. Building security camera. Somebody posted it online. It went VIRAL."

Minghao's stomach dropped. "How viral?"

"Two point three MILLION views."

"TWO point THREE MILLION—"

"Yeah. It's called 'Man Gets Hit By Truck While Photographing Pigeon.' The comments are BRUTAL. But also HILARIOUS. Wanna see?"

"NO!"

"I'm showing you anyway." Tito pulled it up on his phone.

The video was exactly as described:

\- Minghao backing up

\- Phone out

\- Completely oblivious

\- Truck backing up

\- IMPACT

\- Minghao going down

\- Pigeon flying away with churro

\- Perfect comedic timing

The comments:

\@BirdWatcher2000: "Respect to the pigeon for finishing that churro"

\@ComedyGold: "This is the funniest thing I've seen all year I'm crying"

\@NaturePhotog: "As a nature photographer I understand his dedication"

\@EMTLife: "I responded to this call. The pigeon was unharmed. The human… not so much."

\@PigeonArmy: "PIGEON GANG RISE UP! WE RUN THESE STREETS!"

"Two point three MILLION people watched me almost die!" Minghao said, voice rising in pitch. "Two point three MILLION people LAUGHED at my PAIN!"

"It's not pain if you survived!" Carlos offered helpfully. "It's COMEDY!"

"MY life IS NOT COMEDY!"

"I mean…" Big Mike gestured vaguely. "It KIND of is though? You almost died because of a bird. You dreamed you were a KINGPIN. You woke up trying to pimp-walk in CROCS. That's OBJECTIVELY funny."

"I HATE all OF YOU!"

"No you don't," Tito said, grinning. "You LOVE us. We're the only people who know the full STORY and we still showed up to the hospital EVERY WEEK while you were in that coma! We're FAMILY!"

"Terrible family! Mean family! ROASTING family!"

"The BEST kind of family!" Big Mike declared. "The kind that tells you the truth even when the truth is that you got BODIED by a garbage truck because you were OBSESSED with a pigeon!"

Minghao put his head in his hands.

"I can NEVER be Marvelous now. Not after this. Not after everyone KNOWS."

"Milo," Uncle Donny said gently, putting a weathered hand on his shoulder. "Being marvelous ain't about what OTHER people think. It's about what you think. It's about how you move forward. You can let this video define you—let it make you a JOKE—or you can OWN it. Make it part of your STORY. The story of how you survived. How you came BACK."

"How do I own 'I almost died because of a PIGEON'?!"

"You laugh at it. You accept it. You move FORWARD from it. And eventually—eventually you become someone bigger than that one moment. Someone who that moment was just the BEGINNING of their story, not the END."

The table went quiet.

Uncle Donny was SPITTING WISDOM today.

"Also," Tito added, "there's merchandise. People made SHIRTS. 'Team Pigeon' and 'Team Milo.' The pigeon is winning. But it's CLOSE."

"THERE'S MERCHANDISE?!"

"Capitalism waits for NO TRAGEDY!"

Minghao stared at the ceiling. At the flickering fluorescent lights. At his LIFE.

"Fine," he said finally. "FINE. I got hit by a truck because of a pigeon. I dreamed I was a kingpin. I woke up in a 300-square-foot studio apartment wearing crocs. This is my REALITY. This is my TRUTH."

"That's the spirit!" Big Mike clapped him on the back. Hard. Almost knocked him forward into his rice.

"But I'm STILL gonna be marvelous," Minghao added. "Somehow. eventually. Even if it takes years. Even if I gotta BUILD it from NOTHING. I'm gonna be MORE than the pigeon guy."

"That's all we asking!" Tito said. "Just be REALISTIC about it! Be marvelous in reality! Not in your DREAMS!"

"Also," Carlos added, still on his phone, "the pigeon has an Instagram now. Seventeen thousand followers. Someone claimed they found it and it's become a BRAND. There's a book DEAL in the works apparently."

"THE pigeon HAS A BOOK DEAL?!"

"Life ain't fair, Milo," Uncle Donny said wisely. "But it's still life. And you're STILL here. And that's what MATTERS."

Minghao looked around the break room. At these men. His coworkers. His real crew. Not fantasy characters. Not dream people. REAL humans who showed up, who visited him in the hospital, who roasted him MERCILESSLY but also had his back.

Maybe that was worth MORE than a dream empire.

Maybe.

EVENTUALLY.

After he processed the pigeon thing.

"Can somebody PLEASE explain to me why the pigeon needed a whole churro?!" he asked desperately. "Why not just CRUMBS?! Why the WHOLE THING?!"

"Ambition," Uncle Donny said simply. "That pigeon had DREAMS. That pigeon was MARVELOUS."

Everyone laughed.

Including, eventually, Minghao.

Because what else could he do?

The pigeon won.

The pigeon had ALWAYS won.

But Minghao was still HERE.

And that had to count for SOMETHING.

MINGHAO LIU: THOROUGHLY ROASTED BUT STILL STANDING

Status: Knows the truth now (it's WORSE than he imagined)

Viral Fame: 2.3 million views (for all the WRONG reasons)

Nemesis: A pigeon (majestic, churro-eating, VICTORIOUS)

Reality Acceptance: 35% (progress! painful progress!)

Determination: Still present (barely)

CHAPTER 16

More Failed Attempts (or: When Confidence Meets Reality)

⚓

TWO WEEKS LATER - THE WARDROBE EXPERIMENT

Minghao decided that if he couldn't AFFORD a velour suit, he'd CREATE one.

He went to the thrift store on Vermont Avenue with \$23 to his name (payday was in THREE days, rent was due in FOUR, math was HOSTILE).

The thrift store smelled like mothballs and broken dreams. Racks of clothes organized by COLOR not size (who does that? MONSTERS, that's who). Fluorescent lights that made EVERYONE look dead. A cat wandering around like it OWNED the place (it probably did, spiritually).

Minghao hunted through the racks with DETERMINATION. He would find something marvelous. He WOULD rebuild his style. He WOULD—

"Can I help you?" A woman in her sixties, name tag: BRENDA, expression: seen EVERYTHING TWICE.

"I'm looking for something with PRESENCE," Minghao explained. "Something that says 'I'm important.' Something with SWAGGER."

"Honey, this is a thrift store. We got swagger from 1987. That what you want?"

"PERFECT! Vintage swagger is still SWAGGER!"

She led him to a rack in the back. "This here's the 'questionable fashion choices' section. People donate this stuff thinking SOMEONE will want it. Usually nobody does. But you look DETERMINED."

She left him there. Alone. With the QUESTIONABLE CHOICES.

Minghao found:

Option 1: A purple suit. NOT velour. Some kind of polyester that felt like it would MELT in direct sunlight. Three sizes too big. Pants had a MYSTERIOUS STAIN. Price: \$8.

Option 2: A leather jacket. From the 90s. With TASSELS. So many tassels. AGGRESSIVE tassels. The kind of jacket that said "I make bad decisions but CONFIDENTLY." Price: \$12.

Option 3: A Hawaiian shirt covered in pineapples. Unclear how this qualified as "swagger" but it was BOLD. VERY bold. AGGRESSIVELY bold. Price: \$4.

He bought ALL THREE. Total: \$24.

He was one dollar OVER budget.

"You got twenty-three dollars," Brenda said at the register.

"I got twenty-three AND some change!" He frantically searched his pockets. Found: 67 cents in NICKELS.

"That's not enough."

"Please. PLEASE. I need this wardrobe. I need to rebuild my CONFIDENCE. I need to be SOMEBODY."

Brenda looked at him. Really LOOKED. At his desperate face. His coma-recovery pallor. His NEED.

"Fine. Take it. But honey—" she leaned forward. "—no amount of clothes gonna make you somebody if you don't BELIEVE you somebody. Confidence come from INSIDE."

"Inside don't have TASSELS!"

"Exactly my POINT."

⚓

THE OUTFIT DEBUT (PUBLIC HUMILIATION #4)

Minghao wore the purple suit (polyester CONFIRMED, sweat immediately) to the grocery store. Because if you can't debut your new look somewhere IMPORTANT, grocery shopping was the NEXT BEST THING.

He walked in with CONFIDENCE. Head up. Shoulders back. Purple suit gleaming under fluorescent lights (possibly reflecting ALL the light, possibly GLOWING, hard to tell).

People STARED.

He assumed this was RESPECT.

It was NOT respect.

An old woman approached: "Excuse me, young man. Are you okay?"

"I'm EXCELLENT! MARVELOUS even!"

"You look like a GRAPE."

"I look like SUCCESS!"

"You look like a grape that's having an EMERGENCY."

She moved away quickly. Possibly to call security.

A teenager took a photo. ANOTHER teenager took a video. Within minutes, he was being RECORDED by at least SIX people.

"IS this A TREND?!" someone yelled.

"ARE you FAMOUS?!" someone else asked.

"YES!" Minghao answered confidently. "I'M DA MARVELOUS! I'M—"

"You're the PIGEON guy!" A kid recognized him from the viral video. "You're the dude who got HIT while taking pictures of a BIRD!"

The crowd REALIZED. connected. REMEMBERED.

"OH shit, IT IS HIM!"

"PIGEON GUY!"

"MISTER PIGEON!"

"Can you sign my phone?!" someone asked.

"NO!" Minghao yelled. "I'm not pigeon guy! I'm da MARVELOUS! I'm a BUSINESSMAN! I'm—I'm buying GROCERIES with DIGNITY!"

He grabbed a cart. Pushed it forward with CONFIDENCE.

The wheel was BROKEN. Cart pulled HARD to the left.

He fought it. Overcompensated. Cart CRASHED into a pyramid of canned beans.

CATASTROPHIC bean avalanche.

Cans EVERYWHERE. Rolling. Bouncing. MULTIPLYING somehow.

Store manager appeared: "SIR! You need to—are you wearing A PURPLE SUIT TO BUY MILK?!"

"It's called FASHION!"

"It's called DISTURBING the PEACE!"

Minghao left. Quickly. No groceries. Just SHAME.

And possibly another viral video in the making.

⚓

THE DATING APP EXPERIMENT (TECHNOLOGICAL HUMILIATION)

Back in his apartment (still depressing, twin bed still creaking, toilet still down the hall), Minghao decided to try ONLINE DATING.

If Da Marvelous could attract Cherry Bomb, then regular Minghao could attract... SOMEBODY.

He downloaded three apps: Tinder, Bumble, Hinge.

Created his profile:

Name: "Da Marvelous" (Minghao in parentheses)

Age: 28

Occupation: "Entrepreneur/Sanitation Professional"

Bio: "Confidence, swagger, and authenticity. Recently survived a 3-month coma. Have seen some things. Looking for someone who appreciates ambition and doesn't mind that I almost died because of a pigeon. Yes, that's a real thing. Yes, there's video. No, I don't want to talk about it unless you're REALLY interested, then I'll tell you EVERYTHING."

Photos:

\- Purple suit pic (took that morning, looked RIDICULOUS but COMMITTED)

\- Work uniform pic (honest, at least)

\- Hospital pic his mom took when he woke up (looked TERRIBLE but showed he was a SURVIVOR)

\- The pigeon photo (leaning into it, OWNING it)

He hit SUBMIT.

Waited.

Waited MORE.

First match came in EIGHTEEN MINUTES later!

Her name was JENNIFER. 32. Teacher. Pretty. Liked hiking.

She messaged first: "Did you really almost die because of a pigeon?"

"Yes."

"That's the funniest thing I've ever heard."

"It's TRAGIC!"

"It's comedy GOLD! Tell me EVERYTHING!"

They talked for TWO hours. She was nice. She was FUNNY. She thought his story was HILARIOUS rather than HUMILIATING.

"Want to meet for coffee tomorrow?" she asked.

"YES! Absolutely! I'll wear my purple suit!"

"Please don't."

"But it's my SIGNATURE—"

"I will NOT be seen in public with a man wearing a purple polyester suit. That's my one RULE."

"...Fine. Regular clothes."

"Thank you."

They set up a date. 2 PM. Coffee shop in Silver Lake. ACTUAL progress!

Minghao felt HOPE.

REAL hope.

Not fantasy hope.

ACTUAL, date-with-a-real-person hope!

⚓

THE COFFEE DATE (DISASTER IN REAL TIME)

Minghao arrived EARLY. 1:47 pm. Wanted to secure the BEST table. Wanted to look CASUAL, like he was already there, not desperate, not WAITING.

He wore:

\- His ONE button-up (freshly washed)

\- Better jeans (hole-less ones)

\- Sneakers (only pair that didn't smell AGGRESSIVE)

\\- Hair combed (first time in WEEKS)

He ordered a coffee. Large. Needed ENERGY. Needed ALERTNESS.

Drank it FAST because NERVOUS.

Mistake.

Immediate caffeine spike. Heart RACING. Hands shaking. Thoughts ACCELERATING.

Jennifer arrived at 2:03. Looked like her photos. Sundress. Smile. Normal human woman. REAL.

"Minghao?" she said, approaching.

"DA MARVELOUS!" he announced, standing up fast.

TOO fast.

Head rush. Vision SPOTS. Caffeine overload.

Wobbled. Grabbed table for support.

Knocked over the water glass he'd gotten.

Water EVERYWHERE. Spreading across the table. Dripping onto the floor. Creating a SCENE.

"I'm FINE!" he said quickly. "This is normal! This happens SOMETIMES!"

"…Okay?" She helped clean up with napkins.

They sat. Awkwardly. Dampness EVERYWHERE.

"So!" he said, trying to recover. "You're a TEACHER! That's MARVELOUS! I mean— that's great! Teaching is IMPORTANT!"

"Thanks. What kind of entrepreneur work do you do?"

"I'm… I'm PLANNING ventures. multiple ventures. I'm in the development phase. The STRATEGIC phase. The phase where you don't actually have BUSINESSES yet but you're THINKING about them EXTENSIVELY."

"So… you don't have a business?"

"I have CONCEPTS! I have vision! I have—" He leaned forward intensely. too intensely. "—I had a whole empire in my MIND during the coma. A club! A dispensary! Multiple properties! It felt SO REAL! And I'm trying to figure out how to make that REAL in the ACTUAL world!"

She blinked. Processing. "You're trying to… recreate your coma dreams?"

"YES! Exactly! exactly! Because those dreams showed me who I COULD be! Who I SHOULD be! DA MARVELOUS! Not regular Minghao! Not pigeon-watching Minghao! MARVELOUS Minghao!"

"That's..." She searched for words. "That's a LOT."

"I KNOW it's a lot! But I got confidence! I got DETERMINATION! I got—"

His phone RANG. Loud. Obnoxious ringtone he forgot to change.

It was his MOM. He declined.

It rang AGAIN. Still Mom.

"Sorry, I should—" He answered. "Ma, I'm on a DATE—"

His mother's voice, LOUD, in rapid Cantonese, audible to Jennifer: "minghao! You forget rent! Landlord call me! He say you THREE DAYS LATE! You have MONEY?!"

"Ma, I'm BUSY—"

"You NOT busy! You need PAY RENT! You want to be HOMELESS?!"

"I'll call you BACK—"

"NO call back! You PAY NOW! I bring you money! Where you ARE?!"

"MA, NO—"

She hung up.

Jennifer was staring. "Was that... your mom?"

"Yes. She's VERY involved. Very supportive. Sometimes TOO supportive—"

"Did she say you're behind on rent?"

"three days! Only THREE DAYS! That's like... NOTHING in the grand scheme of TIME and EXISTENCE!"

Jennifer stood up. "Minghao—"

"DA Marvelous—"

"—this has been... interesting. But I think you need to maybe work some things out FIRST. Like paying your rent. And maybe accepting that you're not actually a kingpin. And maybe DEFINITELY see a therapist about the coma dreams."

"I AM seeing a therapist! She says I need to 'process the trauma' and 'accept reality'! But what if reality is BORING?!"

"Then you make it INTERESTING! But you don't do that by pretending you're someone you're NOT!"

She left.

Quickly.

Possibly RUNNING.

Minghao sat alone at the damp table.

The barista approached. "Sir, you need to order something else or leave. We need the table."

"Can I just sit here and SUFFER?"

"No."

"Fine."

He left.

Outside, his mother was WAITING. Pulled up in the Honda Civic. Window down.

"GET in! We go PAY RENT!"

He got in. Defeated. Humiliated. DEFLATED.

"Ma, I HAD A DATE!"

"You HAD rent due! Rent more important than DATE! You cannot DATE if you HOMELESS!"

"That's… that's actually TRUE."

"OF course it true! I your MOTHER! I ALWAYS right!"

She drove (aggressively, dangerously, like ALL chinese MOTHERS) toward his apartment.

"Minghao," she said more gently. "You need STOP trying to be this 'Marvelous' person. You need be YOURSELF. Real you. Not dream you."

"But real me got hit by a truck because of a PIGEON! Real me is boring! Real me lives in a TINY apartment and can't pay rent on TIME!"

"Real you SURVIVED!" she said firmly. "Real you alive! Real you has people who love HIM! That not BORING! That IMPORTANT!"

He looked out the window. At the city passing. At REALITY.

"But I wanted to be MORE, Ma."

"Then BE more! But be real more! Not FAKE more! Build REAL life!

Not DREAM life!"

They pulled up to his building.

She handed him an envelope. "Rent money. \$1,350. I take from savings. You PAY me BACK."

"Ma, I can't—"

"YES you can! You pay ME BACK! Twenty dollar a week! For long time! But you NOT BE HOMELESS! You NOT sleep on STREET!"

He took the envelope. Felt the weight of it. The REALITY of it.

"Thank you, Ma."

"You WELCOME. Now go pay LANDLORD before he change LOCKS!"

He got out. Climbed the six flights (no elevator, NEVER elevator, legs BURNING by floor three).

Knocked on landlord's door.

Mr. Chen answered. Sixtieth floor. Suspicious eyes. WAITING.

"Rent," Minghao said, handing over the envelope. "Plus late fee. Plus apology."

Mr. Chen counted it. Slowly. Deliberately. JUDGMENTALLY.

"Three days late."

"I KNOW. I'm sorry. It won't happen AGAIN."

"See that it doesn't. Or you MOVE OUT."

Door closed. FIRMLY.

Minghao went to his apartment. His TINY apartment. His REALITY.

Sat on the twin bed. It creaked. LOUDLY. Possibly DYING.

Looked around at his LIFE.

This was it.

This was REAL.

No velour suits. No gold chains. No empire. No Cherry Bomb. No Larry.

Just Minghao Liu.

Garbage man.

Pigeon guy.

Regular person.

"This sucks," he said to the empty room.

The room didn't disagree.

⚓

MINGHAO LIU: FAILING FORWARD

Status: Every attempt at being Marvelous fails spectacularly

Success Rate: 0% (consistent at least)

Reality Acceptance: 45% (PAINFUL progress)

Next Step: Maybe actually LISTEN to the therapist

Dignity: Somewhere in that puddle at the coffee shop

⚓

CHAPTER 17

Therapy Breakthrough (or: When You Finally Start Listening)

⚓

THREE DAYS LATER - DR. WASHINGTON'S OFFICE

Dr. Patricia Washington's office was AGGRESSIVELY calming. Like someone had gone to IKEA and said "give me EVERYTHING from the 'Peaceful Professional' section."

Soft blue walls. Plants (MULTIPLE plants, all thriving, showing off). Comfortable chairs. A white noise machine playing gentle ocean sounds (unnecessary but COMMITTED). Inspirational poster: "The Only Way Out Is Through" with a photo of a tunnel (very on-the-nose, kind of appreciated).

Minghao sat in the comfortable chair (TOO comfortable, made him want to sleep, not CONFRONT TRAUMA).

Dr. Washington sat across from him, notepad ready, expression: KIND but NO NONSENSE.

"How have you been, Minghao?"

"terrible!" he burst out immediately. No preamble. No small talk. Straight to pain. "Everything is TERRIBLE! I tried wearing a purple suit to the grocery store and people thought I was having an emergency! I went on one date and my mom called about RENT in the middle of it! I work picking up GARBAGE at five in the MORNING! I live in a 300-square-foot apartment with a TWIN BED that JUDGES me! And everyone keeps telling me to 'accept reality' but reality is GARBAGE! Literally! I pick up GARBAGE!"

Dr. Washington wrote something. Probably "patient in CRISIS" or "needs more THERAPY" or "YIKES."

"Tell me more about what's bothering you the most," she said calmly.

"EVERYTHING! But mostly... mostly I miss the DREAM." His voice got quieter. More vulnerable. "I miss being Da Marvelous. I miss Cherry Bomb. I miss my empire. I miss mattering. I miss people KNOWING MY NAME. I miss feeling like I was SOMEBODY."

"And you don't feel like somebody now?"

"I'm MINGHAO liu! I got hit by a truck because I was photographing A pigeon! Two million people watched me almost DIE and LAUGHED! My only claim to fame is being an INTERNET JOKE! That's not SOMEBODY! That's NOBODY!"

"Do you really believe that?"

"YES! The dream version of me had confidence! Had SWAGGER! Had PEOPLE who depended on him! Real me has NOTHING!"

Dr. Washington set down her notepad. Leaned forward. Serious now.

"Minghao, I want you to really THINK about something. Who was Cherry Bomb?"

"My business partner! My right hand! She was an ACCOUNTANT who could sing! She was INCREDIBLE!"

"And where do you think your brain got that character from?"

He paused. "...What do you mean?"

"Your brain doesn't create things from NOTHING. It takes experiences, desires, things you've seen—and recombines them. Cherry Bomb wasn't random. She represented something. Something you WANTED or something you SAW in your real life. Where do you think she came from?"

Minghao thought. Really THOUGHT.

Cherry was practical. Calculating. Always doing the MATH. But also... hidden talent. Hidden PASSION. Buried under responsibility.

"Me," he said quietly, realizing. "She was ME. The part of me that's practical but wants more. The part that does the responsible thing but DREAMS of being BIGGER."

"Exactly. And what about Larry the goat?"

"Criminal goat. Warrants. Rose garden destruction."

"What did Larry REPRESENT?"

"Chaos? Rebellion? The part of life you CAN'T CONTROL?"

"Or," Dr. Washington suggested gently, "the part of you that wants to break FREE. That wants to do what it wants regardless of consequences. That refuses to be TAMED. Your rebellious spirit."

Minghao sat with that. Processing.

"And Pastor Stacks?" she continued. "The man who betrayed you but then found redemption?"

"Oh my GOD," Minghao said, seeing it. "My dad. That's my dad. The man who let me down but I still... I still want to FORGIVE him. I still want him to COME BACK."

"And Da Marvelous himself? Who was HE?"

"He was... he was who I WISHED I could be. Confident. Powerful. certain. Someone people NOTICED. Someone who MATTERED."

"And do you think that person is GONE? Just because you woke up?"

"...What?"

Dr. Washington smiled. "Minghao, that person wasn't just a DREAM. That was you. That was your potential. Your desires. Your CAPABILITIES. All the things you COULD be if you believed in yourself. Da Marvelous wasn't SEPARATE from you. He was the BEST VERSION of you."

"But I'm NOT like him! I'm quiet! I'm awkward! I almost died because of a BIRD!"

"You're quiet because you've been TAUGHT to be quiet. You're awkward because you're anxious. And you almost died because you were distracted—looking for something MORE INTERESTING than your actual LIFE. Just like you said your coworker said. You were looking AWAY from yourself."

She leaned back, giving him space to PROCESS.

"The dream wasn't about ESCAPING yourself, Minghao. It was about becoming yourself. Your brain showed you who you COULD BE. Now you have to figure out how to BE that person in REALITY. Not by wearing purple suits or calling yourself a kingpin. But by finding REAL confidence. REAL purpose. REAL connections."

"But HOW?!" His voice cracked. "How do I do that when I'm just... REGULAR?!"

"You start SMALL. You build slowly. You take the lessons from the dream—the confidence, the determination, the refusal to give up—and you apply them to real life. You don't need a velour suit to be confident. You don't need an empire to matter. You need to believe that YOU, as you are RIGHT NOW, have VALUE."

"But I DON'T have value! I'm a garbage MAN!"

"You're a SANITATION worker who keeps the city clean. Who does essential work that nobody else wants to do. Who shows up at 5 am every day. Who survived a TRAUMATIC INJURY. Who has coworkers who love you enough to visit you EVERY WEEK for three months. Who has a mother who pays your rent because she believes in you. That's not NOTHING, Minghao. That's EVERYTHING."

He felt something CRACK inside. Something big. Something that had been holding for WEEKS.

His eyes got WET. Tears coming. INEVITABLE.

"But I wanted to be MORE than that," he whispered.

"Then BE more. But you don't have to pretend to be someone else. You don't have to CREATE a fantasy. You can be Minghao Liu AND be marvelous. Those things aren't OPPOSITES."

The tears came. FULL force. Ugly crying. The kind that's been building for WEEKS. For MONTHS maybe. For YEARS possibly.

Crying for the empire he lost.

Crying for the people who never existed.

Crying for Cherry's song and Larry's defiance and Pastor Stacks' redemption.

Crying for the man he THOUGHT he was.

And crying for the man he ACTUALLY was—who'd been INVISIBLE to himself for so long.

Dr. Washington handed him the tissue box. Waited. Patient. KIND.

"I miss them," Minghao said through tears. "I miss Cherry and Larry and everyone. Even though they weren't real. They felt REAL. They felt like FAMILY."

"They WERE family. They were parts of yourself that you needed to see. To UNDERSTAND. And you can keep them. In your memories. In your heart. They don't have to DISAPPEAR just because you accept reality. Dorothy didn't forget Oz. She took the LESSONS with her. The courage. The heart. The KNOWLEDGE. You can do the same."

He cried harder. Because that was EXACTLY what he needed to hear. EXACTLY.

"I'm scared," he admitted. "I'm scared that if I accept being REGULAR Minghao, I'll lose the magic. I'll lose the POSSIBILITY. I'll just be... BORING forever."

"Being yourself isn't BORING, Minghao. Being yourself is the only way to find real magic. Real connection. Real purpose. The fantasy was safe. It couldn't hurt you. It couldn't reject you. But it also couldn't grow. It was FIXED. Reality is SCARY because it's UNCERTAIN. But it's also where REAL CHANGE happens. Where REAL RELATIONSHIPS happen. Where REAL MARVELOUS happens."

She let him cry. Let him PROCESS. Let him grieve for what he lost and ACCEPT what he gained.

After a long time, he wiped his eyes. Blew his nose (LOUDLY, ungracefully, HUMAN).

"So what do I DO?" he asked quietly. "How do I start being… REAL marvelous?"

"You start by showing up. For yourself. For your life. Not the life you WISH you had. The life you actually have. You show up for work. You show up for your relationships. You show up for the SMALL things. And slowly—SLOWLY—you build something REAL. Something that can't be taken away by waking up."

"That sounds… slow."

"It IS slow. Real growth is always slow. But it's also permanent. The dream was fast. The dream was EASY. But it wasn't REAL. This will be HARD. But it will be YOURS."

He sat with that. Really SAT with it.

"Okay," he said finally. "Okay. I'll try. I'll show up. I'll be PRESENT. I'll stop trying to be Da Marvelous and start trying to be… the best version of Minghao."

"That's all I'm asking."

"But can I keep some SWAGGER? Like… internal swagger? The feeling of being marvelous even if I'm not ACTING like a kingpin?"

She smiled. "Yes. Absolutely. Keep the swagger. Keep the CONFIDENCE. Keep the belief that you matter. Just ground it in REALITY. Ground it in TRUTH."

"And the purple suit?"

"Burn the purple suit."

"It cost me TWENTY-four DOLLARS!"

"Burn. The. Purple. Suit."

"…Fine."

They both laughed. Real laughs. GENUINE.

"One more thing," Dr. Washington said as their session ended. "I want you to write a letter."

"To who?"

"To Cherry Bomb. To Larry. To Pastor Stacks. To all the characters from your dream. Tell them what they meant to you. Thank them. Say GOODBYE. Not because you're forgetting them. But because you're

ACCEPTING that they were GIFTS your brain gave you to survive. And now you don't need them anymore. Now you have YOURSELF."

"That's gonna make me cry AGAIN."

"That's the POINT."

⚓

THE LETTER (THAT NIGHT)

Back in his apartment, Minghao sat at his folding table with a notebook (borrowed from work, technically theft, would return it PROBABLY) and started writing.

\> Dear Cherry Bomb,

\>

\> You weren't real. I know that now. But you FELT real. You felt like the best business partner anyone could ask for. You were smart, talented, loyal, and you believed in me even when I didn't believe in myself.

\>

\> I think you were the part of me that's PRACTICAL. The part that does the math. The part that PLANS. But you were also the part that has PASSION. The part that SINGS. The part that wants to be SEEN.

\>

\> Thank you for showing me that I can be BOTH. That I don't have to choose between being responsible and being ALIVE. That I can calculate budgets AND chase dreams.

\>

\> I'll miss you. I'll miss your voice. I'll miss the way you always knew the NUMBERS. I'll miss how you GLOWED when you sang.

\>

\> But I'll carry you with me. In every decision I make. In every moment I choose to be BRAVE.

\>

\> Thank you for being my RIGHT HAND even though you only existed in my HEAD.

\>

\> Love,

\> Minghao (Da Marvelous)

He cried while writing it. OBVIOUSLY.

Then he wrote to Larry:

\> Dear Larry (Criminal Goat),

\>

\> You ate SO MANY THINGS you shouldn't have eaten. Documents. Cardboard. Rose gardens. You had WARRANTS. You were CHAOS.

\>

\> But you were also FREE. You did what you WANTED. You didn't apologize. You didn't ask PERMISSION. You just… EXISTED. Fully. Completely. WITHOUT FEAR.

\>

\> I think you were the part of me that wants to REBEL. That's tired of playing it SAFE. That wants to take RISKS even if they're STUPID.

\>

\> Thank you for showing me that sometimes you gotta eat the thing you're not supposed to eat. Metaphorically. NOT LITERALLY. I'm not eating GARDENS.

\>

\> I'll miss your defiant bleats. I'll miss your complete LACK of remorse. I'll miss how you LIVED.

\>

\> Stay wild, Larry. Wherever fantasy goats go when people wake up.

\>

\> Respect,

\> Minghao

Then Pastor Stacks:

\> Dear Pastor Stacks,

\>

\> You betrayed me. Then you CHOSE me. You sold out for money. Then you gave it BACK. You had the BEST redemption arc.

\>

\> I think you were my DAD. The dad I WISHED I had. The one who would come BACK. Who would choose ME over money. Over convenience. Over whatever kept him AWAY.

\>

\> Thank you for showing me that people can CHANGE. That redemption is POSSIBLE. That choosing RIGHT is always an OPTION even if you chose WRONG before.

\>

\> I forgive you. And through you, maybe I can forgive HIM. Eventually. Maybe.

\>

\> Thank you for coming back,

\> Minghao

He cried MORE. OBVIOUSLY.

Finally, he wrote to Da Marvelous himself:

\> Dear Da Marvelous McCall,

\>

\> You were EVERYTHING I wanted to be. Confident. Powerful. CERTAIN. People knew your name. People RESPECTED you. You had an empire. You had PRESENCE. You MATTERED.

\>

\> But you weren't real. You were a DREAM. A beautiful, ridiculous, impossible dream.

\>

\> And I have to let you go. Not because I'm giving up on being MARVELOUS. But because I need to find a way to be marvelous as MYSELF. As MINGHAO. Not as a fantasy.

\>

\> Thank you for showing me what CONFIDENCE feels like. What DETERMINATION feels like. What REFUSING TO GIVE UP feels like.

\>

\> I'll carry those things with me. Forever. Even if I never wear velour suits. Even if I never have gold chains. Even if I spend the rest of my life picking up garbage at 5 AM.

\>

\> I can still be MARVELOUS.

\>

\> I just have to believe it.

\>

\> Goodbye, Da Marvelous. Thank you for everything. Thank you for SURVIVING. Thank you for showing me who I COULD be.

\>

\> Now I gotta figure out how to BE IT.

\>

\> With love and respect,

\> Minghao Liu

\> (Still Marvelous. Just... quieter about it.)

He set down the pen.

Read all the letters.

Cried AGAIN (getting dehydrated at this point, needed WATER).

Then he carefully folded them. Put them in an envelope. Wrote "TO my DREAM FAMILY" on the outside.

And put it in his drawer.

Not to FORGET them.

But to HONOR them.

And to MOVE FORWARD.

For the first time since waking up, Minghao Liu felt something NEW:

Not fantasy confidence.

Not borrowed swagger.

But REAL, genuine, QUIET certainty.

He was going to be okay.

It would take TIME.

It would be HARD.

But he was going to be okay.

And maybe—MAYBE—eventually...

He'd be MARVELOUS.

For real this time.

MINGHAO LIU: BREAKTHROUGH ACHIEVED

Status: Finally LISTENING to therapy

Reality Acceptance: 75% (MAJOR progress!)

Grief: Processed (mostly)

Letters Written: 4 (all tear-stained)

Next Steps: Actually LIVING (novel concept)

Swagger Status: Transforming from fantasy to REAL

CHAPTER 18

Real Connections (or: When You Stop Pretending)

⚓

TWO WEEKS AFTER THERAPY BREAKTHROUGH

Something changed after the letters.

Minghao couldn't explain it exactly. He still lived in the same tiny apartment. Still picked up garbage at 5 AM. Still had \$47 in his bank account (payday was in two DAYS, rent was paid, small victories).

But something SHIFTED.

He stopped wearing the purple suit. (Donated it back to the thrift store. Brenda nodded approvingly. "Growth," she said. "I'm proud.")

He stopped trying to pimp-walk. (His ankle appreciated this decision. So did pedestrians who no longer had to watch him wobble.)

He stopped introducing himself as "Da Marvelous." (Though he kept it in his MIND. Internal swagger. Dr. Washington approved.)

Instead, he just… SHOWED UP.

For work. For therapy. For his LIFE.

And something WEIRD happened:

People started noticing him.

⚓

THE WORK SHIFT (REAL CONNECTIONS BEGIN)

5:47 AM - SANITATION YARD

"Yo, Milo!" Tito called out. "You seem DIFFERENT! Like… lighter? Less insane?"

"I had a BREAKTHROUGH!" Minghao announced, climbing into the truck. "I wrote letters to my imaginary friends and GRIEVED them properly!"

"That's the WEIRDEST thing you ever said. But also... healthy? I think?"

"It WAS healthy! My therapist said so! She said I'm PROCESSING!"

"Look at you! Processing! That's GROWTH!"

They drove the route. Residential neighborhoods. Quiet streets. Sunrise painting everything GOLD.

"Hey Milo," Tito said after a while, more serious. "You know we were WORRIED about you, right? When you were in that coma? We visited every WEEK. Talked to you even though you couldn't hear. Brought you MAGAZINES. Stupid stuff. But we showed UP."

Minghao felt something warm in his chest. Not fantasy warm. REAL warm.

"I know. Thank you. That... that means a lot."

"You our BOY. That's what FAMILY does."

Family. REAL family. Not dream family. actual HUMANS who showed up.

"Hey Tito?"

"Yeah?"

"In my dream, you were a bartender. You made drinks that could kill people. TERRIBLE drinks. Like 70% alcohol."

Tito laughed. "That's hilarious! I can't even make KOOL-AID without messing it up!"

"But you were LOYAL. You always had my back. Even in the dream."

"That part's REAL then," Tito said, grinning. "That part I can DO."

They fist-bumped.

Small moment. REAL moment.

Building something.

⚓

THE HOSPITAL FOLLOW-UP (MEETING CINDY - FULL SCENE)

2:37 PM - MOUNT SINAI HOSPITAL

Minghao had a follow-up appointment. Three-month post-coma check. Make sure his brain was FUNCTIONAL (debatable but TRYING).

He sat in the waiting room reading a magazine (six months old, covered in germs, THRILLING article about refrigerator maintenance that he'd read three TIMES because he was NERVOUS).

Why was he nervous? It was just a MEDICAL appointment. Just a doctor checking if his brain was working. Standard procedure. ROUTINE.

Except the waiting room smelled like ANTISEPTIC and memories. Last time he was here, he woke up thinking he was DA MARVELOUS. Last time he was here, everything CHANGED.

"Minghao Liu?"

He looked up.

A woman in scrubs stood there. Early thirties. Warm smile that reached her EYES. Name tag: cindy martinez, RN. Different from Nurse Jasmine. NEW. Which meant she probably HADN'T heard about the purple suit incident yet. Small mercies.

"That's me! Well, technically Da Marvelous, but I'm WORKING on accepting—never mind. Yes. Minghao." He stood up too fast. Knocked the magazine off his lap. It hit the floor with a slap. "I'm SMOOTH. Very COORDINATED. Medical professional levels of GRACE."

She smiled wider. Not a pity smile. An AMUSED smile. "I can see that. Come on back."

He followed her through the corridors. White walls. Fluorescent lights. That specific hospital QUIET that's never actually quiet—beeping machines, distant voices, the hum of LIFE continuing.

"Room three," she said, holding the door open.

He walked in. Sat on the exam table. It crinkled under him. LOUD. Everything in hospitals was designed to make you feel EXPOSED.

She washed her hands. Pulled on gloves. Started setting up equipment. Professional. COMPETENT. The kind of competence that comes from doing something a THOUSAND times.

"So how have you been feeling?" she asked, wrapping the blood pressure cuff around his arm. "Any headaches? Dizziness? Confusion?"

"I mean, EXISTENTIAL confusion? Constantly. Like 'what is life' and 'why am I HERE' and 'what's my PURPOSE?' That kind of confusion. Medical confusion? Not really. My brain seems to be FUNCTIONING.

Mostly."

She laughed. GENUINE laugh. The kind that makes you want to say MORE funny things just to hear it again.

"Existential confusion is NORMAL. Especially after what you went through. Your brain had a JOURNEY. Three months is a long time to be asleep."

"You know about the coma?"

"Everyone here knows about you!" She pumped the blood pressure cuff. It SQUEEZED. "You're famous! The guy who had the three-month dream life! Nurse Jasmine tells EVERYONE your story! She says you thought you were a kingpin! That you wore a PURPLE SUIT to public places!"

Minghao groaned. "The purple suit was a phase! A brief, regrettable PHASE! I DONATED it! It's GONE!"

"But the LEGEND remains!" She released the cuff. Wrote down numbers. "Blood pressure's good. Heart rate's a little elevated but that could be white COAT SYNDROME. Are you nervous?"

"I'm ALWAYS nervous! It's my default STATE! I'm like a CHIHUAHUA in human form!"

She laughed again. Started checking his reflexes. Little rubber hammer. Tap tap tap.

"So tell me about the empire," she said, focusing on his knee. "What was it like? Being a kingpin?"

"It was AMAZING!" He couldn't help it. Even though it wasn't real, talking about it felt good. "I had a business partner named Cherry Bomb! She was an ACCOUNTANT who could SING! Like professionally! Like make-you-CRY levels of singing! We ran this club called Club Marvelous! Big purple building! Gold letters! Very PRESTIGIOUS!"

"That sounds incredible." She moved to the other knee. Tap tap. "What else?"

"I had a GOAT! A criminal goat named Larry! He had warrants! He destroyed a rose garden! Four thousand dollars in damages! But he was MAJESTIC! He had this LOOK in his eyes like he KNEW he was special! Like he OWNED the world!"

"What was the goat's crime specifically?" She was ENGAGED. Actually interested. Not just doing the polite medical professional thing. GENUINELY asking.

"Destruction of public property! The Washington Park rose garden! He ate SEVENTEEN rose bushes! Made direct eye contact with the park ranger while doing it! zero REMORSE! They had to send Animal Control! It was a whole SITUATION!"

She was laughing now. REALLY laughing. Had to set down her clipboard.

"I love that your DREAM included a criminal goat! That's the most specific detail! Most people dream about flying or their teeth falling out! You dreamed about GOAT CRIMES!"

"Larry was IMPORTANT! He represented my rebellious spirit! My desire to break free! My—" He stopped. "I've been in THERAPY. I know what all the dream people represented now. It's very PSYCHOLOGICAL."

"I bet." She checked his pupils. Little flashlight. "Follow my finger." She moved it left, right, up, down. "Good. Everything looks normal. Neurologically speaking, you're FINE."

"But PSYCHOLOGICALLY?"

"That's above my pay grade." She smiled. "But between you and me? I think you're doing AMAZING."

"Really?"

"Really. You survived a TRAUMATIC injury. Three months in a coma. Massive head trauma. Woke up completely confused. And you're HERE. You're FUNCTIONING. You're making JOKES. That's not nothing. That's EVERYTHING."

She sat down in the chair. Pulled off her gloves. Just... LOOKED at him.

"Can I tell you something?" she said quietly. "I think it's beautiful that you REMEMBER them. Your dream people. A lot of coma patients wake up and the dreams just... fade. Like smoke. Like they were never THERE. But you're HOLDING ON to them. That's special."

"My therapist said it's like Dorothy and Oz," Minghao said, feeling something WARM in his chest. "I'll always remember my friends even though they weren't real."

"EXACTLY!" Cindy leaned forward. "And Dorothy came back changed! She was BETTER because of Oz! She learned about courage and heart and home! You're better because of your empire! You learned about confidence and dreams and—" She paused. "I'm getting PHILOSOPHICAL. Sorry. It's the end of a long shift. My filter's GONE."

"No, I LIKE it! I like that you get it! Most people think I'm CRAZY!"

"You're not crazy. You're PROCESSING. There's a difference."

He looked at her. REALLY looked.

She had laugh lines around her eyes. Tired lines from long shifts. But also WARMTH. The kind of warmth that comes from someone who shows UP for people. Who CARES.

"You know what's WEIRD?" he said. "In my dream, I had this whole life. People depended on me. I mattered. I was SOMEBODY. And then I woke up and I was... nobody. Just regular Minghao who picks up garbage and got hit by a truck because of a PIGEON."

"The pigeon incident," she said, grinning. "Nurse Jasmine showed me the video."

"OF course she DID! That woman is VIOLATING my privacy CONSTANTLY! I'm gonna SUE! I'm gonna—" He stopped. "You watched it?"

"SEVENTEEN times. Showed all my coworkers. We have a group chat specifically for funny MEDICAL STORIES and you're in there. Multiple times. With GIFs."

"That's HORRIFYING!"

"That's HILARIOUS! You backing up for a better photo angle while a TRUCK is coming! The pigeon with the CHURRO! The perfect comedic TIMING of it all!"

"I almost DIED!"

"But you DIDN'T! You survived! And now you're here! Making ME laugh! That's MARVELOUS!" She said it without thinking. Then realized. "Oh. I just—I didn't mean to use your—"

"No, I LIKE it!" He grinned. "Maybe I am marvelous! Maybe not fantasy marvelous. But REAL marvelous! Like... surviving-a-truck-and-still-showing-up marvelous!"

"EXACTLY!" She stood up. "Exam's done. You're cleared. Neurologically perfect. Psychologically processing. Overall: MARVELOUS."

"Thank you, Nurse Cindy."

"Just Cindy." She wrote something on his chart. Then paused. Looked at him. Made a DECISION. "Can I tell you something ELSE?"

"Sure?"

"I saw your chart when you were in the coma. Before you woke up. I wasn't your assigned nurse but I was on the floor one night and I saw: 'Minghao Liu. Three months unconscious. Extensive REM activity.' And I wondered what you were dreaming about. If you were happy in there. If you'd

WANT to wake up."

"That's... that's really KIND of you."

"And when Nurse Jasmine told me you woke up thinking you were a KINGPIN? I knew I wanted to meet you. Because that's the most hopeful thing I ever heard. Your brain didn't give up. Your brain created a whole LIFE. An EMPIRE. That's not CRAZY. That's SURVIVING."

Minghao felt tears coming. Not sad tears. GRATEFUL tears.

"Thank you," he said quietly. "For seeing it that way. Most people think I'm INSANE."

"You're not insane. You're RESILIENT. Big difference."

She handed him a piece of paper. Not his discharge papers. Something ELSE.

A phone number. Written in neat handwriting.

"Text me," she said. "If you want. No pressure. But... I'd like to get coffee sometime. Hear more about Larry the criminal goat. Learn more about the REAL marvelous."

Minghao stared at the paper. At the NUMBERS. At the POSSIBILITY.

"You... you want to get coffee? With ME? The pigeon guy?"

"ESPECIALLY with the pigeon guy. That pigeon had dreams. That pigeon saw a CHURRO and went for it. I respect that level of COMMITMENT."

"The pigeon also ruined my LIFE!"

"The pigeon CHANGED your life. There's a difference."

She walked toward the door. Stopped. Turned back.

"For what it's worth? I think old Minghao—the one who got hit by the truck—wouldn't have asked that girl out at the laundromat. Wouldn't have worn the purple suit even though it was RIDICULOUS. Wouldn't have tried. New Minghao tries. Even when he's scared. Even when he might fail. That's GROWTH. That's REAL confidence. Not fantasy confidence. EARNED confidence."

"How do you KNOW about the laundromat?!"

"Nurse Jasmine has SO many STORIES! Your privacy was violated EXTENSIVELY! It's honestly impressive how much she SHARES!"

Then she left. Door closing softly. Leaving Minghao sitting on the crinkly exam table. Holding a phone number.

REAL phone number.

From a REAL person.

Who KNEW everything.

The pigeon. The purple suit. The coma dreams. The laundromat disaster.

And still wanted coffee.

"Maybe real life IS better," he whispered.

The exam room didn't disagree.

Progress.

⚓

THE TEXT ANXIETY (47 MINUTES OF PARALYSIS)

That night, Minghao sat in his apartment staring at Cindy's phone number.

Gerald the Plant watched (possibly judged, hard to tell with plants).

"Should I text her?" he asked Gerald.

Gerald didn't respond. Because PLANTS don'T TALK.

"What if I say something WEIRD? What if she realizes I'm boring? What if I text the WRONG THING and she regrets giving me her number?"

Gerald remained silent. Unhelpfully.

Minghao typed and deleted SEVENTEEN different opening texts:

"Hi this is Minghao! The pigeon guy!" (Too self-deprecating)

"Hey it's Minghao from the hospital! Want to get coffee?" (Too direct, too soon)

"This is Minghao Liu, the man whose dreams included goat crimes." (Too weird)

"Hi Cindy! This is Minghao. I promise I'm less awkward via text!" (Probably a lie)

Finally, at 7:43 PM (forty-SEVEN MINUTES after getting her number), he texted:

Minghao: Hi! This is Minghao from the hospital! The guy with the criminal goat dreams!

He hit send. Immediately REGRETTED it. Why lead with the goat? Why not something NORMAL?

His phone buzzed. THIRTY SECONDS later.

Cindy: I was HOPING you'd text! I was worried you'd chicken out!

Minghao: I ALMOST did! I stared at your number for like an HOUR! Wrote seventeen different texts! Deleted them all! This was text number EIGHTEEN!

Cindy: That's adorable. And honest. I appreciate honesty.

Minghao: I'm TOO honest! It's a PROBLEM! I have no FILTER! My therapist says it's because I'm 'processing trauma through radical transparency!'

Cindy: Your therapist sounds SMART.

Minghao: She's VERY smart! She explained that Cherry Bomb was actually ME! And that Larry represented my rebellious spirit! And that Pastor Stacks was my DAD! It was very PSYCHOLOGICAL!

Cindy: I want to hear ALL of this. Over coffee?

Minghao: YES! Coffee! When? Where? I promise not to spill water this time!

Cindy: This time?

Minghao: Long story. Involves a previous date. A phone call from my mother. RENT DRAMA. The woman I was meeting RAN AWAY. Literally RAN. Like I was DANGEROUS.

Cindy: Okay NOW I NEED to hear this story.

Minghao: Saturday? 2 PM? There's a place in Silver Lake? Same place as the disaster date actually. I'm RECLAIMING it!

Cindy: RECLAIMING dates! I love it! Perfect! Saturday 2 PM!

Minghao: Wait should I pick you up? Is that a thing people do? I don't know date PROTOCOL! I haven't dated in YEARS! Honestly I might've never ACTUALLY dated! The dream didn't have dating! It just had CHERRY BOMB who appeared fully formed like ATHENA!

Cindy: I'll meet you there. Less pressure. We can see how it goes.

Minghao: Smart. STRATEGIC. You're good at this!

Cindy: I've had practice. Both good dates and TERRIBLE dates. Including one where the guy brought his MOM. To the DATE. His MOTHER.

Minghao: That's INSANE! Who brings their MOTHER?!

Cindy: Mama's boys. Anyway. Saturday! 2 PM! I'm excited!

Minghao: Me too! Should I wear something special? The purple suit is gone but I have a button-up shirt! It's BLUE! Very RESPONSIBLE looking!

Cindy: Perfect. And Minghao?

Minghao: Yeah?

Cindy: Don't wear the purple suit.

Minghao: HOW DO YOU KNOW ABOUT THE PURPLE SUIT?!

Cindy: Nurse Jasmine has PHOTOS. She showed EVERYONE. You looked like a GRAPE. An IMPORTANT grape. But still a grape.

Minghao: I'm going to SUE the hospital for PRIVACY VIOLATIONS! I'm going to call a LAWYER! I'm going to—

Cindy: See you Saturday ☺

Minghao: Saturday! 2 PM! Blue shirt! No purple suit! I'll be there!

He put down his phone. Looked at Gerald.

"I have a date," he told the plant. "A real date. With a REAL person. Who knows about the pigeon. Who knows about the purple suit. Who knows about the coma dreams. And she STILL wants coffee."

Gerald thrived silently.

"You're right," Minghao said. "This IS good. This is PROGRESS."

For the first time in months, Minghao Liu felt something he hadn't felt since waking up:

HOPE.

Not fantasy hope.

Not borrowed hope.

REAL hope.

The kind that comes from someone seeing ALL of you—the embarrassing parts, the broken parts, the WEIRD parts—and still choosing to show up.

"Maybe real life is better," he whispered.

The apartment (and Gerald) finally agreed.

⚓

THE COFFEE DATE (TAKE TWO - FULL SCENE WITH

DEPTH)

SATURDAY, 1:54 PM - SAME COFFEE SHOP, DIFFERENT MINGHAO

Minghao arrived EARLY. Of course he did. Arriving early was his THING now apparently.

But this time he was PREPARED:

✓ Ordered a SMALL coffee (learning from mistakes, GROWTH)

✓ Chose a table with NO water glass (STRATEGIC thinking)

✓ Wore the blue button-up (freshly ironed by Mom, no shame)

✓ Regular jeans (the hole-less ones)

✓ Told his mother he was on a date and to NOT call under ANY CIRCUMSTANCES (she promised, probably lying, but TRYING)

✓ Left phone on VIBRATE (not RING)

✓ Bathroom trip completed (PREPARATION)

✓ Breath mints consumed (CONFIDENCE)

He sat. Waited. Tried to look CASUAL. Failed. Looked nervous instead. Which was at least HONEST.

At 2:02 PM, Cindy walked in.

She looked... BEAUTIFUL.

Not fantasy beautiful. REAL beautiful. The kind that comes from someone who woke up, chose an outfit, did their makeup, and decided to show UP.

Sundress (yellow, cheerful, SUNSHINE). Denim jacket. Sneakers (practical). Smile that made his heart do GYMNASTICS.

"You came!" she said, sitting down.

"Of course I CAME! Why wouldn't I come?!"

"Last time someone asked me out at work, they stood me up! Said they were 'too nervous to go through with it!' Sent me a TEXT an hour after we were supposed to meet!"

"That's TERRIBLE! Who DOES that?!"

"Cowards. People who panic. People who can't handle the REALITY

268

of dating."

"I'm VERY nervous!" Minghao admitted. "My hands are sweating! My heart is doing ARRHYTHMIAS! But I'm HERE! That's GROWTH!"

She laughed. REAL laugh. The kind he'd been hoping to hear again.

"That IS growth! You get credit for showing up!"

The barista came over. Took their orders.

Cindy: Oat milk latte (FANCY)

Minghao: Refill of his small coffee (ECONOMICAL)

Then they just… TALKED.

For TWO HOURS.

About EVERYTHING:

The Coma Dreams (She wanted DETAILS):

"So Cherry Bomb was an accountant AND a singer? How did THAT work?"

"She calculated budgets during the day and performed at night! She had this INCREDIBLE voice! Made people cry! She sang Whitney Houston at our gala and people gave her EIGHT HUNDRED DOLLARS in tips!"

"In your DREAM gala?"

"In my VERY real dream gala! It felt REAL! Everything felt SO REAL!"

"What happened at the gala?"

"We raised twenty thousand dollars! But we NEEDED twenty-three thousand! And then Larry got seized by Animal Control and we paid his fine with the crowd's money and then we came up SHORT and Isabella liquidated everything and I got hit by a truck and woke up and—"

He stopped. Realized he was talking TOO much. "Sorry. I'm RAMBLING."

"No! Keep going! This is FASCINATING! What happened to Larry?"

"He got SAVED! The crowd loved him! They chanted 'free LARRY!' It was BEAUTIFUL! But it cost eighteen hundred dollars and that's why we failed!"

"So you chose the GOAT over success?"

"I HAD to! Larry was family! You don't abandon FAMILY!"

"Even imaginary family?"

"ESPECIALLY imaginary family! They're the only family you get to CHOOSE completely!"

She smiled. Warm. Understanding. "I love that about you."

"What?"

"You're LOYAL. Even to dream people. Even to a criminal goat. That says something about who you ARE."

The Pigeon Incident (She'd Watched It 17 TIMES):

"Okay I HAVE to know," Cindy said, leaning forward. "What were you thinking? When you backed up? What was going through your HEAD?"

"I was thinking: that pigeon is living BETTER than me! That pigeon has a churro! A whole churro! Not crumbs! Not SCRAPS! A FULL churro! And I wanted to CAPTURE that moment! I wanted PROOF that even pigeons can achieve GREATNESS!"

"And then?"

"And then I woke up in a hospital three months later having dreamed I was a kingpin!"

"The pigeon CHANGED your LIFE!"

"The pigeon RUINED my life! Two point three million views! merchandise! The pigeon has an INSTAGRAM! The pigeon has a BOOK DEAL!"

"The pigeon has a book deal?!"

"SEVENTEEN thousand followers! The book is called 'Churro Dreams: One Pigeon's Journey!' I'm NOT making this up!"

Cindy laughed so hard coffee almost came out her NOSE. "That's the most ABSURD thing I've ever heard!"

"Welcome to MY life! Where pigeons win and I LOSE!"

"You didn't lose! You're HERE! You're alive! You're having coffee with ME!"

"That's... that's actually TRUE."

Therapy & Processing (She Got It):

"My therapist helped me understand what everyone MEANT," Minghao explained. "Cherry was my practical side that also had hidden passion. Larry was my rebellious spirit. Pastor Stacks was the father I WISHED I had. And

Da Marvelous was... me. The best VERSION of me. The version I wanted to BE."

"That's BEAUTIFUL! And kind of heartbreaking?"

"It WAS heartbreaking! I wrote them letters! I cried SO MUCH! I was DEHYDRATED!"

"You wrote them letters?"

"Goodbye letters! Thanking them! Telling them what they meant! It was very EMOTIONAL! Very cathartic! My therapist says I'm 'processing trauma through structured grief!' Which sounds FANCY but really just means 'ugly crying into a notebook!'"

She reached across the table. Touched his hand. "That takes COURAGE. Most people would just try to forget. Pretend it never happened. You're HONORING it."

"My therapist said the same thing! Are you SURE you're not a therapist?"

"I'm a nurse! We do SOME psychology! Mostly we just try to keep people alive and somewhat COMFORTABLE!"

Her Life (She Opened Up Too):

"My family's LOUD," Cindy said. "Big Mexican family. Six kids. I'm number four. Middle child. CLASSIC middle child. Always mediating. Always keeping the peace."

"My family's loud TOO! Chinese loud! Which is like... aggressively CONCERNED loud! My mom shows love through CRITICISM and SOUP!"

"SAME! My mom shows love through food and judgment! 'Mija, you look SKINNY, here's TAMALES!' Then five minutes later: 'Mija, you getting FAT, eat a SALAD!'"

"EXACTLY! My mom's like: 'Minghao you need eat more! Also you getting CHUBBY! Also here's MORE FOOD!'"

They laughed. TOGETHER. Finding connection in SHARED EXPERIENCE.

"Why'd you become a nurse?" Minghao asked.

"My abuela—my grandmother—had a stroke when I was fifteen. Spent months in the hospital. The nurses were AMAZING. They were kind. They were patient. They treated her like FAMILY. And I thought: I want to DO that. I want to be that person for SOMEONE."

"That's... that's really BEAUTIFUL."

"What about you? Why sanitation?"

"Honestly? I needed a JOB. I needed benefits. I needed something stable. It's not glamorous. It's not what I DREAMED about. But it's HONEST work. And the people—Tito and Big Mike and Uncle Donny—they're GOOD people. They showed up for me when I was in the coma. Visited EVERY WEEK. That's FAMILY."

"Real family. Not dream family."

"Real family. Which is BETTER actually. Because they're REAL."

Mutual Food Love (The Foundation):

"Okay CRITICAL question," Cindy said seriously. "Tacos: hard shell or soft?"

"SOFT! Obviously! Hard shell tacos are a lie! They're not even tacos! They're SALAD BOWLS with DELUSIONS!"

"CORRECT answer! Korean BBQ: you cook or they cook?"

"I cook! OBVIOUSLY! That's half the FUN!"

"ALSO CORRECT! Okay you're passing all the tests!"

"There are TESTS?!"

"Always tests! Dating is FULL of tests!"

Two hours passed like MINUTES. Coffee cups emptied. Conversations flowed. Connection BUILT.

Finally, the barista started giving them LOOKS. The kind that said "you've been here two HOURS, other people need tables."

"We should probably go," Cindy said reluctantly.

They walked outside. The sun was lower. The afternoon was ending. The date was CONCLUDING.

"Can I tell you something?" Minghao said, stopping on the sidewalk.

"Sure?"

"I was SO scared you wouldn't like the real me. The non-fantasy me. The regular-guy-who-picks-up-garbage-and-got-hit-by-a-truck-because-of-a-pigeon me. But you DO. You actually DO. And that's... that's more AMAZING than anything that happened in my dream."

Cindy smiled. Soft. GENUINE. "But that's the best you! That's the real you! The you who survived! The you who SHOWS UP! The you who writes letters to imaginary friends and frames photos of PIGEONS! That's more impressive than any imaginary empire!"

"You THINK?"

"I KNOW!"

She stepped closer. Looked up at him. Made a DECISION.

And kissed him.

Not on the cheek.

On the LIPS.

Soft. Quick. But REAL.

SO REAL.

When she pulled back, she was smiling. "Text me about date number two. I'm thinking DINNER. Somewhere with no water glasses. Just to be SAFE."

"DEAL! Yes! Dinner! When?!"

"Next Saturday? Same time?"

"Perfect! I'll be there! On TIME! With no disasters! I PROMISE!"

"I'm not worried about disasters. Disasters make good STORIES."

She walked to her car. Turned back once. Waved.

He waved back. ENTHUSIASTIC wave. Possibly too enthusiastic. But HONEST.

She drove away. Tail lights disappearing.

Leaving Minghao standing on the sidewalk. Touching his lips where she'd kissed him.

REAL kiss.

REAL person.

REAL connection.

Da Marvelous had Cherry Bomb who appeared fully formed with no HISTORY.

But Minghao Liu had CINDY who knew his WHOLE story and still showed up.

And Cindy was REAL.

And real was BETTER.

So much BETTER.

⚓

TELLING THE CREW (CELEBRATION)

MONDAY, LUNCH BREAK

"I GOT A GIRLFRIEND!" Minghao announced, bursting into the break room.

Everyone looked up.

"You got a WHAT?" Tito asked.

"A girlfriend! A REAL girlfriend! Not a dream girlfriend! An actual HUMAN WOMAN!"

"MILO!" Big Mike stood up, hugged him. "my boy! YOU DID IT!"

"How you meet her?" Uncle Donny asked, smiling.

"Hospital follow-up! She's a nurse! She knows about the pigeon! She KNOWS about the purple suit! She KNOWS about the coma dreams! And she STILL likes me!"

"That's TRUE love right there!" Tito declared. "Any woman who knows about the pigeon and STAYS is a KEEPER!"

"We going on a second date Saturday! DINNER! I need to NOT mess this up!"

"Don't wear the purple suit," Carlos said, still on his phone.

"I DONATED the purple suit!"

"Good. That was a CRY for HELP disguised as FASHION."

They celebrated. High-fives. Backslaps. REAL happiness for him.

"I'm proud of you, Milo," Uncle Donny said quietly. "You came back from that coma. You processed your grief. You accepted reality. And now you're building something REAL. That's TRUE strength."

"Thanks, Uncle Donny."

"Now don't SCREW it UP by talking about the goat too much."

"Larry was IMPORTANT!"

"Larry was IMAGINARY!"

"Larry was SYMBOLICALLY SIGNIFICANT!"

Everyone laughed.

274

And Minghao realized:

This was BETTER than the dream.

The dream was SAFE.

The dream was CONTROLLED.

But THIS?

This was REAL.

This was UNCERTAIN.

This was SCARY.

But this was also ALIVE.

And for the first time since waking up…

Minghao Liu felt AWAKE.

Truly, completely, AWAKE.

CHAPTER 19

Small Victories (or: When Progress Isn't Linear)

⚓

ONE MONTH LATER - SLOW BUILDING

Real growth, Minghao learned, wasn't DRAMATIC.

There was no MONTAGE. No inspiring music. No sudden transformation from garbage man to success STORY.

Instead, it was:

Showing up. Every day. Even when it was HARD.

Small victories. Tiny improvements. Gradual CHANGE.

Not marvelous yet.

But… MOVING.

⚓

VICTORY #1: THE APARTMENT UPGRADE (SMALL BUT MEANINGFUL)

PAYDAY - \$1,847 (After taxes, after paying Mom back \$20)

Minghao stood in his apartment looking at what \$27 could buy.

In his dream, \$27 was NOTHING. Pocket change. The cost of one DRINK at Club Marvelous (drinks were expensive, very EXCLUSIVE).

In reality, \$27 was a DECISION. A choice between competing needs.

Option A: A pillow. REAL pillow. Not the flat thing he'd been using (which was basically a PILLOWCASE stuffed with REGRET). Actual SUPPORT. Potential neck-pain RELIEF.

Option B: A plant. Living thing. GREENERY. Hope. Something to care for besides HIMSELF.

Option C: A poster. Make the walls less DEPRESSING. Cover the worst stain (mysterious origin, possibly SENTIENT).

He stood there for TWENTY MINUTES weighing options.

Then realized: Why CHOOSE?

He could get ALL three if he was STRATEGIC.

THE HUNT:

Dollar store pillow: \$8 (not great, but BETTER than current situation)

Small succulent (Fred Meyer clearance): \$3.99 (slightly dying but RECOVERABLE)

Motivational poster (thrift store): \$2 (said "BE the change" with mountain photo, EXTREMELY on-the-nose but WHO CARES)

Total: \$13.99

He had money LEFT OVER.

Thirteen dollars and one cent of SURPLUS.

This was WEALTH.

This was PROSPERITY.

This was what GROWTH felt like.

⚓

THE PILLOW CHANGED EVERYTHING

That night, Minghao slept on his new pillow.

Eight dollars of HEAVEN.

His neck didn't hurt for the first time in MONTHS.

He woke up at 5 AM feeling... rested. Actually RESTED.

"This is what rich people feel like," he told his apartment. "This is LUXURY."

The apartment seemed to agree.

Gerald the Plant (he'd named it immediately, BONDING was important) sat on his folding table in the morning light. Looking slightly less dying than yesterday. PROGRESS.

The motivational poster covered the wall stain perfectly. "BE the

CHANGE" it proclaimed. With a mountain. Because mountains are INSPIRING apparently.

"I AM being the change," Minghao told the poster. "I bought a pillow. That's CHANGE."

The poster didn't disagree.

Small victories.

Building.

GROWING.

⚓

VICTORY #2: THE DINNER DATE SUCCESS (BUILDING REAL CONNECTION)

SATURDAY NIGHT, 7:47 PM - THAI RESTAURANT IN LOS FELIZ

Minghao arrived EARLY (his pattern, his BRAND now).

He'd chosen his outfit carefully:

\- Button-up shirt (BLUE one, the successful one from coffee date)

\- Dark jeans (the GOOD ones, no holes)

\- Belt (borrowed from Tito, slightly too big but FUNCTIONAL)

\- Shoes (cleaned thoroughly, looked almost NEW)

Total cost: \$0 (already owned everything, ECONOMICAL)

He waited outside the restaurant. Nervous. VERY nervous.

What if the coffee date was a FLUKE? What if she realized during the week that he was BORING? What if—

"Minghao!"

Cindy walked up. Dress (different from last time, green, STUNNING). Leather jacket. Boots. Smile that made his brain MALFUNCTION.

"You came!" he said.

"Did you think I wouldn't?"

"I have ANXIETY! I think about EVERYTHING! I had seventeen

different scenarios where you cancelled! Including one where you got abducted BY ALIENS!"

She laughed. "No alien abductions. Just TRAFFIC. Los Feliz on a Saturday is TERRIBLE."

"I arrived early specifically to AVOID traffic anxiety!"

"Smart. STRATEGIC. I like it."

They went inside. Small restaurant. Cozy. Authentic. Within budget (he'd checked the menu online SEVENTEEN TIMES, calculated exact costs, planned accordingly).

The waiter seated them. Gave them menus.

"So," Cindy said, "tell me about your week."

And he DID.

For the first time in his life, Minghao talked about his actual LIFE without feeling the need to EMBELLISH:

About Work:

"We had a new guy start Monday. Kevin. Twenty-two years old. TERRIFIED. Reminded me of me six months ago. And I realized I could help him. I knew what to say because I'd BEEN there. That felt... good. Like I had something to OFFER."

"That's LEADERSHIP," Cindy said. "That's GROWTH."

"It's SMALL growth."

"Small growth is still GROWTH."

About Therapy:

"Dr. Washington says I'm making progress. She says I've moved from 'denial and bargaining' to 'acceptance and integration.' Which sounds FANCY but means I'm not trying to be Da Marvelous anymore. I'm just... being ME. With lessons learned from Da Marvelous."

"How does that FEEL?"

"Weird. But also... LIGHTER? Like I don't have to pretend anymore. I can just EXIST."

About Gerald:

"I bought a plant. Named it Gerald. It's slightly dying but I'm

DETERMINED to save it. I water it every three days. I talk to it sometimes. Is that WEIRD?"

"That's ADORABLE! Plants respond to ATTENTION! Science proves it!"

"Gerald is RESPONDING! He grew a new leaf! one leaf! But it's PROGRESS!"

They ordered food:

\- Pad Thai (to share, couple ACTIVITY)

\- Tom Yum soup (spicy, ALIVE)

\- Spring rolls (fried, commitment to CALORIES)

\- Thai iced teas (sweet, DELICIOUS)

While they waited, Cindy told him about HER week:

About the Hospital:

"We had a patient Wednesday. Fifty-seven years old. Heart attack. Survived. Woke up and the first thing he said was 'I've been wasting my life.' Just like that. REVELATION. Said he'd been working seventy-hour weeks for twenty years. Hadn't seen his daughter in six months. Hadn't taken a vacation in five YEARS. And almost DYING made him realize: what's it all FOR?"

"What happened?"

"He QUIT. Gave two weeks notice right there from his hospital bed. Said he was going to spend time with his family. Move somewhere quiet. Live SMALLER but BETTER."

"That's... that's BRAVE."

"That's what almost DYING does sometimes. It clarifies things. Like your coma. You woke up DIFFERENT. BETTER."

"I woke up thinking I was a KINGPIN!"

"But then you PROCESSED it! You learned from it! That patient might've just gone back to his seventy-hour weeks. But HE chose change. Like YOU chose change."

The food arrived. They ate. They talked. They LAUGHED.

Minghao told her about the pigeon having MORE followers now (23,000, GROWING).

Cindy told him about her sister's wedding drama (dress disasters, family CHAOS).

He told her about Uncle Donny's wisdom drops (man was full of INSIGHTS).

She told him about her abuela's recovery (slow but STEADY, much like his own).

They found RHYTHM. Natural rhythm. The kind that comes from two people who actually like each other. Who aren't PERFORMING. Just… EXISTING together.

THE SERIOUS CONVERSATION (IT HAPPENED NATURALLY):

"Can I tell you something?" Minghao said, halfway through the Pad Thai. "Something I haven't told many people?"

"Of course."

"My dad left when I was nine. Just… LEFT. One day he was there. Next day he wasn'T. No explanation. No goodbye. He just VANISHED."

Cindy put down her fork. Gave him her FULL attention.

"I'm so sorry."

"I think that's why I dreamed about Pastor Stacks," Minghao continued, surprised at himself. He'd never told ANYONE this. Not even therapy yet. "The man who betrayed me but came back. Who chose ME. Who said 'I'm sorry.' My dad never said that. Never CAME BACK. But Pastor Stacks DID. Even though he was IMAGINARY. My brain gave me the dad I NEEDED. Even if he wasn't REAL."

"That's not imaginary," Cindy said softly, reaching across the table to hold his hand. "That's your brain showing you what you DESERVED. What you still deserve. That's BEAUTIFUL. And sad. But also HOPEFUL."

"How is it HOPEFUL?"

"Because you KNOW now. You know what you needed. What you deserved. And that means you can recognize it when it shows up in real LIFE. You won't accept LESS than what Pastor Stacks represented. You won't accept abandonment. You won't accept BETRAYAL. You'll expect LOYALTY. You'll expect people to CHOOSE YOU. That's POWERFUL."

Minghao felt tears coming. Blinked them back.

"Why are you being so NICE to me? I'm a mess. I live in a 300-square-foot apartment. I pick up garbage. I almost died because of a pigeon. I'm thirty-THREE years old and I just bought my first REAL PILLOW last week."

"Because you're REAL," she said simply, squeezing his hand. "You're not pretending. You're not trying to impress me with fake swagger. You're not lying about who you are. You're just... you. And I like you. I like that you named your plant Gerald. I like that you help new coworkers even though you're scared. I like that you frame PIGEON PHOTOS. I like that you're honest about your struggles. That's not a MESS. That's HUMAN. That's REAL. And real is what I WANT."

"Even the pigeon thing?"

"ESPECIALLY the pigeon thing! That pigeon had vision! That pigeon knew what it WANTED! That pigeon is my HERO!"

They laughed. Through tears. Through FEELINGS. Through CONNECTION.

The waiter came with the check.

Minghao paid. \$47.82 (including tip, he'd budgeted CAREFULLY).

They walked outside. Cool Los Feliz night. Stars barely visible through city LIGHTS.

"Can I walk you to your car?" Minghao asked.

"I'd like that."

They walked. Slowly. Not wanting the night to END.

"So," Cindy said, "I have a question."

"Okay?"

"Are you falling for me? Because I need to know. I need HONESTY. I've had relationships where people weren't honest about their feelings and I wasted MONTHS. So I'm just... asking. Directly."

Minghao stopped walking. Looked at her. REALLY looked.

"Yes," he said. Simple. True. "I'm falling for you. I think I started falling for you in the exam room when you laughed at my goat story. And I fell more during coffee when you understood about Dorothy and Oz. And I'm falling MORE now because you let me talk about my dad without making it WEIRD. So yes. I'm falling. HARD. Is that... is that OKAY?"

She smiled. "It's MORE than okay. Because I'm falling too."

She kissed him. REAL kiss. Not first-date kiss. second-date kiss. The kind that promises MORE dates. The kind that says "this is GOING somewhere."

When they pulled apart, they were both smiling.

"Text me tomorrow," she said. "Tell me about Gerald's progress. Tell

282

me if the new pillow is still LIFE-CHANGING. Tell me EVERYTHING."

"I will. I PROMISE."

She drove away. He walked to the bus stop (couldn't afford car yet, PUBLIC transportation was FINE).

Sat on the bench. Touched his lips. Smiled like an IDIOT.

REAL relationship.

REAL feelings.

REAL future possibility.

Better than any dream.

⚓

SETBACK #1: THE PANIC ATTACK AT WORK (REALITY CHECK)

TUESDAY, 7:23 AM - MID-ROUTE

It hit WITHOUT WARNING.

One moment Minghao was lifting a trash bin. Normal routine. Regular Tuesday. Nothing SPECIAL.

Next moment: CRUSHING chest pain. Can't breathe. Vision TUNNELING.

The trash bin fell from his hands. Hit the ground. LOUD crash.

"Tito—" he gasped. "Tito, something's WRONG—"

Tito pulled over. FAST. Emergency stop. Hazards ON.

"Milo! MILO! What's wrong?!"

"Can't— can't BREATHE—"

"You having a HEART ATTACK?! Should I call 911?!"

"No—I think—panic attack—had them BEFORE—in the HOSPITAL—"

Tito got him out of the truck. Sat him on the curb. Street corner. 7:23 AM. Morning commuters passing. WITNESSING his breakdown.

"Breathe with me, man. IN. out. IN. OUT. Look at me. Focus on ME."

Minghao tried. STRUGGLED. Everything felt wrong. Like dying. Like ending. Like being hit by the truck ALL OVER AGAIN.

His hands were TINGLING. His heart was racing. His brain was SCREAMING.

"You're OKAY," Tito kept saying, voice steady, grounding. "You're NOT dying. This is anxiety. You're SAFE. You're with ME. I got you."

Slowly—SLOWLY—it passed.

Five minutes. Felt like FOREVER. But it PASSED.

Minghao sat on the curb. Breathing. SHAKING. Embarrassed. MORTIFIED.

"What TRIGGERED it?" Tito asked gently, sitting next to him.

"I don't... I don't KNOW. We were just working. Routine stuff. And then I thought about the accident. About the truck. About almost DYING. About waking up in the hospital. About how FRAGILE everything is. And then my brain just... PANICKED."

"That's PTSD, man. That's trauma. You got hit by a truck. You were in a COMA for three months. Your brain is still PROCESSING. This is NORMAL."

"It doesn't FEEL normal! It feels like I'm BROKEN!"

"You're not broken. You're HEALING. And healing ain't linear. It's messy. It's up and down. But you're still BETTER than you were. You're still MOVING FORWARD."

Tito radioed dispatch. Explained the situation. Asked for coverage for the rest of the route.

"I'm SO sorry—" Minghao started.

"Don't APOLOGIZE! You had a panic attack! That happens! You think you're the first person on this crew to have a mental health moment? Big Mike had one last YEAR! Carlos sees a therapist for DEPRESSION! Uncle Donny is on anxiety medication! You're not ALONE in this!"

"Really?"

"REALLY! We don't talk about it because we're men and we're STUPID. But everyone's dealing with SOMETHING. You just dealing with it more PUBLICLY. Which is actually HEALTHIER."

They sat there. On the curb. Taking time. BREATHING.

"You need me to call someone?" Tito asked. "Your therapist? Your girlfriend? Your MOM?"

"Can you… can you just sit with me? For a minute? Until I feel MORE okay?"

"I can sit with you FOREVER, man. That's what FRIENDS do."

They sat. Traffic passing. Life continuing. The world NOT ending even though it FELT like it was.

After ten minutes, Minghao felt STABLE enough to stand.

"You want me to take you HOME?" Tito asked.

"No. I want to FINISH the shift. I don't want to let this win. I don't want to RUN AWAY."

"You SURE?"

"No. But I'm doing it ANYWAY. That's GROWTH, right?"

Tito smiled. "That's DEFINITELY growth."

They finished the route. Slowly. Carefully. With breaks when needed.

Progress wasn't LINEAR.

But it was still PROGRESS.

⚓

SMALL VICTORY #3: THE PROMOTION OPPORTUNITY (HOPE APPEARS)

FRIDAY AFTERNOON, 3:47 PM - SUPERVISOR'S OFFICE

"Minghao Liu!" Supervisor Anderson called him in after shift. Big guy. Ex-military. FAIR but TOUGH.

Minghao's stomach DROPPED. Was he getting fired? Did someone complain about the panic attack? Did he mess up SOMETHING?

"Yes, sir?"

"Sit down. I got a PROPOSITION for you."

Minghao sat. Nervous. Prepared for BAD NEWS.

"You've been here three years," Anderson said, leaning back in his chair. "Good worker. Show up on time. Don't complain. Your crew LIKES you. Tito says you helped the new guy Kevin settle in. That's LEADERSHIP."

"Oh. Um. Thank you?"

"I'm looking for someone to train for crew lead. It's a step up. More responsibility. More HOURS. But also more PAY. Twenty percent increase. That's about \$8,000 more a year."

Minghao's brain STOPPED. "\$8,000 MORE?!"

Eight thousand dollars MORE.

That was:

\- Better apartment (one with bathroom INSIDE)

\- Car possibility (used, but WHEELS)

\- Savings account (actual SAVINGS)

\- Paying Mom back (all of it, with INTEREST)

\- Dating budget (dinner without calculating to the PENNY)

That was EVERYTHING.

"You'd have to go through training," Anderson continued. "Three weeks intensive. Pass some tests. Prove you can MANAGE a crew. But I think you got potential. You're steady. You show UP. Even when shit gets hard—like Tuesday with your panic attack—you keep GOING. That's the kind of person I want LEADING."

"You KNOW about the panic attack?"

"Tito reported it. Protocol. But he also said you finished your shift anyway. Said you didn't want to LET it win. That's CHARACTER. That's what I need in a crew lead."

"I..." Minghao felt tears coming. Happy tears. GRATEFUL tears. "I'm interested. Very interested. YES. Absolutely YES."

"Good. Training starts next month. Three weeks intensive. Early mornings. Weekends. It's HARD. Some people wash out. But if you PASS, the position's yours."

"I'll pass. I'll WORK. I'll do WHATEVER it takes."

Anderson smiled. Rare smile. GENUINE. "I believe you. Now get out of here. See you Monday."

Minghao left the office. Walked to the parking lot. Pulled out his phone.

Called Cindy.

She answered on the second ring. "Hey! How was your day?"

"I GOT A promotion OPPORTUNITY!"

"WHAT?! That's AMAZING!"

"Twenty percent raise! EIGHT thousand MORE DOLLARS!"

"That's like... over SIX hundred DOLLARS more every month!"

"I can get a BETTER apartment! I can pay back my MOM! I can have SAVINGS!"

"I'm SO PROUD of you!"

"Training starts next month! Three weeks! It's gonna be HARD but I can do THIS!"

"You can DEFINITELY do this! You're going to be AMAZING!"

They talked for twenty minutes. About the opportunity. About the training. About what this MEANT.

When he hung up, Minghao stood in the parking lot feeling something he hadn't felt in MONTHS:

PRIDE.

Real pride.

Not fantasy pride.

EARNED pride.

⚓

SETBACK #2: THE FATHER EMAIL (COMPLICATION ARRIVES)

That night, Minghao checked his email (rarely, because who emails ANYMORE, mostly spam about miracle weight loss and Nigerian princes).

One new message.

Subject: "From Your Father"

His stomach DROPPED.

He stared at it for FIFTEEN minutes. Cursor hovering over DELETE.

Then opened it:

\> Minghao,

\>

\> I heard about your accident. Your mother told me. I wanted to reach out sooner but I didn't think you'd want to hear from me.

\>

\> I know I haven't been a father to you. I know I LEFT. I know I was WEAK. I was dealing with my own problems and I took the coward's way out. I abandoned you and your mother when you needed me most.

\>

\> I don't expect forgiveness. I don't expect ANYTHING. I just wanted you to know I think about you. I've thought about you every day for nineteen years. And I'm proud of you. For surviving. For THRIVING. For being the man I never was.

\>

\> If you ever want to talk, I'm here. But I understand if you don't.

\>

\> - Dad

Minghao read it seventeen times.

Each time it hurt MORE.

Nineteen years of SILENCE. And now this. Now he's proud? Now he WANTS TO TALK?

Where was he when Minghao was NINE? When he needed a father?

Where was he when Minghao was FIFTEEN and being bullied at school?

Where was he when Minghao was TWENTY-FIVE and struggling to find work?

Where was he when Minghao was in a COMA for three months?

NOWHERE.

And now he wants to TALK?

Minghao called Dr. Washington. Emergency therapy session. Tomorrow. NEEDED.

Then called Cindy.

"My dad EMAILED me."

"Oh no. What did it SAY?"

"He's PROUD of me. He wants to talk. He says he was WRONG."

"How do you FEEL?"

"ANGRY! And also... relieved? And also confused? And also EVERY EMOTION AT ONCE?!"

"That's NORMAL. That's healthy. What do you want to DO?"

"I don't KNOW! Pastor Stacks came back and it was beautiful! But Pastor Stacks was FAKE! This is REAL! What if he hurts me AGAIN?!"

"Then you'll SURVIVE. Like you survived the coma. Like you survived the pigeon. Like you survived EVERYTHING. You're stronger now, Minghao. You can HANDLE this. Whatever you decide."

"Can I?"

"YES. And I'll be right HERE. Whatever you decide. I'm HERE."

He cried. She listened. For an HOUR. Just... THERE.

REAL support.

REAL relationship.

REAL LIFE.

⚓

END OF MONTH CHECK-IN (PROGRESS ASSESSMENT)

By the end of the month, Minghao had:

Not marvelous YET.

But MOVING.

Building.

GROWING.

Small victories adding UP.

Real victories that couldn't be taken away by WAKING UP.

Because he was ALREADY awake.

And being awake—truly, GENUINELY awake—

Was better than any dream.

⚓

CHAPTER 20

Real Marvelous Emerging (or: When You Choose Yourself)

⚓

SIX WEEKS LATER - TRANSFORMATION IN PROGRESS

The crew lead training was KICKING his ASS.

Not because it was TOO HARD.

But because it required something Minghao hadn't done in YEARS:

BELIEVING he was CAPABLE.

⚓

TRAINING DAY 15 - THE LEADERSHIP TEST (PROVING HIMSELF)

"Liu!" Instructor Davis barked. Former Marine. Voice like GRAVEL mixed with BROKEN GLASS. Zero tolerance for WEAKNESS. "You're crew lead today! Six people! Three trucks! Two routes! Make it HAPPEN!"

Minghao stood in front of five other trainees. All staring. All WAITING.

Old Minghao would've PANICKED. Would've doubted. Would've imagined Da Marvelous doing it and felt INADEQUATE.

New Minghao took a breath. Remembered Dr. Washington: "You ARE capable. You just have to BELIEVE it."

And Cindy: "Just show UP. That's all you need."

And Tito: "You got this, boss man."

He looked at the five trainees. NERVOUS faces. First time being led. Waiting for CONFIDENCE. Waiting for DIRECTION.

"Okay," he said. Voice STEADY. Not Da Marvelous loud. Just... confident. "Rodriguez, you're on truck one with Chen. Residential route, north side. The hills are STEEP and the brakes on truck one are SENSITIVE. Pump them EARLY. Don't wait until the last second. Pride isn't worth a COLLISION."

Rodriguez nodded. Taking notes.

"Williams, you're with me on truck two. We got commercial—restaurants, offices, heavier LOADS. We go slow. We double-check weight distribution. An unbalanced load will SHIFT and that's how people get HURT."

Williams gave a thumbs-up.

"Jackson and Martinez, you're on truck three. South route. Watch for the elementary school zone—speed limit drops to 15mph from 7:45 to 8:30 AM. Cops love that zone. I've seen three tickets written there this MONTH. Also, parents doing drop-off don't LOOK before backing out. Expect CHAOS."

Everyone nodded. ENGAGED. LISTENING.

"Any questions?"

"What if we fall behind schedule?" Rodriguez asked. The NERVOUS one. Minghao recognized that anxiety. He'd LIVED that anxiety.

"Then we COMMUNICATE. We radio in. We don't rush. Rushing gets people hurt." He touched his head where the scar was. Small gesture. But MEANINGFUL. "I know that PERSONALLY. Better to be late than INJURED. Better to be safe than SORRY. This job isn't worth your LIFE."

Silence. RESPECTFUL silence.

"Anderson will be monitoring. He's watching to see if I PANIC. If I freeze. If I make bad decisions. So let's show him what GOOD looks like. Let's show him SAFE. Let's show him SMART."

They loaded up. Started the routes.

Minghao drove truck two. Williams navigated. Everything SMOOTH.

At each stop, Minghao demonstrated:

\- "See how the bin is OVERLOADED? That's a two-person lift. ALWAYS ask for help."

\- "Check your mirrors EVERY time. Cars don't expect us. WE have to be alert."

\- "Set the parking brake EVERY time. Even on flat ground. ESPECIALLY on flat ground. Complacency KILLS."

Williams absorbed everything. Asked questions. LEARNED.

"You're a good teacher," Williams said during a break. "Better than training. You make it make SENSE."

"I remember being NEW. Being SCARED. Not knowing if I'd mess up. So I know what helps."

"Were you always this confident?"

Minghao laughed. REAL laugh. "no. Six months ago I was in a coma. Woke up thinking I was a kingpin. Tried to wear a PURPLE VELOUR SUIT to a grocery store. Got hit by a truck because I was PHOTOGRAPHING A PIGEON."

Williams stared. "You're JOKING."

"There's VIDEO. Two million views. I'm internet famous for all the WRONG reasons. The pigeon has a BOOK DEAL."

"But you're... you're so TOGETHER now. So CONFIDENT."

"That's EARNED confidence. Not borrowed. Not fake. I showed up. Every day. Even when I was broken. Even when I was LOST. And slowly— SLOWLY—I became the person I pretended to be in my DREAMS."

Williams processed that. "That's... that's actually really HELPFUL."

"Stick with me, kid. I got WISDOM now. And trauma. lots of trauma. But also WISDOM."

At the end of the shift, Instructor Davis approached.

Stone-faced. UNREADABLE.

"Liu."

"Yes, sir?"

"Good work today. SOLID work. Your crew came back safe. On time. No incidents. No COMPLAINTS. You delegated effectively. You communicated clearly. You LED."

"Thank you, sir."

"You got command presence. Not LOUD. Not flashy. But solid. People trust you. That's 90% of leadership right there. The OTHER 10% is knowing when to admit you DON'T know something and asking for HELP. You do both."

Minghao felt something WARM in his chest. PRIDE. Real pride.

"You passed. Training complete. Official promotion starts January first. Congratulations, CREW LEAD Liu."

Minghao stood there. STUNNED.

He DID IT.

He ACTUALLY did it.

Not as Da Marvelous.

As HIMSELF.

As MINGHAO LIU.

Crew Lead.

Twenty percent raise.

\$8,000 more per year.

EARNED.

Not fantasy earned.

REAL earned.

The kind that LASTS.

⚓

CELEBRATING WITH REAL PEOPLE (CHOSEN FAMILY)

That night, they ALL went out.

Tito, Big Mike, Uncle Donny, Carlos, AND Cindy (who took the night off to CELEBRATE).

Cheap Mexican restaurant (Mom-and-Pop place, AUTHENTIC, plastic tablecloths but good FOOD).

Margaritas: ONE for Minghao (responsible), three for Big Mike (CELEBRATING HARD), ZERO for Uncle Donny (driving, WISE).

Tacos: SEVENTEEN consumed collectively (they lost count after twelve).

"TO milo!" Tito raised his glass. "crew lead! boss MAN! NO LONGER THE LOWEST ON THE TOTEM POLE!"

"I'm STILL pretty low!" Minghao protested.

"But you HIGHER! That's progress! That's GROWTH! That's CHARACTER DEVELOPMENT!"

They toasted. Drank. CELEBRATED.

"You know what's WILD?" Big Mike said, waving a taco for emphasis. "Six months ago you were in a coma dreaming you were a kingpin with a criminal goat. Now you ACTUALLY got promoted. REAL promotion. EARNED promotion. That's a STORY. That's a JOURNEY."

"The CHARACTER arc!" Carlos added, still on his phone but ENGAGED. "The TRANSFORMATION!"

Cindy squeezed Minghao's hand under the table. "I'm SO proud of you."

"I'm proud of ME too," he said, surprising himself with how easy it was to say. "Is that ALLOWED? Am I allowed to be proud of MYSELF?"

"HELL yes you're allowed!" Uncle Donny said, emphatic. "You EARNED this! You showed UP! You did the WORK! You BELIEVED in yourself even when it was HARD! That's EVERYTHING!"

Minghao felt tears coming. HAPPY tears. GRATEFUL tears.

"Thank you," he said to everyone. "Thank you for not giving up on me. When I was CRAZY. When I was trying to wear purple suits and call myself Da Marvelous and pretend I was someone I wasn'T. Thank you for STAYING."

"We FAMILY," Tito said simply. firmly. "Family don't leave. Family shows UP. Even when it's HARD. ESPECIALLY when it's hard."

Not like his father.

Family STAYS.

Minghao looked around the table. These PEOPLE. This crew. His girlfriend. His FAMILY.

"I need to tell you all something," he said. Voice QUIET but everyone heard. "My dad emailed me. Six weeks ago. Wants to meet. Wants to APOLOGIZE. Wants to try to BUILD something."

Silence. HEAVY silence.

"What you gonna DO?" Uncle Donny asked gently.

"I'm going to MEET him. Tomorrow. With my therapist. In her office. supervised. With boundaries. With an exit PLAN. Because I need to KNOW. I need to hear what he has to SAY. But I'm not doing it ALONE. And I'm not doing it WITHOUT support."

"That's BRAVE," Cindy said. "That's REALLY brave."

"I don't FEEL brave. I feel TERRIFIED."

"Brave doesn't mean NOT scared. Brave means doing it ANYWAY."

"You want me to come?" Tito offered. "I'll sit in the waiting room. I'll be BACKUP. Just in case."

"Me too," Big Mike said.

"All of US," Uncle Donny added. "We'll be THERE. You ain't doing this alone."

Minghao looked at them. REALLY looked.

"Thank you. I don't—I don't deserve—"

"STOP," Cindy interrupted. firm. "You do deserve. You deserve SUPPORT. You deserve FAMILY. You deserve PEOPLE who show up. Don't EVER say you don't deserve that."

They stayed at the restaurant until CLOSING. Talking. Laughing. PLANNING.

And Minghao realized:

This was his CREW.

Not dream crew.

REAL crew.

Better than ANYTHING in his fantasy.

Because they were HERE.

Because they STAYED.

Because they were REAL.

THE FATHER MEETING - PART 1: WAITING (THE ANXIETY)

SUNDAY, 1:47 PM - DR. WASHINGTON'S OFFICE WAITING ROOM

Minghao sat in a chair that was TOO soft. Sinking into ANXIETY.

Cindy sat next to him. Holding his hand. GROUNDING.

In the adjacent waiting area (different entrance, DR. WASHINGTON'S PLANNING):

\- Tito (reading a magazine upside down, NERVOUS on Minghao's behalf)

\- Big Mike (eating a sandwich, PREPARED)

\\- Uncle Donny (sitting calmly, SOLID PRESENCE)

"They're HERE," Minghao said. "My whole crew is here. For THIS. That's… that's INSANE. That's AMAZING."

"That's FAMILY," Cindy corrected.

At 1:58 PM, a man walked in.

Minghao recognized him IMMEDIATELY even though nineteen years had passed.

Older. Grayer. Thinner. SMALLER somehow. Like all those years had DIMINISHED him.

But still: DAD.

Their eyes met.

The man's eyes filled with TEARS immediately.

"Minghao," he said. Voice BREAKING. "You look… you look so GROWN. So…"

He couldn't finish.

Dr. Washington appeared. Professional. CALM. "Gentlemen. Please come in. Let's BEGIN."

⚓

THE FATHER MEETING - PART 2: THE CONFRONTATION (FULL SCENE)

Inside Dr. Washington's office:

Three chairs arranged in a TRIANGLE. Neutral space. EQUAL positioning.

Dr. Washington sat at the top. Minghao on the left. His father (richard, his name was RICHARD, Minghao had almost FORGOTTEN) on the right.

"Ground rules," Dr. Washington began. FIRM. "This is a mediated conversation. I'm here to facilitate SAFETY. Either person can leave at ANY time. No OBLIGATION to continue if it becomes too much. Understood?"

Both men nodded.

"Richard, you asked for this meeting. You SPOKE. Minghao gets to respond. Or NOT respond. His CHOICE. Are you ready?"

Richard took a breath. DEEP breath. Hands SHAKING.

"Minghao, I don't know how to START. I don't know what to say that will make ANY of this better. But I need to try."

Silence.

Minghao said NOTHING. Just WAITED.

"I left when you were nine years old. I told your mother I was going to the STORE. I never came back. I walked out on you, on her, on our family. And I've carried that SHAME for nineteen years."

"GOOD," Minghao said. First word. sharp. "You SHOULD carry it."

Richard flinched. But nodded. "You're RIGHT. I should. I DO."

"Why?" Minghao's voice was QUIET but intense. "Why did you LEAVE? What did I DO? What was WRONG with me that made you—"

"NOTHING!" Richard interrupted. emphatic. "Nothing was wrong with you! YOU were perfect! You were NINE! You were my SON! The problem was ME!"

"Then WHY?!"

"Because I was DROWNING!" Richard's voice broke. completely. "I was depressed. I was drinking. I was failing at everything—my job, my marriage, my life. And every time I looked at you I saw disappointment. I saw my OWN father's face telling me I wasn't GOOD ENOUGH. And I COULDN'T—I couldn't watch you grow up seeing me FAIL. Seeing me BROKEN. So I RAN. I chose the COWARD'S path."

"You chose YOURSELF over ME!"

"YES! I did! And it was the WORST decision I ever made! It was UNFORGIVABLE! It was—"

"Then why are you HERE?!" Minghao stood up. pacing. "Why now?! After NINETEEN YEARS?! Why do you think you get to just SHOW UP and—"

"Because you almost DIED!" Richard was crying now. fully crying. "Your mother called me. Said you'd been in an accident. Three months in a coma. Might not wake UP. And I realized I might lose you FOREVER without ever telling you I was SORRY. Without ever explaining. Without ever TRYING to make it right."

"You CAN'T make it right! You can't give me back those years! You can't FIX what you BROKE!"

"I KNOW! I know I can't! But I can tell you the truth! I can tell you that leaving you was the biggest MISTAKE of my life! That not a DAY went by that I didn't think about you! That I didn't WONDER who you became! That I didn't MISS you!"

"You have NO right to miss me! You CHOSE to leave!"

"You're ABSOLUTELY right!"

They stood there. Both BREATHING hard. Both crying. Both BROKEN.

Dr. Washington spoke softly: "Minghao, what do you NEED to hear right now?"

"I need—" His voice cracked. "I need to know if he LOVES me. If he ever loved me. Because I spent nineteen YEARS thinking maybe I was UNLOVABLE. Maybe I did something WRONG. Maybe I wasn't ENOUGH."

Richard moved forward. INSTINCTIVE. Stopped himself.

"Can I—" He looked at Dr. Washington. "Can I approach him?"

She looked at Minghao. "Is that OKAY?"

Minghao nodded. BARELY.

Richard stepped closer. Not TOUCHING. Just CLOSER.

"I have ALWAYS loved you. From the moment you were born. You were perfect. You were EVERYTHING. And my leaving had nothing to do with you. nothing. You were—you ARE—the BEST thing I ever did in my WORTHLESS life. And I threw it away because I was WEAK. Because I was BROKEN. Because I didn't think I DESERVED you."

"You DIDN'T deserve me! You were my dad! You were supposed to STAY!"

"I KNOW!"

"You were supposed to FIGHT for me! You were supposed to CHOOSE me!"

"I KNOW!"

"I dreamed about you!" Minghao was SOBBING now. All the years. All the pain. "When I was in that coma! I dreamed I had a friend named Pastor Stacks! He betrayed me! He took money to sabotage me! But then he came back! He CHOSE to do the RIGHT thing! He said 'I'M SORRY' and I FORGAVE him! Because that's what I WANTED from YOU! I wanted you to come BACK! I wanted you to CHOOSE me! Even in my DREAMS I couldn't imagine a world where my father STAYED!"

Richard was BREAKING. Completely BREAKING.

"I'm so sorry. I'm so, so SORRY. I can't—there aren't words. There's no APOLOGY big enough. Nothing I can SAY that will make this OKAY."

"You're RIGHT! There ISN'T!"

"But I can show UP now. Going forward. I can be here. I can TRY. I can do the WORK. I'm four years sober. I'm in therapy. I'm STABLE. I'm not the man who left. I'm TRYING to be the man you DESERVED to have."

Minghao wiped his eyes. ANGRY wipes. FURIOUS wipes.

"I don't know if I can forgive you."

"I don't EXPECT forgiveness."

"I don't know if I CAN trust you."

"You SHOULDN'T trust me. Not yet. Not until I EARN it."

"I don't know if I WANT you in my life!"

"That's YOUR choice. Completely YOUR choice."

They stood there. EXHAUSTED. broken. HONEST.

Dr. Washington spoke: "Minghao, what would you need—WHAT specific THINGS would you need—to even CONSIDER building a relationship with Richard?"

Minghao thought. HARD.

"Boundaries," he said finally. "CLEAR boundaries."

"Such as?"

"Once a month. Coffee. PUBLIC place. one hour maximum. If he's late more than twice, we're DONE. If he cancels more than ONCE, we're done. If he drinks ANYTHING alcoholic ever, we're DONE. If he makes EXCUSES for what he did, we're done. If he tries to make ME responsible for HIS healing, we're done."

Richard nodded at each point. "I ACCEPT. All of it. Completely."

"And THERAPY. Together. With Dr. Washington. Once a month. For at LEAST six months. Then we REASSESS."

"Yes. Absolutely."

"And you don't get to meet my GIRLFRIEND. Or my crew. Or my mom. Not until I decide you've EARNED it. They're MY family. You're not PART of that yet. Maybe never."

"I understand."

"And if you hurt me AGAIN—" Minghao's voice was steel now. "If you leave again. If you DISAPPEAR. I will NEVER forgive you. We will be DONE. Forever. No second CHANCES after this second chance. You understand?"

"I understand. And I won't. I PROMISE I won't."

"Promises don't mean ANYTHING. Not from you. You have to SHOW me."

"Then I'll show you. Every day. Every MONTH. Every YEAR. However long it takes."

Dr. Washington looked at Minghao. "How do you FEEL right now?"

"angry. Still ANGRY. But also... maybe... a little bit relieved? That he came? That he TRIED? That he didn't make EXCUSES? I don't KNOW. I'm CONFUSED."

"That's OKAY. All those feelings can exist together. You can be angry and willing to try. You can be hurt AND open to POSSIBILITY. That's not WEAKNESS. That's STRENGTH."

"It doesn't FEEL like strength."

"The HARDEST thing is giving someone a chance to hurt you again. That takes more courage than walking away. BOTH choices are valid. You chose to TRY. That's BRAVE."

Minghao looked at Richard. REALLY looked.

"First coffee is two weeks from now. Saturday. 10 AM. The place in Silver Lake. You're fifteen minutes early or we're DONE."

"I'll be there."

"And Dad?"

Richard's face BROKE at the word. "Yes?"

"This doesn't mean I forgive you. This doesn't mean we're OKAY. This just means I'm willing to see if we can BUILD something. From scratch. Like we're STRANGERS. Because we ARE strangers."

"I understand. Thank you. Thank you for giving me this CHANCE."

⚓

AFTERMATH - PROCESSING WITH CINDY (BREAKING DOWN)

In the parking lot, Minghao COLLAPSED into Cindy's arms.

Just... BROKE.

All the CRYING he'd held back. All the years. All the PAIN.

She held him. TIGHT. Didn't say anything. Just HELD him.

Tito, Big Mike, and Uncle Donny stood nearby. Not INTERFERING. Just present. Just THERE.

After ten minutes, Minghao pulled back.

"I did it," he said. Voice WRECKED. "I actually DID it."

"You were AMAZING," Cindy said. "You were so strong. You set boundaries. You told the TRUTH. You didn't let him make EXCUSES. You OWNED your feelings."

"I feel like I got hit by a TRUCK. Again."

"Emotionally, you DID. But you survived. Like you always DO."

They drove to Cindy's apartment. Made tea (chamomile, CALMING). Sat on the couch.

"You know what's WEIRD?" Minghao said after an hour. "In my dream, Pastor Stacks' redemption was clean. SIMPLE. He came back. He apologized. I forgave him. DONE. Beautiful ARC."

"And in reality?"

"In reality it's MESSY. It's complicated. I don't know if I can forgive him. I don't know if I WANT to. But I'm willing to TRY. And that's... that's HARDER than the dream version. But also MORE real. MORE honest."

"That's because it IS real. Real relationships are messy. Real forgiveness takes TIME. Real healing isn't LINEAR."

"I'm learning that. The hard way."

She kissed his forehead. "I'm SO proud of you. For showing up. For being honest. For setting BOUNDARIES. That takes more STRENGTH than anything Da Marvelous ever did."

"Da Marvelous never had to face his father. Da Marvelous had it EASY."

"Da Marvelous wasn't REAL. But YOU are. And you're more MARVELOUS than he ever was."

Minghao looked at her. REALLY looked.

"I love you. I'm IN love with you. Not fantasy love. real love. The messy, complicated, TERRIFYING kind."

"Good," she said, smiling. "Because I'm in love with you too. The real you. The MESSY you. The you who cries and panics and tries anyway. That's the BEST you."

They held each other. PRESENT. together. BUILDING something REAL.

And Minghao understood:

Being marvelous isn't about having it ALL together.

It's about showing UP when you're falling APART.

It's about TRYING even when you're TERRIFIED.

It's about building something REAL even when the fantasy was EASIER.

That's the REAL marvelous.

That's who he was BECOMING.

⚓

CHAPTER 21

The Hero Moment (or: When You Save Someone Without Thinking)

⚓

TWO WEEKS AFTER THE FATHER MEETING - FIRST DAY AS CREW LEAD

MONDAY, 6:47 AM - SANITATION YARD

Minghao arrived thirty minutes early. (New position. New RESPONSIBILITIES. Need to be PREPARED.)

His NEW uniform had embroidered on the chest: crew LEAD - M. LIU

Official. REAL. EARNED.

He stood in front of the assignments board. Deep breath. NERVOUS breath.

Today he'd be training a NEW GUY. Kevin Martinez. Twenty-two years old. Fresh out of training. First real job.

Tito walked up. Grinned. "BOSS man! Look at you! Looking all OFFICIAL!"

"I'm TERRIFIED! What if I mess up? What if I'm a bad LEADER? What if—"

"Milo. BREATHE. You passed training. Anderson chose you. You got THIS."

"But what if Kevin asks me something I don't KNOW?"

"Then you say 'I don't know, let me FIND out.' That's LEADERSHIP. Admitting you don't know EVERYTHING. Being HONEST."

At 6:55 AM, Kevin Martinez walked in.

Young. Nervous. Hands SHAKING as he approached.

Minghao recognized that terror IMMEDIATELY.

Because six months ago, that was HIM. Scared. Uncertain. Pretending to be confident while being terrified INSIDE.

"Kevin Martinez?" Minghao asked.

"Yes, sir!"

"Don't call me sir. I'm MINGHAO. Or Milo. Everyone calls me Milo. You ready for your first day?"

"Yes s— I mean, yes Milo!"

"You NERVOUS?"

"No!" Kevin lied. OBVIOUSLY. Voice cracking. "I'm good! I'm READY! I'm—yeah, I'm TERRIFIED."

Minghao smiled. GENUINE smile. "That's normal. First day is always scary. But you got TRAINING. You got SKILLS. And you got ME. I'll show you the ropes. We'll take it SLOW. SAFE."

"You sure? I don't want to mess up—"

"Everyone messes up. I knocked over a PYRAMID of beans my first week. two pyramids actually. Different stores. I'm BANNED from one. Still not allowed back."

Kevin laughed. Nervous laugh. But REAL.

"You'll be FINE," Minghao said with CONFIDENCE. Real confidence. Earned confidence. "I got you."

⚓

THE ROUTE - TEACHING MOMENT (BUILDING TRUST)

They started the route. Residential area. Quiet streets. SAFE. Minghao's PLAN.

First day should be EASY. Build confidence. Not throw them into CHAOS.

As they drove, Minghao explained EVERYTHING:

"See how the bin is OVERLOADED? That's a two-person lift. Don't try to hero it. You'll throw out your back. I've seen guys out for MONTHS because they tried to lift something too HEAVY alone. Pride isn't worth PAIN."

Kevin nodded. Taking mental NOTES.

"Check your mirrors CONSTANTLY. Every three seconds. Cars don't expect us. They're on their phones. They're DISTRACTED. WE gotta be

ALERT. Our JOB is dangerous if we're not PAYING ATTENTION."

"Got it. Mirrors. Every three seconds."

"Always set the parking brake. ALWAYS. Even on flat ground. especially on flat ground. Trucks roll. I know a guy who lost three TOES because he forgot the brake and the truck rolled over his FOOT. Three toes. GONE. Because of COMPLACENCY."

"Oh my GOD."

"That's why we follow PROCEDURE. Every time. No shortcuts. No exceptions. safety first. ALWAYS."

They worked through the morning. Smooth. EFFICIENT. Kevin was good. Careful. Attentive. LEARNING.

During a water break, Kevin said: "You're a good teacher. Better than training. You make it make SENSE."

"I had good teachers," Minghao said, thinking of Tito and Uncle Donny. "And I remember being NEW. Being SCARED. So I know what helps."

"Were you always this confident?"

Minghao laughed. REAL laugh. "no. Absolutely not. Six months ago I was in a coma. Woke up thinking I was a KINGPIN. Had a whole EMPIRE in my head. Business partner who could SING. Criminal GOAT with WARRANTS. The whole THING."

Kevin stared. "You're SERIOUS?"

"Completely serious. Then I tried to be that person in REAL life. Wore a purple velvet SUIT to public places. People thought I was a GRAPE having an emergency. It was TRAGIC. I have VIDEO EVIDENCE of my SHAME."

"But you're... you're so TOGETHER now. So CONFIDENT."

"That's earned confidence. Not fantasy confidence. Not borrowed. EARNED. By showing up. Every day. Even when it was hard. Even when I wanted to QUIT. Even when I felt like a FAILURE. I showed UP. And slowly—SLOWLY—I became who I needed to be."

Kevin absorbed that. "That's... that's actually really HELPFUL. Thank you."

"Anytime, kid. Stick with me. You'll be FINE."

They continued the route. Building TRUST. Building CONFIDENCE.

Until 8:47 AM.

⚓

THE MOMENT - PART 1: THE SETUP

They were at a commercial stop. Back of a restaurant. Three dumpsters. HEAVY loads.

"I got this one," Kevin said, eager to prove himself. "I can handle it."

"You SURE? That's a heavy bin—"

"I got it!" CONFIDENT. Too confident. The kind of confidence that comes before experience teaches you HUMILITY.

Minghao recognized it. Let him TRY. (Learning meant doing. Not just WATCHING.)

Kevin approached the first dumpster. Started positioning himself. GOOD form. He'd learned WELL in training.

Minghao walked to the truck. Needed to check the compactor. It had been making a GRINDING noise. Maintenance issue. Needed to DOCUMENT it.

He opened the compactor panel. Checked the mechanism. JAMMED slightly. Needed adjustment. Pulled out his phone to take a PHOTO for the maintenance report.

Then he heard it:

BEEP BEEP BEEP

Backing alarm. TRUCK reversing.

His head snapped up. INSTINCT.

A delivery truck. Big. HEAVY. Backing up into the alley. FAST. Too fast.

Driver looking at his PHONE. Not his mirrors. Not his SURROUNDINGS. Just his PHONE.

And Kevin.

Kevin was behind the truck. Between the dumpster and the VEHICLE. Wearing his HEADPHONES.

(Against regulations. Minghao would address that LATER. If there WAS a later.)

Kevin was OBLIVIOUS. Focused on the dumpster. Calculating the lift. Not hearing the ALARM.

The truck was BACKING UP.

Kevin wasn't MOVING.

FIVE SECONDS until impact.

Everything SLOWED.

Time dilated. Like before. Like his OWN accident. Like the garbage TRUCK that changed everything.

Minghao saw EVERYTHING:

The driver's face (distracted, TEXTING, completely UNAWARE).

Kevin's face (concentrated, FOCUSED on work, completely OBLIVIOUS).

The distance (CLOSING, fast, DEADLY).

The trajectory (DIRECT impact in three SECONDS).

The outcome (Kevin would be HIT. Kevin would be hurt. Kevin might DIE).

And in that moment—that SPLIT second moment—Minghao Liu had a CHOICE.

Freeze. (Like most people do. Panic. HESITATE.)

Or ACT.

Not as Da Marvelous (fantasy hero, make-believe COURAGE).

Not as crew lead (following PROTOCOL, calling for HELP).

Just as MINGHAO.

HUMAN. present. CHOOSING.

He RAN.

⚓

THE MOMENT - PART 2: THE SAVE (REAL HEROISM)

"KEVIN!" Minghao screamed. Voice ripping from his throat. "MOVE!

MOVE NOW!"

Kevin looked up. Confused. Turned his head. Saw MINGHAO running.

Didn't see the TRUCK. Headphones blocking the alarm. Confusion delaying REACTION.

THREE SECONDS.

Minghao SPRINTED.

Faster than he'd run in YEARS. Faster than crew lead training. Faster than he'd run from Bean Pyramid disasters. Faster than he THOUGHT he could run.

His body SCREAMED. Muscles unused to this intensity. Lungs burning. Heart POUNDING.

But he didn't STOP.

TWO SECONDS.

Kevin finally TURNED. Saw the truck. Eyes going wide. Mouth opening in HORROR.

Started to move. Too SLOW. Too late. Not enough TIME.

The truck was RIGHT THERE.

ONE SECOND.

Minghao GRABBED Kevin. Both arms. wrapped around him like he was DROWNING. Like he was PRECIOUS. Like he MATTERED.

Pulled with every ounce of strength he had. Every muscle. Every FIBER.

They FELL.

Hard. To the side. Away from the truck's PATH. Onto the PAVEMENT.

Minghao felt his shoulder HIT concrete. pain. Sharp. IMMEDIATE.

But they were CLEAR.

The truck's bumper—MASSIVE, steel, DEADLY—passed through the space where Kevin had been standing.

INCHES.

Maybe SIX INCHES.

Maybe FOUR.

Hit the dumpster instead. CRASH. LOUD. Metal on metal. TERRIBLE sound that echoed through the alley.

The truck stopped. SCREECHING brakes. Too late. But they were SAFE.

They were ALIVE.

⚓

THE AFTERMATH - PART 1: IMMEDIATE RESPONSE

Minghao and Kevin were on the ground. Both breathing HARD. Both in SHOCK.

"You OKAY?!" Minghao asked, rolling to face Kevin. Checking for injuries. "Anything broken?! Can you MOVE?!"

"I—I don't—what HAPPENED?!" Kevin's voice was shaking. Whole body TREMBLING.

"Truck almost HIT you! You didn't hear it because of the HEADPHONES!"

"Oh my god. Oh my GOD." Realization hitting. Like a SECOND truck. "I almost DIED!"

"But you DIDN'T!" Minghao held his shoulders. steady. GROUNDING. "You're OKAY! You're SAFE! I got you!"

The delivery driver jumped out. PANICKING. "oh my god! is EVERYONE OKAY?! I DIDN'T SEE HIM! I WAS—" He looked at his phone. Horror on his face. "I was checking my TEXTS! I didn't—I'm SO SORRY!"

"CALL 911!" Minghao ordered. Voice firm. Taking charge. LEADING. "NOW! We need paramedics to check him for SHOCK! And call OUR dispatch! Tell them what happened! Tell them there was an INCIDENT!"

The driver scrambled for his phone. CALLING. reporting. PANICKING.

Kevin was starting to CRY. Shock setting in. REALITY settling in.

"I almost died. I could've DIED. If you hadn't—if you didn't—" Couldn't finish. Just SOBBED.

"But I DID. You're alive. You're HERE. Focus on THAT. You're okay. You're SAFE."

Tito's truck pulled up. SCREECHING stop. "I heard the crash! What—MILO?! KEVIN?!"

"Kevin's okay!" Minghao reported. Voice STEADY despite his hands SHAKING. "Almost got hit. Delivery truck. Driver was texting. Didn't see him."

Tito looked at Minghao. REALLY looked. Seeing something in his FACE.

"YOU saved him?"

"I—yeah. I PULLED him out of the way."

"You could've gotten HIT yourself!"

The thought hadn't even OCCURRED to Minghao. Not in the moment. Not when it MATTERED.

"I DIDN'T think about that! I just—I just saw him and I MOVED! I didn't—there wasn't TIME to think! There was just—ACTION!"

Tito grabbed him in a HUG. tight. "You're a hero, man! You SAVED HIS LIFE!"

THE AFTERMATH - PART 2: OFFICIAL RESPONSE

Paramedics arrived. Checked Kevin (bruised hip, MINOR scrapes, but FINE physically. Shock was the main concern).

Checked Minghao (bruised shoulder, scraped palms, adrenaline crash causing SHAKES, but ALIVE).

Police came. Took statements. Driver got CITED:

\- Distracted driving

\- Failure to ensure clear path

\- Nearly causing a FATALITY

Supervisor Anderson showed up. Face SERIOUS. "Liu. REPORT."

Minghao explained. Everything. The backing truck. Kevin's headphones (would address THAT in training). The split-second decision. The SAVE.

Anderson listened. SILENT. Face UNREADABLE.

When Minghao finished, Anderson nodded slowly. "You saved his life."

"I did what anyone would—"

"NO." Anderson's voice was firm. absolute. "Most people freeze. Most people panic. Most people HESITATE. You ACTED. You put yourself at RISK to save someone else. You didn't THINK about YOUR safety. You didn't CALCULATE odds. You just MOVED. That's the definition of HEROISM."

"I just—I REMEMBERED my own accident. How fast it happened. How NOBODY saw it coming. I didn't want Kevin to go through what I went through."

"That makes it even MORE heroic. You have trauma around this exact scenario. You could've frozen because of your OWN history. But you didn't. You CHOSE to act DESPITE your fear. That's extraordinary."

Minghao felt tears coming. GRATEFUL tears. OVERWHELMED tears.

"Kevin's parents are on the way," Anderson continued. "They're going to want to THANK you. To meet the man who saved their son's LIFE."

"They don't need to—"

"They DO need to. And you need to let them. This isn't just about YOU. It's about THEM. Let them EXPRESS their gratitude."

THE AFTERMATH - PART 3: KEVIN'S PARENTS (EMOTIONAL IMPACT)

Mrs. Martinez and Mr. Martinez arrived THIRTY MINUTES later.

Minghao could HEAR them before he SAW them.

"WHERE is he?! WHERE'S MY BABY?!"

They burst into the area. FRANTIC. terrified. GRATEFUL.

Kevin was sitting in the ambulance. Safe. Wrapped in a BLANKET. Talking to paramedics.

"KEVIN!" Mrs. Martinez ran to him. Grabbed him. held him. SOBBED. "My BABY! My BABY!"

"I'm okay, Mom. I'm OKAY."

"You could've DIED! You could've—" She couldn't finish. Just HELD him tighter.

Mr. Martinez joined them. STOIC but eyes were WET.

After FIVE minutes of hugging Kevin, checking him, touching his FACE like confirming he was REAL—Mrs. Martinez turned.

"Where is he? Where's the man who saved him?"

Anderson pointed. "That's Minghao Liu. Crew lead. First day on the job."

She approached Minghao. DIRECT. INTENSE.

Then GRABBED him in a hug so TIGHT he couldn't breathe.

"You saved our son," she said, crying into his shoulder. "You SAVED him! You risked your life! thank YOU! THANK YOU!"

"I just—I saw him and I MOVED—" Minghao's voice cracked. "I couldn't let him get HIT. I couldn't—"

"Our BABY could've died!" She pulled back. Grabbed his face. Made him look at her. "You gave us back our son. Do you UNDERSTAND? You gave us back the most PRECIOUS thing in our LIVES!"

Mr. Martinez shook Minghao's hand. FIRM. "Whatever you need. anything. We owe you. Forever. You need ANYTHING—job, money, HELP—you call us. You're FAMILY now. You're part of OUR family."

"You don't owe me ANYTHING. I'm just glad he's okay."

"You're a HERO," Mrs. Martinez said. firm. Final. "A REAL hero. Not the movie kind. The REAL kind. The kind that MATTERS."

After they left with Kevin (taking him home, giving him REST, processing the TRAUMA), Minghao sat in the break room.

Alone.

Hands STILL shaking. Adrenaline fading. REALITY setting in.

He could've been HIT.

He could've been INJURED.

He could've ended up back in a COMA.

Or WORSE.

But he DIDN'T think about that in the MOMENT.

He just SAW someone in danger and MOVED.

Not as Da Marvelous (fantasy hero with plot ARMOR).

As Minghao (real person with REAL risk).

And that was MORE heroic than anything Da Marvelous ever did in the dream.

Because it was REAL.

Because it was DANGEROUS.

Because it was a CHOICE.

Because it MATTERED.

CINDY'S REACTION (PROCESSING WITH LOVE)

That night, Cindy came over. She'd heard the news. From Anderson. From TITO. From the entire DEPARTMENT apparently.

She GRABBED Minghao. Checked him for injuries. Found the bruised shoulder. The scraped palms.

"You could've been KILLED!" She was crying. Angry crying. Relief crying. EVERYTHING crying. "You could've been hit! You could've—" She couldn't finish. Just held him. TIGHT.

"I'm FINE! I'm HERE!"

"You could've been in another COMA! You could've DIED! You could've—"

"But I WASN'T! And Kevin's alive! And I did the RIGHT thing!"

"I know! I KNOW you did! And I'm so proud! But I'm also terrified! Because you're brave and you're GOOD and you DO THE RIGHT THING and that means you PUT YOURSELF IN DANGER!"

"Would you want me to be someone who DOESN'T? Who watches people get hurt and does NOTHING?"

She pulled back. Looked at him. REALLY looked.

"No. No, I wouldn't want that. I love you BECAUSE you're that person. Because you act. Because you CARE. Because when it matters, you don't FREEZE. You CHOOSE."

"Then you have to accept that I might get HURT. That loving me means accepting that I'll do scary things when they're RIGHT."

"I know. I KNOW. It's just—" She wiped her eyes. "It's just hard. Loving someone who's brave. Because bravery means RISK."

They sat on his couch. HOLDING each other. PROCESSING.

"You know what I realized?" Minghao said after a while. "When I saw Kevin about to get HIT, I didn't think 'What would Da Marvelous do?' I didn't think about being impressive. I didn't think about being a hero. I just... ACTED. Because it was RIGHT. Because he MATTERED. Because I couldn't NOT act."

"That's the REAL marvelous," Cindy said softly. "That's who you've been this whole time. You just needed to SEE it. To KNOW it. To PROVE it to yourself."

"I think I do now. I think I finally DO."

"Good. Because everyone ELSE already knew. We were just waiting for YOU to catch up."

He kissed her. GRATEFUL kiss. love kiss. The kind that says "thank you for seeing me. For KNOWING me. For LOVING me even when I'm TERRIFIED."

⚓

THE REALIZATION (WHO HE'S BECOME)

Later, lying in bed, Minghao thought about his YEAR.

Twelve months ago: Got hit by a truck because of a PIGEON. Spent three months in a COMA.

Six months ago: Woke up thinking he was DA MARVELOUS. Wore purple suits. Made a FOOL of himself.

Three months ago: Started therapy. Wrote letters to dream friends. Started accepting REALITY.

Two months ago: Met Cindy. Started building something REAL.

One month ago: Promoted to crew lead. Met his father. Started HEALING.

Today: Saved someone's life. Became a HERO. Not fantasy. REAL.

And he UNDERSTOOD:

Da Marvelous was never the MAN he needed to be.

Da Marvelous was the CONFIDENCE he needed to find.

The COURAGE he needed to access.

The BELIEF he needed to have.

And now he HAD those things.

FOR REAL.

As HIMSELF.

As Minghao Liu.

Crew lead.

Hero.

MARVELOUS.

Not because he PRETENDED.

But because he BECAME.

By showing up. By being HONEST. By doing the WORK.

By CHOOSING to act when it MATTERED.

That's what marvelous MEANS.

Not velour suits.

Not gold chains.

Not imaginary EMPIRES.

Just… showing UP.

Being PRESENT.

CHOOSING good.

Even when it's SCARY.

ESPECIALLY when it's scary.

"I'm proud of me," he whispered to the darkness.

And for the first time EVER—

He meant it COMPLETELY.

CHAPTER 22

One Year Later (or: When You Become The Dream)

⚓

PART 1: THE IMMEDIATE AFTERMATH (THREE WEEKS AFTER THE SAVE)

HERO STATUS: UNCOMFORTABLE

Minghao Liu did NOT handle being called a hero WELL.

The local news ran the story: "SANITATION worker saves COLLEAGUE FROM CERTAIN DEATH."

(They used his DMV photo. The worst photo. The one where he looked CONSTIPATED. Naturally.)

The story went VIRAL. (Again. Minghao was becoming internet FAMOUS for multiple reasons now.)

2.7 MILLION VIEWS on the news clip.

Comments:

\- "This is the PIGEON guy! He went from getting hit by trucks to SAVING people from trucks! CHARACTER DEVELOPMENT!"

\- "The redemption arc we NEEDED!"

\- "From meme to HERO! I'm not crying you'RE crying!"

Someone made a COMPARISON VIDEO:

\- LEFT side: Minghao backing up to photograph pigeon, getting HIT

\- RIGHT side: Minghao RUNNING to save Kevin

Title: "The GLOW UP is REAL"

47,000 LIKES

At work, people kept:

\- Shaking his hand (AWKWARD)

\- Calling him "Hero" (WORSE)

\- Asking for PHOTOS (WHY?!)

\- Bringing him COFFEE (unnecessary but appreciated)

"I just DID what anyone would do!" he kept saying.

"But most people DON'T," Anderson replied. "That's what makes it HEROIC."

Kevin returned to work after a week. Still SHAKY. Still processing.

"I owe you my LIFE," he said quietly during lunch.

"You don't OWE me anything."

"I DO. You didn't have to—you could've been HURT—"

"Kevin. Listen." Minghao put down his sandwich. "You're part of the CREW now. We look out for each other. That's what FAMILY does. You'd do the same for ME."

"I WOULD. I will. I PROMISE."

They fist-bumped. SOLID.

Building something REAL.

PART 2: THE FATHER COFFEE MEETINGS (SLOW PROGRESS)

FIRST COFFEE MEETING - WEEK ONE

Richard arrived TWENTY MINUTES early. (Overcompensating. Minghao appreciated it.)

They sat. Awkward. SO awkward. Nineteen years of SILENCE sitting between them.

"How... how was your week?" Richard asked.

"I saved someone's life. It's been on the NEWS. You didn't SEE?"

"I did. I'm so proud—" He stopped. "Sorry. I don't get to be PROUD yet. I haven't EARNED that."

"You're right. You haven't."

They sat in PAINFUL silence for five minutes.

Finally, Minghao said: "Tell me about therapy. What are you WORKING on?"

Richard took a breath. "Understanding why I ran. Understanding my PATTERNS. Learning that running from problems doesn't solve them. Learning to STAY even when it's hard."

"Are you LEARNING?"

"I think so. I hope so. I'm TRYING."

"Trying isn't ENOUGH. You have to DO."

"You're right. I'm DOING. I'm here. I'm STAYING. I'm not running."

Small talk. Surface talk. SAFE talk.

But they showed UP.

That was SOMETHING.

SECOND COFFEE MEETING - WEEK TWO

Slightly less awkward. (Only MODERATE awkwardness. Progress!)

"I'm dating someone," Minghao said. Testing. Seeing if Richard would ASK. Would CARE.

"That's wonderful! What's her name?"

"Cindy. She's a NURSE. She's kind. She's SMART. She knows about the pigeon."

Richard smiled. GENUINE smile. "And she still likes you?"

"She LOVES me actually. She said it. 'I love you.' Those WORDS."

"That's—" Richard's voice CRACKED. "That's beautiful. You deserve that. You deserve someone who sees you. Who CHOOSES you."

Unlike what YOU did, hung in the air. unspoken but PRESENT.

"I'm thinking about PROPOSING," Minghao continued. "Is that CRAZY? We've only been together six months."

"Do you LOVE her?"

"More than anything."

"Does she make you BETTER?"

"She makes me want to BE better."

"Then it's not crazy. When you KNOW, you know."

They talked about Cindy for TWENTY minutes. Richard asked QUESTIONS. Listened. ENGAGED.

Small progress. But REAL.

THIRD COFFEE MEETING - WEEK THREE

"I'm scared I'll be like you," Minghao said. DIRECT. honest. "I'm scared I'll have a kid and I'll LEAVE. I'm scared I'll repeat your PATTERNS."

Richard nodded. Expected this. "That's a VALID fear."

"How do I PREVENT it? How do I make sure I DON'T become you?"

"You already AREN'T me. You show up. You face HARD things. You don't RUN. You're already BETTER than I was at your age. Better than I've EVER been."

"But genetics—"

"Aren't destiny. You get to CHOOSE. Every day. You get to choose to stay. To be PRESENT. To do the WORK. And from what I've seen? You're already DOING that."

Minghao felt tears coming. "I'm terrified I'll fail."

"Everyone's terrified. Being a GOOD person doesn't mean not being scared. It means doing it ANYWAY."

Progress. REAL progress.

Still complicated. Still MESSY.

But MOVING.

⚓

PART 3: THE PROPOSAL (SIX MONTHS AFTER THE SAVE)

JULY - SUMMER EVENING

Minghao had been planning for THREE WEEKS.

Not elaborate. Not FANCY. Just… real. Just THEM.

He took Cindy to the FIRST coffee shop. Where they had their first date. Where she kissed him. Where everything BEGAN.

"Why are we here?" she asked, smiling. "Feeling NOSTALGIC?"

"Something like that."

They ordered their USUAL:

\- Her: Oat milk latte (FANCY)

\- Him: Small coffee (ECONOMICAL but now he could afford large, character GROWTH)

They sat at the SAME table. Where they'd talked for two hours. Where they'd connected. Where they'd started building something REAL.

"Can I tell you something?" Minghao said.

"Always."

"A year ago, I woke up from a coma thinking my life was OVER. I thought I'd lost everything. My empire. My identity. My purpose. And I was DEVASTATED."

"And now?"

"And now I have MORE than I had in the dream. I have you. I have real friends. I have a job I'm good at. I have actual ACHIEVEMENTS. I have—" He took a breath. "I have a LIFE. A REAL life. Better than any fantasy."

"I'm glad. You DESERVE that life."

"But it's not COMPLETE. There's one thing MISSING."

He reached into his pocket. Pulled out a small box. (NOT expensive. He'd saved. But not FANCY. Just... REAL.)

Cindy's eyes went WIDE.

"Cindy Martinez," Minghao said, voice SHAKING. "You saw me at my worst. You knew about the pigeon. You knew about the purple suit. You knew I woke up thinking I was someone else. And you didn't RUN. You stayed. You CHOSE me. Every day. Even when I was MESSY. Even when I was BROKEN. Even when I was SCARED."

"Minghao—"

"I'm not Da Marvelous. I'm not smooth. I'm not IMPRESSIVE. I pick up garbage for a living. I got hit by a truck because of a pigeon. I have panic ATTACKS. I'm TERRIFIED of everything. But I love you. I'm IN love with you. And I want to spend the rest of my life SHOWING UP for you. The way you've shown up for ME."

He opened the box. Simple ring. Silver band. Small stone. AFFORDABLE but MEANINGFUL.

"Will you marry me? Will you choose ME? Forever?"

Cindy was CRYING. Happy crying. JOYFUL crying.

"YES! Oh my god, YES!"

He slipped the ring on her finger. (It FIT. He'd asked her sister for her size. PLANNING.)

They kissed. In the same coffee shop. At the SAME table. Where everything STARTED.

And Minghao felt COMPLETE.

Not fantasy complete.

REAL complete.

The kind that LASTS.

⚓

PART 4: THE PROMOTION CEREMONY (ONE YEAR AFTER THE ACCIDENT)

DECEMBER 10TH - EXACTLY ONE YEAR LATER

Minghao woke up in his NEW apartment.

One bedroom. Actual BEDROOM. Separate from living space. LUXURY.

Kitchen with full stove (not hot plate, PROGRESS).

Bathroom INSIDE the apartment (not shared, PRIVACY).

A window with ACTUAL view (parking lot, but SUNSET-visible).

Rent: \$1,650/month (painful but MANAGEABLE with assistant manager salary).

Savings account: \$3,847 (GROWING, steadily, RESPONSIBLY)

Gerald the Plant (now MASSIVE, possibly sentient) sat on the counter in SUNLIGHT.

Gerald Jr. thrived next to him. (FAMILY.)

Cindy was in the bedroom. HIS bedroom. their bedroom soon. (Moving in together next month. PLANNING.)

"Morning," she said, walking out. Wearing his SHIRT. (Character development: he had shirts now. Multiple. VARIETY.)

"Morning, future wife."

She smiled. RADIANT. "How do you FEEL? Big day."

"Nervous. Excited. GRATEFUL."

Today was the promotion ceremony. Assistant Operations Manager. Official. PUBLIC. In front of everyone.

One year ago he woke up from a coma.

Today he was being PROMOTED.

FULL CIRCLE.

⚓

THE CEREMONY (RECOGNITION)

10:47 AM - SANITATION DEPARTMENT HEADQUARTERS

The room was FULL. Forty sanitation workers. City officials. Local news (ugh). Kevin's parents (HONORED GUESTS).

Supervisor Anderson stood at the podium.

"We're here to recognize EXCELLENCE. To honor someone who exemplifies what this department stands for: service. DEDICATION. COURAGE."

Minghao stood off to the side. Wearing his BEST outfit:

\- Button-up (PRESSED)

\- Tie (first time WEARING one, slightly crooked)

\- Dress pants (NO HOLES)

\- Shoes that MATCHED (consistency!)

Cindy sat in the front row. Crying already. (Happy crying. SUPPORTIVE crying.)

Tito, Big Mike, Uncle Donny, Carlos - entire CREW present.

His MOTHER (brought 47 bags of food, NATURALLY).

And in the back - Richard. His father. PRESENT. Not invited by Minghao but not kicked OUT either. Progress.

"Fourteen months ago," Anderson began, "Minghao Liu was hit by a truck. Spent three months in a coma. Woke up confused, disoriented, dealing with TRAUMA. But he didn't quit. He came BACK. He did the WORK. He HEALED."

Pause. Let it LAND.

"Eight months ago, he saved a coworker's LIFE. Risked his own safety to pull Kevin Martinez out of the path of a backing truck. HEROISM. Real heroism. Not movie heroism. ACTUAL heroism."

Kevin stood up. Clapped. EMOTIONAL.

Everyone joined. STANDING OVATION for Minghao's heroism.

"And for the past eight months, as crew lead, Minghao has shown EXCEPTIONAL leadership. His crew has the best safety record. The highest efficiency rating. The LOWEST turnover. Because people want to work for someone who CARES. Someone who SHOWS UP. Someone who LEADS by example."

More applause.

"So it is my HONOR—and my PRIVILEGE—to promote Minghao Liu to Assistant Operations Manager. Effective immediately. Congratulations."

STANDING OVATION.

Tito was SCREAMING: "that'S my BOY! THAT'S MY BOY!"

Big Mike was ugly crying. PROUD crying.

Uncle Donny nodded. WISDOM in his eyes.

His mother was SOBBING. (Joy sobbing. MOM sobbing.)

Cindy was GLOWING. (Future wife GLOWING.)

Even Richard was crying. (Missed nineteen years but PRESENT for this. Something.)

Minghao walked to the podium. Shook Anderson's hand. Received the plaque:

MINGHAO LIU

ASSISTANT OPERATIONS MANAGER

EXCELLENCE IN SERVICE

He looked at it. His NAME. His title. His ACHIEVEMENT.

EARNED.

Not fantasy.

REAL.

He stepped to the microphone.

"Thank you. Thank you for believing in me. For supporting me. For showing UP when I was at my lowest. Fourteen months ago I woke up thinking my life was over. I thought I'd lost everything. But I was WRONG. I hadn't lost anything. I just hadn't FOUND it yet."

He looked at the CROWD. His PEOPLE.

"I'm not the person I thought I was. I'm not the fantasy person I dreamed about. But I'm BETTER. Because I'm real. Because I showed UP. Because I did the WORK. And because YOU—all of you—didn't give up on me."

He looked at Cindy. "Thank you for CHOOSING me."

He looked at his crew. "Thank you for being my FAMILY."

He looked at his mother. "Thank you for NEVER giving up."

He looked at Richard. Brief. COMPLICATED. But acknowledged. "Thank you for TRYING."

More applause. More TEARS. More GRATITUDE.

And Minghao felt something he'd only felt in the DREAM before:

PRIDE.

But this time it was REAL.

This time it was HIS.

This time it LASTED.

⚓

PART 5: THE MYSTERIOUS ENDING (FULL CIRCLE)

9:47 PM - WALKING HOME ALONE (PROCESSING)

After the ceremony. After the CELEBRATION. After dinner with everyone. After EVERYTHING.

Minghao walked home alone. (Cindy went to her place - packing for the MOVE. Progress. FUTURE.)

The night was COOL. The city was alive. People everywhere living their LIVES.

He stopped at a crosswalk. Waiting for the light. Thinking about his YEAR. His journey. His TRANSFORMATION.

Fourteen months ago: Hit by truck. COMA. DREAMS.

Twelve months ago: Woke up. CONFUSED. Lost.

Ten months ago: Purple suit phase. DENIAL. Embarrassment.

Six months ago: Met Cindy. Started BUILDING.

Four months ago: Saved Kevin. Became HERO.

Two months ago: PROPOSED. Future secured.

Today: PROMOTED. Life transformed.

FULL JOURNEY.

COMPLETE ARC.

That's when he saw him.

Across the street.

A man in a PURPLE velour SUIT.

Gold chains GLEAMING under streetlights.

Mink coat (in DECEMBER, completely IMPRACTICAL).

Sunglasses (at NIGHT, completely RIDICULOUS).

Swagger for DAYS. Confidence for YEARS.

The man looked DIRECTLY at Minghao.

Made eye contact. HELD it.

And WINKED.

Slow. DELIBERATE. KNOWING.

Like he was saying: "I SEE you. I know you. Well DONE."

Minghao's heart STOPPED.

Da Marvelous?

The light changed. Cars passed. BLOCKING view.

When they cleared...

The man was GONE.

Disappeared.

Like he was never THERE.

Minghao stood there. PROCESSING.

Was it REAL?

Was it his IMAGINATION?

Was it his brain's way of saying GOODBYE?

Or was it CONFIRMATION?

That Da Marvelous wasn't GONE.

He was just… TRANSFORMED.

Living inside Minghao.

Part of him.

ALWAYS.

Not as a separate PERSON.

But as CONFIDENCE.

As COURAGE.

As the BELIEF that he matters.

That he's CAPABLE.

That he's MARVELOUS.

Minghao smiled.

Touched his chest. Where his heart was. Where Da Marvelous lived now. Where the CONFIDENCE resided.

He FELT it.

The swagger. The CERTAINTY. The PRIDE.

Not borrowed.

Not fantasy.

HIS.

"Thanks for everything," he whispered to the night. To the memory. To himself. To Da Marvelous. To the DREAM that saved him.

Then he turned.

And walked toward his apartment.

Toward his LIFE.

Toward his FUTURE.

Not as Da Marvelous McCall (fantasy kingpin with impossible EMPIRE).

As Minghao Liu (real person with REAL life).

Assistant Operations Manager.

Hero.

Partner.

Friend.

Son.

And yes—

MARVELOUS.

Always.

In his own way.

For REAL.

⚓

EPILOGUE: SIX MONTHS LATER (THE FULL CIRCLE COMPLETION)

WEDDING DAY - SUMMER

Minghao stood at the altar. Wearing a SUIT. (Real suit. Fitted. not PURPLE. Character growth.)

Tito was best man. (Obviously. FAMILY.)

Big Mike, Uncle Donny, Carlos - all groomsmen. (CREW. family. SAME THING.)

Kevin was there. (Friend now. SAVED. Present.)

His mother was in the front row. (Crying. Obviously. MOM TEARS.)

Richard was in the BACK row. (Invited. Progress. trying. Showed up to SEVEN coffee meetings now. Building something. SLOWLY.)

The music started.

Cindy appeared.

BEAUTIFUL.

Not fantasy beautiful.

REAL beautiful.

The kind that comes from CHOOSING someone. From building something. From SHOWING UP.

She walked down the aisle. Smiling. GLOWING. CERTAIN.

Choosing HIM.

Forever.

When she reached the altar, Minghao whispered: "You sure about this? You could still RUN. I'm the pigeon GUY. I got hit by a TRUCK. I'm MESSY."

"I'm SURE," she whispered back. "You're MY mess. Forever."

They said their vows.

(His were LONG. Rambling. honest. Very MINGHAO.)

(Hers were SHORT. Clear. perfect. Very CINDY.)

They kissed.

MARRIED.

For REAL.

Forever.

As the reception started, Minghao looked around.

Everyone he LOVED. Everyone who showed UP. Everyone who STAYED.

THIS was his empire.

Not Club Marvelous.

Not velour suits and gold chains.

THIS.

real people. REAL love. REAL LIFE.

Better than ANY dream.

"You did it," Tito said, hugging him. "You BECAME the marvelous."

"I think I did," Minghao agreed. "Finally. For REAL."

Later, during the first dance, Cindy asked: "Any regrets? About the dream? About Da Marvelous?"

Minghao thought about it. HONESTLY thought.

"No," he said finally. "The dream SAVED me. It showed me who I could be. But this—" He gestured around. "This is BETTER. Because it's REAL. Because it's EARNED. Because I CHOSE it. And it chose ME back."

"Good answer."

"I'm getting BETTER at them."

They danced. TOGETHER. Building a life. Building a FUTURE.

And somewhere—maybe in his MIND, maybe in the universe, maybe in MEMORY—

Da Marvelous watched.

And approved.

Because the REAL marvelous—

Was always Minghao.

He just needed to BELIEVE it.

THE ABSOLUTE END

MINGHAO LIU - FINAL STATUS:

The Dream: Never forgotten (Dorothy remembered Oz)

The Reality: Better than the dream (REAL, CHOSEN, EARNED)

The Future: BRIGHT (genuinely, authentically BRIGHT)

The pigeon: Still has a book deal (capitalism waits for NO ONE)

Minghao: Also winning (in his own way, FOR REAL)

A NOTE FROM MINGHAO:

They say you can't go home to Oz. That once you wake up, the dream DIES.

But that's not TRUE.

I carry Da Marvelous with me every day. His confidence. His swagger. His BELIEF that he mattered. I carry Cherry's practicality and hidden passion. I carry Larry's defiance and refusal to be TAMED. I carry Pastor Stacks' capacity for redemption.

They're not GONE. They're transformed. Into the REAL me. Into the MARVELOUS me.

Because being marvelous isn't about velour suits or gold chains or imaginary empires.

It's about SHOWING up. Every day. Even when it's HARD. Especially when it's HARD.

It's about being YOURSELF. Honestly. Authentically. Without

PRETENSE.

It's about BELIEVING you matter. Even when the world tells you you're nobody. Even when you're just a regular person who picks up garbage. Even when you almost died because of a PIGEON.

You MATTER.

You're ENOUGH.

You're MARVELOUS.

You just have to BELIEVE it.

And then BECOME it.

For REAL.

- Minghao Liu

Assistant Operations Manager

Hero

Husband

Still Marvelous (just quieter about it)

P.S. - The pigeon STILL has more Instagram followers than me. But I'm okay with it now. That pigeon had DREAMS. We can BOTH win.

END OF MARVELOUS

THE COMPLETE STORY OF HOW MINGHAO LIU
BECAME DA MARVELOUS MCCALL…

…BY BEING HIMSELF.